The Poison Tide

ANDREW WILLIAMS

JOHN MURRAY

First published in Great Britain in 2012 by John Murray (Publishers)
An Hachette UK Company

First published in paperback in 2013

1

A CIP catalogue record for this title is available from the British Library

ISBN 978-1-84854-584-7
Ebook ISBN 978-1-84854-583-0

Typeset in Celeste by Palimpsest Book Production Limited,
Falkirk, Stirlingshire

Printed and bound by Clays Ltd, St Ives plc

John Murray policy is to use papers that are natural, renewable and recyclable products and
made from wood grown in sustainable forests. The logging and manufacturing processes
are expected to conform to the environmental regulations of the country of origin.

John Murray (Publishers)
338 Euston Road
London NW1 3BH

www.johnmurray.co.uk

For Kate

Things fall apart; the centre cannot hold;
Mere anarchy is loosed upon the world,
The blood-dimmed tide is loosed, and everywhere
The ceremony of innocence is drowned.

William Butler Yeats

1914

PROLOGUE

The Patient

THE HOSPITAL TRAIN announced its arrival beneath the smoky vault of the Lehrter Bahnhof with a shriek that set nerves jangling. A column of ambulances was waiting on the platform and to an accompaniment of whistles, the slamming of doors and the barking of the military marshals, the wounded began to step from the train, grey and solemn after many hours in close carriages. Patient faces – the resignation of the helpless – tired faces, some dazed, some distorted by pain, stained and bandaged like the procession at the last trumpet. After four months of war, they were still worthy of comment and the polite applause of civil servants and businessmen on their way to offices in Berlin's government district. Mothers with young children hurried by.

Dr Anton Dilger was used to the suffering of others. He had met a dozen or more hospital trains from the Front. He'd restrained men demented with pain and some had died under his knife. All of these tasks he'd conducted with the necessary professional detachment. But on this freezing December day, Dr Dilger was a spectator, standing among a group of the curious on the platform opposite, gawking with the rest. He was a young man of thirty, clever but restless, inclined more by disposition to action than to thought. To watch, unable to lift a finger, was an exquisite torment and yet the feeling held him there.

A tightness across the chest, fatigue, lethargy, irritability, a lack of concentration, a certain emptiness. His symptoms met a description he'd read in a medical journal of an affliction the British were calling shell shock. But he'd spent no more than a few hours at the battle front as an observer and enjoyed the experience. No, he was ashamed to acknowledge the cause because grief was not a condition he recognised or could treat. The death of his nephew, Peter, had left him with a sense of helplessness – worse – impotence.

Last from the train were the stretchers, the tough cases and the amputees, received by the orderlies with a sharp efficiency that spoke already of great experience. One young man, his head swathed in a turban of bandages, was wearing the greatcoat of his nephew's cavalry regiment about his shoulders. Dilger wanted to shout to him but the words stuck in his throat and then the stretcher was gone.

He left the station with the wounded and walked the short distance to the Charité Hospital. Ambulances were idling at its entrance, nurses scurrying through an evil cloud of exhaust fumes like figures in badly cranked and tinted film. For a few uncertain minutes he stood idly by again, gazing up at the hospital's plain brick face. The invitation had arrived just days after he had learnt of Peter's death and he'd given it no consideration. There had been a second invitation, and a third, and finally a telephone call from the director of his own hospital, all but ordering him to come here. Professor Carl Troester was Germany's leading veterinary surgeon. Why would he wish to see a little-known – no, if he was honest, an unknown Red Cross doctor? His director wasn't able to say.

Troester's young assistant greeted him in the entrance hall with a stiff bow and click of his heels that contrived to suggest a rebuke. The professor was expecting him in Infectious Diseases, he remarked haughtily. 'And to save time, Doctor,

I took the liberty of bringing these.' He thrust a coat and mask at Dilger then turned away, intent on quick-marching him to the stairs.

The isolation ward was stiflingly hot and the sickly-sweet smell of putrefaction made Dilger feel nauseous. Life was being squeezed from the patient. An oscillation of ventilation between apnoea and tachypnoea: a pattern he had witnessed a hundred times. Caucasian male, heavily built, approximately forty. Motionless for what seemed an eternity, then with a jerk his body arched as if tugged by invisible strings, gasping for air, fluid rattling in his throat, lips drawn tightly over his teeth.

'Is this a case of glanders?' Dilger asked, turning to the men in coats and masks at his side.

'*Bacillus anthracis.* Anthrax. A foolish mistake.' Professor Carl Troester peered at the patient through thick pince-nez spectacles, his mask puckering as he spoke. 'One of mine. That is to say, he worked for me at the Military Veterinary Academy. Conducting tests . . .'

Ulceration of the upper respiratory tract. Suppurating sores on the torso, blue tinge to the skin, swelling of the glands beneath the patient's arms: a painful and highly infectious contagion. Death was no more than a few hours away.

'Why was it important for me to see this?' enquired Dilger quietly.

The corners of the professor's small dark-blue eyes wrinkled in what may, beneath the mask, have been a smile or a grimace. Leaning forward to grasp a corner of the stained sheet, he dragged it back across the patient. 'There's someone you must meet, Doctor.'

Professor Troester led him from the ward into a scrub room and they dropped their coats and masks in a steel bucket. 'Burn them,' he instructed the orderly. They washed their hands in silence and Dilger's thoughts drifted again from the nameless patient to his nephew in the noise and filth of battle. Turning for a towel, he caught the professor's eye: 'Is he a casualty?'

The professor tossed his towel into the bucket. 'An accident. Didn't I say so?'

'I've never met a human case.'

'No.'

'My father bred horses . . .'

'Your father was an extraordinary man,' interrupted Troester. He bent into the uniform jacket an orderly was holding to his long back.

'You knew my father?'

'I didn't have the pleasure. Shall we?'

He led Dilger into the corridor, broad like a monastery cloister and restless with the confused echo of military boots, hushed voices, the rattle of hospital trolleys. Half a step in front of him as they turned on to the stairs, the professor-brigadier was tall, parade-ground erect although almost sixty, with a thin leathery face, a distant, academic smile. From the little he had said, his bearing, other small details, it was plain that Troester was a Prussian. On the next landing, they pushed through heavy doors into the administrative wing of the Kaiser Wilhelm Medical Academy – the imperial eagle picked out in tesserae on the wall: a corridor of polished wood and brass nameplates where clerks in crisp olive-grey uniforms had time to acknowledge a superior officer with a salute.

The man Dilger had been brought to meet was standing with his back to the window in the Medical Director's office. The smoke that hung over the desk and the stubs in the ashtray at its edge suggested he'd been waiting a while. Lost at first in silhouette, he came forward to greet them. He was in his fifties with grizzled brown hair, high cheekbones, a large silky cavalry moustache and a general air of quiet authority. He was dressed like any other sober middle-aged servant of the Crown, in frock

6

coat and striped trousers, but a duelling scar high on his left cheek suggested a colourful history. Troester introduced him as Count Rudolf Nadolny.

'I'm grateful for your time, Doctor,' he said with a warm smile, his handshake longer than was customary on first acquaintance. 'I'm sensible of your loss. Colonel Lamey says you were close to his son . . .'

'You know the colonel?'

'We've spoken on the telephone.'

'Peter and I were like brothers, yes . . .'

They stood in respectful silence as if expecting Dilger to say more, but to say more would be to risk saying too much and to say too much would be to lose control.

'Why do you want to see me, Count?' he said at last.

'Has the professor spoken to you of his programme?'

'That is for you to do,' interjected Troester. He looked ill at ease.

Nadolny gave him a reassuring, at-your-service smile. 'Yes, of course. Doctor Dilger, please,' and he gestured to a table in front of the windows. The Count took the chair opposite, with the dying light of the winter day behind him.

'I know a good deal about your family, Doctor. Your father – a distinguished soldier on two continents – and both your brothers-in-law are at the Front?'

'Yes.'

'You could be of great service to Germany too . . .'

'I'm doing what I can. A Red Cross hospital . . .'

'A volunteer surgeon, yes.' The Count leant over the table, his hands together. Dilger noticed the blood-red intaglio signet ring on his left hand – lest anyone doubt his place in the first rank of society. 'But there is more important work,' he continued. 'Work that will help us to win the war . . .'

'I'm a doctor.'

'And a good one, I know. But we have need of soldier-scientists too.' The Count sat back in his chair again, dragging his fists across the polished mahogany. 'Forgive me, but before I say more, I must ask for your word as a gentleman that you will not speak of what you hear or have seen at the hospital today.'

'You mean the patient?' Dilger glanced at the professor. 'I was surprised . . . a rare condition.'

'He was working on our special programme . . . a lesson to us all to be careful, but a clear demonstration of the possibilities too, don't you agree?'

His question was put with the everyday informality of one proposing guests for a dinner party. It took Dilger a moment to grasp his meaning.

'Can we be clear?' he said stiffly. 'You work for Military Intelligence and you want me to work for you – this *special programme*?' Nadolny smiled but said nothing, so Dilger continued. 'I'm sorry, Count, I have no experience, nor do I wish to.'

'You served in the Balkans – I've read your paper on battle-field infections. I'm not a scientist but—'

'Very fine, very fine,' Troester cut in. 'Many valuable insights, and . . .'

'You see,' the Count said firmly, raising his hand with its stamp of authority, 'praise from the professor. You're a specialist in tissue cultures . . .'

'There are scores of doctors in the Empire who know more, and I really . . .' Dilger hesitated. The Count's sharp little brown eyes didn't leave his face for a second, turning, turning the signet ring between thumb and forefinger. 'There are doctors who know more than me,' he added lamely.

'Young men like your nephew, Peter, are giving their lives for the Fatherland. It's important at such times that all of us do what we can.'

'Yes, yes, but this is a matter of conscience too.'

The professor coughed, removed his pince-nez and began to polish the lenses with his handkerchief. Voices in the outer office filled the silence at the table and, from the street, the distant jangling of an ambulance's bell.

'Cigarette? They're Russian.' Nadolny reached inside his morning coat. 'No?'

'It isn't very patriotic to smoke Russian tobacco, Count,' Troester observed with a tense little laugh.

Nadolny ignored him. 'You must understand, this war is like no other, Doctor,' he said with quiet emphasis. 'The choice is either victory or destruction. Victory will be secured by those who prove the fittest – an old struggle but in a new, unforgiving age.' He paused to draw reflectively on his cigarette. He reminded Dilger of a patient fencer, feinting, parrying, probing for a perfect hit. 'Germany will win only if each and every one of us dedicates ourselves to victory,' he resumed. 'We must bend our thoughts to this task. If necessary, think the unthinkable. Everyone is a combatant. Everyone. But we bring different skills. Perhaps there are better scientists in the Empire, better doctors than you, but this is your duty . . .'

'I'm clear about my duty, Count. It is to heal.'

'Your duty, Doctor, is to the Fatherland, your family – to Peter.' There was a new firmness in Nadolny's voice. 'There is no one better suited to this task.'

'I don't understand – there are others . . .' He was angry at the Count's presumption. 'Why is it *my* duty? Why me?'

They let him go with a promise that he would speak with them again. His sister's house in Charlottenburg was dark but for the candle of remembrance burning at a first-floor window. Something wet touched his face as he was collecting himself on the step. The first snow of winter. Lazy flakes were falling on his clothing, expiring in the dark wool, from something into nothing. Christmas Eve tomorrow.

The colonel's old batman answered the door, took Dilger's hat and coat and, with bowed head, informed him that the mistress had retired to her chamber. Colonel Lamey was still at the Front. A stuttering fire in the drawing room had barely taken the edge off the chill. The burgundy curtains were closed and had been for days, the room harshly lit by new electric wall sconces. In Dilger's absence, his sister had stopped the large mantel clock. The silence was complete. Through the prism of grief the house was taking on a subtle new aspect, sad memories clinging to familiar objects like a film of dust. A few months before, his nephew Peter had perched on the couch by the fire with a glass of champagne.

'A toast to victory!' the colonel had said, his hand on his son's shoulder. Cheers for the young soldier, good-humoured teasing, tears on the cheeks of his mother, Elizabeth.

The parcel with Peter's personal effects was lying on an occasional table between the windows. Elizabeth was refusing to touch it. With small, light steps lest he make a noise that she would deem in the madness of grief to be disrespectful, he walked to the table, picked up the parcel and tore it open. Peter's service revolver, a pipe and tobacco pouch, some leather gloves, his green silk scarf – a present from his mother – and some mud-stained letters and photographs. One of the photographs had been taken on the farm of Dilger's father in Virginia. Peter had an arm about Anton's shoulders, his head thrown back in laughter. Like brothers. Dilger's gaze drifted to the pier glass above the table. They had the same high forehead and long face, and the strong Dilger jaw with the curious dimple in the chin. He picked up Peter's scarf and pressed it to his face. There was still a trace of his sister's perfume. What would my father, the old cavalryman, have thought? he wondered. He would have been proud of his grandson, Peter. What would he have wished of his son? The course Dilger had plotted to this point in his life had been easy. But his family's grief, this Count – Nadolny – he had been snatched up in the confusing current of the times, inclination, duty, conscience pulling him to different shores.

'Anton, what are you doing?'

His sister Elizabeth was watching him from the door.

'Thinking of Father. I opened this . . .' and he showed her the scarf. She looked at him, wide eyes ringed with shadow, then turned her face to the side and he could see that she was on the point of breaking. He moved quickly to her and held her shaking shoulder and she took the scarf from him. 'Anton, what will become of me . . . how can I . . . oh God, why . . .'

As she sobbed against his chest he asked himself again: 'Why me?' But he knew the answer: 'Because you are an American.' The Count had slipped from German to speak the words very precisely in English, leaning forward with his gaze fixed on Dilger's face, elbow on the table, right hand balled in a fist. 'You are a German and American doctor, but we need you to be an American.'

1915

1

London

A SPLINTER OF WINTER sun was forcing its way through the curtains on to the wall at an angle that suggested to Wolff he should rouse himself at once.

'Are you awake, Mrs Curtis?'

Drunk, in a hurry, they'd fallen apart with no thought to the morning. Violet's face was lost behind a tousled curtain of hair. There was lipstick on the sheet she had pulled to her chin and she'd chipped her nail varnish. Wolff reached a cold hand to her breast, then thought better of waking her. A shave, a shallow tepid bath, sweeping back his dark-brown hair, a splash of discreet cologne. From his dressing-room wardrobe, a black wool suit, stiff white collar and dark-blue tie. Before the mirror, for the world to see in time, a businessman of means in his late thirties, who, to judge by his dark eyes, was burning too much midnight oil. Slipping on his coat, he was searching for his hat when Violet called to him: 'You *are* taking me to dinner, Sebastian darling, aren't you?'

'I'll try.' Wolff wasn't sure what he would want to do by the evening.

The cab dropped him in Trafalgar Square. He walked briskly into Northumberland Avenue and at the corner with Great Scotland Yard he stopped to light a cigarette, turning to face the way he'd come as if sheltering the guttering flame. Satisfied, he walked on into Whitehall Court. Number 2 was an eight-storey apartment block in the French renaissance style, directly behind the War Office and next to the National Liberal Club. An MP had financed the building with money swindled from those he had described on election day as ordinary hard-working families. Thousands had been left penniless to provide a brash home at the heart of government for civil servants and wealthy businessmen. Its façade of Portland stone and pitched green slate towered over the Embankment, drawing the eye of commuters crossing the river into Charing Cross Station.

In its polished hall the porter slid a register and pen across the desk to Wolff without comment.

'You're new.'

'Three months, sir.'

Wolff pushed it back unsigned: 'I'm visiting Captain Spencer. I know my way.'

The captain's private lift was little more than the width of a man's broad shoulders. The grille slid into place with a rattle and clunk that always reminded Wolff of earth falling on a coffin lid. Apartment 45 was a maze of passages and oddly shaped rooms beneath the eaves of the Court, so difficult to find from the stairway that few residents had any inkling it was there. Its occupant, a short, thickset naval officer, was occasionally seen crossing the entrance hall with companions or walking in the direction of Whitehall. Neighbours who tried to engage him in conversation received no more than the time of day. Only a man with a perfect understanding of the deep reserve of upper-middle-class London and its slavish attachment to the proprieties would have had the temerity to hide the Bureau in genteel Whitehall Court.

'He's waiting for you, Lieutenant Wolff.' The captain's secretary stepped away from the door to let him enter. 'You're late. I telephoned your apartment . . .' A censorious frown was hovering between Miss Groves' finely plucked eyebrows. 'And I spoke to your . . . *friend*.' The word fell to its '*end*' as if Miss Groves had pushed it from the Tarpeian for sexual impropriety. The captain's nice 'gels' cared a great deal about such things.

The naval gentleman whom the other denizens of the Court called 'Spencer' – Captain Mansfield Cumming – was leaning heavily on sticks in his outer office. 'Where the hell have you been?' He glared at Wolff through his gold-rimmed monocle. 'You're still a naval officer, you know? My office in five minutes.' He turned too smartly and one of his sticks locked beneath a chair.

'Damn it!'

Wolff stepped forward to help. 'No, damn it, man, I can manage,' he said, jerking it free. 'And bring us some coffee, Miss Groves. Lieutenant Wolff looks as if he could do with some.'

He stomped slowly towards his office, hunched like a grizzly bear.

'He's doing very well,' whispered Miss Groves reverentially. Pinned in the wreckage of a car, it was rumoured he had hacked off his own foot with a penknife in order to crawl to his dying son. 'It's only been three months. Flinty, isn't he?'

'He loves his work.'

The captain was breathing heavily when Wolff entered, his face a little sallow, elbows resting on a copy of *The Times*. With a curt nod he indicated the chair on the opposite side of his desk. It was a large airy office, simply decorated with naval charts and a picture of French villagers before a Prussian firing squad. He had placed some of the mechanical gadgets he enjoyed tinkering with at idle moments on a table beneath the window. The largest piece of furniture in the room was a huge steel Dartmouth-green safe where he kept his 'eyes only' files. Two of these were on the desk in front of Wolff.

'Have you seen this?' Cumming tapped the newspaper with his forefinger. 'For some extraordinary reason, they launched their first air raid on your part of the world. Killed a boy in King's Lynn.'

'Yes, my mother thought she heard the Zeppelin; it passed over her farm.'

'Quite a coincidence – I mean, after your visit to the factory at Friedrichshafen. That was a fine piece of work.'

Wolff didn't reply.

'No one took the damn things seriously until they read your report,' Cumming continued. 'The PS at the War Office reminded me of that the other day; wanted to know how you'd managed it. Told him to mind his own bloody business.'

Get to the point, for goodness' sake, thought Wolff. He'd been one of C's scallywags for almost as long as there'd been a Bureau, so they could dispense with the customary overture. The captain didn't play it well anyway, too soapy, too obvious.

'It was the reason I was able to get you back from Turkey, of course. That was a bad business.' Cumming shook his head sympathetically. 'But it's been a while now, hasn't it? Nine months?'

'Something like that.'

'Do you think you're ready now?'

'Ready for what, sir?'

'It's the Irish, you see. Or should I say the Irish problem . . .'
He was interrupted by a knock at the door and Miss Groves entered with the tray. They sat in silence as she poured the coffee, Cumming polishing his monocle with a handkerchief. It was his favourite prop. It made him look villainous, like a spymaster in a shilling shocker. Without it he was the sort of stout, elderly military gentleman you passed in the street without a second glance: mid fifties, with thin white hair, a Punch-like chin, a small mouth and keen grey eyes. They had

liked and respected each other once. Cumming had described him as 'a born spy' and he'd meant it as a compliment. There'd been disagreements, difficult times, but Wolff had trusted him in almost all things. In rather too much, as it turned out. Manipulative and as unscrupulous as Genghis Khan, he had reflected in the leisure of his Turkish prison cell, unfettered by personal loyalty, just as he was required to be by the custom and professional practice of his role. The door closed behind Miss Groves.

'What do you know about Roger Casement?'

Wolff shrugged. 'No more than I read in the papers. Champion of native rights in Africa and elsewhere, celebrated servant of the Crown turned Irish rebel— '

'Traitor,' interrupted Cumming. 'He was in America, now he's in Germany. Gave our fellows the slip. New papers, new face – he shaved his beard . . .' He reached for his cup, cradling it in large calloused sailor's hands. 'There's no doubt about what he wants, of course. Guns and men. Force Irish independence at the point of a German bayonet, and succeed or fail, they know that civil unrest at home would draw men from the fighting in France . . .'

'. . . and set a poor example to the rest of the Empire?'

C put down his cup deliberately. 'Do you believe that, or is it the cynicism you effect as one of your clever disguises?'

'Merely an observation, sir.'

'Do you have views on Ireland?'

'I'm not very interested in politics.'

He nodded approvingly. 'It's enough to be a patriot. We're at war.'

'As you say, sir.'

'Which is why I hope you'll agree to my proposition.'

'You haven't made one yet, sir.'

'Haven't I? No, well I know it won't be easy but we need to

know what he's doing in Berlin, you see. Need someone in his circle.' He peered at Wolff intently through his monocle as if hoping to force instant acquiescence.

Wolff returned his gaze with a stony face. *He wants me to go to Germany.* Lifting his cup slowly, he examined then swirled the dregs of his coffee before returning it to the saucer. Really too bitter a blend for his taste.

'Different from your last assignment, of course,' C remarked, shifting uncomfortably in his chair. 'You know Germany. It's your patch.'

'We shoot their spies now, don't we? And they shoot ours.'

'Everything's tighter in war, you know that.'

'Will you explain that to my widow?'

'Isn't she somebody else's wife?' C enquired tartly.

'Have you been spying on me?'

Cumming dismissed the question with a wave of the hand. 'Won't be easy, I know,' he repeated, with a little less sympathy, 'but no one has your experience of operating in Germany. I still trust you to do a good job.'

'Should I be grateful for your trust? What about Landau or Bywater?'

'You're a spy, Wolff. This is what you're supposed to do. Are you refusing to consider it?'

Am I? Wolff wondered. *Did he have a choice?* The room seemed darker suddenly. He turned his head a little to gaze out of the window. It was a miserable grey January day, miserable. Drops of rain were beginning to trickle down the pane. Sooty London rain. 'No, I'm not refusing. I'll consider it,' he said flatly.

'It's all we have on Casement.' Cumming leant across the desk to push the 'eyes only' files closer. 'Use the scallywags' room. Speak to Miss Groves if you need anything else. Two days is enough. We'll meet again on Thursday. But not here – the Clapham safe house. Will you be awake by ten?'

Wolff picked up the files, and rose quickly from his chair. He was almost at the door when Cumming spoke again: 'Perhaps you've no longer the stomach for this sort of work.' His voice was harder. There was a steely glint in his eye, the old pugilist preparing to lead with his remarkable chin. 'I could order you to go.'

'I thought it was a proposition?'

'You're not the only one, you know,' and he lifted *The Times* and shook it at Wolff. 'Don't you read the casualty list? These fellows are only just out of short trousers.' He glanced away, thin lips white with righteous anger. 'The thing is, your country bloody well needs you, Wolff, they need you – don't forget it.'

Bugger Kitchener. Wolff knew he had earned the right to say so. He'd thought nothing of his own safety when he'd accepted his first assignment – nor had anyone else. He'd learnt a lot in ten years.

He was a tall man with the lean, muscular physique of a distance runner. As a boy, he had run in his grandfather's fields, and as a youth, along fenland dykes to the sea, before him always a seamless Lincolnshire sky. At Cambridge, he'd won a blue; as an officer cadet he'd represented the Navy and earned grudging respect from those who didn't consider a grammar-school engineer a proper gentleman. Wolff drank too much, he smoked too much, but he was still in good condition. He wore his suits well and took trouble with his appearance, a practical man but not without vanity. Clean shaven, with the Dutch face of his father's people, women judged him handsome and often mistook him for younger than his thirty-seven years. Something in his demeanour suggested he had seen a good deal of the world and he was often taken for a 'foreigner'; it was an impression he'd found it useful to cultivate.

He read the Casement files carefully, making notes in his own shorthand as an aide-memoire. After lunch, he spent an hour sheltering from the rain in a bookshop on the Charing Cross Road and bought a handsome edition of Conan Doyle's *The Poison Belt*. In Trafalgar Square, a recruiting officer and his sergeants were shouting 'Duty' and 'Honour' at passers-by.

A month before, there had been no need for raised voices; the crowd was five deep at the base of the Column. Now the rush to glory was over. He walked on into St James's Park, the bare branches drip-dripping on his hat and overcoat, a mist thickening to a late-afternoon pea-souper. Somewhere on the still lake a duck struggled to take flight and from the direction of the Palace, the dreary echo of a regimental band playing an imperial favourite. At the bridge Wolff stopped and leant on the wet rail to consider C's 'proposition', but poisonous memories kept looming in and out of his mind like people passing in the fog.

He had resolved to finish with the Bureau. He'd spent almost a year in the Sultan's special prison in Istanbul contemplating an escape to something better, a return perhaps to the submarine service he had helped to pioneer. But by the time the Foreign Office had decided it was worthwhile negotiating his release he'd recognised the impossibility of settling to his old life again. Then the Kaiser had put paid to other possibilities by marching his armies into Belgium. Wolff ran his forefinger along the rail of the bridge, impatiently stroking raindrops into the lake. 'Honour', 'duty', 'sacrifice' were on everyone's lips these days. He'd been doing his bit for ten years. He'd made sacrifices. Violet liked to trace some of them on his skin.

Wolff turned and crossed the bridge, strolling back along the lake towards Whitehall. Bowler-hatted civil servants hurried past on the way to Victoria Station and their tidy homes in the suburbs. The lights in the Foreign Secretary's office were still burning brightly even if they'd gone out in the rest of Europe. Wolff wondered if he'd taken tea there with Casement and listened to his tales of Africa and South America. Casement had been a hero for the new century. Proof in person of Great Britain's civilising influence on the rest of the world. Knighted by his king, as conquerors were before him, but for his work on behalf of Negroes and Indians. Whitehall didn't hold Wolff in very high regard and his work was not of the civilising sort. He didn't give a fig for the Foreign Secretary's good opinion but the irony of being asked to spy upon a man who'd received so much of his approbation made him smile.

Crossing Horse Guards Road, he walked briskly on up the steps into Downing Street. A group of senior army officers was adjusting hats and sticks on the pavement outside Number 10. He followed them into Whitehall and stood beneath the street-lamp in front of the Foreign Office in the hope of attracting the attention of a passing cab. Parliament was lost in the fog and he could only distinguish a muddy halo of office windows on the opposite side of Whitehall. Am I to risk my life in Germany because Casement has so thoroughly disappointed them all? he wondered. 'Here.' The taxi wheezed to the kerb a few yards beyond him. 'Take me to Devonshire Place.'

The trouble with Sir Roger Casement, he reflected as he swung on to the taxi's seat, is that he's no longer the conscience of the Empire but a challenge to its existence.

Mrs Violet Curtis had invited her younger brother and two of his friends to join them for dinner at Rules. A striking figure in pale lavender satin, daringly décolleté, she moved with a graceful swing of the hips that drew the gaze of the gentlemen in the restaurant. There was something carnal in her obvious wish to please.

23

'You're lucky, you know,' she'd told Wolff a few weeks into their affair. 'My friends can't understand what I see in you.'

He was fifteen years her senior and only a year younger than her husband.

'Why don't you say you love me?' she often asked him.

But she wanted him because he refused to and trusted him because he never spoke of the future. When Major Reggie Curtis returned from Belgium she would be waiting to fall into his arms.

Wolff sensed, even before the waiter dropped a napkin into his lap, that it was going to be an unpleasant evening. Violet had taken the seat opposite him and was bubbling noisily, drawing more hungry looks from the gentlemen at adjoining tables. Violet's brother and his friends were in uniform and conversation turned to the war before they'd finished with the menu.

'Do you think they'll bomb London?' they wanted to know.

'Sebastian's mother heard a Zeppelin, didn't she, darling?'

'They killed a fourteen-year-old boy. You see – that's what we're fighting against.'

'They say the war won't last more than another six months . . .'

'Long enough for us to get out there, I hope.'

They talked like rugby-club hearties before a game. It put Wolff in a bad humour. Violet frowned at him as if to say, 'Buck up, why don't you?' She was an astute judge of men's moods and she'd seen him like this before. She smiled and sometimes she giggled but there were anxious little lines on her brow as if she also sensed that the evening would end badly.

He was a portly junior officer with the sort of sly moustache the war had made fashionable. He had been staring at Violet from the moment she'd entered the restaurant but it had taken time and wine for him to find the courage to approach her. Out of the corner of his eye, Wolff watched the man make excuses to his party, rise from his chair and walk unsteadily towards their table. His fleshy face was the colour of a Weissherbst rosé and he was perspiring profusely. Violet was too caught up in her own story to notice him at her shoulder, even when he'd secured the attention of her audience. He cleared his throat nervously and then again with more determination.

'Oh, hello,' she half turned to look up at him.

'Mrs Curtis? My name's Barrett. I have the honour of serving with Major Curtis.'

'Oh? How wonderful.' She blushed and her tiny hands began to wrestle with a napkin. 'Did you hear that, everyone? Join us, Lieutenant, please,' and she tried to summon a waiter for a chair.

'No. Thank you. No, Mrs Curtis.' The lieutenant took a deep shaky breath. He was preparing to step off his precipice.

Violet must have sensed it too because she began to chatter like a small child before an angry parent. 'When did you last see him? My husband, I mean. It's been so long . . .' Her right hand strayed to her lip. 'This is my brother, Adam . . .'

'Out of respect for your husband, I must say, your behaviour, well, he deserves better,' Barrett stammered.

Violet's face began to crumple.

'It isn't my place—' he continued.

'You're right. It isn't,' interrupted Wolff. 'Your place is over there.' He nodded to the lieutenant's table. 'I suggest you rejoin your companions at once.'

Barrett's jaw dropped like a marionette's at rest. 'Who the devil –' he said at last. 'Who the devil are you, sir? My business—'

'Sit down before you make a fool of yourself, why don't you?'

'Please, Sebastian.' Violet gave him a desperate look. Her eyes were shining with tears. 'Please, let him just say what he wants to say and go.'

'Are you the fellow?' Barrett's dander was up, flushed with wine and a righteous resolve to have it out, his right hand in a fist at his side. 'What are you smiling at? Not in uniform, I see,' and he snapped his fingers theatrically in front of Wolff's face.

'Look, steady, old chap . . .' This from Violet's brother. He had dumped his napkin on the table and was rising. Wolff was conscious of a hush in the restaurant, broken only by the tinkle of knives and forks on china and the mumble of waiters serving the tables. The manager was moving swiftly towards them.

'Leave now, Lieutenant,' said Wolff quietly. But Barrett wasn't going to surrender an inch of polished floor to someone in white tie and tails. 'What is your name, sir?' he demanded loudly. 'It is my intention to write to Major Curtis . . .'

'Please, sir.' The manager touched Barrett's elbow and he began to turn towards him. 'I must ask— '

But his words were drowned by a clatter of plates.

'No, Sebastian,' Violet squealed.

It was too late. Wolff was on his feet and lunging for the lieutenant's wrist. Grasping it in his left hand, he thrust at Barrett's head with his right, as if trying to jerk it from his shoulders. The lieutenant whimpered with pain and bent double as Wolff twisted his arm and locked it at right angles to his body, the pressure on the elbow. Then, with a deft turn, Wolff forced Barrett's arm behind his back, pulling him upright by the collar. No one had moved. There had been no time to cry out in protest. It was over in the blink of an eye, accomplished with a sleight of hand worthy of Houdini the handcuff king.

Violet buried her face in a lace handkerchief. Her brother was still hovering over the table with an expression of complete astonishment on his face. Wolff caught his eye. 'Settle our bill, will you?'

'Let me go at once, do you hear.' Barrett had found his voice.

There was a rumble of disapproval as the restaurant began to stir at last.

'Really, I say,' one man shouted.

'This is Rules,' ventured another. 'Let the fellow go.'

Wolff didn't reply. Eyes front, he frog-marched Barrett across the floor, weaving between tables with the rough confidence of an East End landlord at closing time. Manager and waiters fussed about him, a young army officer made a half-hearted attempt to block his way – Wolff brushed him aside – but no one was willing to lift a finger to prevent him reaching the door.

Rain was beating on the restaurant's awning, gusting down Maiden Lane and chasing couples on their way home from the theatre into the shelter of shopfronts. Within seconds Wolff's trousers were clinging to his legs. A passing car sloshed into the gutter and a sheet of dirty water swept across the pavement on to Lieutenant Barrett's perfectly polished boots. The button had come off one of his shoulder boards and it was flapping like a broken wing.

'Let me go, do you hear?' He was almost weeping. 'You haven't heard the last of this, you coward.'

Wolff twisted his arm tighter until he gasped with pain. It would be a simple thing to break it, Wolff thought, and for a moment he wanted to. Why shouldn't Barrett be made to pay?

'Let him go,' screamed Violet, and she tugged at his arm. 'For God's sake, are you mad?'

'How could you?' she asked Wolff repeatedly. She cried and shouted – he had humiliated her in front of 'everyone' – but she refused to go home with her brother. She sat in smouldering silence in the taxicab to his apartment, and fell on him with her tiny fists as soon as he had closed the door, biting, scratching, then kissing – the desperate passion of those who wish to forget. Later, in crumpled sheets, her small round face pressed in sleep to his shoulder, he wondered if it was the darkness she'd glimpsed in him at the restaurant that had aroused her so.

He'd had many affairs. Short, intense, unrestrained and blinding for a time. He had told two women that he loved them but when it was over he couldn't be sure. He cared for his mother. The thought made him smile: the spy and his mother. His father had died when he was five and his mother and paternal grandfather had brought him up, a little foreign boy, an only child in a lonely place – always running.

Violet stirred beside him and he craned forward to kiss her hair. It was damp with perspiration and smelt of her perfume and their sex. He traced the graceful curves of her body beneath the sheet with his fingertips. Would it be different if they were in love? He was sorry he'd upset her at the restaurant. He had wanted to protect her from scandal but all he'd succeeded in doing was inviting more. One day soon the post would travel up the line and there would be a letter for Major Curtis.

'Letter for Major Curtis.'

Wolff could see him there, knee deep in Flanders mud, preparing to lead a raiding party, or in a funk hole under shell-fire. There'd be a big smile on his face – there was always a smile on Reggie Curtis's face. He'd tear the letter open with a dirty fingernail.

I feel it my duty to inform you, Sir, that your wife is fucking your old Cambridge chum, Sebastian Wolff. Yours respectfully, et cetera, et cetera.

Overcome with grief, he would lead a suicidal charge into no-man's-land and be blown to small pieces by a Jack Johnson. Reggie could be the most obliging of fellows.

Wolff shuffled down the bed until his face was close to

Violet's, then leant forward to kiss her lightly on the lips. She smiled but didn't open her eyes, and he felt a surge of tenderness for her. 'Shameless hussy, I'll miss you.' He'd drunk deeply of her, intoxicated by her beguiling smile, the scent of her and the way she seemed to glide through life with effortless grace – those things and more. But it wasn't enough. It was an illusion. He leant forward to kiss Violet again. He would go to Germany and, for as long as he could stay alive, he'd pretend to be someone else, someone who hadn't broken and screamed in agony and begged them to stop. Wasn't that his patriotic duty? Didn't he owe his country that much? C had blown his whistle and he would go over the top with the rest.

2

Cover

THE TEMPERATURE FELL to freezing at dusk and by the time the ship was close to Christiania the mooring ropes were stiff with ice. Wolff watched from the promenade deck as the pricks of light on the banks of the fjord closed into the solid band of the city. The port was quieter than he'd known it before the war, with fewer vessels in passage or waiting at anchor for a berth. The enemy had been pinched out of Norwegian waters. The *Helig Olav* came alongside the pier beneath the curtain wall of the medieval fortress. Although it was late, there was a crowd at the Scandinavian America Line's office to meet her and taxicabs and tradesmen's vehicles were idling on the dockside road, their lamps winking a secret signal as people scurried between them on to the quay. Ropes made fast, stevedores began to swing gangways in place along her side. Wolff peeled his glove from the frozen rail and joined the queue of passengers shuffling towards the companionway.

'You're Mr Jan de Witt,' C had informed him the day he accepted his assignment. 'A Dutchman with a grudge.'

'An Afrikaner?'

'The same thing,' he joked. 'You crossed the Atlantic on an American passport – one of our chaps made the journey for you.'

'You were certain I'd do as I was told then?'

'You're a naval officer, yes,' he'd replied matter-of-factly. Rank and the service he dropped and raised with the incontinence of a tart's knickers. 'Our Mr de Witt works for New England Westinghouse and poses as an American, an engineer adventurer if you like, but on the wrong side. You'll spend a week in Amsterdam visiting business partners – meetings have been arranged for you – then you'll travel to Norway.'

The Norwegians were 'our neutral allies', C had said. It was possible to 'arrange things' in Christiania.

From the second-class crowd at the top of the gangway, Wolff watched an officer in the Norwegian border police examining the papers of passengers disembarking at the bottom. The elderly constable beside him had shrunk inside his greatcoat, his face frozen in an expression of complete indifference. Wolff paused to allow a young woman with two small girls to step in front of him, then followed them closely down the gangway. By some small miracle, the steward he'd entrusted with his case had fought his way off the ship and was negotiating with a cab driver.

The police officer demanded Wolff's passport in perfect English, and turned its pages deliberately, holding the red State Department stamp to his eye. He was older than Wolff, with an intelligent face but the complexion, the small broken veins, of a heavy drinker.

'Your name is de Witt?' he asked at last.

'That's what it says.'

'What is your business here?'

'I'm visiting a client. Paulsen Shipping.'

'And then?'

'And then a meeting in Copenhagen.'

'I see.' The police officer folded the leaf with the stapled photograph of Wolff carefully into the passport and offered it back to him: 'It seems in order.'

But when Wolff tried to take it he wouldn't let go.

'Where will you be staying in Christiania, Mr de Witt?' There was something in the way he spoke the name *de Witt* that suggested he had heard it before, something in his frown and in his little bloodshot eyes, a crack in the veneer of cool indifference that is the part of the experienced minor official everywhere.

'I have a reservation at the Grand Hotel,' Wolff replied curtly. 'So, if you've finished . . .'

The policeman stared at him suspiciously for a few seconds more, then released his passport: 'Thank you, Mr de Witt.' And the mask slipped back into place.

The Grand Hotel was the place to be noticed in Christiania. It wasn't handsome or especially grand but it was on the city's main thoroughfare, a stone's throw from the parliament, palace, National Theatre and university. The hotel of choice for well-heeled travellers and businessmen, and now Europe was at war – for the gentleman spy. Its façade was in the French style and reminded Wolff a little of the Bureau's offices in Whitehall Court. A letter on Westinghouse headed paper was waiting in reception with instructions for his meetings in Christiania and Copenhagen and promising a further communication in Berlin, and Wolff noted that the reservation had been made for him by someone at the company in America. The Bureau hadn't cut any corners. The porter carried his bags to the room and was rewarded with a gratuity generous enough to be memorable. Wolff unpacked his own clothes. They had been bought for him in America but were too crisp and new to risk handing over to a valet. It was just the sort of small thing that might arouse suspicion. There was always someone happy to sell information in a grand hotel: perhaps the maid who emptied the wastepaper baskets of well-to-do guests for only a few krone a week, or the pageboy who delivered their correspondence for even less, or the concierge who summoned the taxicabs and spoke to their drivers later. Policeman or spy, British or German – there was money to be made from everyone in a neutral country. Wolff poured himself a whisky from the bottle he'd brought with him, ran a hot bath and lay sipping and soaking in a cloud of steam.

He'd spent six weeks growing into Mr Jan de Witt's skin.

'I know it isn't long,' C had observed. 'But I'm confident we've thought of everything. You'll need a legend the enemy can follow. Mansfeldt Findlay at the Legation in Christiania can help you with footprints. He's a good fellow. Done this sort of thing for us before. We have him to thank for the informer.'

Wolff lifted a soapy hand to his beard. Jan de Witt's little Dutch beard. It took time to get used to. A beard always changed his appearance markedly; it made his thin face fuller and intensely serious, like the photograph of his father that hung in a thick black frame above the fireplace in the parlour at his mother's farm.

'Damn good thing your beard, you know,' C had teased. 'Traitors have beards.'

'Oh? I thought it was a monocle?'

C had chuckled like a fat schoolboy. 'Makes you look a little like Casement.'

The following morning, Wolff took breakfast at the Grand Café with an old copy of the *New York Times*. At a little before nine he visited the front desk to ask for directions to Paulsen Shipping. It was his intention to walk the short distance to the harbour, he said, and when his business was over he hoped to walk a little further. Taking Baedeker from the pocket of his overcoat, he let the porter trace a route on a map to the city's notable sights. A stiff north-easterly was shaking the hotel's broad awning like the mainsail of a ship, force 6 fresh to rock the steamers anchored in the bay but bright enough for Wolff to step out with his coat over his arm. He walked briskly along Karl Johans gate towards the parliament, then on to the East Station, stopping from time to time to glance in shop windows, and even dashing between trams to a newspaper kiosk on the pavement opposite.

Paulsen Shipping occupied a modest two-storey building of the sort that was being pulled down all over the city to meet the requirements of the brash new century. Its granite-faced neighbours had been built in the ten years since independence and were indistinguishable from many of a similar age in the City of London. A clerk led Wolff from its tiled hall to a large office on the first floor and asked him to wait, with the assurance that Mr Paulsen would be pleased to welcome him soon. It was a large mahogany-panelled room, smoke-filled and gloomy, with only two small windows overlooking the narrow street. A dozen or so brokers and clerks – young men in their twenties for the most part – sat facing their managing director's door like children in a Victorian schoolroom. On the wall behind them, the severe grey countenance of the man Wolff took to be the company's founding father.

'Jacob the First. My grandfather.' The managing director had slipped out of his office and was standing above Wolff with a broad smile on his face.

'I'm the third. Jacob Paulsen the Third,' and he offered Wolff his hand. 'Isn't that how you Americans style it, Mr de Witt? As if you were kings. This is my kingdom,' he said, opening his arms to the room like a music-hall doxy, 'until I'm swallowed up by Olsen or Knutsen Shipping or one of the others. Please . . .' and with a flamboyant sweep of his hand he invited Wolff to step into his office.

'My grandfather was a friend of Henrik Ibsen's, you know,' he said, pulling the door to behind them. 'Helped him with a little money. Sit down, please.' He pulled a red leather armchair away from his desk. A log fire was spitting in the hearth and dancing warmly on the polished panelled walls.

'Peculiar, really, he didn't care for the theatre. All my grandfather cared about was ships and money – we were quite a company in his day.'

His English was perfect but drawled in the languid manner of an undergraduate aesthete. Early fifties, tall and thin, his straw-blond hair streaked with white, the same light-blue eyes as his grandfather, the same thin, almost colourless lips, a smile hovering constantly at the corners. Mr Jacob Paulsen the Third was an easy fellow but not a foolish one. There was a wariness in his glance, in the deliberate way he walked to the drinks cabinet in the corner of the room.

'A celebration,' he said, lifting two small glasses. 'Have you tried our akevitt?'

'Is there something to celebrate?'

'Of course. Always. But our arrangement in particular,' and he placed the glasses and a bottle on a tray and carried them back to his desk. The bottle in his left hand, he opened a drawer with his right, took out an envelope and slid it across the desk to Wolff. 'It's from the minister at your Legation, Mr Findlay . . .'

'Do you know what's in it?'

'Arrangements for your meeting.'

'Do you know where?'

'No.'

Wolff ran the tip of his forefinger along the flap to check the seal. Satisfied, he tore it open and unfolded the note. There were just two lines.

'Have you been to our country before, Mr de Witt?' Paulsen

had poured the akevitt and was settling into his chair with a glass.

'Are you sure you know your part?' Wolff asked impatiently.

He frowned. 'Perfectly. Unlike my grandfather I love theatre and I'm a consummate liar. Your people in London must have spoken to you about me? I have been of service in the past. Now, your very good health.' He raised his glass in salute, then drained it in a gulp. 'Please,' he said, a little hoarsely, and gestured with his glass to the one he'd poured for Wolff. 'Please.'

'They'll send someone to you. He won't be German. One of your own countrymen, probably someone you know. A businessman, perhaps a family friend or a policeman . . .'

'I have everything,' and Paulsen rested the palm of his right hand on a large leather-bound ledger, 'correspondence, invoices. My staff know your name and that you work for Westinghouse but I've handled everything and that will have made them curious, even a little suspicious.'

Wolff nodded approvingly.

'Look to your own part, Mr de Witt; rest assured I know what I'm doing. Now another . . .' and, half rising, he reached across the desk for the bottle. 'And this time I hope you'll join me.'

'Are there references to the rifles in the paperwork?'

'Do you read Norwegian? No, well . . .' Paulsen put down the bottle and picked up the ledger. 'Let me put your mind at rest.' He flicked through it lazily in search of a suitable page. 'Here's something: *The shipment will be hidden in a large consignment of electrical equipment and stamped by the Westinghouse Company* . . . And here: . . . *the client's agent will board in Darwin* . . . *he will make his own arrangements for unloading* . . . You see. Clues. Only clues. But lots of them.'

'Good. To our arrangement then,' Wolff replied, leaning forward to pick up his glass. 'To the success of your performance,

Mr Paulsen. Skoal.' He drank the spirit in one and banged the glass down emphatically on the edge of the desk.

Paulsen smiled: 'And to yours, Mr de Witt.'

Medium height, slight build, brown hair, young – perhaps twenty-five – dressed like a clerk. He was waiting in a doorway a little way along the street from Paulsen's and moved into the cover of the building too quickly. Wolff pretended to consult his Baedeker. Was the tip-off from the hotel or one of Paulsen's people? he wondered. It didn't matter. He had begun leaving a trail a child could follow the moment he stepped from the ship. But make the fellow work a little, he thought. He'd expect that. He closed the guidebook and adjusted his hat. It was only a pity Christiania was such a dull city.

Shuffling too close one minute, racing to catch up the next, bumping into passers-by, spinning round to gaze in shop windows. For a time he made Wolff smile. But what he lacked in craft he made up for in persistence. He was very young. Wolff caught a glimpse of his face in a mirror at the Continental as he was being shown to a table for luncheon. Younger than twenty-five. Twenty. A runner for someone else, that's all. Did he have any idea what he was getting into? Wolff toyed whimsically with the thought of calling him over, sitting him down with a glass of wine and saying, 'Whatever they pay you, my boy, it will never be enough.' But after lunch he took a tram from outside the parliament to the palace and in the course of a stroll through the royal park gave him the slip. To be sure, he caught a second tram in the direction of the smart coastal district of Bygdoy but got off after only a few stops and hopped on to another heading back into the city. It was not until he'd changed twice more that he felt ready to catch one to the St Hanshaugen Park. At the entrance, he consulted his guidebook until he was satisfied that he was still alone, then began to climb through the formal gardens to the reservoir and viewpoint. He'd walked the same route on a summer day fourteen years earlier – a young naval officer enjoying a furlough from his ship. The hill was popular with locals and visitors in the late afternoon. The elderly came to sit and listen to the military band in the pavilion by the lower pond; mothers ambled through the arboretum on its slopes while their children played hide and seek, and courting couples strolled to the top to gaze over the city. It wasn't the sort of place Wolff would have chosen for a clandestine meeting at any time of the year.

The reservoir keeper lived on the crown in a yellow-and-white tower house that Wolff had mistaken on his first visit for a church. Beyond it was the basin with the water supply for the district, the fountain in the centre cascading the colours of the rainbow in the evening sunshine. The stiff breeze was whipping spray across the gravel esplanade and spotted his overcoat as he walked round to the benches on the south side. There was still a nip in the air and as luck would have it the place was deserted but for a Norwegian couple spooning at the rail, too wrapped up in each other to show any interest in Wolff. He sat on a bench and took out his cigarettes. To the east, the wooded slopes of the Ekeberg; Oscarshall and the brick spire of the Uranienborg Church to the west, and beyond it the shimmering sea. But a daft bloody place to meet, just daft. Wolff bent to light a cigarette from the flame guttering in his cupped hands, then rose from the bench and ambled over to the rail, turning his back to the city. It was almost five o'clock. The lovers were drifting along the esplanade. He watched them laughing and kissing with a wry smile of regret. Damn it, didn't they know there was a war on?

A few yards from the keeper's house, they separated as if conscious they were not alone. A moment later, an exceptionally tall figure with the stride of a fairy-tale ogre stalked past them and down the steps to the basin. He was dressed in a bowler hat and black overcoat and used his umbrella as a walking stick as if he was making his way down Whitehall. He was the sort of man it was impossible not to notice and his imperious swagger suggested that he wanted to be. Wolff walked over to a bench and sat down again. A few seconds later Mr Mansfeldt Findlay crunched up the path to stand towering above him.

'Do you think it will rain?'

It was the code he'd suggested in his note.

'I think we can dispense with the formalities, don't you,' replied Wolff.

'All right.' He sounded disappointed. 'Mansfeldt Findlay, Head of Legation.'

'Sit down, Mr Findlay. We'll be less conspicuous.'

'Is something wrong?' His voice was surprisingly high pitched for such a large man.

'You should tell me what you have to tell me quickly, then go.'

'I don't like your tone,' he snapped.

'And I don't like your idea of a discreet rendezvous. But we're here now, so let's get on with it.'

Findlay glared at him for a few seconds, then sat down with the umbrella upright between his legs like a weapon, his enormous hands resting on its ebony handle. A bear of a man in his mid fifties, square jaw, thick grizzled moustache. A man who looked as if he knew how to handle himself in a ring. Queensberry Rules, of course.

'You met our friend Paulsen?' he asked.

'Yes.'

'A good fellow. Won't let us down. Needs the money.'

Wolff frowned. 'It's only the money?'

'Not a bit of it. Anglophile too. A lot of them are, you know. He'll play his part, you can be sure of it.' He paused, then said,

'I've spoken to our friend in the police. Told him a little of my interest in Mr de Witt's activities. His people are looking into it already.'

'How very obliging.'

'Good diplomacy,' he said coolly. 'The enemy has friends here too but our friends are better placed and more sincere. When are you leaving for Berlin?'

'Tomorrow.'

'Good. Make sure it's no later. They're visiting Paulsen tomorrow, then they'll come for you. My guess is the local Germans will have wind of it by the end of the day. They'll know you're on your way to Berlin.'

Wolff took a last draw on his cigarette and ground the butt into the gravel beneath his shoe. 'Tell me about the informer, Adler Christensen.'

Findlay's face wrinkled as if he was recalling an unpleasant smell: 'Came to us at the end of October. He'd struck up a friendship with Casement in New York and was acting as his valet. They were staying at the Grand Hotel and had already made contact with the German delegation in the city.'

Wolff nodded. 'How much did it cost you?'

'A hundred and twenty-five krone. He gave me a contact address in Berlin – here,' and he reached into his coat pocket and took out a small envelope. 'It's a boarding house run by a Norwegian woman. His mother writes to him there. There's a copy of Christensen's last letter too. Damn fellow wants more money. Do you know how you're going to get your information out?'

Wolff took the envelope from him without comment.

'Well, I expect you've met his sort before.' He shook his huge head in disgust.

'What sort? What was he like?'

'Dishonest. Typical Norwegian sailor. Perhaps more dishonest than most. Speaks English like an American. It's all in the file we sent you. Wouldn't trust him further than I could throw him,' he snorted disparagingly.

'Does Christensen like Casement?'

'They're close. He says Casement calls him a "treasure". And I sensed he . . .' His heavy brow gathered in a frown. 'Well, I just didn't like the fellow,' he added, lifting his umbrella to his shoulder.

'Is there something else?'

'I think we should be going, don't you?' Findlay looked uneasy.

'There's something you aren't telling me,' Wolff insisted.

'Goodness, no. No, no. Damn mercenary, that's all. A loathsome creature,' he replied, getting quickly to his feet. 'I don't want to give him another thought,' and he turned deliberately to gaze at the view. It was the hour before sunset, the sky burnt orange and gold like a peach. 'They do their best for us, you know. The Norwegians, I mean.'

Wolff stood up slowly. 'All right. If you're sure you've told me everything.'

'I was only with him for an hour. Glad to get away. A dangerous rascal. Casement too.'

They walked back along the esplanade in silence. When they reached the tower house, Findlay said, 'I'd offer you a lift but . . .'

'No. Thank you.'

Another long silence. The diplomat seemed reluctant to leave.

'We'll get him in the end, you know,' he said at last. 'I just hope the Liberals have the balls to hang him. *Pour encourager*. Can't let Ireland go.'

Wolff couldn't think of anything to say. He wasn't sure he cared.

'Look, good luck.' Findlay offered his hand. 'Be careful, for God's sake. Rest assured your friends here will do all they can.'

He began to walk towards his car but stopped after only a few yards and turned to Wolff again. 'You're a brave fellow,' he said stiffly.

He's written me off already, thought Wolff.

3

A German Scientist

HERR PROFESSOR DR Fritz Haber brushed the chalk from his uniform jacket and turned to face them with an indulgent smile.

'You know a little chemistry.' He didn't wait for Anton Dilger to reply. 'For the benefit of the Count,' he said, pointing to the equation he'd written on the blackboard in a bold hand.

$$Cl_2 + H_2O \rightarrow HCl +$$

'Chlorine is a diatomic element. It combines with most elements but not with oxygen and nitrogen. At certain concentrations, corrosive when it comes into contact with epithelium, forming hydrochloric acid in moist tissue – eyes, nose, throat, lungs and . . .' He picked up the chalk again and wrote the symbol HOCl: 'Hypochlorous acid,' then took a step away and frowned at the board as if the simple act of writing the equation had set his mind to another thread of chemical possibilities.

Is he a genius? Dilger wondered. Some people said so. The first to fix nitrogen from the air. *Brot aus Luft!* Bread out of air. His discovery made fertilisers possible; he'd enriched the soil and fed the world. Yes, there were some who called it 'an act of genius'.

Haber was completely bald, like a wrinkled egg. Late forties, short, his eyes almost hidden beneath a pronounced brow and by pince-nez spectacles. He had a bushy moustache and a large nose. His manner was clipped, even a little haughty. He won't suffer fools gladly, Dilger thought anxiously. He knew he was a little too conscious of the honour Haber was bestowing in speaking to him as an equal. Professor Troester had arranged the visit to the Kaiser Wilhelm Institute. 'I'd like you to meet the director,' he had told Dilger. 'The professor is a great German patriot,' and, more cryptically, 'You'll find him helpful.'

Haber had greeted the three of them – naturally, Nadolny had come too – in his lecture hall. He'd been sitting near the back, almost lost in the rows of empty benches, elbows on his knees, rolling a large cigar between his fingers, his assistants in white coats at the door like monks in attendance on an abbot at prayer.

'I still don't understand a word of it, do you, gentlemen?' remarked Count Nadolny, turning with a wry smile to Troester.

'Of course,' he replied curtly.

'To the director of this Institute, everything is simple,' said Nadolny, acknowledging Haber with a gracious bow. 'I am merely an old soldier.'

'You do yourself an injustice. The Count has a subtle mind, don't you agree?' Haber asked, turning to Dilger with a distant smile. 'In chemistry as in life, Count; few things are as simple as they appear. There are always choices to be made.'

'Tested in the crucible of time, but . . .' the Count paused, flourishing his hand and the red intaglio at the blackboard. 'Perhaps you can demonstrate the practical application of your work here, Professor.'

The late-afternoon sun was casting strange shifting shadows as it streamed through the laboratory windows on to shimmering Bunsen flames and assorted bell jars, flasks and cylinders. It was a long room with a high barrel-vaulted ceiling, the ceramic-topped benches in rows facing the door, glass-fronted cabinets and shelves against the walls. Better equipped than Heidelberg, Dilger thought, and a more orderly environment than the one he'd studied in at Johns Hopkins in Baltimore, but unremarkable except in one respect. The collars and Saxon cuffs beneath the white coats of the young men at the work benches were field grey, and peaked caps were hanging on the stand by the door. On a board next to it was the old saying, *War is the Father of all things*, and in ebony frames on the wall, the Kaiser and the Chief of the General Staff, von Falkenhayn. Professor Dr Fritz Haber's laboratory belonged to the Army and to its industry.

'We discussed the possibility in a general way before the war and I carried out a little research of my own,' he said, leading them over to the workbench nearest the window, 'but it wasn't until we had the money and there was the political will.'

One of his research assistants had drawn a hose from a steel cylinder beneath the bench and was attaching it to the bottom of a large bell jar. In the jar were five albino rats.

'Doctor Hahn is my Pied Piper.' Haber smiled benignly at his assistant, then bent forward to peer at the squealing tangle of white fur. 'Our calculations suggest it will be effective on the battlefield at a concentration as low as one to one thousand.' He paused, his brow wrinkled like an anxious Humpty Dumpty, before adding as an afterthought: 'Of course, we won't be able to determine this precisely until we've tried.'

Then he nodded to his assistant who reached beneath the bench and turned the tap on the cylinder. First a puff as if someone with an evil cigarette had exhaled into the jar, then a steady stream of yellow-green gas. Dilger was surprised that he could see it so clearly. It was heavy, sitting in a cloud at the bottom, the rats scrambling for the top of the bell jar, pink eyes, white fur twisting, turning, clawing at the glass.

'Our dissections show clear evidence of spontaneous pulmonary disease – an increase in the mucus-secreting cells in the bronchial tree,' Haber observed, tapping the glass with his knuckle. 'They drown in their own body fluids.'

'Extraordinary.' Professor Troester leant closer, pocket watch in his hand; 'About a minute and thirty seconds.' The rats were twitching at the bottom of the bell jar. 'Yes, extraordinary. Don't you think so, Doctor?' he asked, glancing sideways at Dilger.

'I . . . yes, extraordinary,' Dilger said, although he didn't know what to think.

The twitching had stopped. 'Extraordinary,' Troester repeated, straightening his long back. 'But will it be possible to ensure a satisfactory result in normal atmospheric conditions, Professor?'

'We will err on the side of caution,' said Haber, polishing his glasses with his handkerchief. 'I have advised the General Staff we will require something like a hundred and sixty tons of liquid chlorine along a front of two or three kilometres. Of course it will depend upon wind speed and direction, but I'm confident six thousand cylinders will be enough and, well, yes, will . . .'

'Secure a decisive breakthrough?'

Haber put his glasses back on his nose and smiled. 'Yes, Count, a decisive breakthrough.'

'Ha! There you have it, gentlemen,' Nadolny declared, clapping his hands together. 'A triumph of German science. What do you think of that, Doctor?' The professor was one of the first to recognise the need for science to keep in step with the people, he gushed, even when they marched to war.

Then Haber led them from his laboratory and along corridors where work was taking place on even more 'interesting' possibilities. On the stairs they saw a uniformed scientist in one of the new gas masks, and in the lecture theatre an excitable member of the director's research team was instructing the first special gas unit on the handling and placing of the new weapon.

'I'm going to supervise the first release myself,' Haber confided to Dilger as they were leaving the theatre. 'I must make my own observations.'

'Do any of the men in your research unit have doubts, Professor?'

Haber stopped abruptly, his hand on the half-open door. 'My dear Doctor,' he said irritably, 'my dear Dr Dilger – they obey my orders.'

'Yes, I see.' But he didn't see. No. He wanted the great scientist and great patriot to explain. Wasn't that why Troester had brought him to the Institute?

'The international agreement prohibiting poison gas, Professor,' prompted the Count, at Haber's shoulder. 'I think Dr Dilger would like to hear your view on the ethical question.'

'The ethical question? Ha. My dear fellow.' Haber was smiling again. 'Yes, of course, in more congenial surroundings.'

The professor invited them to his home and they drank tea with milk and sugar in the English way. He lived a short distance from the Institute in the city village of Dahlem, in a surprisingly modest villa that was painted a sickly shade of yellow like the gas. A Prussian home, too self-consciously so, Dilger thought, placing his cup and saucer on a table by the arm of his chair. Everyone knew that Haber and his wife were Jews who had converted to Christianity. Some said he had traded his religion for a professor's chair, others, to be a better German. Their drawing room was unimaginatively furnished with heavy imperial pieces and landscape prints and in the hall Dilger noticed a full-length portrait of the Kaiser. Frau Haber didn't keep an orderly house. The furniture was new but scruffy, as if she cared nothing for her husband's reputation. It smelt of strong tobacco. The professor was sitting in a swirling cloud of smoke now, his back to the window.

'You see, no one has been able to explain to my satisfaction, Doctor, why dying of asphyxiation . . .' he paused to puff on his cigar, '. . . asphyxiation, is any worse than having your leg blown off and bleeding to death. Is there a moral difference?' he asked, turning first to Troester and then to Nadolny.

'No, of course not,' replied Troester, shaking his head vigorously.

'Morality?' Nadolny dismissed the question with a casual wave of his hand. 'War gives a biologically just decision.'

'No, Count. Victory in the shortest possible time is the correct moral position,' said Haber, shifting earnestly on the edge of his chair. 'Gas warfare will help us win this war quickly. There will be fewer casualties. Battles are not won by the physical destruction of the enemy but by undermining his will to resist – forcing him to imagine defeat. You see . . .' Unable to contain himself any longer, the professor rose and began to pace the length of the drawing room, stooping a little, the black cigar burning between his fingers, '. . . you see, the psychological power of bullets and shells is nothing in modern warfare to the threat of chemicals. There are hundreds of lethal chemicals, each with its own taste and smell, and these poisons are unsettling to the soul. Victory can be won by frightening the enemy, not by destroying him.'

'Professor Haber is correct,' said Troester, turning a little in his chair to address Dilger in his precise laboratory voice. 'The knight on horseback feared the soldier with the gun. In this modern age, the soldier feels the same when confronted by the scientist. It's the scientist who'll bring this war to a speedy end.'

'I couldn't have put it better myself,' said Haber, waving the stub of his cigar triumphantly at Dilger. 'The German scientist.'

A trail of ash marked his passage across the rug. 'And our work is the same, Doctor, your work, my work, there is no difference between us. It is a heavy responsibility but we are the only ones who can carry out this task.'

'Gentlemen, Dr Dilger is still considering our proposition,' said Nadolny quietly and with the suggestion of a reproach.

'Oh?' Haber looked surprised.

'I'm grateful for your guidance, Professor,' said Dilger defensively. He had listened to them with the professional detachment of a doctor at a bedside case conference even though he knew they viewed him as the patient. They had flattered him, confided in him, spoken to him as an equal, and he aspired to be one, but not this way, with this sort of work, not in America. 'It would be an honour to play a part,' he ventured; 'it's just, I feel my duty . . .' He hesitated, aware that his 'gut feeling' was not an explanation the professors would respect. He was spared the immediate trouble of articulating another by a sharp rap at the door.

It would have been easy to have mistaken the woman who entered for a servant but it was clear from Haber's manner that she was his wife and that he was not pleased to see her. They rose to greet her and she offered her hand, but without warmth. Clara Haber was in her forties, short, trim, with a round face that must have been pretty once, tired-looking eyes and a mouth that turned down sadly at the corners. Her faded black dress and the severity with which she had dragged her hair into a bun suggested that she cared no more for her appearance than for the order of her house.

'You've visited my husband's laboratories?' she enquired, settling on a *Kanapee*.

'Professor Haber has shown us some of the work he's carrying out at the Institute, yes,' Troester replied cautiously. 'Remarkable. Fascinating.'

'Do you think so?' There was no mistaking the chill in her voice.

Haber frowned angrily at her but she refused to let him catch her eye. For a few uncomfortable seconds no one spoke.

'Doctor Dilger is a great-grandson of the physiologist, Tiedemann,' Haber remarked at last. 'An American but from a German family . . .'

'Oh?' she cut across him. 'Tiedemann was a great man. You must be proud.'

'Yes, I am, Frau Haber.'

'A great scientist.'

'Yes.'

She leant forward, her gaze fixed intently upon him. 'Are you going to work for my husband, Doctor? If you're an American you can refuse.'

There was another long silence. Haber was squirming in his chair but she paid him no attention. She was watching Dilger with the patient fervour of a mystic at prayer, her dark eyes pleading with him – to do what? The clock in the hall chimed the half-hour.

'Please, Frau Haber.' Count Nadolny was on his feet. 'Gentlemen, I think we should leave. Frau Haber is not herself.'

'Don't you see?' she said quietly. 'You must, Doctor. Someone must say "no".' She leant forward, her hands clasped so tightly her knuckles were pushing white through her skin. 'You're American, you must see how mad . . .'

'I'm a German.' Dilger was angry at her presumption. Was she trying to humiliate him in front of her husband? 'I am a German,' he repeated, raising his voice. 'As a German it would be an honour to serve alongside Professor Haber.'

'An honour!' She spat the word back at him. 'An honour to serve. You're a scientist.' Her eyes were sparkling with fury now. 'It's a crime, a perversion of science. Professor Haber . . . my husband . . . is a criminal.'

'Enough,' Haber shouted, 'enough,' and he tried to grab her arm.

'Gentlemen, really, we must go.' Nadolny was at the door.

'No. I'm leaving,' and she rose quickly from the *Kanapee*. 'I'm leaving,' she said again and this time it sounded like a threat. There were tears on her cheeks but she stared at them defiantly, even with contempt. Then, turning her back, she walked out of the room, her rebuke heavy in the air.

Professor Haber begged them to excuse his wife. She was suffering from a nervous disorder, he said. She had been a fine chemist before their marriage; too clever to settle. She believed the scientist should work for the good of mankind in general, a notion Haber dismissed with a wave of his bony hand as hopelessly naïve. 'Where is the general good in wartime?' he asked them on the doorstep.

Troester patted his arm reassuringly. 'There is nothing beyond victory, my friend.'

As they turned from the house to the waiting cars, Dilger glanced sideways at Nadolny. He was smiling. *I'm a German.* Was that leap of faith ringing in the Count's ears too?

Dilger thought about the visit and their conversation constantly over the next few days. He thought about it on the tram to the Red Cross Hospital and in the director's office as he slid his letter of resignation across the table. He thought about it at dinner with his sister, and even at the Club Noir, eyes fixed on a troupe of scantily clad girls dancing on its brightly lit stage; his mind at the bottom of the professor's bell jar. But most of all he thought about his father in his old cavalry uniform and his cousin Peter's mud-stained scarf, a visit one summer to family graves in Baden and evenings singing old songs with university friends in Heidelberg; a line of Heinrich Heine whispered to lovers in the dark, language, *Kultur*, memory – German, German, German in every fibre of his being. Something he could be sure of and something deeper than his sense of whether it was right or wrong.

Then, one morning, he caught the tram to the Charité Hospital but instead of turning inside he walked further down Luisenstrasse to the low building, like a stable block, that served as the experimental laboratory facility of the Military Veterinary Academy.

4

Wolff in Berlin

'BOERS FIGHT ON *against the British,*' Boyd intoned. 'Seen this?' He thrust the *Morgenpost* at Wolff. 'Are they fightin' for Germany? You know these people, Mr de Witt . . .'

The story was at the bottom of page eight. The British had seized rifles from a ship bound for their colony in the Cape. According to the unnamed source, it was the first of a large consignment purchased for the Afrikaner rebels.

Wolff folded the newspaper carefully and slipped it back on the attaché's desk. 'No, they're fighting for a homeland, Boyd – freedom from the British.'

'A homeland, I see.' Quite plainly he didn't. The trade attaché was an incurious young man. Berlin was his first posting and he was still struggling with what he referred to in his Bostonian drawl as 'the ways of the old world'. Wolff had met him on his first visit to the American Embassy and every day since.

'Happy to be of assistance to a great company like Westinghouse, Mr de Witt,' he had said, accepting Wolff's credentials without question – and he was proving as good as his word. 'There are twenty-five thousand of us here. Do you speak German? If you do risk speakin' English, be sure to wear this,' and he'd pushed a stars-and-stripes lapel badge across his desk. 'They're mad at us for sellin' the British ammunition, so expect some abuse. Oh, and don't speak it on the telephone unless you want the police at your door.'

The city was in the grip of a fever. Suspicion. Exhortations to be watchful for 'the enemy within' were papered on every station wall, to lampposts and kiosks. Symptoms were as uncertain as those ascribed to the medieval plague. Who is he? Where is he? Hiding in the bread queue or behind a newspaper in the works canteen, swinging from a tram strap, the butcher, the baker, the candlestick-maker who betrayed himself with a careless word, just a suggestion of doubt about the conduct of the war?

Englishmen generally considered Berlin dreary and compared it unfavourably with London or Paris. Too modern, they liked to say, its buildings too pompous, or functional, like factories, the streets and parks too well ordered; a city without a soul. They were patronising in a way that only Englishmen know how to be. It wasn't Berlin they disliked but the new German Empire. They were afraid. In the years before the war it was brash, confident and, if you knew where to look, colourful. But within hours of stepping from the train, Wolff had sensed a sadder and a stiffer city.

Files of soldiers passed his hotel every day with 'London' chalked on their gun carriages and Berliners still cheered and sang 'The Watch on the Rhine', but only because they felt they ought to. On his second day Wolff had visited a department store and queued at a counter behind an old man buying a black armband for his coat.

'My grandson,' he'd explained to the shop assistant.

Everyone blamed the British. War with France was almost the natural order of things but no one Wolff spoke to – businessmen, waiters, cab drivers, the old Baron who lived in rooms at the Minerva and spent his evenings talking to strangers in the saloon – no one understood why the British were at war with Germany.

'Why do they want to destroy us?' the policemen who visited

54

his hotel wanted to know, 'and why are you Americans helping them?'

'Because they're frightened of you,' Wolff told them. 'Frightened of losing their Empire.'

The police wanted to know his business. Two solid representatives of the city constabulary carrying out their routine check. Wolff was used to fear. It was a thick band about his chest that loosened and tightened according to circumstance: like the old torture *Peine forte et dure*. Since Turkey, Wolff understood better than anyone that there was only so much a man could bear before he was suffocated by the weight pressing upon him. This time his legend was a good one but would he be able to look them in the eye and, if he did, would it be a hunted look?

In the event, he was calm enough to arouse no more than the curiosity that was his object. De Witt's past was waiting to be teased from him by someone in authority – at the right time.

'The British are decadent,' he told the policemen. 'Germany will win this war,' and they were satisfied with the sincerity of his loathing. After their visit he was ready to make contact with the informer.

It was a fifty-pfennigs-a-day sort of place in a quiet residential street. An elderly man with an unruly shock of grey hair was planting spring flowers in the window boxes on either side of the front door. It was the sort of risk Wolff had revelled in taking once, but as he opened the guest-house gate he was conscious only of being afraid. The outcome was more incalculable than a spinning chamber in a game of Russian roulette. He nodded to the gardener, knocked at the door and handed over to the landlady a note for Christensen. No need to cross the threshold, no need for more than a few words, no police. He felt foolish when it was over, and it was over in less than two minutes. Click. He'd pulled the trigger and heard the hammer fall on an empty chamber.

A reply was delivered to the Minerva the following day. Christensen would meet him beside the fountain in the Spittelmarkt at six o'clock in the afternoon. He was to carry a copy of the *Berliner Tageblatt*. The bellboy brought him the paper and he glanced through it at breakfast: stories of derring-do from the Front, bellicose commentaries exhorting the people to more sacrifices, German soldiers repelling British soldiers in France, Russian soldiers retreating before German ones in Poland. Who could be sure that any of it was true? But there were a few more column inches on the rifles captured before they could reach the Boer rebels in South Africa. The paper's source could reveal that these were manufactured by Westinghouse in America.

'We're seeking clarification from Washington,' Boyd told him when he visited the embassy later that morning. 'If it's proved, I'm afraid it might make your position here difficult.' Wolff agreed that it might.

By six o'clock the junior employees of the state bank and business houses of the Spittelmarkt were streaming across the small square to the U-bahn and home. Christensen stood out like a sore thumb. Wolff watched him from the tram stop as he rolled round the fountain in search of a man holding the *Tageblatt*. He was a big fellow with large hands and stoker's shoulders that shifted in his jacket like a crab adjusting to a new shell. Plain enough he wasn't a gentleman, but there was something studied in his gestures, his expression, in the trouble he'd taken with his appearance, that suggested he wanted to be. The Spittelmarkt was too busy to be sure that he'd come alone. Wolff watched him saunter over to the newspaper kiosk, glance at the headlines, then turn back to the fountain. He didn't notice a prosperous-looking businessman who was hurrying across the square with his arm raised for a cab. They cannoned into each other and the businessman was thrown sideways and on to one knee. Christensen bent at once to offer a helping hand but the man brushed it angrily aside and shouted something abusive. A documents case he'd been carrying under his arm had burst open and his papers were flapping about him like fish on the deck of a trawler. It was perfect. Crossing behind a tram, Wolff began weaving quickly through the crowd towards them, newspaper under his arm.

'Not like that, you oaf,' the businessman shouted, his face puce with rage. Christensen was trying to catch some of the papers beneath his boot.

A young clerk stopped to pick up one or two sheets and a hotel porter in the livery of the Continental was scrambling about the stones too.

'Hold this, would you,' Wolff commanded, pointedly thrusting the end of the *Tageblatt* into Christensen's side. He obeyed without question, as he would have done on his last ship. Wolff took a few steps and bent to scoop up two of the businessman's documents. He could sense that Christensen was watching him closely and turning back he caught his eye at once. There was an enquiring expression on his face and he lifted the newspaper a little in acknowledgement.

'Take these, why don't you,' said Wolff, holding his gaze. 'Do you know the U-bahn stop I will need for the east side of the Tiergarten?'

'The Tiergarten? But I thought . . .' Christensen looked confused.

'Yes. The Tiergarten,' Wolff replied with careful emphasis.

'Leipziger Platz, then you'll have to walk. Are you meeting someone there?'

'Yes, in front of the statue of Gotthold Lessing . . .'

57

'I'll take those,' interjected the businessman, snatching the papers from Christensen. 'Damn fool. Look where you're going next time.'

Christensen wasn't a fool. He was careful. Wolff waited at a shop window and watched him cross from the square and file down the steps to the station. He was an easy man to follow, more than six feet tall, with blond hair, those broad shoulders, and dressed in the sort of green wool suit that was fashionable at country-house shooting parties before the war. Wolff wondered if it had belonged to Casement. By the time he reached the edge of the park it was dusk. Christensen was stalking impatiently to and fro beneath the statue, a streetlamp casting his enormous shadow on its marble plinth.

'Why did we have to come here?' he asked, angrily slapping the newspaper against his thigh.

'So I could be sure you weren't being followed.'

'No one's going to follow me.' He shook his head in disbelief.

'Look, Adler – may I call you that?' Wolff stepped a little closer. 'Let me be quite clear. We're only going to stay alive in this country if we're careful. Very careful. Do you understand?' He paused to look him directly in the eye. 'Do you?'

'Yes, of course.'

'A silly mistake and we'll wind up in a cell at the Alex.' Then to be sure: 'Both of us.'

'Yes, I understand,' he snapped.

But Wolff didn't believe him. He was too young – only twenty-four – and too mechanical. The file said he had run away to sea as a boy. He'd have learnt some tricks and no doubt thought he could slip any obligation. They were all like that – informers.

'Let's walk, we'll be less conspicuous. No, not in the Tiergarten at this hour,' he said, touching Christensen's sleeve. 'At its edge.'

They ambled away from the Brandenburg Gate and the

government district to the broad victory avenue, lined with statues, that cut through the heart of the park.

'Is your real name de Witt?' Christensen asked. Wolff said it was.

'And you've spoken to Mr Findlay?' Wolff said that he had.

Casement was staying at the Eden on the Kurfürstendamm, Christensen said, 'but we'll move soon. He can't afford it.'

'Aren't the Germans paying him?'

'He won't take anything for himself,' he grumbled. 'Only people like him who are used to having money refuse when it's offered.'

'So who's paying?'

'Didn't you hear me? No one. He says he's expecting some from his Irish friends in America.'

'Do you know their names?'

'A man called Devoy, and his sister in New York, I think. He has friends here too.'

'Who?'

Christensen shrugged. 'I don't know. I haven't met them.'

'All right, Adler.' Wolff stopped abruptly. 'Let's be clear. I need names – who he meets and why, and what they're talking about. I need to know who he writes to and what he says. Do you have access to his correspondence?'

'Sometimes,' said Christensen sulkily.

'Who, what, why, when and where, my friend. Understand? Everything. That will be a profitable arrangement.'

He didn't reply and he didn't look Wolff in the eye, but stood there with his head bent, hands thrust in the pockets of his coat.

'Who does he visit here?' Wolff asked, at last.

'You've got to give me more.'

Wolff took a step closer. 'Sorry, I didn't catch that, Adler.'

'You need to give me more,' he repeated – belligerently this time. He took his hands from his pockets and stood a little straighter. 'It's dangerous here. It will cost you more.'

Wolff glanced over his shoulder. They had almost reached the top of the Siegesallee and the Reichstag was only a few minutes' walk away.

'Come with me,' and he tugged roughly at Christensen's sleeve.

'Why?'

'Come on, man, I'm not going to kill you,' he said, impatiently. 'We've been standing beneath this streetlamp for too long,' and he turned and walked quickly into the trees. After a few seconds Christensen followed him.

'Cigarette?'

Christensen shook his head. Wolff bent to light his own, then took a step away. They were only a few feet apart but it was too dark beneath the trees to see Christensen's face. That he felt uncomfortable, even a little afraid, was apparent in his movements. The silhouette of his broad shifting shoulders made Wolff smile: an awkward troll of a man.

'You going to threaten me?' he asked defiantly in New York English.

'Speak German. I'm not going to threaten you, Adler, but we must understand each other. You think you can play me, blackmail me – if I don't pay enough, sell me to the security police . . .'

'I only want to—'

'Don't interrupt,' said Wolff fiercely. 'You can try. They might pay you, but they might lock you up. I think they'll lock you up, or shoot you . . .'

'That's not—'

'I said, don't interrupt. Now, let's suppose they don't shoot you. One of these days you'll leave Germany. Go home to Norway or America. Visit mother. That's when my friends will find you. They won't let you get away with it. It's bad for business.

You can see that, can't you? You'll have to spend the rest of your life here. But they might get you here too.' He paused to draw on his cigarette, dropped it and ground the end into the earth. 'That's just the way it is, Adler. It's your choice. I'll pay you a fair price for what you give me.'

'That's all I want,' Christensen muttered. He sounded hurt. He'd probably convinced himself in the batting of an eyelid that it had never crossed his mind to betray Wolff, and he was incapable of such low behaviour.

God, they're all the same, thought Wolff. Always victims. 'Come on, let's go.'

Christensen followed him back to the pavement and they walked on towards the victory column in Königsplatz in silence.

'He writes some of his letters in a code the Germans gave him,' Christensen declared at last. Reaching into his jacket he pulled out a roll of papers. 'I've copied it out and some of his letters too – here.'

Wolff took the tube and slipped it inside his coat pocket.

'He visits the Foreign Ministry two or three times a week,' he continued. 'The War Office too.'

'Do you accompany him?'

'Sometimes, but only as far as the lobby.'

'Who does he meet?'

'He usually sees a Foreign Office official called Meyer. But sometimes more important people. He's met the Chancellor.'

'Bethmann-Hollweg?'

Christensen nodded. 'Also an aristocrat called Nadolny – something to do with the military.'

'Do you know what they've promised him?'

Christensen said there was talk of men and guns, lots of talk, but all he could say for sure was that Casement was exasperated by how long his plans were taking to finalise. He'd even considered returning to the United States.

'Does he trust you?'

'Oh yes,' he replied; 'we're friends,' and he turned his head to hide a coy smile. It was a tight-lipped, manipulative smile, the smile of someone who takes pleasure in winning, then betraying, a confidence. It didn't matter, of course. Wolff knew he couldn't afford to actively dislike Christensen. Who was he to judge anyway?

'All right, Adler, that's enough for tonight.'

'And what about our agreement?' he asked, a little sheepishly.

'Findlay gave you a hundred and twenty-five krone, didn't he?'

'But . . .'

Wolff grasped his forearm, pinching it tightly. 'Let's not talk about it again. There's nothing more now. Here,' and he handed Christensen a piece of paper. 'It's the address of a café in Wedding. Will you be able to make ten o'clock on Wednesday?'

'I'll try.'

'If you can't, I'll be there at the same time on Friday. By then I'll have read this,' and he patted the front of his coat. 'Don't visit my hotel. Don't send messages.'

'I understand,' he replied gloomily.

They said goodbye and Wolff walked quickly away. Glancing up at Victory holding out her Prussian laurels to the city, he smiled at his own small triumph. But a man like Christensen he would have to fight again and again. He was as slippery as an eel. What use would he be if he wasn't? But what did Casement see in the fellow? Wolff pondered this a little as he strolled back to his hotel but came to no firm view. It was impossible to say until he met Casement.

After dinner he settled at the desk in his room and worked his way through the notes Christensen had given him. But for one short memorandum there was nothing he couldn't glean from the newspapers. It was wrapped tightly in the centre of the roll and had been copied in such haste that it was barely legible.

14 February, 1915
The Chief of the General Staff requests Sir Roger Casement's assistance in contacting reliable and discreet Irish in America for special work of importance in the defeat of our common enemy. The General Staff has sent Captain von Rintelen to New York to make the necessary contacts.

One of the names on the distribution list was a Count Rudolf Nadolny, Section P of the General Staff.

It was of some importance, but how much Wolff couldn't say; nor was he confident that Christensen would be able to help. He made a note of the German cipher, the names, and other important details, in his own code and buried them in the text of a report he'd begun writing on his business meetings in Berlin. Then he destroyed Christensen's papers. When an opportunity presented itself he would send his coded report to Westinghouse by their office in Amsterdam. An agent would pick it up and forward it to the Bureau.

Christensen arrived at the café before him on the Wednesday. He said he knew nothing of 'special work' in America or a 'von Rintelen'. Wolff bought him *Bratkartoffeln* and bacon and he gobbled it down as if he was fighting for his share in the stokers' mess.

'Is that it?' he asked, wiping his mouth on the sleeve of his wool suit. 'My payment?'

'Not necessarily. It depends what else you have for me,' Wolff declared. 'Let's walk.'

That became the pattern: first a plate of food for Christensen, then a stroll through a park. Thoughts came quicker to Wolff on the move. When he tried to explain this, Christensen just shrugged his square shoulders: 'Wherever you like, Mr de Witt – so long as you pay.' But after only a short time he was bored with questions. 'Why do you need to know that?' he complained. 'It doesn't matter why,' Wolff told him curtly. He wanted everything, not just Casement's contacts and his correspondence, but his routine, what he liked to eat and drink, the newspapers he bought, when he went to bed and who he went to bed with – 'No one,' said Christensen with another sly smile, 'only cares about his cause.' Of Sir Roger's personal habits he spoke with authority but he knew little of his mind and nothing of his plans for a rising in Ireland. Casement called him 'friend' but plainly treated him as something less than his equal and certainly not as a gentleman. A nasty word here and there, a certain resentful tone, the narrowing of his light-blue eyes, and it wasn't long before Wolff understood that Christensen's betrayal wasn't just about money: Christensen was a disappointed young man. Why didn't his 'friend' do more to help him? More than an old green suit. His pride was hurt. Doors opened for Sir Roger but he shut them in poor Adler's face. Perhaps he had begun to realise that they would always be closed to someone of his class and blamed Casement for that too.

'He's let me down, you know,' he said at their fourth meeting. 'You can see that, can't you?' Wolff said he could.

Most of the lies Christensen told were to himself but was he any different in that way from anyone else? Wolff did all he could to nourish his grievance. The more he understood the man, the more important it became. For all the childish slights, the bitter words, the pleasure he took in passing on confidences, he was plainly attached to 'Sir Raj-er'.

'He's a great man, an honest man,' he observed, only minutes after railing at Casement's vanity.

The portrait he painted of Casement was of someone naïve,

impulsive, and with an exaggerated sense of his own importance, but principled and generous to a fault. Wolff could see that Adler was as fond of the man he was betraying as he was capable of being of anyone, and that made him even less trustworthy. So Wolff didn't mention the note he left for Casement at the Eden or the visit he received from the security police the following day.

5

Teasing

THEY MUST HAVE been waiting at the hotel but Wolff didn't notice them until he stopped to watch a column of soldiers march by. It was part of his daily routine: faces in a crowd, reflections in shop windows, skipping on and off trams. It was an exchange of glances only but his heart missed a beat. Two powerfully built men in their forties who walked like *Unteroffiziere* and wore their cheap blue suits like uniforms. They followed him into Wilhelmstrasse, working the pavements in tandem and with a professionalism that suggested they were of a different calibre to the state gendarmes he'd encountered so far.

After the note he had sent to Casement, he was expecting something of the sort, but not quite so quickly. He was very relieved to reach the sanctuary of his new country's embassy. 'That's Turkey,' he thought as he climbed the stairs to the trade section on the first floor.

Secretary Boyd was dictating a letter to a clerk. He didn't look pleased to see Wolff.

'I've been instructed not to talk to you,' he said brusquely. 'From Ambassador Gerard himself. No assistance. No contact. Persona non grata.'

'Why?'

'It's best you leave.'

'If you explain . . .'

'I can't.'

'Then I will have to see the Ambassador.'

The trade attaché looked horrified. 'All right, Adams, we'll finish this later.' He dismissed the clerk with a wave and rose quickly from his desk, catching his thigh against its edge. Wolff watched him hobble to the door and shut it firmly.

'The Ambassador won't see you.' He was still gripping the handle, his eyes locked on the floor. 'He's got more pressing concerns.'

'He will see me. I'm an American.'

'Oh?' he snorted sceptically. 'Look, it's somethin' to do with your business, that's all I can tell you.'

'Westinghouse?'

'Yes. No. Instructions from the State Department. Look, I want you to leave at once.'

'But it was a matter concerning Westinghouse?'

'I've said too much already.'

'You haven't said anything.'

'That's not what the Ambassador thinks,' Boyd said, lifting his eyes to Wolff's face at last. 'Unprofessional. Damn stupid,' he barked in the straight-talking manner of Ambassador Gerard, flushing at the recollection. 'There you have it, Mr de Witt. Too much charity.' He frowned unhappily. 'It's that business in the papers, the Boers and their rifles. Made a bit of a fool of me, didn't you?'

Mr James W. Gerard was otherwise engaged and his secretary was unable to find a time in his diary when he wouldn't be. Wolff made his protest to a second counsellor who had no idea what he was talking about and urged him to 'come back tomorrow'.

There was a telegram from Westinghouse at the hotel. The concierge at the desk handed it to him with a butter-wouldn't-melt expression that suggested it had passed through the security police's hands already. They had trailed him from the embassy and watched him take lunch at a restaurant near the Potsdamer Brücke. They'd caught the same tram to the Tiergarten, then wandered with him in the rain, and now they were dripping on the marble floor in the entrance hall of the Minerva.

In his rooms, Wolff hung up his hat and coat, lit a cigarette and stood at the window gazing down at the traffic in the Unter den Linden. He felt calm. The police were in no hurry. There would be time for a bath and perhaps dinner. Only when he'd finished his cigarette did he reach for the telegram. It was from a Mr J. P. Foote of New England Westinghouse, not in the customary commercial code but in hard telegraph capitals that communicated so much more than the two lines of type. 'Look, reader,' they screamed; 'look how angry we are with you. We're very angry.'

SERVICES NO LONGER REQUIRED.
BUSINESS WITH THIS COMPANY TERMINATED
WITH IMMEDIATE EFFECT.

There was virtue in brevity. 'Let your enemy embroider the rest,' C liked to say. Wolff folded the telegram back into the envelope. It was funny how often C's little expressions forced their way to the front of his mind.

By the time Wolff entered the hotel dining room it was almost full. There was no sign of the policemen who had followed him so doggedly. He asked for, and was shown to, a table against the wall. The waiter took his order of fish in a simple hollandaise and a small glass of wine but he had no appetite when it came. He sipped at the wine and smoked a cigarette and watched the other tables. Business sorts in white tie and tails for the most part, laughing, eating, drinking fine wine, two – perhaps three – of the diners bold enough to cock a snook at the new moral fervour of the nation and entertain expensive prostitutes. War was kind to a few.

At nine o'clock, Wolff wandered into the entrance hall and spoke briefly to the concierge about the weather and the latest news from the Front. He expected to see the policemen lounging on the leather benches between the pillars but they had gone. It looked as if they were going to leave him for another day. Damn, he cursed them under his breath; damn, damn, damn, why didn't they get on with it? Once they had you, your senses and every thought were bent on the story and staying alive. Waiting was the worst thing by far. It was fear, not the pain, that had broken him in Turkey.

He considered taking the air, perhaps a walk to the river and the museum island, but it was bucketing down, and the concierge was sure the rain wouldn't stop before morning. He would have to return to his room, to another cigarette, old newspapers, memories, and a small brandy at bedtime.

That the evening was going to end differently was plain the second the attendant slid the lift cage open on the fourth floor: the police *Unteroffiziere* were standing in the corridor and the door of his room was ajar.

'Well?' Wolff asked, walking purposefully towards them. 'Did you find what you were looking for?'

They gazed at him blankly as if it wasn't their place to say, and before he could repeat the question a young man with the hauteur of a recently commissioned officer stepped out of his room to stand beside them.

'Who the devil are you?'

'Herr de Witt?' he asked, looking Wolff up and down very deliberately. 'We are policemen.' Then, after a pause, 'But you know that. Passport, please.'

'Don't you have it?'

'Find it for me.'

Wolff brushed past him into the sitting room. His passport was still in a drawer of the escritoire but not in quite the same place.

'Here.'

The young officer pretended to scrutinise it but his eyes kept flitting to Wolff's face. They were large and almost colourless, an unnervingly light shade of blue. Very like the eyes of a submariner Wolff knew who'd cracked and run amok at three hundred feet.

'You must come with me,' he said, slipping the passport into his overcoat.

'At this hour?'

'Yes.'

'Are you arresting me?' Wolff sounded incredulous. 'You've seen my passport.'

'Some questions, that's all,' he ventured. 'If you wouldn't mind . . .'

He was struggling to be polite. It wasn't expected of secret policemen. Wolff guessed he had been instructed not to break the head of a neutral.

'I do mind,' he said impatiently. They – whoever they turned out to be – would expect him to mind.

'My orders are to fetch you,' the officer glanced over his shoulder to his men, 'whether you wish to co-operate or not . . .'

At the front of the hotel, an Opel with curtains across the windows, the driver in a uniform he didn't recognise. The rain was bouncing off the pavement and dripping through the hotel awning on to Wolff's hat and coat. It reminded him of the evening at Rules and the morning at the safe house in south London – the morning he'd caved like a wet paper bag. C had rubbed his hands and chuckled like Bunter with a cake. 'They'll be intrigued by Mr de Witt, we'll make sure of that,' he'd promised.

They escorted Wolff to the car in the rain and he sat in the back between their damp shoulders, trousers clinging to his legs. When they turned right along the canal and passed the palace he knew they were taking him to the Alexanderplatz Police Headquarters.

'Make them tease it from you,' C had observed. Wolff had listened to his plan at the window of the safe house, gazing across acres of wet slate. He remembered reaching for his handkerchief and catching the scent of Violet's perfume.

'Did you hear me?' C had upbraided him. 'Do you want to stay alive? Concentrate, for God's sake.' Concentrate.

The police driver cursed as he braked for a man scuttling across the road beneath an umbrella. It was almost ten o'clock but the lights were still on at Tietz's on the north-west side of the square. In front of the department store, a banner with the slogan 'God Punish England' was wrapped around the statue of the city's protector, the wind lifting it immodestly from her full figure. They turned and Wolff glimpsed the dome of the Police Headquarters over the driver's shoulder. In the course of one of his operations he'd passed it on foot, resisting the urge to walk faster and walk away. He remembered wondering if there was a country in the world with a larger police station: 19,000 square yards of neo-Gothic brick, according to Baedeker – all you needed to know about the new German order. He had stepped from its shadow into the square confident that he would never be obliged to visit the place. In his early twenties he was sure of a lot of things.

'Do you mind if I smoke?' he asked, as the car drew up to the security barrier. The officer didn't reply. A brief exchange with the guard and they were moving again, passing beneath a high arch into a courtyard, then on into another. 'This is all part of the scheme,' he told himself. 'Keep your faith,' C had said at their last meeting. But he'd said the same thing before the Turkish operation.

The car stopped at the bottom of broad steps and guards stepped forward to open the doors.

'Out, out, out,' the young officer shouted, a little hysterically.

Wolff smiled. Poor fellow's wound even tighter than me, he thought. The anxiety and anger of others always made him feel calmer. Sliding across the seat, he stood in the rain with his hand on the door and with a sergeant at his back, grinding his cigarette into the gravel of the immaculately swept yard.

'All right, let's get on.'

6

Inside the Alex

'YOU'RE NOT AN American, Herr de Witt. Who are you, I wonder?'

'I have an American passport.'

'Easy for a resourceful man like you.'

'I can't imagine what you mean,' Wolff retorted impatiently.

The officer didn't explain but stared at Wolff intently as if the past could be read in the lines of his face. Foreign Office or General Staff, Wolff guessed. He had introduced himself as Lieutenant Maguerre; lieutenant of what, he didn't say. Too well spoken and cultivated for a junior police officer, he was resting his fingertips on the table like a pianist, and his suit was cut in Paris. Mid to late thirties, of slight build, his name and fine Gallic features suggested a family tree that criss-crossed the border. He looked like the sort of fellow who'd have felt at home in any drawing room in Europe – before the war.

'No one knows you're here, Herr de Witt,' he said at last, 'and would Ambassador Gerard care if he did?'

'What do you want?'

'What are you doing here?'

'I'm here for Westinghouse, you know that.'

'Don't lie to me. I'm not a patient man. If you want to behave like a spy I can arrange for the policemen . . .' he enunciated the word contemptuously '. . . who generally carry out their business in this room to treat you like one. You see—'

'For God's sake,' interrupted Wolff. 'I'm a consulting engineer.'

'Enough.' Maguerre's chair screeched as he pushed it sharply from the table. He stood glaring at Wolff for a few seconds, then turned and walked over to the chimneypiece. Picking the poker from its stand, he began stirring the embers so vigorously that the last of the heat was quickly lost from the fire. It was a bare brick room, stripped of anything that might distract from the pursuit of truth: windowless, timeless, its vaulted ceiling in shadow. 'They'll only believe in Herr de Witt if they smoke his story from you,' C had counselled. In the Alex, only lies were held to be simple and offered freely. The truth was spoken on the edge, mumbled sometimes through cut and swollen lips. Wolff was relieved when Maguerre put the poker down and returned to the table.

'Well?'

'I've told you,' said Wolff sulkily. 'I'm a consulting engineer and sometimes I work for Westinghouse, or I used to.'

'Our people say no one at Westinghouse knows what you're doing in Germany.'

Wolff frowned. 'I don't suppose it matters. I've lost my job,' he muttered. 'I was involved in a little private business. It didn't go . . .' he hesitated. 'It didn't go quite as I'd hoped and, well, that's why I'm here.'

'And what was the nature of this private business?'

'May I have a cigarette?'

'Come on, come on.' Maguerre leant forward, his elbows on the table. 'Your private business?'

His right hand was balled in a manicured fist but he wasn't the sort to swing a punch – that he would leave to the regulars at the Alex.

'Your private business,' he persisted.

'A small matter . . .'

74

'A small matter of guns?'

Wolff flicked the ash from his cigarette and said nothing.

'All right.' Maguerre bent to pick up the briefcase at his feet. 'The story's everywhere.' Taking out a leather-bound file, he opened it and slid a small cutting across the table. 'From *The Times* of London.'

'Oh?' Wolff glanced at it for a few seconds, then pushed it back.

'Is it you?' demanded Maguerre.

'Who?'

'What are you hoping to gain from this nonsense?' He was losing his temper. Good interrogators never lost their temper.

'Are you the man the British are looking for?'

Wolff looked at him coolly. 'No.'

'You're lying.'

'That isn't polite.'

'Please, Herr de Witt . . .' He shook his head in exasperation. 'This is foolish. The rifles. They're your rifles – for your people in South Africa, General Maritz's forces – the Boers. Your shipping agent in Norway told us everything – for a price, of course. A thousand rifles hidden in a shipment of mining machinery. The M-1891 Westinghouse is making for the Russians. You see?'

'If you're right, I don't believe it's any of your business,' replied Wolff belligerently.

'You know the old saying: "My enemy's enemy is my friend". We help our friends.' Maguerre paused and looked down at his hands. Then, lifting his eyes to Wolff's face again, 'But perhaps it's a clever story and you're a spy.'

Wolff shrugged. 'I might be. I'm not Germany's friend or enemy. I'm a businessman.'

'But you hate the British?'

'Yes,' he said under his breath.

'What did you say?'

'I said "yes", damn it. Yes, I hate the British. Satisfied?'

Maguerre gave a short laugh. 'I don't understand why . . .'

'Why I'm discreet?' Wolff dragged a hand through his hair in frustration. 'I don't want to be chased across Europe. I don't want a reputation for trouble. I don't want to be a face in a secret policeman's file.'

'Too late, you've made your choice,' Maguerre said, lifting the cutting. 'Isn't that why you're here in Germany?'

'I'm here for my health,' replied Wolff with a wry smile. 'When it improves I'll return to America.'

'It won't improve in the Alex, Herr de Witt.'

Wolff sighed.

'All right.' Maguerre got to his feet wearily and drifted to the door. 'Hey,' he shouted, rapping it with his fist. It was opened by the more solidly built of the *Unteroffiziere* who'd followed Wolff the previous day. Christ, thought Wolff, his body tensing, that ape isn't necessary, and for a couple of seconds old images, fists, boots, faces, flashed through his mind like a fairground whirligig.

'Fetch us some coffee, would you,' demanded Maguerre ungraciously.

The door closed quietly behind the policeman.

'Why was it necessary to conduct this business in the middle of the night?' Wolff enquired fiercely, his skin still prickling with sweat. A more observant man than the lieutenant would have noticed his discomfort.

Maguerre scratched his temple thoughtfully. 'I think you know the answer. But we'll come to that later,' he said, easing behind the table again. 'You're not an American. Your German is excellent; your Dutch too?'

Wolff nodded.

'Who are you, Herr de Witt?'

Who? What? Why de Witt? Your life, de Witt, like a babbling stream through the early hours.

'Who am I? Dutch, I suppose,' he told Maguerre. 'My father and mother were Dutch, from Maastricht, but they lived in England with my grandfather for a time.'

The story was as close to his own as he could make it, and he'd rehearsed it until it became his life entirely, first with C, then with Bywater and the old South Africa hand, Landau. Jan Cornelius de Witt, the only child of farmers, religious zealots quick to recognise the Devil in their neighbours and sometimes in their son. School in England and Holland, then the polytechnic college in Delft. It was 1900 and in South Africa the Boers were fighting the British.

'It was the romance of David and Goliath – farmers fighting an empire for their freedom,' he explained to Maguerre. 'And I was bored of narrow streets and flat country, the smallness, the tidiness of everything. Bored with the polytechnic. It wasn't a difficult choice – I joined the Dutch Volunteers.'

There were others – Germans, Frenchmen, Americans, a few Russians; de Witt had served alongside MacBride's Irish for a time. The Dutch didn't see much action. They did see crops and homes burned, the bodies of farmers shot in their fields, their wives and children dying of hunger and disease in concentration camps. That's when de Witt learnt to hate the British. In the autumn of 1900, he was taken prisoner and sent to a camp in Ceylon. He was twenty-two when he left it, no money, no prospects, no country to speak of, but resolved to make his way in the world, harder and with that ember still glowing inside. No, Lieutenant Maguerre, hatred wasn't too strong a word; hatred not just for the British but for all empires, and for all who refuse to acknowledge the rights of small nations. With the outbreak of war in Europe, the Boers under General Maritz were fighting again. Westinghouse trusted him, the opportunity to send arms was there and Wolff had taken it even though he was sure this rebellion would fail too. Why he'd decided to risk so much he found it impossible to say.

Did Maguerre believe him? At a little before four o'clock he was joined at the table by a man with a face baked and wrinkled by the sun. He said his name was Cronje and that he'd served in the 'last war' and had the honour to be Maritz's representative in Germany. He looked as if he'd just ridden in from the Highveld in his long tweed waistcoat and jacket, and after a few minutes he slipped into the *taal*.

'Don't take me for another of your farmers,' Wolff replied curtly in Dutch.

But Cronje wasn't a simple Boer. He gazed at Wolff with the dispassionate eye of the experienced interrogator, the eye of one who has witnessed the worst a man can be. For an hour he picked at the threads of Wolff's story, his questions always to the point, probing, probing for the smallest inconsistency to threaten the fabric of the whole. Perhaps he thought he'd found it because he kept returning to the identity of de Witt's go-between for the arms shipment. A name, he insisted in his tight-lipped South African way, a name.

'Maritz's people call him "the Stork",' Wolff said at last.

'And only you know his real identity, Herr de Witt?'

'That's right,' he replied. 'You know in Holland, Herr Cronje, the stork is . . .'

'The bringer of treasure.'

'Yes.'

'And who paid for this treasure?'

'Friends who trust me to keep my mouth shut.'

'Who has that sort of money?'

'I've told you, I won't say,' he snapped.

'We're friends here.'

'Øh?'

'Yes, yes,' interjected Maguerre. He'd been wriggling impatiently for a while, breaking into exchanges to insist they were repeated in German, making no effort to stifle his yawns. It was plain that he had no time for the Boer. 'We have enough information to speak to the Count,' he said, rising from the table. 'If you'll excuse us, Herr de Witt.' He gazed down his nose at Cronje for two or three seconds, then turned to the door.

Cronje didn't move, he didn't reply. His face was inscrutable, with only a suggestion of colour rising to his cheeks. His dark-brown eyes were fixed on Wolff, his rough hands clasped on the table. Then, slowly, theatrically, he looked away and down as if he were itching to spit on the stone floor.

'Herr Cronje, we mustn't keep the Count waiting,' commanded Maguerre from the door.

The Boer caught Wolff's eye again. 'Shit,' he muttered in the *taal*. 'Shit.' He stroked his chin thoughtfully with his thumb and forefinger, then, dropping his hands to his knees, he gave a heavy shrug to suggest that he suspected him but didn't care: his 'Shit' was a plague on both their houses.

Once, as a small child, Wolff had lost his way in a fenland mist, conscious that a step from the path might be his last, alive to every sound, the reeds rustling on the banks of the dyke, a large bird breaking its waters, his pulse racing, and yet floating, detached, as if in a dream. Stretching on his bed in the hotel the following morning, he reflected that he'd found his way through his interrogation in much the same way. After Turkey, he'd wondered if he would be able to. Self-belief was a spy's armour. Other performers could draw confidence from the approbation of an audience but no one slapped a spy on the back after his turn. Spies pulled their tricks alone. Only a job for the right sort of person, C liked to say. 'That, sir, is a meaningless cliché,' Wolff had once had the audacity to remark. 'Who is the right sort of person?'

'You're the right sort of person, Wolff. An adventurer, clever, resourceful, patriotic . . . ah, you scoff, but—'

'A loner,' Wolff had interrupted. 'A morally ambivalent loner actually, or is that just what you become after a while in the Service? Someone who loses himself in his disguises.'

C had leant forward to examine his face more closely, pinching the edge of his monocle. 'That isn't the right sort of person, Wolff,' he'd commented. 'That's a professional hazard. The right sort of person holds on to himself.'

Wolff rolled on to his side and reached across to the bedside table for his drink. He was too tired to sleep and still a little on edge. It had ended so suddenly and not at all as he'd expected. Maguerre had escorted him down the stairs at dawn and spoken as one gentleman to another. Apologies for the lateness of the hour . . . one or two points to clear up another time . . . and they'd walked with lazy steps as if reluctant to say goodbye. Through a window, he'd glimpsed a car in the courtyard with its acetylene lights burning, waiting perhaps to take him to his hotel. It felt wrong. Surely they weren't going to let him go without asking him? Perhaps they weren't going to release him after all. All sorts of possibilities had flitted through his mind.

The Count must have watched him saunter down the stairs, coolly appraising him as only spies and clever tarts know how, processing every detail of his carriage, every flicker of emotion in his face, considering his likely qualities. Lying on his bed, tinkling the ice in his glass, Wolff could picture him in the shadow of the vast entrance hall like a magician in the wings. Click, click, his shoes had echoed round the empty hall as he approached them with a smile.

'Count.' Wolff had greeted him with a stiff bow. 'It's you I have to thank for my detention here, I suppose.'

'And for your release too, Herr de Witt,' he'd replied.

'For that, I'll reserve my thanks.'

He said his name was Rudolf Nadolny and that he worked for the Foreign Ministry, but with one half of Europe at war with the other he was of more service at home than in an embassy.

'Rescuing innocent foreigners from our police,' he added smoothly.

Wolff raised his eyebrows sceptically.

'You are innocent, aren't you, Herr de Witt?'

'It depends who you ask.'

Nadolny scrutinised him closely. There was the suggestion of a smile on his lips but not in his eyes. He wanted an answer and it wasn't necessary to say so. But for the scar on his left cheek he looked like the middle-ranking diplomat he claimed to be, and yet the force of his personality was quite out of the ordinary. Wolff had found himself blustering that he was a businessman and an American, that he was tired and he would be grateful if the Count would arrange to deliver him to his bed.

He closed his eyes and pulled a face at the recollection. He had wanted to present himself to them as a steady sort, discreet, reliable.

Nadolny had accompanied him to the motor car. Waiting in the beam of its lamps was the young police lieutenant who'd lifted him from the hotel eight hours before. The sun was creeping up the wall of the building they had left but in the courtyard it was still dark and would be until the summer. Above the rattle of the Opel's engine and the crunch of gravel, Wolff had heard a confused echo, a man shouting a single word over and over, perhaps a name. As he walked round the car to the passenger door it became distinct enough for him to be sure it was coming from a barred window somewhere near the top of the block facing him.

'Someone less fortunate than me?' he'd observed to Nadolny.

'Yes.'

The second the Count acknowledged the shouting, it stopped, as if at his command someone had lifted a phonograph needle from a disc. Bastards, Wolff thought.

'You aren't planning to leave Berlin, are you, Herr de Witt?'

'No, Count.'

'Good,' and he'd offered Wolff his hand. 'The Minerva, isn't it?'

'Yes.'

'Yes.' He had glanced away as if trying to recall something he wanted to ask. The passenger door on the other side opened and shut and the engine roared as the driver slipped the Opel into gear. 'Yes, there was one thing . . .' the Count said at last, his voice barely audible. 'Why did you visit . . .'

'I'm sorry, what did you say?'

' . . . the Eden?'

Nadolny was still holding his hand firmly, gazing at him with a quiet authority that would have stripped an unprepared or weaker man to the bone.

'The hotel? I served in South Africa with Major MacBride – Maguerre must have told you?'

The Count didn't reply. He had moved his head a little and the reflex from a lighted window shone in his eyes.

'You see, I'd heard Roger Casement was staying at the place,' Wolff continued.

'Oh?'

'Thought he might have word of my old comrade, MacBride,' he paused. 'May I have my hand?'

'Who told you Sir Roger was staying at the Eden?'

'I'll tell you when you let go of my hand.'

Nadolny gave a small smile and loosened his grip.

'Thank you.' Wolff would have liked to step away but the car was at his back. 'Everyone knows he's here in Berlin, of course. I don't remember who mentioned the Eden, perhaps someone at my hotel,' he hesitated, as if to consider further, 'no, the embassy. The fellow I deal with . . .'

'Secretary Boyd?' Nadolny enquired.

Wolff raised his eyebrows in a show of surprise. 'Yes, Count, Secretary Boyd.'

The intimacy of those last few minutes in the courtyard had shaken Wolff. As the car drove him from the Alex, he'd discreetly wiped the perspiration from his palms on his trousers. The Count was a sleek cat waiting to pounce on his mouse. 'This mouse has escaped – for now,' he muttered, and reaching for the edge of the counterpane he pulled it across himself and rolled on to his side in a cocoon.

He was woken three hours later by a persistent knocking at the door.

'What is it?' he shouted blearily.

'A letter, sir.'

'A moment.'

Rolling from the bed, he tucked in his shirttails and walked a little unsteadily across the sitting room. He half expected the letter to be from Christensen but the envelope was written in a cultured hand he didn't recognise.

'All right,' he said, tipping the pageboy.

'But the gentleman asked me to deliver a reply.'

A foreigner who doesn't speak German, the pageboy reported for a few pfennigs more. He was waiting in the hotel foyer. Taking a paperknife from the desk, Wolff opened the envelope, then stepped over to the window with the letter. It was in English.

My Dear Sir,

   *It appears we have at least one acquaintance in common
and in an alien country in time of war that is quite enough
to permit the possibility of friendship. I hope you will be
free to join me for luncheon here at your hotel in half an hour.*

   Yours faithfully,

   J. E. Henderson

'Please tell Herr Henderson I would be delighted to join him
for lunch,' Wolff said, folding the letter back into the envelope.
'In, say, twenty minutes.'

There was only time for a shave, a stand-up wash and change
of clothes. He took Mr Henderson's invitation to be a good sign
but there were other possibilities; thankfully he didn't have
the time to explore them. The family lawyer, he thought, gazing
at himself in the mirror. A well-cut but sober suit and tie, hair
combed off the forehead with only a little oil, expensive but
understated and trustworthy.

Mr Henderson was sitting in the foyer with his legs crossed,
snoozing with his chin on his chest. He was taller than Wolff
imagined and thinner. Christensen was standing at his side, an
adolescent scowl on his face. As Wolff approached, he bent to
whisper in Henderson's ear. He rose at once and came towards
Wolff with a smile.

'Mr de Witt,' he said, shaking his hand warmly. 'I'm very
pleased to meet you.'

'And I you, Sir Roger.'

He smiled a little shyly. 'Please excuse my small deception.
I know it's ridiculous but my friends tell me I must be careful
with my name – even here.' He paused, his grey eyes catching
Wolff's gaze for a moment. They were deep set and a little sad,
as if the thought that someone might wish him harm was still

a surprise and a source of pain. 'The English have their spies, I'm sure you know,' he continued. 'My friend, the Count, says you may be one. Are you a spy, Mr de Witt?'

'Would you believe me if I said "No"?' Wolff asked. 'Make up your own mind over lunch – if you're prepared to take the chance?'

He gave a little laugh. 'I'm prepared to take the chance.'

7

A Hard Street

H E DIDN'T EAT much and chose the least expensive dish on the menu. Christensen said he was short of money. Or was it habit? Someone had noted in the Bureau's file that he recorded even the cost of his newspaper in an account book. He was fiddling with his knife and his cigarette case, and Wolff recalled that the same report described him as 'restless', 'impetuous', 'unstable'. But that was the view from Whitehall *after* his fall from grace.

'Have you visited Ireland, Mr de Witt?' he asked, as the waiter drew the cork from their wine.

'No, Sir Roger, I'm afraid I haven't,' Wolff lied.

'Then your mission is bound to fail.'

'My mission?'

'To report to Whitehall on my state of mind.'

'That mission.'

'*Many that have been free to walk the hills and the bogs and the rushes will be sent to walk hard streets in far countries,*' he intoned softly. 'Yeats.'

'Ah.'

The file had mentioned that Casement wrote a little poetry but not that he spoke it like an English gentleman, with only the trace of an Irish accent.

'You do understand, don't you?' he prompted.

'Ireland isn't the only country fighting for its freedom, Sir Roger,' Wolff replied reprovingly.

'Are you fighting for the freedom of your country, Mr de Witt?'

Wolff shook his head a little. 'I'm fighting for myself now. If I have a country it's the land of the free.'

'But you fought in Africa. Isn't that what you told our friend the Count?'

'For a short time.'

'And you're here because you've upset the British again.'

'I thought I was a British spy. Or have you made up your mind about me already?'

Casement smiled apologetically. 'My friends tell me I'm too trusting, Mr de Witt. I find it difficult to be any other way. Here in Berlin, especially. One is always grateful for companions on this hard street.' He paused, still turning the cigarette case in his right hand. 'I like the Germans but . . .' his candid frown suggested he'd thought better of sharing a confidence; 'well, you know the expression "Your enemy's enemy is your friend", I'm sure; it's on everyone's lips today. But we're still foreigners, and foreigners are only tolerated in a war for as long as they're useful.'

Wolff nodded.

'I'm fortunate in Adler, of course,' he continued. 'He speaks German, you see.'

'Adler?'

'My man, Adler Christensen. I hope I haven't hurt his feelings – I should have introduced you.'

The waiter returned to their table and they sat in silence as he served the hors d'oeuvre of smoked goose. Casement gazed abstractedly at his plate, then into the body of the room. There was a diffidence, something half apologetic in his manner, that hadn't made it into the file. He looked older than the photographs too, still handsome, in good condition for fifty, his thin face tanned by his years in Africa and South America, his black curly hair and beard tinged with silver. Everyone commented on his eyes. He noticed Wolff watching him and smiled. They were a dreamy grey. He wasn't as Wolff had imagined him to be – sadder. A sad sort of rebel.

'Do you think they mind us speaking English here?' he asked when the waiter had gone.

'Does it matter, Sir Roger?'

'No, I don't suppose it does,' he said, picking up his knife and fork. 'Now, I believe you know Mr John MacBride. Perhaps you would do me the courtesy of telling me how you met.'

While they waited for their next course, Wolff spoke of the African war, of MacBride and his brigade, of the brutality of the British camps, of women and children dying of disease and malnutrition. The story was the one he'd served his interrogators but he told it to Casement with a quiet fury that had the Irishman dabbing the corner of his eye with his napkin.

'I should have done more. But I had no idea at the time,' he explained. 'I was in Africa . . .'

'The Congo.'

'You were fighting the British Empire and I was its servant.'

'Your service was to humanity, Sir Roger.'

'Do you think so?' he asked, a little plaintively.

'Yes, of course,' Wolff assured him. 'You will always be remembered for your humanitarian work there.'

They slipped into a pattern. Casement asked him about his childhood and his work with Westinghouse, and within minutes Wolff deflected the conversation to Ireland and the evils of imperialism. It wasn't difficult because the Irishman wanted to talk. Something better must come out of this war, he declared, an end of empires and oppression. He spoke well and with passion, eyes blazing, preacher rather than politician, his plate cold, oblivious to the disapproving glances of their German neighbours.

'I'm sorry,' he said. 'But people don't want to speak of liberty and social justice here. The Germans are only interested in Ireland if she helps them into the next trench. But I must be careful what I say.'

Wolff smiled. 'Of course, the British spy at the next table – or at this.'

'Yes . . .' he replied pensively, 'or a German one.'

When they had finished lunch Casement didn't want to let him go.

'Do you walk, Mr de Witt?' he enquired.

'I run.'

'We can compromise on a brisk pace.'

He had a long stride and was reluctant to break it even on a busy Berlin pavement. They walked in silence until they reached the river, when, seduced by the late-afternoon sun on the water, they fell into companionable step.

'Will you be giving the Count a report of your afternoon?' Wolff enquired.

Casement coloured a little. 'Do you mind?'

Wolff turned slightly and pointed to the railway bridge they had just passed under. 'If you look carefully, you'll see one of them under the arch. He's bending to tie his laces. And over there,' he said, gesturing to the river, 'the big fellow on the bank opposite, in front of the electricity works – turning his back. Do you think they're watching me or both of us?'

Casement closed his eyes and pressed a hand to his forehead as if suffering from a migraine. 'How did you know?'

Wolff shrugged. 'It isn't the first time I've enjoyed this sort of attention.'

'It's shabby,' he said, gazing down at the river.

'Don't be concerned on my account, or is it on your own?'

He sighed heavily. 'I'm tired, that's all, tired of living with deceit, tired of this place and of the times. Did you read about the gas attack in this morning's paper?' he asked, turning to face Wolff. 'The Germans broke the British line at Ypres by releasing a cloud of poison gas. Can you imagine anything more terrible?'

Wolff said he'd not had an opportunity to read the newspaper.

'Germany will win the war, of course. Will the world be a better place? What do you say?'

'I say, "perhaps".'

'If Ireland is free, if Britain is brought to her knees – I pray to God it will be so,' and he clasped his hands and shook them fervently.

They strolled on to the Reichstag, then along the calm grey curving river to the Tiergarten. They didn't speak of politics or war but of Casement's childhood in Ulster, of his travels, the cruelty he had witnessed on the rubber plantations in Peru, of the dark heart of man. He said he regretted his knighthood and most of all the manner of his acceptance. 'My letter to the King was too obsequious,' he explained. 'Silly, I know, but it haunts me.'

By the time they reached the Brandenburg Gate again it was five o'clock. He refused Wolff's offer of a taxicab. 'I've talked far too much, Mr de Witt.' He turned to look at their police escort. 'What do you think the Count will say?'

'What will you say to the Count?' Wolff asked with a smile. 'Tell him you didn't pass on any secrets.'

'I did enjoy our conversation. Adler is a dear friend but he hasn't enjoyed the benefit of quite the same . . .' he hesitated; 'well, Ireland and politics in general bore him.'

They parted without making a commitment to meet again, Casement climbing the steps of a crowded tram. As it pulled away he gave a shy little wave that Wolff answered by tipping his hat. Sir Roger was most obliging. Careful to say nothing of his plans, it was true, but he was too hungry for reassurance from a stranger, and the air of melancholy in his demeanour lingered like stale sweat, no matter how hard he tried to disguise it.

Wolff couldn't see the policemen among the crowd at the tram stop but he was sure they could see him. He was going to have to take his time, work through a routine; his mind was so blunted by fatigue that it would be easy to make a mistake. He strolled beneath the gate to the Adlon and drank a cup of coffee in its palm house. Then he walked up the Unter den Linden to the *Chicago Daily News* office and browsed through the papers in its public reading room. He left after forty-five minutes and took a horse cab to Spandauer Strasse. Outside the City Chambers, he hailed a motor cab and paid the driver two marks and twenty pfennigs to take him to the theatre on Schumannstrasse. After enquiring about tickets for a revue, he walked across the river and into the Tiergarten. It was half past eight by the time he reached the statue of Lessing and fine rain was falling again. From the tree stump at the edge of the gravel path, he counted one hundred paces due east. They'd chosen a distinctive-looking cherry with a fork high in the trunk, but it wasn't easy to locate in the dark and he ripped the pocket of his coat pushing through the undergrowth. Reaching up through the branches, he felt inside for the flat head of a drawing pin. Having found it, he carefully released a strip of damp paper. He made his way back to the path and stopped beneath a streetlamp to glance at the note. The damn fool had written it in ink and it was barely legible.

Café Klose

Wolff knew the place – first floor, corner of Leipziger and Mauer – too smart, too central, but at least Christensen was still in business. Rolling the paper into a ball, he flicked it into the gutter.

*

It took a while to give the security police the slip the following morning and he was late for their rendezvous. Christensen was at a corner table with a coffee and was plainly in an evil temper. His mood didn't improve when Wolff refused to discuss their business in the café. They left separately and caught trains to the old cemetery on Chausséestrasse where they wandered about the graves of the famous in the spring sunshine. Why had Wolff missed their rendezvous the other day? What did the Count say? It was too dangerous, he said, they must stop. Wolff knew he didn't mean to. He was greedy and for all his blustering he enjoyed the cast-iron confidence of a youthful chancer.

'You shouldn't speak to Sir Roger,' he protested. 'He likes me, trusts me. You can leave it to me.'

They stopped at a philosopher's grave and Wolff crouched forward as if to read the inscription. 'You're offering me scraps,' he said. 'I need to know what he wants from the Germans and what they want from him.'

Christensen waited until Wolff rose to stand at his side again. 'I do have something.' He looked pleased with himself. 'It's worth a lot.'

'I'll be the judge of that. Well?'

But he wouldn't be drawn for less than forty marks and a promise of forty more. 'You understand the risk . . .' he said. 'It's a fair price. Roger told me why he thinks you're useful . . .'

'Not here,' interrupted Wolff. 'We've been here too long.' They ambled along the path into an unfashionable corner of the cemetery some distance from the gate.

'This will do,' Wolff nodded to an ugly granite temple dedicated to an architect and his family. It was gloomy and damp inside and someone had used it as a lavatory. 'Is this necessary?' Christensen gave a little shudder.

'Are you afraid of ghosts?'

'No, but . . .'

'Here,' Wolff offered him the marks. 'Tell me what you know and we can leave.'

'It was the Count,' the Norwegian muttered, slipping the money into his pocketbook. 'What I mean is, the Count told him you were in South Africa. That you'd served with an Irishman . . .'

'MacBride.'

'Yeah, MacBride. That's why he wanted to speak to you.'

'That's it?' He stared at Christensen for a few seconds, then reached for the lapel of his coat, pinching its edge as if testing the weight of the cloth. 'Is that all?'

'Sir Roger was excited.'

'I know,' he snapped.

'No. You don't understand. I mean, yes, he likes this man MacBride, but it's the brigade. Like the one you served in . . .' he frowned. 'If you did. He's trying to, well, form his own Irish Brigade.'

Wolff let go of his lapel. 'Here?'

'Yes. Irishmen in the British Army, prisoners – the Germans have captured some – thousands.'

Wolff looked at him sceptically.

'Hundreds.'

He didn't know how many.

'To fight in Ireland?'

'I suppose.' He shrugged his square shoulders. 'Why else?'

'You're sure about this?'

Christensen said he was certain. He had listened to Sir Roger explaining his plans to a man who'd arrived from Switzerland. An Irishman, someone important, he said. No, he didn't catch his name nor did he hear mention of a date for a rising.

'All right.' Wolff patted his arm. 'Good. See if you can find out.'

Christensen smiled. 'I told you. You can leave it to me. You will leave it to me, won't you?'

'What does it matter, if I pay you?' he replied.

It was impossible to avoid Casement even if he had wished to. They met for breakfast and walked through the Tiergarten again, then on the following day for dinner. He insisted on taking Wolff to the theatre and arranged for an invitation to a soirée in Count Blücher's rooms at the Esplanade. Would you fight again? he asked. What might you risk to bring England low? He hated injustice, he hated the prejudice of his own class, he hated intemperate sacrifice, the machine grinding relentlessly on the Western Front. He hated all those things, and yet he spoke to Wolff of 'England' without reason, raging at her 'perfidy' and the 'moral debauchery' of her public servants, rejoicing in the thought that she would be made to 'pay' in time.

Did Wolff like him? Ordinarily it was a question he didn't ask himself. As they walked the same circuits, round and round, he listened and recognised a man twisted to distraction by doubts: charming, funny and fragile. 'Spies follow me everywhere too,' Casement observed at dinner. Was he imagining it? There was always a policeman trailing Wolff so it was impossible to say. 'I'm worse than a refugee – an outcast,' Casement continued. 'My friends despise me, the Germans don't trust me, and the rest of the world wants to hang me.'

'You're respected as a man of principle,' Wolff assured him, but it wasn't true.

He noted it first at the Blüchers' soirée. The Count and his wife were old friends from Casement's London days. 'People of our mind,' he remarked breezily, but a few minutes later he was urging de Witt to accompany him into the 'lion's den'.

The Esplanade was a new hotel in the French style, brash,

opulent, a favourite of the Kaiser's before the war and, since, a refuge for the rich returning from abroad.

'Do you think I look well?' Casement asked as they presented their hats and coats to a footman.

'Of course.'

He smiled appreciatively. 'I'm sure it will be a pleasant evening,' but he didn't sound sure.

The Count's suite was one of the finest in the hotel, with French windows opening on to an elegant courtyard garden of trimmed box borders and pine. Some of his hardier guests were smoking on the terrace but most were sipping champagne in his drawing room: gentlemen of middle years and their ladies in expensive, sombre dresses, black and grey the new fashion, with only a little discreet jewellery. The Countess glided towards them like a ship in full sail.

'Sir Roger says you're American and Dutch.' She offered Wolff a cold hand. Her English was as finely cut as the room's Venetian chandelier. 'Americans are always something else as well, aren't they?' She turned her head a little to gaze at Casement, a small frown on her brow. 'But in this ghastly war all our loyalties are being tested.'

'I pray something worthwhile will come from it,' ventured Casement.

'I can't imagine what you think will be worth the sacrifice, Sir Roger,' she replied stiffly. 'Mr de Witt . . .' she caught Wolff's eye. Her dark looks and no-nonsense manner reminded him of his mother. 'There's someone I'd like to introduce you to, another of your countrymen.'

Weber was a middle-aged Californian, a gruff soldier with a shaggy blond moustache like General Custer's. He talked incessantly about the war in a deep and somnolent voice, pausing only to sip his champagne. Wolff let his plans for a 'knockout' blow in the West wash over him, his eyes on

Casement as he drifted from circle to circle. Weber must have followed his gaze. 'That's Sir Roger Casement,' he said, a hand to his face, as if sheltering a secret from the room. His breath smelt of alcohol and strong tobacco. 'You've seen his name in the papers, I reckon?' Wolff admitted that he had. 'People say he's raisin' a brigade to fight against the British. You heard that? The thing is . . .' and he edged closer still. 'It leaves a bad taste, don't it?' Wolff raised his eyebrows quizzically. 'Course I want Germany to win this shootin' match, but a fella who's betrayed one country won't fuss about betrayin' another.'

Drawing-room whispers, sideways glances, and Wolff saw the backs of one small circle turned like a wall. In his crude way, Weber spoke for them all. Sir Roger wasn't Sir Roger any more. The Count had invited his old friend for what he'd been, not what he'd become. His wife put it more bluntly.

'He says you're his friend,' she remarked to Wolff as she led him away from Weber into the chill air. 'Persuade him to go back to America.'

'I don't understand,' Wolff said, genuinely perplexed.

'Sir Roger's making a fool of himself; you do see that, don't you?'

'Why?' he asked coolly.

'He's humiliating himself. My husband says no one here is sure they can trust him – traitors, spies, who can be certain of the difference? You've heard of his Irish Brigade?'

'No.'

'Madness. He's being used and I'm sorry.' Her regret sounded genuine. 'You know I am, well, I *was* very fond of him.'

'Whether he's being used or not, I can't say,' replied Wolff. 'I confess, I barely know him, but I do believe him to be courageous and, yes, a good man. A good man fighting, as he always has – for liberty and justice, but this time for his own people – for Ireland.'

'Then you are as foolish as Roger,' she declared haughtily.

They left the party a short time later, police spies in tow. Casement looked strained and said little. To their surprise, Christensen was slumped on a couch in the lobby of the Minerva, his face flushed with drink. He fussed over Casement, adjusting his silk scarf, summoning a waiter for a glass of water.

'You see how Adler looks after me, de Witt.' Casement's voice shook a little.

'You're a lucky man.'

Christensen scowled at Wolff indiscreetly.

'Really? Do you think so?' asked Casement sadly.

As soon as they'd gone, Wolff went up to his room to rescue the note beneath his door. They had arranged to make their drops at the cemetery but he knew Christensen was angry and frustrated and was at the hotel to say so. The damn fool was going to give them away. Heart thumping, he checked the powder he'd lightly dusted on the door handle – no sign of a print. Christ, he could see a corner of the paper under the door. Thankfully Christensen had written no more than a time.

Calmer, settled in shirtsleeves, Wolff stood at the window of his sitting room with a cigarette, gazing down on the empty boulevard, a gathering wind rattling flag ropes, shaking the spring limes, sickly in the lamplight. He'd been in Berlin almost six weeks and the only thing he knew for sure was that Casement was recruiting a brigade – it seemed to be common knowledge in some circles – no numbers, no dates. C liked to be kept informed, if only to be sure his agents were alive and still on 'our side', but that was before the war when everything was simpler. Of course, C would know from his bank account at Deutsche in New York that he was alive. Wolff could imagine him poring over the statements and fuming to his secretary that he'd heard nothing for weeks and wasn't getting his money's worth. He was as hot as hell about money. 'Serves him bloody well right,' Wolff muttered, grinding his cigarette into an ashtray.

The following morning he visited the bank and withdrew another hundred marks, then registered at the police station as foreigners were required to do. It took a little longer to lose his tail. At the cemetery a work party was polishing the tombs and raking the paths. Wolff nodded to the foreman, thankful that he'd taken the trouble to buy a small wreath at the station florist. He wandered for a while in the sunshine, stopping every now and again to read an inscription. Satisfied at last that the police weren't hiding among the monuments, he made his way to the architect's temple. Christensen arrived a few minutes later, short of breath, his face red and a little swollen.

'Too used to the good life,' Wolff teased. 'You're out of condition.'

He was bent double over his knees, his wool jacket stretched so tightly across his broad back that its seams were easing apart.

'Have you the forty marks you owe me?' he gasped at last.

'Not here – inside.'

The little temple smelt worse. Wolff waited until his eyes had adjusted to the gloom, then hoisted himself on to a ledge.

'Can't we meet somewhere else?' grumbled Christensen.

'Next time. What do you have for me?'

'Where's my money?'

Reaching into his jacket, Wolff took out his cigarette case and offered it to him: 'All in good time.'

Christensen waved it away irritably. 'I don't want to do this any more.'

'Got a better offer?'

'You don't need me.' He took a step away, reaching up to a marble bust of the architect's wife, running his large forefinger down her nose. 'I told you to leave it to me,' he added resentfully.

'Are you jealous?'

'If you can do it on your own, why don't you?' he said, turning to gaze at Wolff.

'Belt and braces, Adler, I need you. Of course I do.'

'Roger likes you. He's spending too much time with you.'

'You've spoken about me?'

Christensen nodded.

'Damn stupid. One small mistake and we'll end up here.' Wolff gestured angrily to the view of the cemetery beyond the temple columns. 'But not before a lot of pain.'

'You're wrong.'

'Don't be a fool.' Wolff slipped off the ledge and took a step towards him. 'This is a dirty business, you can't imagine.'

'Sir Roger wouldn't let them.'

He sounded very sure – cocksure. Wolff glared at him until he looked away.

'He isn't going to fall on his knees and beg them to spare you, Adler.'

'No? Why not?' His finger was trailing over the architect's wife again, from her hair, to her forehead, to her nose, to her lips. 'He's fallen on his knees for me before, you know.'

Wolff felt a frisson of disgust before he was entirely sure why. 'I don't know what you mean and I'm not sure I care to know.'

'Yes you do, I can see you do,' he said, smirking. 'That's why he'll always want *me*, not you, you see – for what I let him do.'

Wolff stared at him coldly: filth. A liability. He would have to go. In the Grünewald forest perhaps, the body in the Havel.

For a few seconds Wolff wanted to do it. Of course that fool Findlay should have told him.

'You see . . .' prompted Christensen, watching Wolff closely. 'Leave it to me. Keep away. I'll get you what you want.'

'Shut up, Adler. Shut up.' Wolff grabbed him by the collar and shook him. It wasn't easy; he was a big man. 'Do what you and Casement do . . .' he paused, '. . . if you must, but you're a bloody fool if you think he'll save you. They don't give a damn about him. If they catch me, they'll probably shoot him too.'

'Get off me,' Christensen said, brushing Wolff's hand from his collar. His eyes had narrowed to slits beneath his heavy brow. 'They care about him. He's helping them, here and in America.'

Wolff took a step back and leant against one of the columns. 'How?'

'Are you going to pay me?'

'So you're still in business?' He stared at Christensen for a moment, then reached into his jacket for his wallet. 'It better be good.'

'I copied it from his diary. You'd be surprised what there is in there,' he said with a little chuckle. 'All sorts of little secrets.'

'Oh?'

'But nothing that would interest you,' he added sheepishly.

'It might.'

'No, it wouldn't. Look, here are my notes.' He was suddenly keen to talk about something else.

Wolff glanced at them, then at Christensen.

'From his diary, you say?'

'Yes. He copies important documents into his diary.'

'Word for word?'

'Yes.'

It was the text of a minute from the Chief of the General Staff of the Army.

Erich von Falkenhayn, Chief of the General Staff
to Rudolf Nadolny

Secret

General Headquarters, 12 February, 1915

The American leaders of the Irish and Sir Roger Casement have agreed to the following proposals:

1) To separate all Catholic Irish prisoners of war from the other prisoners as quickly as possible and to unite them in a place where Sir Roger Casement can encourage them to join an Irish Brigade to fight against England.
2) In the event that he succeeds, an Irish Brigade shall be organised under the command of some English-speaking German officers. The Brigade will be equipped with uniforms and guns.
3) A further 20,000 rifles and 10 machine guns with ammunition and explosives will be provided for a rebellion in Ireland.
4) The German Empire will furnish transport for the Irish Brigade to Ireland for the rebellion. Sir Roger Casement is certain that such measures will lead to a total halt of British recruiting in Ireland and, possibly, to mutinies of Irish troops in France.
5) In return, Irish American leaders undertake to provide men and assistance for a sabotage campaign against British interests in the United States and Canada, the sabotage to cover all kinds of factories for war materials, in particular ammunition, railroads, dams, bridges, banks

and other buildings. The German Embassy in Washington is not to be compromised by direct contact with those involved in sabotage plans, which are to be handled by Captain von Rintelen.

6) Following the decree of 5 November 1914 Nr. 8525 IIIb, I herewith order that Captain of the Reserve, Nadolny of Section P, will take over the handling of this matter.

Falkenhayn

'It's word for word?' Wolff asked again. His voice cracked a little. 'Word for word?'

'Yes, didn't I say so? From Falkenhayn.'

'Yes.' Wolff folded it carefully into his pocket.

'It's good – isn't it?' prompted Christensen.

Wolff smiled at him. A few minutes earlier he had wanted to finish their arrangement. Now he was hungry for approbation. Knowing how to please was his living.

'It's good, Adler, yes. It's very good. First rate.'

It was worth the forty. More. Much more. Even a tight bastard like C would say so.

8

Of Madness

S HE'D TAKEN HABER'S army revolver from the desk, stepped into the garden and shot herself in the chest. The boy had found her by the light of an almost full moon. His face was still covered in her blood three hours later, eyes wide, uncomprehending, ignored by everyone.

They had carried his mother into the house but she'd died before the doctor could arrive. Nadolny was dining with the Foreign Minister and Count Blücher when the police rang to notify him. He made an excuse and left at once. He didn't care a fig for Frau Haber. In so far as he'd formed an opinion of her, it was of a clever but hysterical woman whose outbursts were distracting the professor from his work. She had solved that problem.

It was a little before midnight when he arrived at the house. No one had thought to clean her blood from the steps or the porch, and it trailed along the hall into the drawing room. Haber was in his study with a police inspector, ashen faced, chewing on his cigar, puzzled and a little shocked but in control of his emotions. One of the desk drawers was open and he was showing the inspector where he had kept the revolver.

'My dear Professor, I'm so very sorry,' Nadolny said, advancing across the carpet to greet him.

'Count . . .'

'No, please don't get up.'

He pulled a chair closer to the desk and listened as the inspector asked his questions. 'She said she couldn't bear it – I'd betrayed her, and I'd betrayed science.' Haber gave a heavy sigh, pressing the ball of his thumb to his forehead. There were more angry words, it seemed; a nightly occurrence in the week since Haber's return from Ypres.

'Shouting in front of the servants. I was at my wits' end. "Gas is a perversion and you're a criminal," she screamed at me when Baron Kiehlmann came to dinner. He must have thought she was mad.'

'My dear fellow, she was unwell, that much is obvious,' replied Nadolny carefully.

'Then, tonight, she begged me to stop. Begged me. "Stop this madness," she said. I was leaving for the Russian Front in the morning, you see, our first release in the east. But the tears, the threats . . .'

There was nothing for the inspector to discover. Nadolny impressed upon him the need for total secrecy: nothing in writing, his men to speak to no one, the servants to receive the same instructions. Frau Haber was very ill, he said; the war was having a terrible effect on people; another casualty, a tragic business.

'There's the funeral to arrange. Can you send a message to my unit?' Haber asked when the policeman had gone. He was slumped in his chair as if the stuffing had been pulled from him, his uniform jacket crumpled, ash on his sleeve.

'My dear fellow, I'll make the arrangements.' Nadolny patted his arm. 'When is your train?'

Haber looked at him for a moment, then away. 'No, Count, I have to stay. Hermann, my son, he found her, you know. He's only twelve.'

Nadolny stood up and walked slowly about the room, stopping to gaze at the thick green spines on the shelves. The only work of literature was a copy of Heine's *Buch der Lieder*. There wasn't much poetry in the professor and he guessed the book must have belonged to his wife. Yes, her name was on the flyleaf and the inscription: *To Fritz on his birthday, with the hope that these songs will touch his heart.*

'Captain Haber, it's your duty as a German officer,' he said, slipping the book back on the shelf. 'The Field Marshal won't attempt to break the line without a gas attack. After Ypres, it's only a matter of time before the Russians start issuing their soldiers with respirators.'

Nadolny walked back to stand above Haber, his hand on the back of the chair.

'It's a question of the maximum tactical advantage.'

'And Hermann?' Haber asked, looking up at him uncertainly.

'You have family? Then I will arrange for Hermann to visit them. Now when is your train?'

The boy was sitting alone in a corner of the drawing room, his gaze fixed on the revolver. The police had left the weapon on a table just out of his reach. At least they'd had the sense to unload it, Nadolny thought, picking it up and wrapping it in his coat.

'You must go to bed, Hermann.' Haber held out his hand. 'Come.'

Was it the first time they had spoken since the death of the boy's mother? Nadolny wondered.

He watched Haber lead his son upstairs, then instructed the servants to have the car ready at six o'clock. A maid was on her knees scrubbing the steps in the moonlight when he left: everything would be in order by the morning.

*

Clara Haber's death wasn't reported in the newspapers. Her neighbours were instructed to forget the crack of the shot and the policemen at her door in the night. Her husband's colleagues at the Kaiser Wilhelm Institute knew better than to ask questions, and there was no need for an autopsy. So Frau Dr Haber was buried without fuss in a quiet corner of the cemetery at Dahlem. The small congregation of family and a few friends heard the pastor speak of her role as the wife of a great chemist and as a mother. It was just as the professor would have wished it to be. It was a pity that important duties kept him at the Front: 'a noble sacrifice,' the pastor remarked in his sermon. Nor was Count Nadolny able to pay his respects. As the final prayer was recited, a clerk was escorting him along a corridor at the Military Veterinary Academy.

Professor Troester was sitting in silhouette with his back to a long window, sunlight pouring across his desk, dappling the polished floor and the glass cabinets that lined two sides of his office.

'Does Doctor Dilger know?' Nadolny asked, dispensing with pleasantries.

'I haven't told him,' Troester replied defensively. 'Does it matter? The woman was mad.'

'I think it would be wise to say nothing. I hope the good doctor will be in America by the end of the month.'

'He's grown his first cultures,' Troester picked a handbell from the edge of his desk and rang it; 'but it isn't difficult in a laboratory environment.'

With a tinkle of china cups a clerk came into the room and placed the tray on a bureau.

'How much equipment will he need?' Nadolny enquired.

'Nothing out of the ordinary – nothing an American doctor won't be able to acquire. Coffee?' He nodded to the clerk.

'Setting up a laboratory won't be difficult, but he will have to carry phials of the bacilli to America – that is troubling. If his luggage is searched and they're discovered, well, you can imagine the consequences . . .'

They sat in silence while the clerk served the coffee then slipped from the room.

'On reflection, the consequences are quite unimaginable,' Troester added. 'I'm not a politician but America, international opinion, the law . . .' He frowned and his gaze dropped to his hands.

'My dear Professor, don't trouble yourself with matters that aren't your concern.' Nadolny picked up his cup and held it to his mouth. 'Our task is to help him execute this operation without being caught,' he sipped his coffee, 'and I've assured the Chief of the General Staff he won't be.'

'Yes, well, I'm sure I know my duty, Count,' he replied, tetchily. 'I have something to show you.' Rising from his desk, Troester stepped over to a filing cabinet and lifted a stiff brown leather case from the top of it. 'We've prepared this for the operation,' he said, carrying it back to his desk. 'As you can see, it looks something like a doctor's bag, but the sides, well, they're more robust and . . .' he slid open the two brass locks, '. . . there's a hidden compartment here.'

Nadolny got to his feet and bent to look inside. 'Most ingenious,' he muttered. 'Isn't it rather an unusual shape?'

'Do you think so? He'll be able to carry two phials of E and of B.' Troester gazed over his pince-nez at Nadolny. 'That will be sufficient to culture enough of both pathogens to meet your requirements – if he isn't—'

'But you've found the perfect solution,' interrupted Nadolny, waving his ring at the case.

'No, no, you don't understand. If it's handled roughly by a steward or the police, one or more of the phials will break and, well, you'll lose your spy . . .' he closed the bag, snapping the locks back into place, '. . . and a good number of other people too.'

'That would be unfortunate. We won't find anyone more suitable than our friend the doctor.'

'Yes, I can see that, yes. It's only . . .'

'Please, Professor,' prompted Nadolny. 'There's something else?'

'Probably nothing.' Troester took off his glasses and examined them thoroughly. 'Only that he's an American.'

'Yes, that's why we've chosen him. I'm sorry but you'll have to explain.'

'Simply, will he have the necessary resolve to go through with it when he's there?'

Nadolny pursed his lips thoughtfully. 'Yes, I believe so,' he said at last. 'One of my men followed him to a patriotic review and noted he was singing and cheering with the rest – louder than most.' He smiled. 'And he has quite a following in Berlin society, never short of an invitation – dining at the Kempinski, a regular at the Fledermaus, always gracious, especially to a lady. Often to be seen in the company of Frieda Hempel.'

Troester looked uncomprehending.

'The opera singer, my dear Professor, the opera singer – really, you should enjoy life a little more,' he teased. 'Yes, he's been observed at Frau Hempel's apartment in the sinful hours. So, setting aside his late cousin and his other family ties for a moment, I think I can say with confidence that he's embracing Berlin life to the full.' Nadolny paused to lift his cup again. 'And, as good fortune would have it, Frau Hempel has an apartment in New York too.'

They talked a little longer of the need for great care, of the timetable and final preparations, and the professor wanted to know who else Dilger would call upon to help carry out the operation in America. But that, the Count informed him with smooth assurance, was not his business.

9

A Ticket Home

AN EXCITED BELLBOY stopped Wolff in the corridor with the first news, and the old Baron who haunted the lobby accosted him with more a few minutes later. At Reception, an American woman from the International Peace League was trying to make sense of the front page of the *Zeitung*. 'Yesterday, the 7th of May. A passenger liner from New York, the *Lusitania*,' the assistant manager explained to her in fractured English. There was great loss of life, a thousand people or more, some of them Americans. 'Regret, madam,' he said, 'sunk by one of our German submarines.' He didn't sound in the least sorry.

'A catastrophe,' Casement declared at lunch a few hours later, 'can you imagine? Our enemies will be having a field day in the American papers – the influential ones are all for the British.'

Acres of newsprint would be devoted to the ordeal of the families on board, heart-wrenching stories of separation and loss, pictures of dead mothers and small children.

'They'll tar our cause, tar me with a German brush,' he complained. 'It was a mistake to come here.'

He was a picture of misery, self-pitying, diminished, fallen. For God's sake, thought Wolff, you're supposed to be a threat to our great British Empire: be a man. He was surprised that Casement's weakness irritated him so. Then it occurred to him that was precisely what a true friend should say: 'Stop feeling sorry for yourself, Roger.'

Casement lifted his eyes from his plate.

'It's a hard street, remember?' Wolff continued. 'It was you who said so. Don't you have the stomach for it any more?'

'I . . . of course . . .' Casement was shocked.

'Pull yourself together, man. Your people are relying on you. You've known difficult times before.'

'Yes, I have,' he snapped, dumping his napkin on the table. 'Yes, and I don't need to be told by you.'

He was angry now, pulling at his beard like an Irish Elijah. They glared across the table at each other. Have I gone too far? Wolff wondered. Before he could throw an olive branch, Casement's expression softened and he looked away.

'It's so easy to lose oneself here, isn't it?' he observed.

Wolff smiled sympathetically.

' . . . you know, lose any sense of perspective.' He gave an embarrassed little cough. 'I've hardly given a thought to those passengers. First, air raids on towns, then this barbarity at sea. Poison gas. There don't seem to be boundaries any more.'

'Were there ever any?' asked Wolff.

'But in this modern age it's worse. I suppose all any of us can do is follow . . . well, follow what our consciences instruct us to be our duty.' He paused and smiled at Wolff. 'You were right, Jan, to remind me of mine.'

De Witt cared for his good name. Those few impatient words convinced Casement that a companion he wouldn't have given the time of day to in Dublin was the best sort of friend, who was prepared to tell him what he didn't want to hear. A few minutes later, he confided that he was visiting a prisoner-of-war camp in the morning and asked Wolff to accompany him. 'There's so much a man like you could do for our cause,' he said. Wolff reminded him that it wasn't his cause. 'For me, then,' he replied with a shy smile, like an old lover.

No doubt history would remember the *Lusitania* as a tragedy but Wolff couldn't help musing that the confusion of waves left by the sinking ship presented him with an opportunity to escape. It was two days since his last meeting with Christensen and he was still sitting on the intelligence. He'd coded the Falkenhayn minute into another business report at once and buried it in a thick file, and that was as far as it had gone. No one in Whitehall was going to shower him with praise for proof that the enemy was promising rifles for a rising, but a network of saboteurs in America and a list of the British interests it was going to target was worth an official handshake or two. 'First class, first class, Wolff, good fellow,' C would say, bouncing in his chair.

Only, Wolff was very reluctant to send the report. The security police followed him everywhere. The instant it left his hand it would be picked up and delivered to their cryptographers. The Bureau's man, Bywater, had given him the name of a courier he'd used before the war, an odd-job man at a hostel in the Moabit district. But Wolff didn't like the look of the place. Just an uneasy feeling, but a feeling was quite enough. You're behind the lines, he told himself, sometimes it isn't possible to deliver – he felt guilty nonetheless. The hope that his new best friend was going to fill in the missing pieces at the prisoner-of-war camp made it possible to rest a little easier with his coded report still 'on file'. Finish the job and escape, he told himself, that's the answer.

It was a shock to find his interrogator waiting for him in the hotel lobby the following morning.

'I'm to escort you to the camp today,' Maguerre said with a wry smile. 'We'll have the journey to discuss a few matters'.

He didn't waste time on pleasantries. 'You keep giving my men the slip, Herr de Witt,' he observed the moment the motor car pulled away.

'I don't like being followed.'

'Do you have something to hide?'

'Oh, I expect so.' Wolff reached into his jacket. 'Cigarette?'

Maguerre dismissed the offer with a flourish. 'Cronje doesn't like you, Herr de Witt. He says you can't be trusted.'

'Look, I don't want someone breathing down my neck every minute of the day,' Wolff explained irritably. 'It wasn't difficult to lose your men, so I did. Understand? You'd probably do the same.'

Maguerre stared at him intently. Was he satisfied? It was impossible to say. He began to talk about the Boer rebellion. Was Herr de Witt following the papers? It had fizzled like a damp firework and now it was over. 'You don't seem very surprised,' he remarked. Wolff said it had ended just as he'd expected it to.

'If that's true, why did you go to so much trouble?'

'For the money,' he said casually.

'Money?'

'Yes.'

'But you told me you hated the English.' Maguerre frowned. 'And Sir Roger says . . .'

'I do hate the English.'

'And Cronje – you told him the rifles were paid for by friends who wanted the same as you.'

'They were. They paid me too.'

'You made a profit?'

'Naturally.'

Maguerre began to chuckle, then to laugh out loud, and he slapped the leather seat between them so hard that the driver slammed his foot on the brake.

'But why didn't you tell us it was for the money?' he enquired when the car was moving again.

Wolff shrugged. '"My enemy's enemy is my friend," you said to me, and it's true.'

Maguerre evidently remembered because his tone became a little warmer.

'Sir Roger says you're kindred spirits, that you share his high ideals. He thinks you'll help him.'

Wolff didn't reply, but drew on his cigarette and turned to gaze out of the window. They were crossing the bridge into Spandau, the citadel to his right, and in a few minutes they'd be in open country.

'What is your opinion of Sir Roger?' Maguerre asked carefully.

'Do I respect him, do you mean? Yes. And I share some of those high ideals, but . . .'

'Yes?'

'Well, I've told you before, I'm a businessman.'

'An engineer or a gun runner?'

Wolff looked at him steadily but said nothing.

'Are you prepared to help him?'

'He doesn't need my help.'

Maguerre leant forward and tapped the driver on the shoulder. 'Slow down, would you. No need to hurry.'

'Look, what do you want, Lieutenant?'

'All in good time.' He paused and scratched his nose thoughtfully. 'And his man, Christensen, what do you think of him?'

Just his name made Wolff tense. 'I don't know him really.'

'Why would you? Ah, we're almost there.'

They were approaching a checkpoint in the perimeter of a military training zone. It wasn't the sort of place foreigners were invited to visit, even in peacetime, but Wolff had heard that the open heathland to the north-west of the city was used as a proving ground by the Army. The car stopped at the barrier and Maguerre got out to speak to a stout-looking reserve officer. Through the open door, Wolff could hear a blackbird trilling in the stand of birches behind the guard post. The sun was blinding through the windscreen, bleaching the red leather seat, almost too hot to touch, and for a few seconds Wolff closed his eyes to soak in its warmth.

'A perfect spring day,' said Maguerre as he slipped back on to the seat beside him. The car pulled away, but was forced to slow again minutes later while a work gang of prisoners broke step and cleared the road. They weren't much to look at, Russians for the most part, a few British and French, uniforms dusty and torn; some had lost their boots and were wearing clogs.

'I hope none of them are Irish,' Wolff remarked laconically.

The irony was lost on Maguerre who assured him that the Irish had been separated from the rest.

'And you, Herr de Witt, when will you be returning to America?' he enquired archly.

'Soon, I hope. In the next week.'

'I see.'

They drove in silence through a collection of large red-brick barracks buildings to another checkpoint where they were directed to the gate of the Döberitz camp. It was much larger than Wolff had expected and he said so. Ten thousand prisoners, Maguerre informed him, other ranks only. It reminded Wolff of a Klondike mining town he'd visited years before, on shore leave from his first ship: behind the ten-foot wire fence, one-storey wooden shacks as far he could see, and not a blade of grass. Icy in winter, oppressively hot in summer.

Casement was waiting in the commandant's office, plainly out of sorts. He was as surprised as Wolff by the travel arrangements, and angry that the Army wasn't prepared to issue a security pass for 'poor Adler'. A bureaucratic oversight, Maguerre assured him, too smoothly for it to be anything but a lie. Before they left the office, the charmless old aristocrat who was in charge of the camp insisted on 'instructing' them on how to speak to the prisoners. The English were lazy and troublesome, a dirty and ill-disciplined mob; if only they were prepared to work like the Russians. Casement tried to remind him that they were there to meet Irishmen but he didn't recognise the distinction.

Eighty or so men in a ragtag assortment of uniforms were gathered in one of the camp canteens. Wolff recognised the cap badges of Irish regiments but also the artillery, engineers and the naval division. They got reluctantly to their feet when the commandant and his party entered the room but made no effort to fall into line. Nor did they welcome the patriot. Casement was on edge. He'd taken off his trilby and was gripping it firmly in both hands.

They were all a long way from home, he said. Was anyone from Ballymena? Oh, how he longed for the soft wind from the west on his cheek, to stride out at first light, the bright mist dissipating in the glen, scald crows cawing, the comfort of family, craic with 'our friends'. Then he told them why he was an exile in Germany. Irishmen should only give their lives for their own country. The war against Germany wasn't their concern, the slaughter, the waste, for what? Let England fight her own battles. They must save their strength for the rebuilding of their nation. He spoke with quiet passion; he spoke with the colour and romance of one who loves the timbre of words; he spoke of their Christian duty; he spoke in his soft, educated English accent; he spoke like a gentleman, and they listened in attentive silence but they listened without respect. Hands aggressively on hips, shuffling their feet; Wolff could see from the frowns, the sideways glances, that they thought little or nothing of the man. Regulars, they owed their duty to the uniform and when the lousy war was over they would be content to draw an army pension.

'You've all heard tell of MacBride and his Irish in Africa. Mr de Witt here,' Casement placed a hand on Wolff's arm, 'fought alongside MacBride. Now Irishmen like you are volunteering for a new brigade. Germany will win the war . . .'

He was interrupted by an angry murmur. Someone shouted, 'Shame.'

'. . . but it isn't our war,' continued Casement. 'Let England fight for the extension of her Empire. What matters is that . . .'

'Sir Rah-jer,' drawled a sergeant at the front. He had a Belfast accent you could cut with a knife and the squashed features of a fist fighter.

'Yes?'

'Sir Rah-jer, Sir Rah-jer,' he chanted. 'Sir Rah-jer, Sir Rah-jer . . .'

Some of the others began to laugh.

'Sir Rah-jer, Sir Rah-jer . . .'

Casement coloured. 'Just Roger.'

The big fella smirked. 'I wuz seein' what it was like, you bein' a knight an' all. Sir Rah-jer the black traitor knight.'

'How much are the Germans paying you?' someone shouted from the back.

'I'm here for my country,' he replied with quiet dignity.

'Bloody traitor dog, ye,' said another.

'Not to Ireland.'

But it was too late for reason. The gate was opening and through it bitterness poured in a yelping, howling chorus. Casement the enemy's friend – Wolff could hear it plainly: the hard labour and short rations, the loneliness, the neglect, the careless cruelty of camp life. The big Ulsterman was full of menace, little eyes darting to and fro as he warmed to his comrades' anger, an old pugilist anxious to please his crowd. It was going to end badly. Casement must have sensed it too. He'd given up trying to be heard. Wolff jogged his elbow: 'Roger, we must go.'

'I . . . yes, we must,' he said, but he didn't move.

It wasn't going to be easy; his countrymen wanted to punish him. A private in the engineers pushed his shoulder, someone else spat at him.

'Come on, Roger,' insisted Wolff. Casement was standing in a stupor, a thread of spit clinging to his beard. 'Come on.' For goodness' sake, stop playing Christ. The Ulster sergeant was sweating, biting his lip, edging closer. Then he threw his punch, with a right hand heavy enough to fell a horse but slow. Wolff managed to shove Casement aside and the big man was at full stretch. Before he could find his balance Wolff caught him with an upper cut.

'I'll fix ye, ye bastard,' he raged, and he lunged at Casement again. This time Wolff took the blow just below the collarbone. Before the sergeant could throw another, he grabbed his throat, digging nails into his windpipe, jabbing at the soldier's side with a kidney punch. Gasping with pain, he crumpled and Wolff struck him under the chin with his knee.

Someone was pulling at Wolff's shoulder but for a few seconds he was trapped in a heaving scrum of fists and boots, his face wedged against a shoulder, rough wool against his cheek and the smell of stale sweat and cabbage. Then curses shouted in German, a rifle butt driven at a face as the camp guards forced the circle open. Wolff dropped to one knee but strong hands reached down to haul him back to his feet.

'I'm fine, Roger, really,' he said. 'Just a little dazed.'

They didn't say much in the car on the journey back to Berlin. Casement stared out of the window, his hands wrestling in his lap. As soon as they'd left the military zone, Wolff wedged his shoulders between the seat and the door and shut his eyes. His chest was sore and a prisoner must have kicked him in the melee because his right knee was aching. Mad, bonkers, round the bend, so mad he wanted to laugh. Hands off my traitor, he thought. Exchanging punches with British soldiers: perfect – or it would have been if he'd thought it through, if it had been cold policy. It had been an impulse of anger and of sympathy. He opened his eyes and looked at Roger, his shoulders bent, his face turned away with just the faint sad reflection of his frown in the window. He'd scratched the back of his left hand with his nails. Wolff shut his eyes again. Damn it, now he knew how it was with the prisoners, yes, he felt sorry for the man – just the man.

'Will you take dinner with me later?' Casement asked suddenly.

Wolff smiled warmly. 'A pleasure, Roger.' Then, catching his eye, 'An honour.'

They dined in Casement's rather down-at-heel rooms on a simple meal of boiled chicken, cabbage and potato: it was that sort of hotel. Conversation was a struggle. Only when the plates were cleared and they were sitting by the fire in easy chairs was Casement ready to speak of the camp.

'Thank you,' he said simply, and choked with emotion he rose to stand at the chimneypiece with his back to Wolff. 'I haven't been myself these last few weeks. I've been awfully low,' he said when he'd collected himself. 'You came to my defence. It was a truly Christian act . . .'

Wolff didn't suppress a little smile.

'It was a fine thing,' Casement protested. 'You're a good man, Jan.'

'Because I traded punches with a British soldier?'

'Irish. At no small risk to yourself – you shake your head but you're the sort of fellow who's prepared to step forward to help others.' He lifted a trembling glass to his lips to disguise his feelings. 'I won't forget it.'

They sat quietly for a minute. Was his emotion sickening or touching? Wolff wondered, gazing into the heart of the fire.

'You can see how difficult it's going to be to raise a brigade,' Casement declared at last. 'But there are other ways – I have plans, but I need help, someone I can trust.'

He waited a few seconds but Wolff didn't reply.

'There's Adler, of course. I've given him the evening off. Yes, Adler, but there's only so much I can ask him to do. And . . .' he hesitated. 'Well, you see, our German friends don't trust him.'

'Why ever not?'

'I don't really know.'

Wolff could see the lie in his face.

Fifty prisoners had volunteered for the new brigade, he said. He'd designed a smart olive-green uniform with emerald facings. The Germans promised rifles and machine guns for the rising but it wasn't enough: they needed money and more men, and the only place they could hope to find enough of both would be in America.

'I've spoken to the authorities here. There are thousands of young Irish in America who'll fight for the cause,' he explained. 'They can travel here. The Germans will train them well and when the time is right, land us all in Ireland. A brigade like MacBride's.'

He rose from his chair and stood facing Wolff, the fire flickering about him like an apostle at Pentecost.

'It will take a little time, of course,' he continued. 'We must prepare – we won't be ready until next year. I'm sorry.' He bent to pick up the wine from the hearth, leaning forward to fill Wolff's glass. 'What do you think?'

'Think of what?' he asked.

'Will you do it?'

'Roger, I don't know what you're talking about.'

'Will you speak to them for me, the Irish leaders? You're going back to America, aren't you? You told Maguerre . . . I need someone I can trust, a friend. Adler's going but . . .' he hesitated. 'Someone they'll respect, I may as well say it, someone our friends in America, the Clan, will respect more than Adler.'

His grey eyes were shining with excitement. Wolff didn't know what to say so he frowned, turning, turning the stem of his glass on the arm of the chair. Comic but also sad, a wild flight of fancy: the Germans had given Roger his new olive-green uniform but they knew it was a piece of nonsense. They were using him.

'Well?' prompted Casement.

'I'm flattered, Roger,' he replied cautiously. 'It's just . . .'

Mercifully, he was interrupted by a loud knock at the door. It was Christensen and he was soused.

'Roger, it's your Adler,' he slurred, and with the drunk's gift for the obvious, 'I'm back.' He looked as if he was going to fall on Casement like a sailor's tart.

'Mr de Witt's here, Adler,' said Casement sharply.

Christensen swayed, taking half a step to steady himself. His tie and waistcoat buttons were undone and there was a large stain at the top of his trousers.

'You better sit down.' Casement took him by the arm and steered him towards a chair. He collapsed into it like a sack of potatoes.

'Him,' he sneered, blinking lazily at Wolff. 'Don't worry about him. He knows, Roger, he knows . . .'

'Be quiet, Adler,' Casement demanded, a note of panic rising in his voice.

The damn fool was too pie-eyed to be sure what he was saying. Which of our secrets is he intent on betraying? thought Wolff. I'm not going to let the bastard give *me* away, no – and he leant forward, ready to spring.

'No, Roger, I mean . . .' Christensen frowned, trying to concentrate on what he wanted to say.

Casement was intent on shutting him up, too. 'Come on, I'm putting you to bed,' he said, dragging him roughly from the chair. Wolff jumped up to help: 'Allow me.' But Christensen was off balance. He lurched forward, clutching at the edge of a small occasional table to check his fall. Arm straight, it toppled under his weight, sending glasses and cups crashing to the floor.

'Oh, for goodness' sake,' exclaimed Casement, prodding him with his foot. 'Get up, why don't you?'

But the man was out cold, sprawled like a fallen tree on a carpet of shards and splinters, and there was a little blood where his head had struck the hearthstone. For a few seconds Wolff wondered if his – or was it their? – problem was over. Casement began fussing guiltily, falling to his knees like a Magdalene, loosening Christensen's collar, smoothing the hair from his brow. 'He is all right, isn't he?' he asked plaintively.

Wolff bent to feel the pulse in his neck but before he could confirm life, Christensen stirred, then lifted his head a little and vomited on the rug.

'Sorry, Roger,' he coughed. 'Sorry.' He sounded like a little boy again.

Another reason to say goodbye to Berlin, Wolff reflected as he crossed the hotel lobby five minutes later. He'd been lucky. Christensen had served his purpose: it was time to go before he knew it. Casement was offering Wolff the excuse – America.

He expected another summons the following morning and the bellboy brought one to his rooms as he was taking breakfast. But the note wasn't from Casement – it was from Count Nadolny, an instruction courteously disguised as an invitation to visit him at the General Staff Building at a little before ten; and, to be sure, the young lieutenant with the mad blue-grey eyes and two security policemen were waiting in the lobby to escort him there.

10

Necessary Work

T HERE WAS NOTHING remarkable in his appearance. More smart New England academic than engineer, tall, straight military back, neatly cropped beard; the sort of fellow Dilger might pass on a New York street without a glance.

'If you don't trust him, Count, why are you sending him to America?'

'With men of his sort, Doctor, one is obliged to take a risk,' Nadolny observed. 'I'm merely easing his passage with a little money.'

From their vantage point in the General Staff Building, they gazed down upon de Witt in the gloomy courtyard below, pacing a few yards of gravel, smoking, and exchanging occasional words with his escort. Could he sense there was someone watching him? Ordinarily, no one waited for a motor car at the building the locals called the 'Red Hat': Prussian time-keeping was famously precise.

'Sir Roger Casement says he's a man of principle. Maguerre says he is a businessman . . .' Nadolny enunciated the word with disdain, '. . . a profiteer, a mercenary – but we use these people. Keep away from him. He'll be travelling with two companions. There's no reason why your paths should cross in America.'

A black Opel pulled up to the steps and de Witt climbed inside.

'Shall we?' the Count asked, gesturing to the door.

His office was on the other side of the building with a view of the Reichstag, dark even on a bright day and furnished with uninspiring mahogany pieces. The paintings of battles and officers and the Kaiser belonged to the room but there was also a small scene in a bar at night, painted with heavy brushstrokes in the modern French style. 'Do you like it?' he enquired.

Dilger nodded politely. 'But I'm afraid I don't know anything about art.'

'You're interested in music?' the Count remarked, indicating the armchair in front of his desk.

'Not especially.'

'But you're a friend of Frau Hempel's?'

'I can't see how that can be a concern of yours, Count.'

'Your safety is my concern,' he said coolly. 'She'll be in New York at the same time as you?'

Dilger nodded curtly.

'She has many friends, not all of them are reliable.'

'I don't like your . . .'

'Doctor,' interrupted Nadolny, 'I merely observe it would be wise not to be seen too often in public with her. You will draw attention to yourself.' He bent over his desk, opened a drawer and took out a buff envelope. 'Your contact is Mr Paul Hilken of the Norddeutscher Lloyd Line. Under no circumstances visit our embassy in Washington. We must assume the British follow its movements closely.' He paused, elbow on the desk, his thumb stroking the band of his red signet ring. 'Perhaps the Americans too,' he added with an old-world smile. 'Now, I have something for you.' Rising from the desk, he presented the envelope to Dilger with a small bow.

'Who . . . ?'

'Open it, why don't you?'

It was a short handwritten note from the Chief of the General Staff.

Herr Doktor Dilger . . . the great service you do your
Fatherland . . . sensible of the danger . . . most necessary
work . . . following in the footsteps of your illustrious father
. . . a great honour . . .

Signed simply, *Falkenhayn*.

'You see.' The Count was standing at his side. 'Your work is important enough to command his personal attention.'

'He knows of my father?'

'He would have liked to have spoken to you in person, but official duties . . .' The Count held out his hand. 'May I?'

Dilger didn't understand.

'The General's letter,' the Count explained. 'It has to be deniable – you understand.'

Do I? Dilger wondered as he was escorted from the building. The purposeful click of military boots filled the broad marble stairs as young men in field grey passed him without a glance, proud of their uniform, with nothing to deny. The following day he would make his last secret visit to the Military Veterinary Academy to take possession of the case. Until then, he wished to stroll in the May sunshine without fear of being jostled by a careless passer-by; sip coffee and eat cake at the Aschinger, meet friends, visit the cabaret, drink champagne – forget. But Frieda was in America already and he found it difficult to be merry without her. His friends wanted to know why he'd left the hospital. 'We need you,' they said, and in a drunken exchange one of them had accused him of desertion. The memory made him wince.

In the end he walked slowly home to his sister, rehearsing his goodbye. Since his nephew's death, Elizabeth had relied on him so. The colonel never left the Front, the house was always empty, no visitors, no parties, just the servants, and she was losing the butler and the footman to the war.

She greeted him in the hall with a kiss. 'I thought you were at the hospital.'

'I have to talk to you,' he said, leading her by the hand into the drawing room.

'Should I ask for some coffee?' Her voice trembled a little. 'I've had a letter from the colonel. He writes that he's well – is there ever anything else worth saying?' She rang for the maid, then sat beside him with her small hands resting lightly in her lap. 'What is it, Anton?' Her anxious brown eyes fixed on his face. More mother than sister; was there anyone in the world who knew him better? He'd left Virginia to live with her when he was a teenager.

'You're going to the Front,' she said, raising her right hand a little in alarm.

'No, no,' he assured her. 'I'm going home, to America.'

'America?' For a second she was relieved. 'For how long?'

Before he could answer there was a knock at the door and the maid entered with a tray. The china rattled as she brushed the back of a chair. Elizabeth sighed irritably. She'd been impatient with the servants since Peter's death, and it was a wonder they had any. Good staff were hard to come by since the start of the war. There was going to be a shortage of pretty much everything.

'It's too dangerous,' she declared, handing him a cup. 'What about the British and – well – the *Lusitania*?'

That his mission might be sunk by a German submarine made him smile.

'No. Please, think of it,' she demanded. 'Why now, when we're at war?'

'It won't be for long.'

'It isn't necessary,' she persisted. 'Is it Emmeline? Is she sick? She hasn't said anything to me in her letters.'

Their sister Emmeline was well, all the family in America were well, he assured her, but there were things he must attend to.

What sort of things? she wanted to know. What could be so important that it would take him away from his work at the hospital and from his sister? Did she remember the last time they had visited their father's farm at Greenfield? he asked her. Peter was old enough to ride. They'd spent hours on horses in the woods and meadows above the house. He had taken his nephew to New York City and they'd stared in wonder at 15 Park Row and the new Singer Building.

'Why, Anton?' She wasn't to be deflected. 'Tell me,' she said with a stamp of her foot; thin straight lips, jaw set, the little Dilger dimple in her chin – a face full of determination. Just like mine, he thought.

'Sister, I can't tell you,' he replied firmly.

She stared at him for a few seconds, the thumb and forefinger of her right hand plucking distractedly at her black skirt. 'Don't go, Anton,' she pleaded. 'Please don't.'

'It won't be for long.'

Biting her lip, turning her face away: he reached for her hand but she pulled it away, fumbling with her sleeve for a handkerchief. 'I can't lose you . . . not you as well.'

'You won't.' He gave a little laugh but it sounded strained. 'Elizabeth – I'll be back in a few months.' She wasn't to be reassured because she knew him too well. Why couldn't he speak of it? It was something dangerous. Stay, said the siren voice, stay in Berlin, please stay; and he wanted to. What's more, she knew he did.

'Come back,' she sobbed, her face wet with tears. 'Please come back to me, Anton.'

But he left the house after lunch and walked all afternoon. In the evening he telephoned one of Frieda's friends, a banker, a self-satisfied profiteer, boring, rich. They went to a cabaret and he drank too much wine. The following morning he took a taxicab to the Veterinary Academy. Half an hour later he left in another, his right hand resting firmly on the brown leather case.

Blighty

THE BORDER POLICE ignored their military passes. A spy was attempting to leave the country, they said; everyone to be questioned, luggage searched – no exceptions. They were older men and cripples, unfit for the Front, grateful for a uniform, punctilious in the prosecution of their duties – Germany had more than its fair share of the type, even in peacetime – and they were thorough because they received the same 'intelligence' every day. Foreigners were escorted from the train to the station ticket office to wait their turn on low backless benches. Wolff sat between Christensen and the priest, briefcase and trunk at his feet. Like a music-hall joke, he thought, drawing heavily on his cigarette; by imperial appointment, misfits and conspirators. Ten miles from the border, a ticket to New York, money, the promise of more – they were so close that it frightened him. He had always said he didn't believe in any luck he didn't make for himself, but it felt too easy. On his last night in Berlin he'd copied the guts of his report on to sheets of tissue paper and sewn them into the lining of his coat with the dexterity of an experienced sailor.

The coat was lying across his knee when the police called him; over his arm as they rummaged through his luggage. They went through the pockets of his suits, tapped the heels of his shoes, felt the lining of his briefcase, handed his files to a police clerk, emptied his shaving kit and brushes on to the table; they fingered and peered at his possessions until the only pieces he had left were on his person, and then they searched him too. In the seconds it took the sergeant to go through the pockets of his coat he felt his skin prickling cold with fear. Later he wondered if the Count had planned a final check within spitting distance of the border to catch his guard a little lower. It was the story he knew he'd tell in his memoirs. Everything would have to be part of a great conspiracy in his memoirs.

The police didn't ask many questions. He refused to answer any. Speak to Berlin, he said, and they didn't press him for more. At a little before midday the train rattled across the border into the Netherlands, and for the first time in months he felt something like happiness. What is happiness, if not an absence of anxiety and pain?

'A hostile place,' Father Nicholson observed, leaning forward to peer out of the window at the cultivated farmland of the Overijssel. Wolff was still smiling.

'Mr de Witt, I've heard stories of the British snatching people from here,' the priest explained indignantly.

'I don't doubt it, Father,' he replied, 'but this is my home.' At least, that was how it felt, like stepping out of the shade. Mr de Witt had done all that was asked of him – more. Coat neatly folded on the rack above Christensen's head.

'I know the fella in Rotterdam, Ryan – the American consul. Another one of us,' said Nicholson. 'He might be useful. We'll be safe with him until we sail.'

'You'll be all right,' muttered Christensen, eyes closed, head on chest. He'd lost patience with the priest too. Wolff didn't judge as a rule; with priests he made an exception. It was the Dutch Protestant prejudice of his mother. Nicholson had sweated up the platform and offered his flabby hand like the next Pope. His holy mission was England's 'lasting defeat'. In

Germany he'd talked like a young hero. 'Important men' trusted him and 'fine ladies' shared their confidences. 'He's a good man but a little garrulous,' Casement had warned. 'Look after him, please, he's going to recruit in Boston for us.' Casement tried to see the best in everyone. Father John was the sort of Irish cleric who was only inclined to love a neighbour wearing the green. Most of all he was in love with himself. Wolff listened to his fatuous pronouncements with patience before they crossed the border; once across it, the strain of months got the better of him and he fell into a deep sleep. He woke with a start as they pulled into Rotterdam, the priest standing over him like a fat crow.

They took a taxicab from the station to the Holland America Line pier. The Germans had booked tickets for them in second class because they were less likely to be noticed there. C would have done the same but to save money. She was the SS *Rotterdam*, twin-screw, four-cylinder quadruple expansion engines, displacing 15,000 tons.

'Slower than the *Lusitania*,' observed Wolff with a wry smile.

Christensen squinted at her with a stoker's eye and nodded. 'By ten knots.'

'And older than the *Titanic*.'

Father John looked a little white. The queues at the gangways were shorter than before the war. No one was making the trip for fun. Wolff glanced at his watch. It was five o'clock. She would sail at seven, her lights blazing to distinguish her as a friend to all: there was just time. 'See to my luggage, will you?' he said, pushing his trunk with his foot.

Christensen scowled but said nothing. Things were different now they'd left Germany. But Nicholson was alarmed: 'Are you going? What can be so . . . there isn't time.'

It was a personal matter, Wolff said, and no, it couldn't wait. He would be aboard before she sailed, there was no need to fuss. And coat in one hand, briefcase in the other, he walked quickly away from the pier. He knew C's man, Tinsley, had an office above a warehouse somewhere in the docks. He had little more than an hour to find it.

Dilger was at the *Rotterdam*'s rail in time to watch him leave. There were only twenty passengers in first class and they were already comfortably settled topside. He'd left the case in his cabin, relieved to be free of it for a time, and found a place on the promenade deck with a view of the pier. The priest was easy to spot, fussing over his luggage, the circle widening round him and his exasperated companion. Steerage was still filing aboard when de Witt returned an hour later. Dilger watched him approach the gangway, lost for a moment among the flat caps and ready-to-wear suits, Dutchmen for the most part, their new lives in cardboard suitcases. He walked with a regular, purposeful stride, like a soldier trying not to march, still carrying the briefcase but not his coat. Strange, the Count hadn't described a careless man.

Dilger saw him again at dinner. He had the blond Norwegian in tow but not the priest. They were shown to a table beneath the gallery at the opposite end of the dining saloon. Dilger was closer to the ship's orchestra, too close, caught between a loud New York banker and a charmless textiles manufacturer from Lille, and as soon as it was decently possible he made his excuses and left. It was a clear night with a fresh breeze from the north-west, the last of Holland twinkling on the port side. He took a turn about the deck, stopping only to help a woman from the American Peace League with directions to the Palm Court. She was touchingly grateful but too plain and earnest to be worth engaging in conversation. Her scent reminded him of his Frieda. He wasn't labouring under the illusion she was just *his*, of course; he wasn't a fool.

He flicked his cigarette over the side, the tobacco glowing brightly as it swept to stern on the breeze. Somewhere – perhaps in the ballroom – a band was playing rag tunes. Such a pity, he liked to dance.

In his cabin the war felt closer. He found it difficult to keep his eyes off the case. Struggling out of his shirt, untying his laces, carefully folding his trousers – he'd had to dispense with the services of a valet – he even glimpsed it in the mirror while he was washing his face. He climbed into bed and switched off the light but he could still sense it there in the rack at his feet. Damn. It would be such an easy thing to drop it over the side, and wouldn't his conscience be clearer? He followed its arc: smack on the surface, phials splintering, spilling their poison into the ocean. Yes, the Dr Dilger who refused to bring war to America. But wasn't it too late? He would be casting so much of his life away with the case. Duty, conscience, he was weary of worrying about a choice he'd already taken and impatient with himself. I want to dance with a pretty girl, he thought, turning on his side, and he tried to imagine her fingers touching the back of his hand as they swept about the floor, an adoring look in her eyes.

He was woken by an urgent knocking at a door and raised voices in the passageway. No, they were banging on more than one door. Switching on the cabin light, he glanced at the case, then at the clock. Half past two in the morning. Something was wrong. The ship was barely moving. He jumped out of bed and reached for his trousers. The *Lusitania* had sunk in minutes. He was doing up his laces when someone knocked sharply: 'Andersson, sir. You must get up.'

It was the young Swede who'd settled him into the cabin.

'What is it?' he shouted, stumbling towards the door. 'Are we sinking?'

'No, sir,' came the muffled reply. The steward was smirking when Dilger opened the door.

'First class to the library, sir.' He turned to rap at the cabin door opposite. 'A British cruiser, you'll see her on the port side. No need to worry, sir.'

'What do they want?'

Either Andersson didn't hear him or wasn't able to say.

Stay calm, remember, the British won't be looking for someone like you, the Count had advised.

'Come on, don't just stand there.' It was an old lady in a lobster-green silk dressing gown and a life preserver, her grey hair caught in a net. 'Oh, for goodness' sake,' she huffed, pushing past with her elbows. Further along the passageway a young woman was trying to arrange two bleary-eyed children in her arms and he recognised the New York banker, struggling into a coat.

'Do you know your way, sir?' a steward asked.

In the end, Dilger left the case sitting in the middle of the table in his cabin. If they found it hidden in a cupboard they would examine it more carefully. If they knew what he was doing, his number was up anyway. How could they know?

The British were aboard. A young lieutenant with a 'rules-the-waves' air was sitting at a table in the library, the passenger list in front of him, two marines with revolvers at his back.

'American,' he said, glancing up from Dilger's passport. 'On the way home, from where?'

'Germany.' Nadolny had instructed him to tell the truth.

'Your business there?'

'Family business,' he replied. A few weeks with his sister and now he was returning to his practice in Virginia.

The lieutenant considered him carefully for a few seconds, then slid his passport back across the table. 'All right, please take a seat.'

Everyone looked bored, everyone looked weary, and the little textiles manufacturer was wearing a hole in the rug, restless with anger at the affront to his dignity, a Frenchman, an ally. Dilger stood at the green marble mantelpiece with his back to a fire. Stewards glided about the room with drinks and *saucissonages* and he accepted a glass of water, but only minutes after draining it his mouth was sticky with anxiety again. They'd been waiting half an hour when the lieutenant rose from his table. No regrets, no apologies, with the superciliousness of an Empire Englishman he informed them that the *Rotterdam* had been taken under escort; that they could return to their cabins to finish dressing but they were to gather in the library again in half an hour, and that was all his orders permitted him to say.

'They're looking for German stowaways and spies,' the steward informed Dilger at his cabin door.

'But the ship's on her way to America.'

The Swede shrugged philosophically. The same thing had happened to the *Noordam* a few weeks before, he said; forced to anchor off Ramsgate while some of her passengers were questioned ashore. 'It will add at least a day and a half to the journey,' he grumbled.

'Where on earth is Ramsgate?' Dilger enquired.

First-class passengers were permitted to take the air at daybreak, the coast just visible through a grey sea mist, the cruiser a few cables to stern. At seven o'clock they were served breakfast in the dining saloon, the captain and the first officer drifting between tables with words of reassurance. No more than a day or two in Ramsgate, they said, and while they were anchored the passengers would stay aboard.

'All except the spies,' observed the little textiles manufacturer. 'They'll be going ashore.'

Dilger smiled politely. But at nine o'clock the British lieutenant read out the names of first-class passengers who were to be taken ashore.

'Just a formality, Doctor,' he said coolly. 'Our people would like to talk to you – no, no, not under arrest, just a few questions – a little information.'

Dilger protested that he was an American, spitting that their war was none of his goddamn business, to disguise his fear. What information? He was visiting his sister and there was nothing more to say; a private matter, damn their formality, they were treating him like an enemy. Were they going to rifle through his belongings too? Damn them.

The lieutenant held his hands open like Pilate. 'I'm sorry for the inconvenience but you must understand – the war.'

The launch was hanging from its davits a little below the rail. Steerage in the bow, to judge by their jackets; they were in for a good soaking. The real spies were second class, a score or more in coats amidships, de Witt and his companions among them, the priest the colour of old lace. First class were handed down into the stern.

'Steady with my medical bag,' Dilger shouted to the crewman offering it to him on a safety line. 'There are bottles . . . steady, steady . . .'

He could hear the glass tinkling. Pray God they wouldn't be able to tell the difference between one phial and another.

12

The Club

T HE GRILLE SLID back with an emphatic clunk.

'Lieutenant Wolff?'

'Who the devil are you?'

A jangling of keys and after a few seconds the cell door swung open.

'Fitzgerald. I'm to take you to London.' He looked fresh out of school, a good school naturally, one with a tie that the doorman at the Ritz would recognise and with old friends in Whitehall.

'Call me de Witt here, and keep your voice down.'

Fitzgerald blushed. 'Sorry.'

'Where are you holding the rest?' he asked, gathering his jacket from the bench.

'Most of them are still at the harbour Clock House.'

Wolff stopped at the door to look him in the eye: 'Make sure they're unpleasant to the priest, will you? God, he deserves it. Oh, and he's carrying letters from Casement in the lining of his cassock – he rustles like a pig in straw. Tell them to ignore those.'

They caught the one o'clock from Ramsgate Station. Fitzgerald found an unoccupied carriage and wanted to talk 'tradecraft'. He was too impressed, too Boy Scout – they'd all been like that once. 'Learn on the job,' C used to say, and it wasn't a problem before the war – except for Turkey; you couldn't make a mistake there.

'Chuck it, will you, I'm tired,' Wolff declared, settling into his corner.

Fitzgerald woke him as the train rattled across the Thames.

'Fine view of the Court. Look, I say . . .' he turned from the window to Wolff with a diffident smile. 'Do you mind if I ask you one thing – why did he do it? I met him once, you know.'

'Why did who do what?'

'Roger Casement.'

Wolff lifted his briefcase from the rack. The trunk was still on the ship; the last of Mr de Witt – dress coat, three pairs of black shoes, two of brown, six white shirts, four aggressively American suits. Poor man, lost to the bloody British, the colonial oppressor. The first thing he was going to do now he was home was get rid of the beard.

'He came to stay at our house in Ireland, you see,' Fitzgerald continued. 'I liked him, admired him.'

'Has the Chief sent a car to the station?'

Wolff hated Cumming's club. It reminded him of a mausoleum, pompously ornate in the Venetian style, of the last century, a waiting room for old soldiers, some old sailors, a gallery for dusty weapons and portraits of Empire officers who had won their battle honours against spear-carrying tribesmen. Not a place where the 'temporary gentlemen' of the new armies were made to feel welcome: it suited C perfectly. The staff knew how to look after a fellow like C.

The porter took their coats and hats and arranged for a footman to escort them up the stairs to a private room on the first floor.

'My dear chap, come in, come in,' C bellowed, struggling to rise from a low chair. 'We're the reception committee. You look exhausted. Are you hungry, some sandwiches? Beef all right? And something to drink . . . see to it, Fitzgerald, will you.' He advanced on his sticks to offer his hand. 'Congratulations. Jolly fine work,' and his voice shook a little. A good lunch, thought Wolff.

'Sit down,' C said. 'Let's begin. We haven't much time.'

'Oh?'

'You know Admiral Hall.'

Yes, Wolff knew Hall; he'd served under 'Blinker' in Naval Intelligence. Naval aristocracy: his father had been director too. Bloody old Blinker.

'Well done, Wolff,' Hall said, peremptory as ever. He reminded Wolff of a Jack Russell. Short, balding, mid forties, never still, eyes darting about the room suspiciously, always blinking.

'The bank told me you were alive,' C remarked, easing back into his chair. 'Good hotel, wasn't it?'

'Prices in Berlin keep rising,' Wolff replied with a wry smile. They'd directed him to the leather couch, face to face like a review board, just the Persian rug and the empty grate between them. 'Did you say there was a drink?' he asked.

'The report you left with Agent T in Amsterdam – you mentioned a brigade . . .'

'I don't trust Tinsley.'

'Too late to worry about him,' interjected Hall impatiently. 'This brigade?'

'It won't come to anything.'

'And a rising?'

'I can't be sure. He hears everything second hand, you see. My guess, for what it's worth, not this year.'

'Second hand?'

'All his news of Ireland comes through America. I'll help myself, shall I?' he asked, gesturing to a bottle on the mantelpiece.

'You're forgetting yourself, Wolff.' Blinker was losing his temper; it happened quite often.

'Forgetting myself is how I stay alive, sir.'

They watched him pour a whisky. A few minutes later Fitzgerald returned with a plate of sandwiches and a bottle of the club claret. Then Wolff told them of Casement's failure in the camps and of his fairy-tale hope that recruits for his brigade would be found in America. The Germans were using him for propaganda, he said. When the time came, they would let him have a few rifles for his rising, but they didn't expect it to come to anything. 'No, they don't have much faith in the Irish.' He paused to light a cigarette. 'Actually, Casement says he isn't sure they want a rising.'

C grunted incredulously: 'Why on earth not?'

'He says the Germans are like us – like him . . .' Wolff gestured with his cigarette to the portrait of a cavalry colonel in foreign parts, hanging over the chimneypiece. 'At first he believed they were enemies of the British Empire – God Save Ireland the same as God Save Germany. He's very religious.'

'Bloody fool,' barked Hall. 'Realises he's made a mistake then.'

'He's been very low.'

C leant forward to peer at Wolff through his monocle. 'Do you like him?'

Silence. 'I don't know,' he said at last. 'Does it matter?'

'No, it bloody well doesn't.' Hall shifted restlessly in his chair. 'What matters is that we bring him down . . . anything, letters, bad habits, vices – women, does he drink? Anything useful . . .'

Wolff thought of Christensen.

'Well?'

'Only what I've told you,' he replied coldly.

'Sure?' There was a glint of steel in C's eyes.

Wolff picked up his glass. 'Yes.' He sipped his whisky slowly, then bent low to place it on the hearth.

'Then we must talk about America,' said Hall. 'This German fellow, von Rintelen, you mention in your report – is he going to contact you?'

'I don't know. I am to be one of Casement's representatives, that's all we agreed,' Wolff explained. 'The Count said there might be an opportunity to make some money – wanted me to contact a Dr Albert at the Hamburg America Line on Broadway.'

'Good, very good.' Hall was blinking furiously. 'We know Dr Albert, don't we, Cumming? Holds the purse strings in America. Haven't been able to get near him . . .' He exchanged a glance with C.

'Our chap, Gaunt, has been keeping an eye on him,' he continued. 'Says Albert doesn't get his hands dirty, no, that's why they've sent this man von Rintelen . . . marvellous opportunity, Wolff, marvellous.'

Wolff nodded. He wasn't ready, not yet.

'Yes, yes.' Hall got up to stand on the rug in front of the fire. 'Known for a while that they're building a network in New York. Sabotage – all in the report you sent from Amsterdam,' he declared, rattling it in incisive bursts like a machine gun. 'We're going to have to fight this war with American shells . . . not making enough of our own – scandal really. Not just shells . . . rifles, lots of things – horses. That's what this fellow Rintelen is about. Looks as if he's going to be able to count on the bloody Irish, and New York's full of 'em.' He took his cigarette case from his jacket pocket and stared at it distractedly for a few seconds, then put it back without taking one. 'The thing is, Wolff, Rintelen isn't the only man they've sent to America, there's another. There are two of them,' he said at last.

'Two of them?'

'Two of them, *sir*,' snapped Hall. '*Delmar* – at least that's his code name. Heard of him?'

'No, sir.'

'Your Count, well, someone in his Section P has sent him – top secret, highest classification, separate arrangements, separate contacts – he's going to a lot of trouble – why? Like to hazard a guess?'

'No idea, sir.'

'You can see how important this is,' Cumming interpolated quickly. 'We can't rely on the Americans.'

'Amateurs,' said Hall, shaking his head contemptuously.

'We're not supposed to be operating there,' Cumming continued, 'but we have this opportunity . . . a marvellous opportunity . . . safer than Berlin, of course.'

Wolff didn't reply. He wasn't going to make it easy. God, he was sick of their club-smoke intrigue, sitting there on the edge of their seats; sick of the Kipling talk they were preparing to give him on his duty.

'You can have a little time, twenty-four hours all right?' C took out his monocle and rubbed his eye with his forefinger. 'Shore leave, if you like. Time to get a few things straight. The *Rotterdam*, isn't it?'

Wolff nodded and drew on his cigarette. For a time no one spoke.

'You might like to see your friend, Mrs Curtis,' C said at last, putting his monocle back. 'I believe she's had, well . . .'

'How do you know about this Delmar?' interrupted Wolff.

For once C looked a little thrown. Hall was blinking furiously. 'None of your damn business,' he growled.

'It is if you sent someone else out there – to Germany, I mean,' Wolff replied hotly. 'But you'd have told me. No, you're into their codes? Then you don't need me.'

'Damned impertinent, Wolff.' Blinker was bouncing with indignation on the balls of his feet. 'You're a naval officer.'

'I wasn't sure I'd be able to manage it, well, not after . . . anyway, I did. You said yourself it was good work . . .'

'A job half done, Wolff, half done.'

Wolff closed his eyes and shook his head slowly; he didn't want that lecture on duty from a bugger in a club armchair. For a few seconds no one spoke. Someone in the corridor was chuntering in a parade-ground voice.

'Is that the time?' said Hall, glancing at his watch. 'I have an appointment at five. Don't get up, Cumming . . . talk some sense into him.'

Abandoning the rug at last, he strutted to the door, right hand in his jacket pocket, then turned to glare menacingly at Wolff once more.

'Isn't over, not by a long chalk. Don't care what you think of me, Wolff . . . can't walk away from your duty. Don't you know what's happening out there?'

And with that he was gone. Wolff drew heavily on the last of his cigarette, and half rising, flicked the end in the grate. He could sense C watching him closely, perhaps expecting instant acquiescence now that Hall had left them, something like, 'You've had your say, vented your spleen. Game over.'

'I know what you're thinking, Wolff,' C said at last, a sly suggestion of sympathy in his voice. 'You're thinking "I've been out there again, risked my life, I can forget Turkey, forget what happened there. I can walk with a clear conscience."' C paused to let Wolff speak but he couldn't. 'Go home. Sleep. You'll feel different in the morning. My car's outside, I'll drive you.'

'Like that?' Wolff asked, nodding at C's sticks.

'Damn cheek. I'm not a cripple,' he replied irritably, 'I'll thank you not to treat me like one.'

They didn't talk much in the car. C drove like a madman, careering along Park Lane, his hand hovering over the horn. Turning into Marylebone, they narrowly missed a cyclist, C wailing at him like a banshee, schoolboy glint in his eye again. Driving his Rolls always put him in a good humour. 'Funniest thing, Wolff,' he shouted as they swung left into Wimpole Street. 'Got the fellows at University College to come up with the perfect invisible ink. Know what they say? Ha, ha, you won't believe . . . semen.' He was shaking with laughter. 'Semen. They swear by it. Just think, no problem hiding it, fellow always has it on him . . . just so long . . . ha, ha . . . just so long as he's careful not to overdo it.' Tears were streaming down his cheeks and he took his hand off the wheel for a moment to reach for his handkerchief. It was a relief when a few minutes later they took another left into a mews lane and came to a halt a discreet distance from Wolff's door.

'I'll say it again, fine work.' He switched off the engine and shuffled about to face him. 'Hard to go back, I know, but you can be proud of what you achieved for your country.'

For your country. No higher praise. His voice was gruff with sincerity. It was almost touching. Goodness, yes, clapping and hurrahing at the rope. A fine innings. But the match isn't over, Wolff, oh no. No, no.

'Thank you for the lift, sir,' he said, fumbling for the door.

'Fitzgerald will call for you at ten tomorrow. Ramsgate train at eleven. He'll brief you, he's a good fellow . . .'

Wolff nodded.

'One more thing.' He frowned and his gaze slipped to an indeterminate point somewhere over Wolff's right shoulder. 'Your friend, Curtis – you won't have heard – killed a few weeks ago . . . gas attack. Heard his widow was trying to reach you . . . thought you should know.'

'Yes, thank you.'

Silence. Wolff couldn't think of anything more to say. God, he hoped Reggie didn't know.

'Well, good luck,' said C briskly. 'And when you're there, keep me informed, no reason why you can't in America.'

*

He was disappointed to find that his apartment was just as he'd left it. He felt the same after every operation. The maid had left a few letters on his desk, two of them from his mother. It was six o'clock in the evening; he was hungry, tired and generally low. He had a little under seventeen hours in London, and no appetite for any sort of social gathering, even dinner in a restaurant. 'All right,' he sighed, and he walked to his drawing-room sideboard and poured a whisky.

After fifteen minutes, the operator put him through. His mother wasn't surprised to hear his voice, although it was six months since they'd last spoken. She had never asked him where he was or what he was doing, even as a small boy home from the fen after dark, wet to the skin, late for supper. 'Don't you care?' he'd shouted once. 'God will guide your steps,' she'd replied. No doubt she thought the same still, but in her quiet way she was pleased to hear from him, wanted to tell him of the farm – 'your farm' she called it, more in hope than expectation. She was worried there wouldn't be young men for the harvest, she said, and everything was so dear; she was putting two of the fields to bulbs; one of the neighbouring farms had invested in a tractor, perhaps she should do the same. They didn't speak for long because she struggled with the telephone, obliging him to repeat everything two, three times. 'May the Lord keep you, Sebastian,' she shouted in Dutch. 'I pray for you always.' She didn't ask when he would visit. When she'd gone, he followed her in his imagination, from the dark farmhouse hall to the kitchen, the heavy ticking of the Black Forest clock, her spaniel in a basket in front of the range, a black shawl about her shoulders, a little bent now – she was almost seventy – busying herself with her embroidery or her supper, something without meat because it was Friday.

Wolff poured another, stiffer drink, then cranked the telephone for a second time.

'Kensington, double six-three-five, please, operator.'

Yes, Mrs Curtis was at home; would he wait just a moment?

'Violet, it's me,' he said, before she had a chance to ask. 'I'm so sorry about Reggie. I've only just heard.'

The line crackled menacingly, for four, five, six seconds – more.

'How are you managing?' he asked at last. 'I'm sorry I haven't . . .'

'You bastard.' Her voice shook with quiet fury.

Silence again.

'I'm sorry, Violet,' he ventured again.

'Bastard.'

'I wish I could . . .'

'Bastard.'

Another silence.

'Perhaps I should . . .'

'Bastard, bastard,' louder this time.

'All right . . .'

'What do you want?'

'Nothing, I . . .'

'Then leave me alone,' she shouted, tears in her voice.

'Yes, of course, I'm . . .'

Clunk, the line went dead. Bloody stupid, he should have written to her. First-class bastard, she was right; left without a word of explanation or even a goodbye. He picked up one of the unopened letters on his desk, then tossed it back again. Poor old Reggie. God, he'd made a mess of things, but dammit, she was responsible too. After a long bath and another whisky he dressed in an old suit and walked round the corner to a restaurant. He ate a little, drank a lot and brooded for the best part of an hour. Then he ambled to the Langham and ordered another whisky. At eleven he reeled home, content at least that he didn't have to keep looking over his shoulder. He hauled himself up the stairs by the banisters, then bounced along the corridor to his bedroom and was blearily considering removing his trousers when there was a sobering knock at the door.

'Who is it?' he shouted, in a distant voice.

'Me.'

'Violet?'

Head to foot in black, her small round face covered by a veil, she was rocking backwards and forwards like a Jew at the Wailing Wall: drunk.

'Where have you been?' she whined. 'Where? I'm so lonely.'

'You better come inside,' he said softly.

'No,' she snapped.

Wolff shrugged. 'As you wish.'

For a few seconds an awkward silence, then she began to cry. 'I loved him, you know,' she sobbed, 'in my way. But he wrote to me, he wrote . . .'

'Come on,' he took her gently by the arm, 'not here.'

She unlaced her boots and curled her feet beneath her as she'd done many times before on his couch. She wanted another drink, the glass rattling against her teeth as she shook with tears, and when she'd emptied it she was able to tell him in a small voice that Reggie 'knew'. Knew she was fucking his friend. He knew.

'But he didn't need to, did he?' she asked, in a small voice.

'Need to what?'

'Die.' Her face crumpled again.

'No,' he said, wiping a tear from her cheek with his forefinger, 'didn't need to die.'

Fraught with emotion, too much wine, she asked him with bedroom eyes if they should, and he wanted to although he knew it was a mistake. Later, beneath a tangle of sheets, her warm body pressed to his, her little face framed by damp blonde hair, she smiled up at him and whispered, 'I love you.'

He bent to kiss her forehead so she couldn't see his face.

'I like your beard,' she giggled; 'it tickles. You look like a king.'

He stroked a strand of hair from her cheek.

'We can be together now, can't we?'

He kissed her again.

'You'd like that, wouldn't you? No . . .' she pushed his face away; 'wouldn't you?'

'I have to leave in the morning,' he told her, and no, he couldn't say where or for how long. A job, that's all, a job for the Navy. No, she couldn't ring or write.

'You don't love me,' she said, rolling away from him. She'd always wanted him to love her a little, but only a little, and now Reggie was dead she wanted more.

He leant forward and kissed her shoulder. 'I'll always love you.'

'Will you?'

'Of course.'

Why not say so? He knew she'd forget him after a few days, comfortable in her grief, content with five thousand a year, young and desirable – widow's weeds suited her – a little lace handkerchief at the corner of her eye at the mention of 'poor Reggie'; seconds later the smiles and laughter of a most resilient heart. But afterwards he regretted saying he loved her, even if she knew it wasn't true. It was another lie, he reflected, watching her curled warm against him. Reggie had choked to death knowing his wife was fucking his friend; it might have been his last yellow image. Violet wasn't to blame, she was wired in a different way; she knew no better, a happy creature of instinct who never lay awake worrying about purpose or her future. No, it was his betrayal, his lie. Violet, Reggie, Roger Casement, they all met him in a no-man's-land where there was no right or wrong, only something his masters called 'duty'.

In the morning, she fussed about him, brushing a suit jacket, straightening his tie, barely exchanging glances. 'I'll wait for you,' she whispered as he kissed her goodbye.

And on the train, he was happy for Fitzgerald to talk all the way to Ramsgate.

They'd questioned Dilger in a desultory fashion, opened his case, held a few bottles to a dim light, then apologised for the inconvenience. It was over, the ship was under way, the case was in his cabin again. The moment had passed, fear and a conscienceless opportunity to sink it in the briny. Doctor Anton Dilger, physician, was returning to the New World from the Old with his glass phials, no more obstacles, no possible excuses, plain sailing to New York. He was relieved and he knew he should be pleased. The others had escaped too. He'd watched the priest hoisted, skirts flying, from the steam pinnacle. De Witt had managed it like a sailor but looked worn out, crumpled, as if the British had interrogated him through the night. But if they had discovered he was an arms smuggler the ship would surely have sailed without him. Dilger didn't see him in the dining saloon that evening or at the card tables. He drank a little, gambled a little, then retired to his cabin. The wine, the worry of the last few days, it was some time before he was able to sleep, and then it was only for a short while. At three o'clock he woke gasping for breath, his sheets wet with perspiration, and reached a trembling hand for the glass of water he'd left on his bedside table.

Fool, he murmured. Bloody fool. Just a dream. Only a dream.

13

Irish America

WOLFF CHECKED INTO the Algonquin on West 44th Street, a quiet room at the rear of the hotel with discreet access to the fire escape, comfortable enough for a few days, too expensive for Christensen. They'd crossed from the Jersey City side together but parted at the ferry terminal. Father Nicholson was staying at a Manhattan church house, Christensen in Harlem with 'a friend' who, to judge by his sly smile, he was expecting to pay in his usual way. Ever mindful of Casement's holy cause, the priest had undertaken to arrange a meeting with Irish leaders at once. But for a few hours Wolff was free to stride along Broadway, relishing the June heat and his own company, craning up at the office buildings with an engineer's eye. From blinding midday sunshine into shade, a canyon street of skyscrapers alive with the noise of the motor car, monumental, brash, full of inexhaustible optimism. Let the old world tear itself apart, the new century belonged to America. His spirits had lifted as the *Rotterdam* passed through the Narrows, Liberty on the port side, Manhattan dead ahead, teetering at the edge of the bay like a sailor's sweetheart in high heels, changed beyond recognition since his last visit – or was that the impression the new Woolworth Building made on the skyline? Like sloughing necrotic skin – Christensen, his palm always open, the priest with his righteous prattle, Violet, the Bureau, all the refuse of the teeming shore he'd left, and if it was only an illusion – after all, wasn't he here with his own poison? – well, for as long as it lasted it was welcome.

At Wanamaker's he bought some light shirts and was measured for a summer suit, then he visited a barber for a haircut and a shave, to emerge an hour later with a new face, a new name, no longer Mr de Witt with his short Dutch 'v' but an American with a long city 'w'. By then there was a late-afternoon breeze on Broadway and a fresh urgency in the step of office workers that anticipated the end of the working day. Wolff took a cab to the corner with Chambers Street and walked at the same businesslike pace across the park to the post office. In its cool hall he wrote a short note to a Mr Spencer in London, queued at the counter, paid for the postage and watched it drop into the bag. A little further along Broadway, he visited the Western Union office and sent another by messenger to Mr Ponting at the Yacht Club.

By the time he got back to the Algonquin it was half past five and Christensen was fidgeting impatiently in the lobby. Where had Mr de Witt been? They must hurry, it was arranged for that evening: the priest was going to meet them at 51 Chambers Street – ask for Justice Cohalan. He was on edge in the cab, keen to ingratiate himself, complimenting Wolff on his clean shave. 'You know, there's a lot I can do here,' he added plaintively. 'I know New York . . . I could help you, help in your . . . work.' Perhaps they could meet later, a meal or a drink, he knew a bar where there were – and he leant across to whisper behind his hand – girls. His breath smelt of beer and fish. Wolff sighed. Ah, Adler, you know you don't have anything to offer here but your silence and you're in too deep for that to be worth more than a few dollars. It was always difficult saying 'goodbye' to the Adlers. 'I don't want to go back to Berlin,' he explained as the cab came to a halt, 'not yet . . . Tell them that, won't you . . .'

'Why don't you tell them yourself?'

Number 51 Chambers Street was a new limestone skyscraper in the beaux arts style, paid for by interest earned on the savings of two generations of Irish emigrants. Above the vast banking hall where tellers behind bronze grilles counted thousands in and out every day, were several floors belonging to Holy Mother Church. With her special dispensation, Justice Cohalan occupied rooms on the tenth. 'He's a passionate fellow for a lawyer,' Casement had said; 'a fine man, knows everyone, and close to Devoy.' Veteran republican, friend of Parnell, jailbird and journalist, gun runner, foreign legionnaire, implacable enemy of the British for more than half a century: 'Devoy *is* Irish America,' Casement said; 'he's the one you must explain things to.' They were Roger's delegation, the collective voice of his reason: priest, prostitute, spy. Comic and yet strangely appropriate, each of them represented something particular of the man. The part that the spy had rehearsed promenading the *Rotterdam* was loyal friend and businessman.

Father Nicholson greeted them in the lobby. 'It's most of the executive of Clan na Gael,' he said, hunting round anxiously for an ashtray. 'I've given Sir Roger's letter to Mr Devoy already.' He filled the elevator with incense and sweat. There were a dozen of them round a boardroom table, heavy, middle aged or elderly, distinctly Irish in the self-conscious way of the American exile, all of them men but for a young woman in her early twenties who was there to take the minutes and was pretty enough to draw Wolff's eye. From the head of the table, Justice Cohalan spoke a few cool words of welcome and indicated that they should take the empty chairs at the bottom. How was Sir Roger faring? he asked, broad shoulders wriggling uncomfortably; they had read his letter with concern. Concern was written deeply in his remarkably long face. He was a tough-looking man who might have made his living with a pick and a shovel. Wolff's gaze wandered round the table as the priest spoke of Casement's hopes for the brigade, of its spirit, of its new green uniform, of the need for more young Irishmen to fight alongside 'our brothers'. Nicholson spoke with passion – more perhaps than he managed on a Sunday – and they listened with the respect they would offer any priest, but with no warmth. There was a long silence when he finished, only the scratching of the secretary's pen.

'He doesn't seem himself, you know . . .' Cohalan observed at last. 'Disappointed, angry even, at least that's what I read in his letters.'

Nicholson said he thought Casement was in good spirits. But short of money, Christensen chipped in. Sir Roger wasn't able to stay at the best hotels and didn't eat like a gentleman.

'Like a gentleman, you say?' John Devoy leant forward, turning his shaggy grey head to stare menacingly down the table at them.

'He has expenses,' Christensen ventured nervously. 'The grand circles he must be in . . . some costs . . . clothes . . .'

Devoy snorted sceptically.

'. . . clothes . . .' Christensen repeated, nonplussed.

The priest came to his rescue. 'He lives very modestly, Mr Devoy, but he must put our case to the German leaders, their Chancellor and high command.'

'Father, we've sent him six and a half thousand dollars – he's no reason to complain,' replied Devoy, softly spoken, distinctly Irish, too old to mince his words.

Cohalan patted his arm. 'He's out there dealing with these fellas on his own, John, it's a tricky business; they've larger fish to fry than us . . . You've been very quiet, Mr de Witt.

153

What do you say? You're here to speak on Roger's behalf, aren't you?'

'Before he does, I'd like to know who he is,' Devoy remarked, and there was a murmur of assent round the table.

Wolff reached lazily into his jacket pocket for his cigarette case, took one out and rolled it lightly between his fingers. 'I'm a private man, Mr Devoy. Roger Casement trusts me because he knows me.'

'He says in his letter you fought the British in South Africa with MacBride.'

'That's right, Mr Cohalan . . .' Snap. His lighter burst into flame; '. . . but that's no sort of bona fide, I'm sure you'll agree. I'm here to present Roger's view, to answer the questions I can – my past is none of your business.' He paused again to remove a strand of tobacco from his lip; 'if you don't respect Roger's choice I have no business here—'

'I don't,' interrupted Devoy.

'Let's hear him out,' the judge said.

'The Germans won't help you if you don't do anything for yourselves,' Wolff continued. 'That's Roger's opinion. He wants young Irishmen from here and someone, an Irishman, to command the brigade. Then they might believe you've got the guts to do more than sing about dying for old Ireland.'

'You're sneering at us,' someone said. They were angry now, too angry to care who Sir Roger's representative might be.

'He's wasting his time with the brigade,' Devoy shook his head. 'Vanity, that's what it is . . .'

'So you say,' Wolff pressed on, 'but what proof do the Germans have that there's any cause in Ireland they can count on?' There were more complaints. 'Gentlemen, they want you to show some spirit.'

It was the judge who brought them to order. The battle was won: Mr de Witt was allowed to speak his mind because they were Irish rebels for whom it was a great virtue, and perhaps after years of sentimental talk they were inclined to believe what he said was true. But if de Witt's role was to speak for his friend Roger, what of the spy Wolff? A patina of mistrust, a little more of Casement's reputation lost, the suggestion of a man close to a breakdown; goodness, it was easy enough. The man's letters, his soul-baring letters, and the facts that de Witt presented to them, were all that the spy, Wolff, needed because they spoke for themselves. It was Roger's view that hundreds, thousands of Irish Americans might be recruited to the brigade, and Roger was sure they could cross the Atlantic in disguise, and Roger had been promised rifles and a ship to carry them all to Ireland. Mr de Witt declined to give his own view. He did speak with passion of his friend's faithful heart, of his frustrations, the slights he bore without complaint and his much reduced circumstances. With too much passion, C might have said. He would have been wrong. Wolff could see it in their heavy Irish faces. They had no faith in the brigade – what was it Casement called his men? – no faith in his 'Poor Brothers' – and they were going to leave them, like it said in the song, hanging on the barbed wire. But if some passion helped Mr de Witt's friend to have a little more money in exile, good meals, a comfortable bed, then Mr Wolff was content too.

'We must send more, of course,' declared Justice Cohalan. 'You will carry it back, de Witt . . .'

Wolff shook his head. 'I'm not returning to Berlin.'

'Oh?'

'This isn't my cause, although I pray it succeeds in time and have faith that it will. I have a living to make here – Roger's friend is to act as a courier,' he said, half turning to Christensen.

'Yes, perhaps,' the judge replied without enthusiasm.

'Our cause will succeed without *your* prayers,' growled Devoy.

Wolff smiled sardonically. 'I hope you're right because I'm not a man who prays a great deal.'

They glared at each other for a few seconds but with difficulty. 'I felt sure you weren't that sort of man,' Devoy chuckled mischievously. 'Sorry, Father.'

With a smile on his face, the old man reminded Wolff of a grey Casement – the man he might become if he slipped the hangman's noose. The priest blew out his cheeks and waved his hand, relieved to see a little sunshine.

After the smiles, they wanted Wolff to go. There were handshakes, thanks, a promise that the Clan would be in touch – the Algonquin, wasn't it? Was there anything they could do for him? Perhaps, he said; he was a businessman.

'Be gentle with Roger. Your country has no more devoted servant,' he told them. It was meant as a parting shot and he was turning to the door when the young woman spoke to him.

'Mr de Witt, will you find time to visit Sir Roger's sister while you're here?'

He'd presumed she was just the girl who took the minutes: early twenties, not married – he always looked for a ring – educated East Coast voice, fine features, intelligent face.

'Yes, perhaps tomorrow,' he said.

'I know Mrs Newman is very anxious for news of her brother.'

They made eye contact and she offered an embarrassed smile then looked down, turning her notes deliberately.

'All right, gentlemen.' Justice Cohalan clapped his big hands together. 'For now . . .'

14

More Friends and Enemies

THE FOLLOWING MORNING Wolff visited the offices of the Hamburg America Shipping Line on Broadway. 'Contact Dr Albert, he will have something for a man like you,' Nadolny had said to him. But Albert wasn't there and his clerks pretended they didn't know when he would be. Wolff left a note with his name and address, mentioning their 'friend' in Berlin.

It was another blue day and with nothing particular to do until the afternoon he walked to Battery Park and sat in the sunshine watching the traffic along the waterfront, a liner creeping upriver to Hoboken, freighters in and out of the Jersey wharfs. Busier than he remembered it, with a score or more ships waiting for a berth, smoke and steam drifting north-west on a warm breeze. Horses, cattle, grain, iron, guns, ammunition to stoke the fire in Europe. In the name of peaceful commerce, of course. Stocks at the Broad Street exchange up again. No wonder the Germans were raging. Like children in a sweetie shop, everything for sale without discrimination, but with no possibility of slipping the British naval blockade of the Atlantic. If they couldn't dip into the jar, the best they could do was stop the enemy doing the same. Sabotage made sense. But not Dr Albert; he was the man with the purse strings, the commercial attaché in Washington before the war. No, he would pass Wolff's note to someone else – if he decided it was worth the trouble. What were his instructions from Berlin? The sun slipped behind cloud; somewhere in the outer bay a ship was sounding its horn, three, four, five urgent blasts. Rising from the bench, Wolff ambled by the river rail in the direction of the pier and a line of taxicabs. For now it was Casement, quietly losing his mind in Berlin, sad, desperate, lonely Roger, who was still his passport.

Wolff telephoned Casement's sister later that morning and arranged to visit her at four. Not just for King and Country, he liked to think, but out of a sense of duty to Casement too – or was he deluding himself? Mrs Agnes Newman lived in a prosperous tree-lined neighbourhood of Brooklyn among bank clerks and city accountants, a modest single-storey house, neat white picket fence and garden. Her bell tinkled impatiently. She answered the door herself and he was struck at once by the family resemblance. A little greyer, fuller in face and figure, but the same fine features and brooding deep-set eyes.

'Roddy wrote to us about you,' she said, stepping from the door. 'I'm worried about him, you must tell me everything . . . please . . .' She led him into her sitting room.

'You met Miss McDonnell?'

'Still to be properly introduced,' he said. It was the young committee secretary of the night before. 'Miss McDonnell.' He gave a stiff bow.

She smiled in amusement: 'Mr de Witt.'

'Sit down, sit down, please.' Mrs Newman patted the only armchair. It had been positioned in the middle of a tight circle of wooden ones like a throne. The room was crammed with furniture, none of it interesting, the atmosphere alive with dust, swirling impatiently in the sunlight pouring through the lace curtains.

'Laura says you spoke well,' said Mrs Newman, taking a seat opposite. 'Those people don't understand Roddy – such a pity his friend, McGarrity, from Philadelphia wasn't there.'

She leant forward, hands clasped in a big fist, almost touching his knees, but gazing at his face too intently to notice. 'His last letter . . . I'm worried, Mr de Witt.'

'I have another,' he said, reaching into his jacket. She took it from him, turned it over twice, three times, as if reading it with her fingertips, then put it to one side. 'I want to hear from you first, everything – where is he living, is he eating well? . . . he wrote to say he'd seen the Blüchers.'

Wolff told her a little of the party, an account so anodyne it might have been another event. Then he described Casement's life in Berlin, his hotel and routine and the sympathetic hours he'd spent walking with Roger in the Tiergarten, friend and confidant. 'He likes to walk, Mrs Newman . . .'

'Yes, of course he does,' she said irritably. 'What I want—'

He cut across her, '. . . and walking is free.'

'. . . to know . . .'

She lifted an anxious hand to the nape of her neck, her mouth opening and shutting like a trout's. 'I know he's short of money,' she said, finding her voice again. 'Be frank with me – how is he managing? He seems so very low.'

Wolff nodded. 'I think he's lonely. He doesn't trust the Germans and they don't entirely trust him, Mrs Newman. Do you know anything of his plans for a brigade?'

The two women exchanged glances. Plainly it was Clan business and she wasn't supposed to know. Laura McDonnell was avoiding his gaze.

'He's loyal to his men but he must doubt, well, he has black times. He's so alone. I think that's why we became friends – ships in a storm . . . you're right to be concerned for him.'

She looked away, discreetly brushing a tear from the corner of her eye. 'I knew it,' she said fiercely. 'He gives so much – people don't understand – he'll sacrifice himself.'

What could they do to help him? The Clan must answer his

rallying cry with recruits and money. For the good of Ireland, for freedom, for liberty, for Roddy – Mr de Witt, don't you agree? Mr de Witt was careful not to pour cold water on his 'friend's' high hopes, not in sister Agnes' sitting room. Miss McDonnell chose her words with care and said very little. He was conscious of her watching him closely, watching him nod, watching him smile, perfectly insincere, the smile he'd practised in front of a mirror, a 'whatever you're buying I'm selling' smile, the friend, leader, hero, saint smile. Ah, dear Agnes, if only you knew about me, he mused. May I call you 'Nina'? Your brother calls you 'Nina' in his letters, doesn't he? Nina, you're passionate like your brother but a bit of a bully. But, Nina, the world is so full of duplicity and confusion. There are things you don't know, even about your Roddy. Yes, wipe away that tear and I'll tell you. Imagine him bent over his dear sweet Adler. Yes, giving it to the Empire in Ireland's name. It's true, really. That much is true. Can't you read it in my eyes? Of course he couldn't, no; couldn't stir the dust in the room.

'Tea, Mr de Witt?' she asked after a while.

When they were alone, Miss McDonnell observed, 'You're very . . . discreet, Mr de Witt, careful – practised, like a lawyer.'

'You disapprove, Miss McDonnell; what would you . . .'

'Laura, please, I really do prefer it.'

'What would you have me say, Laura?'

'You should tell the truth,' she said quietly.

'Do you? You were at the meeting – is your committee going to recruit young men here in America for Roger?'

She shook her head sadly.

'Roger isn't going to recruit any there, you know – in Germany – but he might go mad trying.'

They sat in silence, Laura trying to avoid his gaze. Short, curvy, well dressed but not expensively, with the easy confident manner of someone older. Content to say nothing, a smile close to her lips and a twinkle in her blue-green eyes; a rich mane of dark auburn hair – proud of her hair, she wore it loose, turning her head out of habit to present it to advantage.

'And you, Mr de Witt . . .' it swept towards him as she looked him in the eye at last, 'what about you?'

'There are always jobs for engineers.'

'And gun runners.'

He raised his brow quizzically. 'Who have you been talking to, Laura?'

She gave a mischievous laugh but didn't answer, and a moment later Mrs Newman came into the room with a tray. The conversation returned to Casement and childhood tales. Plainly dear Nina had always known what was best for her brother. There was no mention of Mr Newman. Out of politeness she asked Wolff about his own childhood and his time in South Africa and listened to his answers with an expression entirely empty of curiosity. But when he rose to leave, she made him promise to visit her again soon so they could settle what 'our Roddy' should do. 'He needs his family,' she said, '. . . and friends,' she added with less conviction. Laura made her excuses too and left with him.

'She loves him very dearly,' she said apologetically, as he held the front gate open for her.

He offered to find a taxicab but she wanted to use the subway.

'Sir Roger's the most honest man I've met and courageous,' she said with feeling as they walked to the station on Atlantic Avenue. 'He's given so much, followed his conscience no matter how difficult the journey – I think of him as Ireland's conscience.'

Wolff nodded respectfully.

'But the Clan is in touch with others,' she said cautiously. 'Men you don't know, leaders in Ireland.'

'I understand.' He was careful not to push her.

'Men like Patrick Pearse. Did Roger speak of him?'

'A little,' he lied.

'Of course everyone respects Roger.'

They walked in silence until it was apparent to Wolff that she wasn't going to say more about the men he didn't know. Then he asked her how she had become involved with the Clan. Her parents were from Kildare like Devoy, she said, but she was brought up in Philadelphia, her father a builder, a pillar of the Church and a leading light among the Irish there. He was a traditional Fenian who knew the Church had betrayed Parnell but wouldn't tolerate anyone saying so; a woman's place was home, excepting his daughter who always got her own way.

'I'm spoilt, Mr de Witt, an only child, you see.' There were tears when she insisted on moving to New York to do law at Albany, she said. She had finished her degree and wanted to practise at the Bar, but for now her time was spent working for the Clan and for women's suffrage. 'My father tolerates the work I do with votes for women because I make myself useful to the Clan. What about you, Mr de Witt . . .'

'Jan.'

'Do you believe a woman has the right to vote?'

'Certainly.'

She stopped suddenly and turned to him. 'I'm not sure I believe you. Do you tell lies?'

'Do you?'

'I'm sorry, that was impertinent,' she said, purring the word in her educated East Coast way.

'You've no reason to doubt my sincerity,' he said.

'No. I'm sorry.'

'Although I don't think about it often – perhaps I should.'

She had a ticket but waited at the barrier while he bought one. There was a problem with a train and the station was crowded with pink-faced families returning from the park with their picnic baskets, Jew and Gentile, the voices of old Europe, Russian, German, Italian, Pole, and a language everyone called English.

'Are you hoping to take a job in New York?' she asked, as they stood facing each other on the platform.

It was his intention to let things settle, he said with a wry smile; there was no hurry, he could draw a modest income from savings. Then how would he occupy himself? she wanted to know: idleness was plainly unthinkable. Renew old acquaintances, he told her, and he would need to find rooms; there was so much of the city to explore, even a little sailing. She frowned and looked away. Close beside him in the crowd she seemed younger, smaller, trapped, her hands fluttering about her dress. He caught her eye and she coloured a little.

'Do you know New York well, Laura?'

'Quite well.'

'Would you be my guide, perhaps one afternoon?'

'Oh, there are better guides than me,' she replied hastily. 'I'm sorry –' she pulled a face; 'that was rude.'

He laughed. 'I'm sure you're too busy.'

'Yes.'

Seconds later the train was upon them. He found Laura a seat and stood beside her, glancing down discreetly at her hair, her hands, the lines of her face, the fall of the dress about her thighs. Perhaps he would see her again at Mrs Newman's home. Eight minutes only under the East River to Bowling Green. They changed trains and for the short journey to Grand Central they were able to sit together but made no effort at conversation.

'Take this,' she said suddenly, bent over her purse. The train began to squeal. 'Oh, dear. Ah. Here,' and she brandished a card at him. 'If you don't find someone better.'

He smiled. 'I'm sure I won't.'

She blushed. 'Well, goodbye, Mr de Witt.'

The carriage doors opened and he touched the brim of his hat.

'Goodbye, Miss McDonnell.'

He caught the man at the corner of his eye as he was turning to wave to Laura. It was only a glance. Eyes flicking to Wolff and away as he stepped from the next carriage. Twenty yards, no, thirty, a face among many that kept walking for the stairs, but Wolff's heart beat a little faster. Five-ten, heavy, dark greasy hair, dark jacket, collarless shirt, swarthy. He didn't look very Irish. Laura acknowledged his wave with a smile, the carriage jolted forward, then the train began to gather speed and she was gone. Wolff turned towards the stairway. Grand Central was big and busy, with more than one exit from the subway, so his tail would wait close by. I've been complacent, Wolff reflected; the roundabout never stops spinning. The man was at the top of the first flight of stairs, pretending to tie his bootlace, passengers flowing round him like an awkward rock. Up the second flight of stairs, through the barrier, out on to 42nd Street, and Wolff walked at a leisurely pace back to the hotel for a hot bath. Irish or German, no reason to hide, he'd given the name of the Algonquin to everybody. He was hoping for a little attention, just as long as it didn't end with a knife in the back.

Wolff didn't see the man or anyone else who looked like a runner when he left the hotel for dinner a few hours later. To be sure, he caught a taxicab to the restaurant and insisted on a corner with a view of the other tables. It was an Italian, lively, popular with the young, the food good but not expensive – the sort of place an engineer of modest means might choose to eat alone. He'd brought his copy of *The War of the Worlds* with him to America and he flicked through it between courses. The rustic red he ordered with his meal reminded him of a run ashore he'd enjoyed in La Spezia, a seedy marker in his passage from university engineer to officer and gentleman. He'd left a lot of nonconformist baggage on the quay at La Spezia: amusing after fifteen years. Whistles and crisp white uniforms, hearts of solid oak eager for action, and my goodness they'd found it. 'Wolff . . . Wolff, the things we . . . we do for king . . . and cun . . . cunt-ry,' Thompson had slurred, a bottle of the very same wine pressed to his bottom lip. 'God bless 'im . . . 'is Maj . . . Majesty.' Ah, yes, God bless him, thought Wolff, raising his glass to drink a silent toast.

It was half past ten when the cab dropped him back at the hotel. While the driver fumbled reluctantly for change, he glanced along the street for the subway man or one of his kind, but there were too many shadows, too many doorways to be sure. At the desk the clerk handed him his key and a small buff envelope.

J. de Witt Esquire

The clerk informed him it had been delivered by a messenger-service boy but not one of the regulars. Wolff opened it with the desk's knife: two lines on plain paper, a terse invitation for drinks at a mid-town address the following evening, signed by a Mr Emile V. Gaché.

'Has anyone asked for me?' he enquired. 'I'm expecting a friend.'

It had been a busy day, but no, the clerk couldn't recall anyone. Wolff slipped him a dollar. A little grease and the machine was turning, for in the time it took to walk to the elevator word reached the porters that Mr de Witt was a proper gentleman who would make it worth their while. 'Big man, about seven o'clock, sir,' the bellboy recalled. 'Face like a boxer, but in a white uniform. He wanted to know your room number.'

'So you told him.'

'No, sir,' he lied. He got his dollar all the same.

Wolff was on the ninth floor. Too high to survive a tumble, he'd joked when the bellboy delivered his luggage. 'This is New York, sir,' he'd replied laconically. The elevator opened on to a broad landing, pot plants, theatre mirror, leather couch. His room was to the left, halfway along a bright, thickly carpeted corridor. An elderly American couple were bickering at their door, the man struggling to turn the key with arthritic fingers. A little further along, a lady was arranging her shoes for the shine. Everything in order, everything as it should be in a good seven-dollar-a-night hotel – and yet, and yet . . . there was something amiss – a spy's sixth sense, a chill: he'd felt it before they arrested him in Berlin; in Turkey too.

Without hesitating, he walked past his room and round the corner to the door at the end of the corridor. He'd checked and knew that it opened on to a fire escape gantry. Removing his shoes first, he stepped out lightly and quickly, counting the windows, seven to the corner of the building, then five more to his room. The curtains were still open, a light inside but a small one, perhaps the desk lamp. Conscious that he was casting a dim shadow, he stooped low and shuffled under the sill, listened for a few seconds – nothing – then glanced inside. A man was sitting a few feet from him at the desk beneath the window. Wolff couldn't see his face, only his legs, one crossed over the other, his forearm, a hand that disappeared as he drew on his cigarette – and through the smoke the silhouette of a revolver. He crept away from the window and back along the fire escape. Manhattan was still humming, steam rising from rooftops nearby, the night sky lost in the glow of the city firmament, like something in one of Wells' dystopian stories. In the corridor once more, he didn't trouble to step lightly and opened the door to his room with no particular care. The intruder was still at the desk, large right hand covering the revolver.

'Lieutenant?' he asked.

Wolff pushed the door to and switched on the chandelier. 'Never call me that: plain *Mr* de Witt, if you please. You should have left a message.'

'You should have left a message, *sir*,' he replied angrily.

Wolff ignored him, shrugging off his coat and throwing it on a chair.

'Gaunt, *Captain* Gaunt,' he rose from his chair; 'but you know.' He gripped Wolff's hand too tightly, squeezing it like a boarding-school bully. 'Look, old fellow, calm down, no one saw me.'

'I'll stick with *Mr Ponting*,' Wolff replied.

'No point. I'm the naval attaché, for God's sake. Everyone knows me here – well, the people who matter do.'

'I'm sure. That's why it was damn stupid to come to the hotel.'

'Who the blazes do you think you're talking to?' He took another step forward, big right hand balled in a fist. Just itching for a fight, always itching for a fight; it was in the hard lines of his face, lantern jaw, gazing down his beak at Wolff, thin, almost colourless lips, all prickly self-regard; captain cum old-fashioned boatswain cum spy, but a spy who wore a crisp white uniform, took rooms at the New York Yacht Club and never missed a diplomatic party. 'He's one of theirs,' young Fitzgerald had said, quoting C directly, by which he meant Naval Intelligence. 'He'll tell you America's his patch, senior service and all that . . .' Gaunt enjoyed his role too much to let a lieutenant fifteen years his junior kick sand in his face.

'Drink?' Wolff asked. 'Only whisky, I'm afraid.'

'I've got everything sewn up here.' Even after twenty years in the Navy there was the trace of a colonial accent. 'I need to be kept informed – clear lines of sight – understand?'

'Perfectly.' Wolff offered him a tumbler. 'I'm anxious not to bugger things up – I'm anxious to stay alive.'

'Too anxious, I hear . . .' he interjected maliciously; 'at least, if that business in Turkey is anything to go by.'

Wolff settled in the only armchair, casually balancing his glass on his knee. 'Trying to put me in my place?'

'They say you gave them Chambers and some of the Turks.'

Wolff sipped his whisky and swallowed hard. Was that how they boiled it down? Bureau chap squealed: a poor show. 'I think we should talk about why I'm here,' he said.

'I know why you're here,' Gaunt snapped at him. 'Who do you think sorted out your cover, squared the people at Westinghouse, the leaks to the newspapers . . .'

'It was an excellent story,' Wolff raised his glass in salute, 'worked a treat. It's kept me alive – so far. Thank you.'

He gazed at Wolff, trying to decide if this small peace offering was enough to satisfy his injured pride. 'All right, what do you need?' he asked, pulling his chair closer.

Wolff took the letter from his jacket and offered it between thumb and forefinger. 'Recognise the name?'

'No. But West 15th, that's Martha Held's place – for Germans with the money to spend on parties and pretty girls. Their military attaché, von Papen, uses the place when he's here. If you're thinking of going, watch your step.'

Not everyone who could afford to pay for the good time Martha promised her guests was a gentleman, Gaunt said. Some of the regulars were merchant captains, their ships bottled up in East Coast ports by the British naval blockade. 'Met Dr Albert?'

Wolff said he hadn't had the pleasure.

'He's their purser. Once a week, a procession of these captains visits his office on Broadway. I wager they'll have something to do with your sabotage campaign.'

Albert paid the bills; the orders came from someone else. Gaunt's people were hearing whispers of a new 'fellow on the block'. 'Perhaps this Rintelen or Delmar,' he observed; 'anyway, the new man seems to have put old Papen's nose out.'

'The military attaché?'

'Queer bird. Gave me a present when I arrived in Washington. Got to have some sympathy . . .'

Wolff looked at him quizzically.

'Fellow from Berlin pushing him aside,' Gaunt explained with a rueful smile. 'The enemy and his friends in Congress are doing all they can to keep America out of the war, sucking up to anyone with an axe to grind against the Empire; every bloody tribesman between here and Timbuktu,' he remarked with a disparaging grunt. An attempt had been made to stir up the 'bloody' Irish on the docks; there had been a few suspicious fires on ships carrying rifles and shells to the Allies, an explosion at an ordnance factory in New Jersey. Gaunt had recruited a network of runners to keep an eye on the docks: 'The enemy have got our Irish; we've got their Czechs and Poles.' Wolff could call on them for assistance, 'but you come to me first, old boy. They'll do the job for you, trained them myself – if you need someone followed or frightened, drop a fellow in a hole, and here . . .' he got up and stepped over to the table '. . . your chaps asked me to find one . . .' – lifting the trigger guard of the revolver with his forefinger and swinging it back and forth like a steel cradle. 'American, I'm afraid. A little clumsy. Careful who you point it at, we don't want to upset our hosts.' He placed it back on the table. 'You'll have a job hiding that in a jacket.'

'I won't take it to dinner.'

'You have the telephone number at Whitehall Street?'

'Not on the telephone.'

'Then a coded note to Mr Ponting,' he said, reaching for his overcoat. 'I'll leave by the fire escape. Can jump back when I reach the first floor.'

For a few seconds, he listened at the door. Satisfied, he turned the handle and was opening it carefully when Wolff reached forward to close it again.

'One last thing,' he whispered, looking Gaunt in the eye. 'Your gypsy, the fellow who picked me up this afternoon . . .'

He offered a taut smile. 'Careless of him – just to be sure you come to no harm, you understand.'

'Well, call him off. It isn't easy judging friends from enemies in this business . . . *sir.*'

15

Dilger Family Business

H IS SISTER JOSEPHINE found the house in Chevy Chase. Nothing grand; two-storey brick colonial, a living room, parlour, small backyard – and the basement for a laboratory. An unremarkable house in an ordinary street, in a neighbour-hood they were still building, where no one had lived long enough to be nosy. Strangers pretending they were friends, fresh faces, fixed American smiles, shallow backyard conversa-tions: Chevy Chase was perfect. A stone's throw from downtown Washington, six miles from Mr Wilson in the White House, but he may as well have been on the moon. Affairs of state troubled no one on 33rd Street, where life in August was lived at the plodding pace of the milkman's horse. Nor did the neigh-bours care about the war; wasn't Wilson promising to keep them out of it? Dilger might have hidden from it too – best Berlin suits hanging in the wardrobe – if he hadn't brought it with him in a hard leather bag.

It troubled him less because America didn't feel like 'home'. He had belonged to her aboard the ship, sleeping, waking, worrying if he was doing his duty or committing a crime. Symptoms he diagnosed later as cabin fever. He'd drunk too much, gambled too much because he was a German and he was an American.

'Welcome home,' one of the officers said to him as they steamed into New York.

'Good to be home,' he replied, although he was simmering quietly with anger.

From the *Rotterdam*'s rail, he counted a dozen enemy freighters in the bay, a dozen more along the waterfront, and as he drew closer he heard, then saw, the cranes swinging boxes of matériel aboard, and a column of lorries from the ordnance factories upstate, tankers, colliers, a bulker loaded with grain, longshoremen driving cattle from a train into the gaping side of a White Star steamer. The spirit of free enterprise, he told himself, but he resented it nonetheless. It wasn't just a question of money. The newspapers were still full of the *Lusitania*, the sympathies of most with the Allies. There was barely a mention of the blockade to starve Germans into submission – women and children too. Dilger felt like an alien, and perhaps he wanted to feel like one, reducing America to childhood memories, the past to a foreign country, everything simple, everything clear, free to execute his mission with purpose. By the time he reached Washington he was cured of his cabin fever and able to ask his sister, with the passion he'd felt in Frau Haber's drawing room, 'So what do you think of your German brother?'

'So proud,' Josephine whispered as she hugged him, so clever, so handsome, such beautiful old-world manners. She spoke German like an American these days. It was six years since his last visit – the summer he'd spent studying at Johns Hopkins – but she had written to him every few months. 'I'm here to see you all,' he told her because the less she knew, the safer she would be. On his second day they visited the cemetery and held hands before their father's stone. 'Oh Anton, he would have been so proud,' she said again, wiping away tears with a tiny lace handkerchief that was not up to the task. 'Oh, how hateful America is becoming – someone spat at Mrs König last week . . .' and she told him she was pleased the old Civil War

172

hero hadn't lived to see the country he served with distinction turn its back on their Fatherland.

Just a few months, he said, when she asked him how long he would stay, and although she was sorry, she understood: of course he must return to his medical duties, those poor wounded men . . . If only she could leave her Adolf and serve alongside him as a nurse – and, yes, their sister Elizabeth in Berlin needed him too.

On the third day he caught a train into the foothills of the Blue Ridge. His older brother, Butzie, was waiting at the station and drove him in a gig along the twisting dirt highway to the farm, a memory round every corner, at the top of every rise; beautiful still, but sadder, as if his father had taken the spirit of the place with him to the grave. The old house had burned to the ground, family pictures, books, swords, medals, the piano they'd gathered round to sing of home, all lost, and the new place was Southern-style ordinary. The Army had purchased most of their fields for its own horses; what was left lay fallow, rain dribbled through the roof of the great barn, and the stone walls they'd bent aching backs to build were crumbling and choked with weeds. Even Butzie was going to seed, struggling to contain his stomach in his filthy overalls. The old man would never have allowed his son to dress that way.

'He isn't going to be able to keep the place up, Anton,' his sister Emmeline confided after supper. 'You know Butzie, he isn't a clever one like you.'

Emmeline was weary of tending the family flame. Years of selfless fetching-and-carrying for her father, then her brother, were beginning to show in the lines of her face, and her crown of thick blonde hair – once so admired by the young men on the neighbouring farms – was streaked with grey. She was still attractive, with their mother's large sad eyes, a German lady fading like the elegant blue silk fauteuil in the drawing room, a ghost of former times. 'Come to Washington with me,' he had said. 'We'll make new friends together and you will be close to Josephine and Adolf.'

Early the following morning he rode the bounds of the farm, a warm breeze in his face, swishing through the long grass. He sensed it was the last he would see of the hills that even his sister in Germany still talked of as home. Family should be home, he thought; only the war is requiring us all to choose another. At five, his father had taught him to ride in the paddock by the house, at the age of eight to jump the high stone wall in the valley; and before his son left for school in Germany, he had fought the Civil War for the benefit of Anton in the seven-acre, hard-riding his old mare like a man half his age. Dilger's chest ached with memories and to outpace them he spurred his horse into a gallop that left them both shaking.

When he left the farm, Emmeline went with him. 'Just for a few months,' she promised Butzie, but by the time they reached Washington, she said she felt ten years younger. Josephine met them with the keys for the house in Chevy Chase. Her husband Adolf had clopped about the capital in a cart, collecting the pieces Dilger needed for his work.

'For your surgery?' Emmeline asked.

'For my research,' he replied.

'Anton's working on infections,' Josephine explained.

'It's my hobby.'

'More than that, Anton,' Josephine added with the warmth that never left her voice when she spoke of him. 'Helping the sick is God's work.'

On their first night in the house they drank beer and laughed and told stories of Father and Mother and how it used to be. They were only sad when Dilger reminded them of the games he'd played on the farm with their nephew Peter.

'You were like brothers,' Josephine declared, drying her eyes with her tiny hankie.

'Elizabeth says so too,' he said quietly. They toasted Peter, they toasted their sister, they toasted Germany and 'victory', then Adolf sang a song of home and they joined him in the chorus.

The following morning Dilger rose early. He dressed in the velvet hunting breeches and jacket he used to wear on the farm, then crept downstairs to the cellar. Twenty-five feet by twenty-five, the size of a comfortable parlour, with a polished oak floor, plain white walls, sink, trelliswork bench, desk, and ever-obliging Adolf had arranged for a carpenter to fit some shelves. There was a door from the kitchen and one into the yard, and two windows high in the wall, a few feet from the ceiling. Adolf had found most of the things on his list: an incubation oven – tick, sterilising machine – tick, phials and Petri dishes, burner and a wire cage – the guinea pigs would be arriving in a couple of days.

'Come up and have some breakfast, Anton,' Emmeline shouted from the kitchen at a little before nine.

'Were you feeling unwell?' she asked when they were seated at the table. 'I heard you on the stairs at five o'clock.'

Just an impulse, he assured her, scientists keep their own time. She smiled and patted his hand indulgently, but he wasn't to forget they were taking tea with the nice couple across the street later. He said he wouldn't, although he didn't care much for tea.

'Well, you'll have to pretend,' she laughed, wagging her finger at him. 'Mustn't offend our new neighbours.'

In the cellar, sunshine was streaming through the stained windows and shimmering on the floor beneath the workbench like bacteria on a slide. Dilger stood for a time at the foot of the stairs listening to his sister washing the dishes in the kitchen above. She was humming a lively tune, something by Mozart.

'All right,' he muttered, and taking a deep breath he reached for the white coat he'd left on the peg by the door.

The leather travelling case he'd nursed from Berlin was on the bench top. Slowly, very slowly, he opened the compartment in its side, took out the velvet padding and placed the phials in a tube rack: two marked *B* and two marked *E*. Thank God they had survived the journey. 'All right,' he sighed again, 'all right,' and he picked up a pair of surgical gloves. A crash in the kitchen above made him start. Emmeline must have dropped a plate. Damn it, he hadn't locked the basement door. Gloves, face mask, Bunsen flame, culture dish, he was ready. *Bacillus anthracis*. The anthrax microbe was the most challenging of the two. He took a phial of *B* from the rack and held it up to the light. A pale-yellow gel to the naked eye, distinctive rod-shaped bacilli beneath a microscope; so extraordinary, so simple, so efficient, so resilient, so deadly. Carefully, he drew the stopper. He'd carried out the procedure at least a dozen times in Berlin but it still made his heart beat faster. Always in his mind's eye at this moment, an image came to him of the man in blood-stained sheets he'd seen at the Charité Hospital.

'That's it.'

Placing the phial in an empty rack, he picked up a length of wire with a small loop at the end and held it in the Bunsen flame. When he was sure it was sterile, he dipped it in the phial, turning the loop once, twice, three times. With his left hand he lifted a Petri dish of growth medium from the shelf above. Then, removing the contaminated wire from the phial, he drew it slowly back and forth across the dish. He repeated the procedure with a second dish. Then he placed both of the new cultures in the incubator.

'Shit.' He smiled. God damn, he was shaking a little. Why? He knew what he was doing, it was simple. He dropped his gloves in the sink, soaped his hands well and selected another pair. Phial *E* for *equus. Burkholderia mallei.* The glanders microbe. A fresh wire and dish, a different growth medium for this culture – ox blood – but the procedure was the same. Infection, by inhalation or ingestion, or perhaps through an abrasion to the skin. The symptoms: coughing, fever, chest pain, followed by septicaemia and death.

'Have you finished, Anton?' Emmeline called from the top of the stairs.

'For now,' he replied. 'I'll be right up.'

At four o'clock they stepped across the street to take tea with young Mr and Mrs Mitchell. He was something in insurance; she was expecting their first child. What a fascinating place Europe must be, they said, so many fine buildings, so much history. How sad its great nations were at war. It made the insurance business very tricky, Mr Mitchell confided chirpily.

'I'm sorry, Anton,' Emmeline said later. 'Not your sort of people.'

Dilger smiled and took her hand, so rough from the farm pots and pans. 'We'll make friends, don't you worry.'

After supper he left her sewing curtains in the parlour and caught a tram along Connecticut Avenue into town. He got off just beyond the Dupont Circle and walked the last three blocks.

The Grafton was the sort of comfortable but ugly modern hotel favoured by businessmen on a budget. No one stayed long enough for the staff to remember a name and no one gave Dilger a second glance as he walked across the lobby. The hotel telephones were in a booth close to the desk, mounted on the wall and a little low. He chose the one at the end, cranked it and asked the operator for a Baltimore number.

'Tell Mr Hilken it's Dr Dilger,' he instructed the servant who answered his call.

The empty line crackled for two, three, four minutes and he

was on the point of hanging up when he heard a bang and someone curse.

'Sorry, the receiver. Are you still there?'

'Mr Paul Hilken?'

'Delmar? I got your telegram,' he replied in German. He spoke it well, plainly a cultivated and youngish man.

'Call me Dr Dilger. Look, you'll need to send someone to me in two weeks, someone reliable.'

'It's all organised – Captain Hinsch will be your contact, but why don't you visit us here?'

'No. He must come to my house. On the fifteenth. He'll need some instruction.'

'All right, then, come here after you've made the delivery,' he said pleasantly. 'Do you like the theatre?'

'And money. I need some money.'

'I'll send it with Hinsch. Don't worry, everything is in order.'

Dilger gave him the address. 'My sister's staying with me.'

He was surprised. 'So it's a family business?'

'She doesn't know.'

'I see. Well, is there anything else I can do for you?' Hilken enquired politely.

'Not yet. We must wait for nature to take her course.'

For a few seconds there was only the line. Then he laughed nervously. '"*That I may smite thee and thy people with pestilence . . .*"' His voice sounded shaky and he laughed again to disguise his embarrassment. 'Well, goodbye, Doctor. Take good care.'

16

Unholy Alliances

H E SAID HIS name was Mr Emile V. Gaché. He said he was Swiss but even Martha Held's 'ladies' knew that was a lie. He said he was a banker, also a barefaced lie. He said he was a friend to Germany and in that at least there was truth.

'What do you want from me?' Wolff asked him after an hour of questions and lies.

'You do not feel comfortable?'

'It's very intimate . . .' Wolff waved his hand languidly at the waitress serving drinks and displaying her cleavage to the gentlemen on the couch opposite.

'It is safe. Martha is a patriot,' and he raised his glass to the spirit of the large operatic lady who was their hostess. 'And you, Mr de Witt?'

'Me? A businessman, I told you. More of a businessman than you, I think.'

He laughed – a strange, strangled laugh like a yelping dog. 'An entrepreneur in the spirit of our times,' he offered; and he was dressed like one, in an expensive suit and spats, fashionable middle-aged businessman or broker – more than a disguise or affectation; military in his bearing but in everything else trade, second or third generation – a new patriot. Convincingly good humoured for a vain man and a German officer. A little older than Wolff, early forties, with a large straight mouth, thin hair swept from a high forehead and sharp little eyes.

'Our mutual acquaintance, Count Nadolny—'

'Yes, the Count did mention you,' he interrupted. 'I like to make up my own mind.'

'So do I,' replied Wolff, rising impatiently from his chair.

'Mr de Witt,' he leant forward, his arm raised; 'wait, please.'

Wolff stared at him for a moment, then resumed his seat.

'Thank you. More wine.' He turned to look for one of Martha's girls, then got to his feet, fastidiously smoothing imaginary creases from his perfectly pressed trousers. 'So, please, I will be just a minute.'

Wolff watched him weave across the drawing room to where Miss Held was holding court at a table. Fifties, full figure, auburn wig and frills; madam by night, German matron by day. Front of house an ordinary brick row, drawing room sinful Parisian silk and velvet, with couches so soft a small man might drown. Martha's young ladies – coy smiles and laughter, '. . . *everything light, darling . . .*', squeezing the hand of a burly German businessman, draped on the arm of a sailor's chair, 'Champagne! More whisky!' Oh, such *Mädchen.*

'Correct. I'm not a banker,' he said in a low voice, sitting beside Wolff again. 'Champagne?' He began to pour. 'Captain Franz von Rintelen of the Imperial German Navy at your service.'

Wolff raised his glass in salute.

'You're a man who enjoys taking risks, correct?'

'For the right price.' Wolff put down his glass, took out his cigarette case and offered it to Rintelen. 'No?' He lit his own and reached for the ashtray. 'I do have *some* principles.'

'Of course, you are an associate of Sir Roger Casement.'

'He doesn't like to use the title,' said Wolff, ignoring his ironic smile. 'I've told you something of my history. If I can be of service to Germany, well . . .'

Rintelen's sharp little eyes flitted about Wolff's face like a persistent bluebottle. 'So, I may have something that will suit you,' he said at last. 'There is someone I want you to meet first, another . . . entrepreneur.'

Captain Friedrich Hinsch was playing skat in the room above. He'd drunk too much, he was losing, he was in a foul temper, and the table breathed a collective sigh as he scooped what was left of his money into a sweaty palm and rose to join them. He was big and rough and rolled like a steamer in a gale, weather-beaten, a beetle brow, black calf-length boots over a grey suit, soap beneath one ear, a shock of blond hair, careless with his appearance, and the sort of man who would enjoy squaring up to anyone foolish enough to say so. He was expecting them and knew a little of de Witt's story but was plainly unimpressed. 'Don't trust a man with more than one country,' he grumbled.

'Captain Hinsch is an . . .' Rintelen slipped apologetically into English, 'old salt.'

'Hey, a beer.' Hinsch waved to one of the girls.

'And Mr de Witt is a man of principle.'

'Principle.' Hinsch spat it back sceptically.

'But at a price,' Rintelen continued. 'He is an engineer, and he has experience of handling explosives.'

'You *have* been talking, Mr Gaché.'

Rintelen coloured a little but ignored the jibe. 'My associate is the master of the *Neckar*. He has been here since the begin-ning of the war . . .'

'Almost a year,' Hinsch interjected.

'His ship is, what do the Americans say – "interned" – interned in Baltimore, a prisoner of the British blockade. But you have not been idle, Captain Hinsch, have you? Ah. Here we are.'

As the girl served Hinsch his beer, his eyes wandered proprietorially from her face, down her long neck to her chest – daringly décolleté, of course – and he tipped her like a regular.

'An engineer, you say?' He paused to wipe froth from his mouth with the back of his chubby hand. 'Know about ships?'

'I've worked my passage a few times,' Wolff replied coolly, 'when things were difficult. Know my way about an engine room, know why the *Titanic* sank.'

'Ah, very good.' Rintelen picked up the champagne and leant forward to fill his glass. 'But would you have been able to sink her?'

'A little thought, a lot of explosive.' He shrugged. 'No such thing as unsinkable, is there? Some of us never forgot that.'

'Easy for the right man, perhaps,' Rintelen sucked his teeth, 'sadly, there are too many of the wrong sort.'

'Too many stupid buggers,' barked Hinsch.

'Good people are not easy to find,' Rintelen observed with a weariness that suggested he'd tried.

With that, they seemed to have said all they wanted to say about ships and explosives and began to crawl through de Witt's life again, family, war, his work – 'the Dutch East Indies, you say, and after that?' He'd told the story so often that it was his own; like flicking a switch in the brain, his memories now, every taste, every smell, the dust of the Highveld scouring his face, engrained in his pores.

'But now you must enjoy yourself,' Rintelen said when he had finished scribbling in his pocketbook. Meet Clara. Clara would be his friend for the rest of the evening. 'She's a good girl,' Hinsch whispered like a beery pimp. Poor Clara. Slender, twenties, small breasts, sweet round face, tired combat eyes. Too bored and drunk to be their spy. What would Martha Held say about the drink? It wasn't good for business. But Clara could still manage it, sweating and groaning, faking it for a few dollars; it just took practice. The lie was all part of the service, that's why it was a profession. Wolff knew the routine, knew the tricks, goodness, wasn't it the same? Didn't the Bible say so somewhere? Clara could probably perform in her sleep. But not with him, not this time.

'Brought up by a God-fearing mother,' he whispered to her, removing her fingers. 'Here,' and he offered her a few dollars.

'No, no,' she protested, placing her hand firmly back on his thigh.

'Yes, yes, take it. And, Clara . . .' His gaze drew her attention to Hinsch. 'Stay away from him. He isn't a nice man.'

She didn't understand but smiled weakly and took his money.

The clock in the lobby at the Algonquin struck two while he was collecting his key at the desk. In the corridor, a shine was placing the shoes he'd cleaned at their owners' doors. Cowboy boots for a country boy; a young couple at 903, small feet, perhaps Italian or Spanish; and Wolff's neighbour was an Englishman, his shoes from a Jermyn Street shop. At his own door he bent and ran fingertips over the carpet: the grit he'd sown was trodden deeply into the pile and the hair he'd fixed across the lock was on the step.

The following morning he sent a coded message to Mr Ponting at the Consulate office in Whitehall Street. They met in the dark corner of a downtown restaurant a few hours later, and he told the naval attaché the little he'd learnt at Martha's.

'I suppose Rintelen is checking your story,' Gaunt observed, stirring a third spoonful of sugar into his coffee.

'Most likely.'

'It's watertight, don't worry.'

Wolff frowned. C had used the same words before the fiasco in Turkey.

'Something the matter?' Gaunt asked.

'He has a monstrously high opinion of himself, but he isn't a fool. Perfect English. Energetic. Can't keep still. Likes everything to be "correct". Let's hope he's in a hurry.' Picking up his coffee spoon, Wolff peered at his reflection in the back of it. 'If he is, I'll get the job. If he isn't, he'll kill me.'

'You sound a little windy,' Gaunt scoffed. 'Don't overdo it. Look, got an address? I'll put someone on to him, Hinsch too.'

Wolff smiled. 'He's your neighbour – staying at the Yacht Club.'

'Bloody hell!' Gaunt choked on his coffee. 'He's a German.'

Wolff decided to prepare for the job by moving somewhere more discreet. He settled on a comfortable first-floor apartment in a red-brick house on the Lower East Side, at the edge of *Kleindeutschland*. The landlord was a Jew from Lvov, his neighbour a voluble Italian; there was a Russian family upstairs and a bent old lady from Posen lived on the ground floor with her cats. Not a patch on the Algonquin but the sort of place an out-of-work engineer counting his coin might wish to rent for a while. Shabby but respectable, furnished with dark old-world pieces his landlord had accepted as rent from the previous tenants. Terms included a maid and a kosher meal if he wanted it, typically *lokshen*, *gefilte* fish, or something made with chopped liver. His sitting-room window looked over East 5th, one broad stone stair to the front of the house, fire escape into a dark courtyard at the rear, private telephone in the hall, sturdy locks and a bolt.

Before he left the hotel, he sent notes to Ponting and Gaché. The first telephone call he made from the apartment was to Miss Laura McDonnell.

'I thought you would choose somewhere . . .'

'Smarter?'

'Downtown.'

'Yes.'

The line crackled for a few seconds, then they began to speak at once.

'I interrupted, please,' he said.

'Only that Nina, Mrs Newman, thought – thinks you've forgotten her.'

He smiled with secret pleasure. 'Sorry. You know, looking for the apartment, making contact with business people . . .'

'I'm sure she understands . . . when you have the time.'

He said he would write to her at once, and he hoped Miss McDonnell remembered her promise to act as his guide to the city. She said her name was still Laura and it wasn't a promise – but she agreed to meet him nonetheless.

Coats and scarves already, a breezy blue September day with white horses in the bay, struggling to hold the *Tribune* open, the front page full of the first British gas attack in France.

'It isn't the city,' she said, when he proposed they catch the ferry to Coney Island. 'I thought you wanted a guide to the city. What about Liberty Island? Have you been?'

'No,' he lied.

They caught the ferry from Battery Park pier.

'Oh dear, if only I'd known we would be on the river,' she declared, trying to hold her hair beneath her hat.

'You're regretting it already.'

'Yes,' she said, with a teasing frown.

She made him climb to the top of the green lady so she could number the buildings on the Manhattan skyline from the balcony. He was happy to listen, prompting her with a question from time to time even when he knew the answer. She was conscious that he was gazing at her and tried not to catch his eye. Why have you come, Laura? he wondered; did they tell you to? But his instinct told him 'no', that she was smart but guileless, and intrigued by Mr Jan de Witt.

'The first of the New World,' she said as they strolled round the platform, their heads bent into the wind. 'You know, my father says he cried when he saw this statue from his ship. Ah, you smile. Sentimental Irishman, is that it? Doing what he was supposed to do? My father doesn't cry.'

'Look.' He pointed to the flame above their heads. 'A bit battered and tarnished, isn't it?'

'You're joking, I see,' she observed tartly. 'Bit of an old cynic. Does Roger know?'

'I don't know; "perhaps" to both.'

She turned towards him, small gloved hand on the rail, the Jersey shore at her back. 'Then you're sure to think me a fool. You see, I have faith in our journey. I'm an optimist. I believe in this . . .' she lifted her arms like a vestal beseeching a goddess. 'Think what you like. Naïve American if you like. I believe in progress.'

'Why?' He closed his eyes for a second and shrugged. 'It isn't inevitable. Here, read today's newspaper.' He tried to present it to her but she ignored the offer.

'Horrible. They're as bad as each other,' she insisted, impatiently sweeping a loose lock of hair from her face. 'But when this madness is over, well, we'll build something better.'

'For the world or just for Ireland?'

'Here and in Ireland; everywhere in time – for women too. Universal suffrage, liberty, equality; that's our trajectory, our duty, isn't it?'

She was trembling with passionate intensity, her green eyes indecently large. He wanted to kiss her. She didn't give a fig what the other visitors thought of her. Perhaps they were like him and couldn't see more from the balcony than the stains on Liberty's copper skin.

'You've risked your life for freedom.'

He shook his head a little, as if to say 'what of it'.

'Stop it,' she commanded, letting go of the rail. 'Cynicism is poison. You're trying to provoke me.'

He smiled. 'I wouldn't dare. But you're confusing me with Roger.'

But wasn't that who he should try to be – if that was who she wanted him to be?

'Is everything all right?' It was the plump keeper of the flame in his green uniform. Perfectly all right, thank you. Goodbye, they said.

'It isn't attractive, is it? I mean, an old cynic.' He plunged his hands into his pockets, drawing his coat tightly round himself like a rueful schoolboy. 'Is it the world or me? Don't you protect yourself from disappointment by expecting the worst?'

She smiled and stretched out her hand, checking the impulse before she touched his arm. 'As long as there are, well, right-thinking people in the world, things will change – you'll see. We have to take risks, don't we?' She paused, biting her lip for a second; 'haven't you ever been in love?'

He laughed. 'What a question.'

'Well, haven't you? That's a risk, giving so much.'

'Have you?'

She shook her head. 'Not yet, but you're . . .'

'Older?'

She blushed. 'I'm sorry.'

'Why?' He frowned intently. 'You know, I don't know if I've been in love.'

'You don't know?' She sounded a little shocked.

'I've forgotten,' he said with a fresh laugh. 'Yes. Forgotten. Come on . . .'

They wandered round the balcony once more and this time she drew his attention to a finger of land on the Jersey shore.

'That's the Black Tom yard. Do you see? Yes, there. All of it for the British.'

Piers protruded at right angles from a main dock like flanges on a mace. Wolff counted eight, nine, ten ships alongside, cranes swinging boxes of shells aboard in rope slings. Look, she said, a freight train crawling on to the wharf with ammunition from the factories upstate, and millions more pounds of explosives in the yard's sheds awaiting shipment. 'Guns, bullets, oh, I don't know, horses, food . . .' Arms open wide as if she were ready to embrace him; '. . . whatever they need to fight their war. The docks along the river, in Boston, Baltimore, Newport News, Norfolk . . .' she shook her head angrily; 'that's one way to change the world for the better.'

'Stopping it?'

'Yes. Look, can we go?' She was struggling to hold down her hat. 'I do believe it's getting worse.'

Wolff didn't move. He was still gazing across the narrow stretch of water.

'We might have time for the next ferry,' she prompted.

'Do you think they'll try to stop this?' He nodded in the direction of the yard.

'Stop it? Who? No. This is the land of the free, remember, free capital, free enterprise. A lot of people are becoming very rich. Our friends in . . .'

'I don't mean government . . .' He glanced round to be sure no one was in earshot. 'The Clan. Won't Clan na Gael try?'

'No,' she bridled at the suggestion, 'no' – and shook her head angrily. 'Don't ask me about the Clan. Not here or anywhere – oh, now look what you've made me . . .' she was tugging on the rim of her hat so hard it looked like a circus bowler, auburn curls breaking free and dancing in front of her face.

'Come on, let's find some shelter.' He tried to take her arm, but she shook it free, 'No . . .', and stamped her foot in frustration. Hat pulled down over her eyes, head bent, she began to shake, and it was a moment before he realised she wasn't crying but laughing heartily.

'Very . . . unladylike,' she managed to gasp.

He laughed too. 'Nonsense, really.' Yes, it was nonsense. He thought she was very fine. 'And what kind of gentleman takes a lady on the water in a gale?'

'You're right,' she said, 'just what kind of gentleman?'

Only when she was in the cabin of the ferry, pinning up her hair, did she mention the Clan to him again. If there was something he wanted to know, she said as quietly as she could over the throbbing of the engine, he must speak to Mr Devoy, because the British have so many spies, Jan, you know how careful everyone must be. Wolff leant forward to gaze out of a port at nothing in particular.

'I'm the girl who takes the notes, that's all – you do understand, don't you?'

He turned and bent his head to look sideways at her. She returned his gaze but with a hesitant smile.

'I met a Mr Emile Gaché, do you know him?' he asked, leaning closer. 'His real name is von Rintelen. He's a German spy.'

She frowned and looked away. 'I don't want to know.'

'But you do, don't you?'

She gathered her skirts to rise. 'Excuse me, Mr de Witt . . .'

'A minute, please,' and he reached across to her arm.

Her jaw dropped in amazement, staring down at his hand holding her discreetly but firmly in her seat.

'You need to know that I know.' He took his hand away. 'Friends must be honest and open with each other,' he said earnestly. 'Please don't be offended but, well, I want us to be friends – it's important.'

Biting her lip uncertainly, avoiding his gaze, she wasn't used to being touched, that much was clear, but he sensed that she liked him, was intrigued, excited; she wasn't going to waltz off in high dudgeon. He watched her struggling for something to say, her body turned stiffly away, loose strands of auburn hair at the nape of her long neck, eyes to the front and rows of polished benches. Before she could make up her mind the ferry drew alongside the pier, passengers crowding into the gangway between the seats.

'I must be going,' she said the moment she stepped on to the quay.

'But you're my guide.'

'It has been interesting;' her eyes were twinkling with amusement.

'I'm glad.' He hesitated. 'Have I spoken out of turn?'

'Yes, you have. Don't pretend to be sorry, I won't believe you.'

He offered to escort her home. She said she wasn't going home, and no, she didn't need a taxicab.

'Will you be my guide again?' he asked.

She looked at him coyly. 'I don't think you need a guide.' She gave a little laugh. 'Perhaps, if I bring a chaperone.' Turning to walk away, she checked and glanced back as if there was something she'd forgotten to say: 'I'm sure we *will* be friends,' and with a shy wave, '*Slán go fóill.*'

'And what, pray . . .'

'Ask an Irishman.'

'Until the next time,' said the man from Cork in the grocer's store a block up from Wolff's apartment. The next time was only three days later. By then he'd kept his promise and caught the train to Brooklyn to see Casement's sister. She was restless, the house too small to contain her anxiety and a litany of woe. 'He's in hospital, Mr de Witt,' she confided. 'It's too much for him, he's so sensitive. He has these black moods, you see – he was the same as a boy.'

They walked to the park and she told him of a new 'unpleasantness'. The Clan had caught Christensen frittering away the funds they'd entrusted to him on a wife he'd kept a secret from everyone. 'He came to see me. I could tell he was no good,' she said in a strained and unhappy voice. 'I'm like that, you know. I look at people and I know at once. I see who they really are.' She wiped away a tear and gave Wolff a shaky smile. 'Dear Roddy's done so much for that young man. He's going to be dreadfully hurt.' Yes, he would be, thought Wolff, and he regretted it deeply. 'Does he need to know?' he asked. 'Of course,' she replied emphatically and with the conviction of the biblical stone-thrower for whom truth is always pure and simply an end in itself.

The summons from the Germans was delivered to him the following day. The author had stolen an idea from a dime-store novel and signed it 'The Dark Invader':

> Take the ferry to Hoboken, then a tram to the park across the street from the Norddeutscher Lloyd Line piers. Be there at 1900 on the 29th – tell no one.

Wolff telephoned Mr Ponting with the news.

'Sure it's Rintelen?' Gaunt asked.

'Dark Invader? It's too ludicrously vainglorious to be anyone else.'

'My people followed him to a trade-union office on the New Jersey side yesterday. Stirring up the Irish on the docks to strike, I shouldn't wonder.'

'Another of his "enterprises".'

'Best go armed,' he advised.

But Wolff was glad he'd left the revolver nailed beneath the floorboards; it was too cumbersome for a light coat on a warm autumn evening, pressed between the worsted shoulders of longshoremen on the tram from the ferry, a sharp smell of stale sweat and beer. Everyone was going the same way, rumbling and cussin' like a crowd before a football game, with Billy the barrack-room lawyer from Belfast – a true son of the city – threatening to kick anyone 'up the arse' who didn't join the strike, and a fella from '*Jerzee*' who was booed and thumped for complaining that it wasn't his war and who was going to feed his family if he joined a walk-out? 'Who the hell are you?' someone asked Wolff as they approached the Norddeutscher terminal. 'NYPD?'

'Dressed too smart for the police,' growled Billy. 'Look at that suit there; from Paris, I wouldn't wonder.'

'Berlin,' he replied, and it didn't seem to be necessary to explain more.

In their tackety boots they clattered from the tram in front of the terminal, and hurried across the street into the park. Beyond the first belt of trees, a crowd of several hundred longshoremen was gathered about a small dais; on the sidewalk close by, a dozen bored-looking police officers. No sign of a 'Dark Invader'. Turning his back on the park, Wolff walked towards the long, low red-brick terminal building where many thousands of passengers had set foot in the New World for the first time, eerily empty now the Atlantic was closed to German shipping lines. Beyond the terminal, the topmasts of the steamers laid up at the piers for the rest of what was going to be a long war. A small car appeared at the angle of the building and accelerated across the parade towards Wolff, but the driver swung left through the gate without giving him a second glance. From the park, a murmur of recognition and applause as the speakers stepped on to the platform. Facing the crowd alone on the sidewalk, Wolff felt like a hooker touting for business. The attention wasn't healthy. He walked across the street and through the trees, drifting at the edge of the gathering until he could see the booming Irishman who'd just begun to address it.

'. . . you have the power to strike a blow for freedom,' he told them, his 'freedom' echoing effortlessly across the park. John Devoy was standing at his back.

'You know me. Big Jim Larkin cares no more for kaisers than for British kings. But Germany's cause is now our cause – this is for Ireland.'

More cheering. 'You men are the ones who load British guns and shells, the horses, the food they need for their war . . . and you are the ones who can say, "No, enough, we'll not serve your bloody purpose any more. Leave our country."'

Some men near Wolff began to chant, 'Strike, strike, strike.'

'That's right,' Larkin pointed in their direction. 'Those men there have it – strike for auld Ireland, here in New Jersey.'

The cry was taken up: 'Strike, strike, strike,' and Wolff was clapping with the rest, or trying to, only someone was tugging at his sleeve. Half turning to look, he discovered Laura smiling up at him.

'What on earth . . .'

She shrugged and put her hands over her ears, then she shouted something but it was lost in the noise of the crowd.

'To meet an associate,' he said – or did she know already?

She shook her head blankly. The man beside her was bellowing inarticulately, like a punter cheering home the favourite: Big Jim was heady stuff. They were all drunk with excitement at the prospect of breaking strike laws in the service of auld Ireland.

'Strike, strike, strike.'

Wolff touched her elbow and with a tilt of the head suggested they move away. She smiled weakly and nodded.

'Those who come out can draw from a strike fund for their

families,' Larkin told them. 'Mr John Devoy from Clan na Gael is here to tell you how . . .'

They walked just far enough for conversation to be possible.

'Is it like this at your suffragette rallies?'

She laughed lightly. 'Noisier.'

'Do you mind if I smoke?'

She shook her head.

'You don't seem surprised to see me,' he observed, tapping a cigarette on the back of his case.

She looked away, the colour rising to her neck and face. 'Mr Devoy thought you might be here.'

'I wonder how he knew.'

'From his German friends, I expect.' Her gaze led him discreetly to where three, perhaps four men were standing beneath the canopy of a weeping cherry. They were twenty yards away, their faces hidden by the tree, but Wolff recognised one of them at once. Shifting awkwardly as large men do, his back turned towards them and his right arm raised to a branch above his head – the master of the *Neckar*. He was listening to someone in his shadow, nodding vigorously. Then he turned towards the meeting and Wolff caught a glimpse of the Dark Invader behind him.

'Your Mr Gaché?' she asked.

'And some of his business associates, yes.'

'I thought so.' She bit the corner of her bottom lip, something she did when she was uneasy. 'It's a good turnout; quite a few men here,' she said, catching his eye.

'But only one woman.'

She laughed and looked down, self-consciously sweeping a loose strand of hair behind her ear. 'I'm perfectly safe. Sir Roger says the only true gentlemen are Irishmen; they are gentlemen by instinct, not by an accident of birth.'

'Then there's no hope for me.'

'There might be exceptions,' she said with another light laugh, the tinkle of fine crystal. 'After all, you are Roger's friend.'

'An honorary Irishman, then.'

'That must be right.'

They stood for a few seconds in silence, she with half an eye to the meeting; he to Hinsch and Rintelen and their companions.

'You'll have to excuse me, Jan,' she said at last. 'There's something I must do.'

He raised his eyebrows enquiringly.

'I'm taking the names of men who will need strike pay.'

'From their Swiss banker?'

She frowned and bit her lip. 'If you mean your Mr Gaché, I don't know.'

A burst of applause and cheering. Devoy was shaking hands with the platform party, slapping 'Big Jim' on the back, celebrating their little victory, an unholy alliance of Irish muscle and German money, an unofficial walk-out, a few days lost, some bullets, some shells. The goddamn price of famine, C would say. But no one at the Front would notice, the killing would go on as before, and sooner or later big American business would speak, no, shout, 'Enough', and the strike would be broken by a bribe or by policemen enforcing the free traffic of goods and services with the hard round end of a 'paddy-whacker'.

'I must go,' said Laura, picking up her skirts.

'Will I see you soon?' he called after her.

Grinding his cigarette end into the grass, he turned with a sigh and strolled towards the little group of conspirators beneath the trees. As he approached, a very fat man detached himself from it and began to waddle away. He cast a furtive glance at Wolff, his face florid like a Bavarian butcher's, chins rolling on to his chest, head rocking from side to side. Ageless, as fleshy people often are, and guilty, Wolff thought, the perpetrator of an unspeakable crime that would be discovered in the fullness of time.

'Well met, Mr de Witt.' Rintelen stepped out from beneath the tree to offer his hand – or was it to distract Wolff from his associate? 'I saw you talking to Miss . . .'

'McDonnell.'

'An Irish lady?'

'And American.'

'What does Miss McDonnell think of our strike?' His own view was plain enough, written boldly in his face.

'Our strike?'

'Another of Mr Gaché's enterprises,' he explained smugly.

Wolff nodded. 'Mr Gaché is a resourceful man. Actually, he asked me to meet him here.'

'To consult you on . . . let's say, a technical matter.' Rintelen looked carefully around the park. The meeting was over, the longshoremen were drifting home or chatting and smoking in tight circles. At a trellis table to the left of the dais, Laura and other members of the Clan were taking the names of those hoping to benefit from Gaché's munificence. 'I have an office, we can talk there,' he said.

'But first it was necessary to drag me out here.' Wolff's voice was heavy with sarcasm.

Rintelen laughed his short yelping laugh. 'No, no, Mr de Witt, patience, patience, you shall see.'

17

The *Friedrich der Grosse*

S HE WAS BATHED in the last golden light of the setting sun like a large soprano taking her curtain call at the Hofoper.

'Our piece of Germany,' Rintelen observed as they walked along the quay towards her.

'Fifteen knots?'

'So, always the engineer,' he replied coolly. 'Yes, fifteen, with a fair wind.'

Top-heavy, thought Wolff, her fine Atlantic lines spoilt by too much amidships, with all the passenger cabins in the superstructure: uncomfortable in a high sea. Two yellow funnels, probably two sets of quadruple expansion engines – that would be typical of her class – two minutes to walk from stem to stern, half a block on Broadway. Once the pride of the Norddeutscher Lloyd fleet, idle and rusting at a pier, the largest ship in a graveyard of ships.

A hefty sailor, a stoker once perhaps, was guarding the foot of the gangway. Instinctively he stiffened, his arm rising in what would have been a salute but for Rintelen's sharp 'Nein'.

'A good German crew,' he said as they walked up the gangway. 'They know how to keep their mouths shut and von Kleist works them hard for me. So, welcome aboard the *Friedrich der Grosse*, Mr de Witt.'

A junior lieutenant had scurried down from the bridge to greet them. Did the *Kapitän* require assistance? he panted. The captain required two stout seamen to guard the passageway to his office. Just a precaution, he said with a strangled laugh, to be sure no one listened at the door, a British spy.

Wolff concentrated on his smile. Water-bloody-tight? Christ, it better be.

'She's perfect for my enterprise,' Rintelen continued. 'Is there a general at the Front in France with a finer headquarters than the *Friedrich der Grosse*?' Cabins, kitchens, workshops, one way on, one way off, impossible to approach undetected by day, and no one to hear a prisoner scream, Wolff thought, or discover a body weighted and buried according to the customs of the sea. Watertight? The damnedest thing; if his cover story leaked like an old bucket he wasn't going to have an opportunity to take it up with Gaunt.

'His Majesty stood where you stand now, Mr de Witt.' Rintelen turned to the young officer, 'A famous day, Braun.'

'Yes, sir.'

'Fifteen years ago.' Rintelen shook his head as middle-aged men seeking the sympathy of peers at the passage of so much time are wont to do. 'And you were fighting in South Africa?'

'On my way.'

'Different times. But the Emperor saw this day. He knew there would be war in Europe.'

'Everyone saw this day, Captain,' said Wolff curtly. No point in pretending de Witt had any affection for their Kaiser.

'Not just that there would be war, but here, aboard the *Friedrich der Grosse*,' said Rintelen, tapping his foot and pointing animatedly to the few feet of deck between them. 'He predicted how it would be fought, Mr de Witt. War in our time.'

'I see. Well, when the cheering stops,' replied Wolff sarcastically.

Rintelen's smile came slowly. 'I forgot – you are a practical man – and an impatient man. So,' he said, with a gracious sweep of the hand, 'we are ready.'

From the shelter deck, the lieutenant escorted them into a polished-panel passageway and up the main companionway to a stateroom on 'A' deck. 'The dark invader's office,' said Rintelen without any trace of irony.

It was no more than a large first-class cabin with two ports on the starboard side, flock wallpaper, black lacquer furniture, and the bed had been replaced by three large oak filing cabinets. Rintelen walked over to the middle one and took out a folder and a cylinder of paper which he unrolled and anchored to the table. It was a draughtsman's drawing of a cargo ship.

'A technical matter, Mr de Witt. She is not the *Titanic* but an associate of mine thinks he has come up with a plan to cripple her rudder at sea – here . . .' he nudged the file. 'What do you think?'

'And for this advice?'

He lifted his chin haughtily. 'You will be compensated – *if* you are the engineer you claim to be.'

Wolff nodded and reached for the file. 'A glass of water, please.'

'Whisky?'

'Yes.'

Careful notes, some sketches, a simple plan on paper; its architect knew what he was doing. Attach the charge to the rudder of the ship. In the tip of the charge, a needle-shaped pin to connect to the rudder shaft. Shaft turns, pin turns, boring its way into the mercury fulminate, detonating an explosion powerful enough to blow the rudder. Ship left helpless.

'Well?' Rintelen set the whisky on the table in front of Wolff.

'It's technically possible, yes.'

'You do not sound sure.'

Wolff lifted his glass, squinting reflectively at the plans through the twinkling crystal. 'It is possible.' He raised it to his lips but lowered it again without taking a sip. 'Is it a good plan? No, it isn't a good plan.'

'Ha,' exclaimed Rintelen, sweeping his hand above the table in a grand gesture. 'Enlighten me.'

'You want to sink or damage the enemy's supply ships, but this—' Wolff was interrupted by the door. Hinsch rolled into the room, tossing his coat over a chair. 'Well?' He nodded curtly towards Wolff. 'Is he any good?'

Rintelen ignored him. 'Please, Mr de Witt.'

'Simply because it will be very difficult for the diver to fit the detonator without being caught,' Wolff's hand trailed over the drawings, 'and what about the water in winter? There are easier ways.'

'A little more?' Rintelen held up the whisky bottle.

Wolff shook his head. 'And the diver would need to know what he was doing with the charge.'

Rintelen nodded thoughtfully. 'So, what would you suggest?'

'Don't you know? You're the Dark Invader.' Yes, of course he knew; Wolff could see it in his face. 'Just light the touchpaper, Captain. These ships are waiting to go off.'

'The ammunition?'

Wolff laughed. 'Enough. No more games. You know that's what I mean, and you've tried, haven't you?'

Silence as they stared at each other. A tinkle of ice. Hinsch was fixing himself a whisky American-style. Rintelen's eyes flitting around Wolff's face. He wanted to swot them away. One step forward and slap.

'So, here . . .' Rintelen looked away at last. Reaching for the file, he took out a copy of the *Shipping News* and spread it on the table in front of Wolff. 'This report. The English ship, *Beatus* – lost with all hands and many tons of ammunition.' He was fidgeting with the edge of the paper excitedly. '*Our* success, Mr de Witt. *Ours.*'

'You sank her?' Wolff raised his glass in salute. 'Congratulations.'

'There have been other English ships, but many failures.'

Hinsch snorted disdainfully. 'Twenty-two.'

'Too many, yes.'

'The detonator?' Wolff asked.

Rintelen shook his head. 'The detonator is good . . .'

'The Irish,' interjected Hinsch. 'The Irish are stupid . . .'

'That is why we need you, Mr de Witt,' Rintelen continued. 'It could be profitable for both of us.' He lifted the draughtsman's plan from the table and began to roll it into the cylinder. 'If I can trust you, of course.'

'Isn't it a bit late to decide?'

Rintelen was pretending to concentrate on the tube, long fingers scrabbling it tighter. 'There!' he remarked with a chillingly false nonchalance. He lifted the tube and his gaze to Wolff. 'Not too late, Mr de Witt.'

'No, I suppose it isn't.'

'But I *can* trust you . . .'

'Yes, of course. Correct.'

'Good.' Scooping up the rest of the papers, he walked over to the filing cabinet and locked them back in the top drawer. 'Now, Hinsch,' he turned back to them both with his little smile, 'let us show our new comrade the stock.'

Half-lit companionways from carpeted 'first' to steerage, into the echoing body of the ship and down to the boiler room; a stoker keeping vigil, tending the flame of a single furnace; plating clatters, bulkhead doors icy to the touch. Cursed by idle darkness, they walk in silence or whisper like intruders at the heart of a mountain, in a place where it is impossible to say 'to thine own self be true', until they come at last to a workshop, buried in the ship like the embers of a dying fire, full of noise and light that breathes, a dozen seamen grinding away at lathes, sparks and shavings showering the deck and their heavy workboots.

'I bought the machinery through one of my companies,' Rintelen shouted above the noise. 'You see – Gaché is a proper businessman.'

Wolff picked up a strip of lead tubing from one of the work-benches. 'Detonator casings?'

'The business of destruction, Mr de Witt.' He was revelling in the role he'd cast for himself. 'Your Westinghouse, yes? I'll buy what I can and blow up what I can't.'

'You attach some sort of timing mechanism?'

'No, no, much better.' He nodded to the chief petty officer and stepped back into the passageway. 'So you see.' He was still shouting, his voice ringing in the emptiness. 'We set the detonator to go off when the ship leaves American waters. I will show you how, but not here.'

'Yes, that would be useful if you want me to set them for you.'

This time Rintelen detected the irony and frowned disapprovingly, his small close-set eyes lost beneath his brow. 'I am not short of people, Mr de Witt. I have people here and in Baltimore, Boston – in every port. But I need someone who can show them where to place the charges. My travelling representative, if you like.'

Wolff nodded slowly. 'And for this service you will pay?'

'I will pay well.'

A fine rain was falling, the lights of Manhattan almost lost in a soft mist. Rintelen tried to persuade him to stay because there was no possibility of a taxicab at that hour. Safer not to, Wolff replied.

'You are careful,' he remarked approvingly. 'You are right to be. The English have spies, and the New York police sometimes. You need money?'

'I want money.'

'Visit Dr Albert. He will see you this time.'

'You know how to contact me, Captain,' Wolff said, pulling up the collar of his mackintosh.

'Yes, I know how to contact you.' His handshake was surprisingly limp and cold.

'Goodbye.' Wolff stepped on to the companionway.

'The Emperor said we must be like the Huns, Mr de Witt, ruthless in pursuit of our victory.'

Reluctantly Wolff turned to face him again.

'Here on this deck,' Rintelen moved closer. His cheeks were shining wet in the ship's lights, sallow like a Chinaman's. 'No prisoners. No quarter. I am a gentleman but this is not a business for gentlemen. I have become the Dark Invader.'

The preening villain again, von Brüning in *The Riddle of the Sands*, but Wolff was too afraid of him to laugh. 'Your point, Captain?'

Rintelen's sharp brown eyes were dancing about Wolff's face again, his mouth hard and straight like an iron bar. 'I'm sure we understand each other, Mr de Witt.'

The rain was quickening, heavy drops thundering on to the steel companionway steps, and Wolff was soaked to the skin by the time he reached the quay.

'But my God, you look rough,' observed Gaunt in his typically bluff fashion the following morning. He had arranged a room at the Prince George Hotel, between Madison and 5th. 'The assistant manager's son is on our side,' he explained; 'have to pay him, of course.'

The window was open, the room reassuringly full of the street three floors below.

'Seen the papers?' he enquired. 'They shot Edith Cavell.'

'Oh?' Wolff didn't have the slightest notion what he was

talking about. 'Is there any coffee?' he asked, dropping into an easy chair. A shaft of sunlight burst through the window and he closed his eyes.

'Wake up, for God's sake, man,' Gaunt commanded. 'The British nurse . . . you must have read about her – here.' He thrust a cup at Wolff. 'She helped chaps caught behind enemy lines. Bad business.' Standing above Wolff in his white uniform, bone-china cup almost lost in his fist, thin lips pursed in thought, '. . . but good in a way – it's upset the Americans.'

He gazed down his long nose at Wolff for a few seconds more, then sat down, perching on the edge of the chair. 'A fine-looking woman for her age,' he noted between sips of coffee; 'jolly fine.'

'Heard of a ship called the *Beatus*?' Wolff asked. 'She was lost with all hands sometime around the twenty-first.'

Gaunt checked his cup a few inches from his mouth, then lowered it slowly on to the saucer. 'Christ. They managed that? How?'

Wolff told him; some of it at least. He began by describing the strike meeting and how Rintelen was encouraging the Irish to stir up trouble in the ports. No need to worry about that one, Gaunt remarked imperiously; he was bankrolling people in the union too – they would sort out the Irish. Then Wolff told him of the *Friedrich der Grosse*, the network of saboteurs the Germans were putting in place, and that they'd sunk a number of ships already. 'He's set up a company to buy what he needs and . . .'

'Cedar Street,' interjected Gaunt. 'Import–export – E. V. Gibbons Inc. My people followed him there.'

'Emile V. Gaché,' Wolff muttered to himself.

'What?'

'E. V. G. Not very imaginative.'

'My Czech fellow says his company has spent a king's ransom buying ammunition and other things, just to stop us getting our hands on it. Doctor Albert writes the cheques.'

Wolff reached into his jacket. 'I have an appointment with him this afternoon. Damn . . .' He held up a damp and crumpled cigarette. 'Would you mind?'

The naval attaché leant forward with his case. 'I want you to find out about this network.' He looked at Wolff earnestly, belligerently, as if to say: 'I am the commander of this operation and don't you forget it when you are out there on your own.'

'How are they smuggling the detonators past the guards?' he asked, his mind rolling at the pace of a traction engine. 'And this Agent Delmar – London has asked again.'

'The Admiralty?'

'Your lot.' Rising quickly, he walked to the window, his shoulders wriggling in his uniform jacket. Wolff watched him as he gazed into the street below, a slight twitch at his eye. 'Your lot are sending someone. God knows why,' he spoke as one for whom resentment is a habit. 'Here . . .' Taking an envelope from his jacket he tossed it to Wolff like a petulant schoolboy. 'Bloody nonsense.' It fell at his feet.

Wolff gazed at it for a moment, then picked it up and slipped it in his jacket.

'Aren't you going to look at it?'

'Later.'

'Later, *sir.* I'll tell your fellow we don't need anyone; wasting his time. I have it all in hand,' he said, his senior service vowels slipping a little. 'Perhaps we will have this sewn up by the time he arrives.'

Wolff raised his head enquiringly.

'It's obvious, man: the filing cabinets in his cabin. It's in there, isn't it? – the network, Delmar . . . everything.'

*

Dr Albert was typical of that stratum of middle-class men who are no more than the sum of their working lives and are only able to conduct relationships with others according to the rules and practices of their chosen profession. A man of precedents and privileges whose patent for life had been drawn up in a law faculty somewhere thirty years before. Pinched and dry, with bad skin and a scrappy grey moustache, he looked as if he had reached middle age without finding either just cause to laugh or demonstrative evidence for love.

He wanted no more involvement with de Witt than was necessary for the conclusion of a 'satisfactory arrangement' and was a little vexed to find that he was dealing with the sort of man who usually commanded his respect. 'Most of Mr Gaché's associates are . . . well, they are not educated men, Mr de Witt,' he explained.

They were sitting in an office on the first floor of the Hamburg America building on Broadway, panelled like the stern cabin of a German clipper. 'I have drawn this up on behalf of my client,' he said, taking a file from a drawer and pushing it across the desk to Wolff.

It was the draft of a formal contract of employment with the company E. V. Gibbons Inc. 'You are an engineer? Shall I say for "consultancy services"?' He picked up his pen to make amendments. 'Is something wrong?'

Wolff was smiling with amusement at the absurdity of a contract to commit acts of sabotage.

Dr Albert shook the knot of his tie irritably. 'An initial period of three months?'

'Is there any danger of you taking me to court for breach of contract?'

'No, it isn't likely,' he replied slowly. 'I expect my client would seek another form of redress.' He examined his nails for a moment to allow Wolff time to consider the tenor of this observation. 'Most of my client's associates prefer to be paid in cash, of course, but he thought a professional man would need . . .' he paused again, searching his lexicon for a legal euphemism.

'An alibi?'

'A more formal arrangement.'

Wolff pushed the contract back across the desk. 'No.'

He stared at Wolff coldly for a moment, then put the file back in his drawer. 'As you wish.'

They did agree on terms. A payment of four hundred dollars into the account of a Mr R. Curtis at J. P. Morgan on Wall Street. Albert pressed him to sign an invoice and he agreed, writing a false address and another false name. Every dollar had to be accounted for, Albert insisted. 'It's a process, you see.'

And when the process was over, his secretary escorted Wolff down to the lobby where half a dozen Hamburg America clerks sat twiddling their thumbs. At a desk a few yards from him was the fat man whom he'd seen slinking away from the strike meeting in the park. He looked just as guilty, perspiring with the effort of being alive. The clerk pushed a piece of paper towards him and he bent to sign it, resting his weight on his outstretched arm. Wolff guessed it was one of the fastidious Dr Albert's receipts for cash-in-hand associates. Conscious that the fat man would see him if he glanced to his right, Wolff turned and fastened on a clerk for the address of an uptown restaurant. From the corner of his eye, he saw the fat man pick up an envelope and slip it into the pocket over his heart. Then, head rocking, he lumbered towards the door and out on to Broadway.

He was a surprisingly difficult man to follow. He moved warily in the shadows, his shoulder almost brushing walls and shopfronts, forcing sidewalk traffic to his left like a boulder at the edge of a fast-flowing stream. Catch me and the game's up, Wolff thought; Dr Albert would write him off as a bad debt. But instinct and the envelope suggested it was something he couldn't ignore. He didn't expect a man that size to walk far. Sure enough, after a couple of blocks he hauled himself up the steps of the elevated at Fulton Street. Wolff held back for a few minutes but it was a busy station and he couldn't afford to leave it for as long as he would have wished. He bought a five-cent ticket for the line, dropped it in the chopper, then drifted on to the platform. There were a dozen or so people waiting for the next train.

The fat man had wandered a few yards off but was still uncomfortably close. Wolff ambled in the opposite direction until he found a map of the elevated train network posted on the wall of a shelter, which he pretended to consult. He was considering what he should do next when the track began to sing. It was a Line 3 train all the way to Bronx Park with a score or more stops on the way. 'Christ!' He'd forgotten some of them pulled only a single carriage. 'Lucky for once,' he muttered under his breath: this time there were three. He watched the man climb into the first, then joined the last. At the next station he hovered by the door to confirm that the man was still on the train. The second stop was busy Chatham Square. For a moment he was distracted by an old Polish lady who pressed him to be a good citizen and help her from the carriage. The platform was crowded with commuters waiting for an express to take them across the Harlem River and it was not until the guard had blown his whistle and the train had taken up the slack that he noticed the fat man's head swinging towards the barrier.

'Hey buddy,' protested the guard, as he stepped from the moving train.

Wolff followed the big man down the steps and waited in the gloom beneath the rumbling iron arches of the elevated as he crossed the square to a dingy café. It was a neighbourhood of cheap saloons, flophouses and hucksters' stalls at the edge of the old Five Points slum: crowded brick tenements and alleys hung with grey washing; shoeshines, rag pickers and beggars. The first stop after Ellis Island for families without a dollar to their name and for those who weren't particular how they made their money; as squalid as the old-world streets they had left in search of liberty from poverty. Too good now for Germans and all but a few of the Irish, it was the jetsam of the new century who lived, copulated and died in this babel, the Italians and the Poles, Jews and Chinamen. The sort of district, Wolff reflected, where it was possible to find any number of men who would be ready to stick you in the back – or blow up a ship. Was that the fat man's business?

There was a small Italian market in the corner of the square only a few yards from the café. It wasn't an easy vantage point; he was too well dressed, a little too Anglo-Saxon. Fortunately, the market was restless with late-afternoon trade, the stallholders in duckbill caps and boaters, barking out their bargains in the Sicilian dialect, while young women in brightly coloured shawls queued for a few cents' advantage and local urchins joked and shouted insults from the tailboard of a passing cart. From beneath the canopy of a boot store, Wolff could see through the confusion to the fat man in the café, his shoulder pressed to the grimy window. In no time at all he'd ordered a plate of something and was devouring it mechanically.

Someone jogged Wolff's elbow: 'Shine, miss-ter?' It was a swarthy-looking boy in a grubby shirt and braces, his trousers hoisted a foot from his boots.

'Can you do it here, in front of the shop?'

He gave Wolff a toothless grin. 'Is my uncle's store,' he lisped. 'Sit yerself.'

Wolff was particular about placing the chair.

At a little after five, the fat man was joined by a cheap suit, short, with a dark complexion and a thin waxed handlebar moustache. Hungarian perhaps; he might have been a waiter in a small-town *Bierkeller* somewhere in the Habsburg Empire. They shook hands, a little reluctantly on the small man's part, Wolff thought. He refused the waiter's offer of drink or food and appeared anxious to get on with whatever business he was there to transact.

'Finished!'

'Here.' Wolff flipped another dime to the shine. 'Do them again, will you – and another coin if you don't ask me why.'

But Rintelen's man wasn't in a hurry. A second plate of food was placed in front of him and he polished it off with the same ugly relish. His contact watched in distaste, fiddling impatiently with a knife. Replete at last, the fat man wiped his mouth on his sleeve, then fished the envelope from his jacket. It rested beneath his heavy hand as he leant over the table confidentially. For a couple of minutes he spoke in what must have been a whisper while his companion made a note in a pocketbook. Business concluded, he slid the money across. With just a curt nod, the contact left the café and drifted through the crush around the market stalls to the kerb. After a few yards he stepped from the sidewalk and turned across the square in the direction of Wolff.

God, he's seen me, he thought with a surge of anger and disgust.

'All right!' He jerked his shoe savagely from the shine's hands and got to his feet. But he was wrong: the little man with the waxed moustache slipped between an empty cart and a stall selling straw hats and crossed to a door just three down from the uncle's boot store.

'Here.' Wolff tossed the shine a quarter. 'This is a good day for you, yes?'

The boy flashed his toothless smile. 'Again?' he asked, glancing down at Wolff's shoes.

'No, no, bravo. Just one thing . . .' and he held up another coin. 'Can you read?'

'Multo bene,' he replied indignantly.

'The door there, the green one, run over and tell me the names on the bell.'

He chuckled. 'There justa one.'

'Oh?'

'G-r-een's Dee-tect-if A-gen-zee,' the boy enunciated slowly.

'Green's Detective Agency?'

'Si, signore.'

Rintelen's man settled the check and left a few minutes later. It was almost dark, a sharp October chill in the air, and the streetlamps glowed soft with the threat of rain. On evenings like this the city ticked a little quicker. Manhattan pulled down its hat, turned up its collar and lengthened its stride for home; and those travelling further, uptown or across the East River, were grateful for the fug of a smoke-filled carriage. The fat man walked only as far as Bowery, then caught a tram to East 2nd. Little Germany. So they were neighbours. Wolff tracked him from the opposite side of the street, just another Joe trailing home from a factory or department store to a plump wife and children, bills, boiled potatoes, and that day's *New Yorker Staats-Zeitung*. Two blocks down only, across from the city's Marble Cemetery, the fat man let himself into a tall tenement of the sort common on the Lower East Side – black iron fire escapes clinging to its brick face like a cancerous growth. Wolff waited in the shadow of a doorway for a few minutes to see if a light came on at the front. No such luck.

The caretaker took his time to answer the door. He was an old man, bent and grey. His shirtsleeves were rolled up and he was holding a kitchen knife; he must have been cooking his supper. Wolff thought he detected the faint whiff of incontinence.

'Yes,' he asked suspiciously.

'There's a man, a fat man who lives here,' Wolff replied in German. 'Short black curly hair, grey suit, lots of chins,' and he held his hands to his neck to demonstrate.

The old man blinked at him but said nothing.

'I have something for him.' Wolff paused, inviting a response. 'Well?'

'Not here.'

'You're Swabian?'

'What of it.' He began to close the door. Wolff reached out to catch its edge. 'Just a minute . . . look, he dropped something.'

'Are you police?'

'No, didn't I just say – he dropped some money. I want to give it back to him.'

The caretaker stopped trying to force the door. 'How much?'

Wolff took five dollars from his wallet. 'It may have been more.' Then, after a pause, 'You understand?'

He gave a sharp nod and stepped aside. 'I thought you were the police.'

'Why?'

'They've been here too.'

He led Wolff round behind the stairs into his own small first-floor apartment. His front room smelt of cabbage. There was a suggestion of a woman's touch once: a sewing machine, dirty lace curtains, the china figure of a shepherd girl on the mantelpiece.

'Well?'

'He's Paul Koenig,' he said, holding out a wrinkled yellow palm. 'I'll give him the money. You sure you're not the police?'

'Koenig. And he lives here?'

The old man shook a crooked finger at him cantankerously, then held out his hand again. Wolff gave him the five dollars.

'You can trust me,' the caretaker remarked lamely; 'we're all Germans. Last of the buildings round here. The rest are full of Jews and Italians.' He stuffed the money into his trouser pocket. 'Yes, he lives here. Third floor at the back. Has done for years. Works for Hamburg America, or used to. Something to do with their security.' He gave Wolff a hard, unfriendly stare. 'You look like a cop.'

'What did they want to know?'

But only when Wolff counted out another five was he prepared to say more. Not the ordinary police, he said. They were watching Koenig; searched his room. 'They didn't say why. Is he in trouble?'

'How would I know?' Wolff replied.

You're wrong, Gaunt, he thought, as he walked back to his apartment. New York's finest did have some inkling of what was going on under their noses.

He tried to warn Gaunt the following morning but the attaché was too excited to listen.

'Never mind the police, Wolff,' he said, pacing their room at the Prince George. 'Never mind that.'

'But we're no better, are we . . .' Wolff persisted.

'Forget the police.'

'Will the police recognise us as friends?'

'For God's sake, man,' Gaunt's temper flared; it was on the lightest of triggers. 'They haven't heard from the *Fiscus* for two days. Left here on the twelfth. Lost. Sunk. Gone. Cargo and crew. Seven thousand tons with shells. Blinker's hopping.' He stopped pacing abruptly. 'That's the fourth we know of for sure. Got to do something,' he declared. 'We're not waiting for your Bureau chaps to arrive, do you hear?'

18

Tony's Laboratory

THEIR VISITOR PARKED his car with two wheels on the sidewalk. Emmeline watched as he dropped his cigarette end in the front yard, grinding it into the grass that Anton had cut and weeded carefully the day before. Suit trousers stuffed carelessly into seaman's boots, and why didn't he run a comb through that shock of blond hair? There was nothing in his demeanour to suggest he was genial, as large men often are, but something unkind in his face. Not the sort she wanted neighbours to see swaggering to their door.

Stepping away from the curtain, she walked into the kitchen. 'Your guest is here.' There was no reply. 'Anton?' He'd closed the cellar door. 'Anton?' she shouted, and took a step down the stair. She didn't like to go further. 'Anton.' Her voice sounded a little plaintive; and there was that evil smell again. 'My beef broth,' Anton liked to joke. 'Your visitor is here!'

This time he opened the door, mask around his neck, white coat and rubber gloves. 'Just finishing,' he replied with a distant smile. 'Entertain him, would you? Just for a few minutes.'

'Please hurry,' she pleaded.

Their guest was smirking on the doorstep. 'I saw you so I didn't bother to ring,' he said in German. 'Is he here?'

'I assume you mean my brother, Dr Dilger. Yes, he is here,' she said stiffly. 'Please come in.' The sooner he was inside the better. 'My name is Miss Emmeline Dilger – Dr Dilger's sister.'

'I know.' He offered her his calloused hand. 'This is Tony's place. Where is he? In the laboratory?'

'Would you like some tea? He'll be with you in a minute, Mr . . . ?'

'Captain. Captain Hinsch. At your service.'

She led him into the drawing room and left him examining their family photographs. When she came back with the tea, he was perched on the edge of a low chair, his broad knees almost at his shoulders. He'd removed a picture from the wall above the secretaire and was scrutinising it closely.

'Big family,' he observed. 'You here?'

'Yes,' she said, placing the tray on the table beneath the window.

'Show me.'

She finished pouring the tea.

'Is that you?' he asked, poking the glass with his forefinger.

Setting a cup on a lace doily beside him, she turned and bent over the picture. 'No, that's me.' He smelt fusty, like an old couch. 'That's Anton; and my father, Mr Hubert Dilger; and there in the middle row, my mother's father, Dr Tiedemann from Heidelberg.'

He grunted. 'Family of doctors.'

'No. My father was a soldier. May I,' she tugged at the picture, jerking it from his hands; 'if you don't mind.'

He didn't seem to notice the hostility in her voice. 'A soldier, eh? Against the French?'

'No. For the Grand Duke of Baden's horse artillery, then here in America – in the Civil War,' she said, polishing the glass with her handkerchief.

He grunted again, this time with a little more interest. 'My brother's fighting,' he said.

'Oh? My brother-in-law too, and Anton was serving in a hospital.'

For some reason he found this amusing, reaching for his cup with the same smirk with which he'd greeted her on the step. She was relieved to hear Anton in the hall, and a few seconds later he joined them.

'Only tea,' he reproached her affectionately; 'but the captain would prefer something stronger, I'm sure. How about that good German beer Josephine brought us?'

She frowned. Why was he going to the trouble?

'So this is Tony,' said Hinsch, levering himself from the chair.

'This is Dr *Anton* Dilger,' she retorted crossly.

She left them to become acquainted while she fetched the beer and the old stoneware mugs she had brought from the farm. Rattling around the kitchen, opening and shutting the same cupboards, fretting that her brother was involved in something he shouldn't be. 'The acquaintance of a friend in Berlin,' he'd told her, but she could see he wasn't being frank. Goodness, it wasn't a matter for her. Please just drink your beer and leave, she thought; leave us in peace.

They were still speaking of the family when she returned to the drawing room. Anton's eyes were twinkling wet with pride as he told of the horse shot from beneath their father at the Battle of Chancellorsville. Such a marvellous raconteur – all their neighbours said so – the dinner guest of choice. Folks in Chevy Chase appreciated proper manners and Anton brought a little old-world sophistication to their homes with his stories of life in Berlin – just as long as the conversation didn't turn to war. Of course she felt the same but she knew not to lose her temper. 'Americans don't understand Germany,' she'd told him; but he'd upset Mr and Mrs Proctor, dumping his napkin and some forthright opinions on their table before walking out unceremoniously. Not that it really mattered; old Proctor was only a storekeeper.

The war would have broken their father's heart, Anton was

saying. 'There's too much stupid sentiment here about democracy, you see.' His beer mug hovered at his lips. 'I was shocked when I got back. The newspapers – the Kaiser's a despot, we're Huns and the despoilers of Belgium . . .' he paused to snatch a sip. 'Is the Tsar a democrat? Do the British care a fig for the rights of small nations? What about the British Empire? I tell you, Captain, I'm worried.'

'About what?' Hinsch asked, shifting impatiently in his chair.

'That the United States will become embroiled.'

'Isn't it already?' He glanced at his watch. 'You know we should get on?'

Anton caught Emmeline's eye and smiled apologetically. 'The captain wants to see my experiments.'

'Oh?' she remarked sceptically. 'Are you interested in science, Captain?'

'Very,' replied Hinsch, bending to stuff a trouser leg back in his boot.

'All right.' Her brother put down his mug and stood up hurriedly. 'Shall we?'

Emmeline followed them into the kitchen with the tray. As they clumped down to the cellar she heard Hinsch say, 'And this is Tony's lab.' Then, a moment later, 'Don't I need a mask?' The door banged shut because it was stiff; she would speak to Anton about shaving a little from the jamb.

She'd asked the Mitchells from across the way for supper. Anton had found a good butcher and she was going to cook *Schweinshaxe*. Taking a sharp knife from the drawer, she scored the flesh of the pork and began to press in the garlic. Pity there wasn't time to soak the knuckle in brine. Hinsch was talking, now laughing. He had a quarterdeck voice – boom, boom, boom – but she couldn't make out more than a few words and was cross with herself for trying.

If only Anton would join a medical practice in Washington. Handsome, charming, still only thirty; his list would be full in no time. But he pulled a face when she mentioned the possibility, and when she had pressed him he said he wasn't interested in that sort of medicine. 'I'm too selfish, Em,' he joked; 'patients would bore me.' She'd scolded him lightheartedly: 'It must be a terrible trial living with me.' He denied it, of course, squeezing her hand affectionately.

She began shredding the cabbage. You couldn't have pork without sauerkraut. Everyone made a joke about it these days. Anton said they were calling Germans 'Krauts' in the newspapers. She wished he wouldn't bother reading them. What was he doing down there with Hinsch? He'd told the family he was exploring ways to control infections, some research he had begun in Berlin. But before today, before Hinsch, he'd avoided speaking to anyone else of his work, skilfully deflecting their neighbours' questions. At first she was glad he had found something worthwhile to do, she had even learnt to live with the smell of his foul 'broth', but the squealing of the guinea pigs – that she was sure she would never get used to. 'It's cruel, An,' she complained, but to no avail. He was adamant that he needed the animals for his experiments. When they died, he wrapped them in tarred canvas and buried them in the border furthest from the house, and she was under strict instructions not to garden there.

Slipping the pork into the hot oven, she turned to tidy the vegetable peelings from the table. '. . . Yes, yes, in a safe at the Hansa Haus. Don't worry, Doctor,' she heard Hinsch say at the cellar door. 'We'll begin in Newport News, the British have a large operation there.' Then her brother said something she didn't catch and a second later the door opened with a jerk and they began to climb the stair to the kitchen.

'I asked Captain Hinsch to join us for supper but he must

return to Baltimore by nightfall,' Anton said with an insincere little smile.

She answered him with one of her own: 'Perhaps another time, Captain.'

'Yes.' Hinsch was cradling a boot box of brown cardboard, tied with string. She caught Anton's eye but he looked away, stern like their father, his thin mouth turning down a little at the corners, skin stretched tight across the family jaw. 'I'll see you to your car, Captain,' he said.

'Best not. Goodbye, Miss Dilger.' He nodded curtly to her.

'Goodbye, Captain.'

Then Anton led him to the end of the hall and they stood there for a moment in conversation. From her place at the kitchen door she heard snatches of Hinsch: '. . . if you need more money, Hilken can make arrangements'; and a moment later, 'Aren't you tired of this place? If you want some life, come to Baltimore, or join us in New York. Hilken says it's perfectly safe; he knows . . .' but the rest was lost as he turned his back to the hall. A few seconds later the door opened and she heard Hinsch leave. From the window in the parlour she watched him lumber across the grass to his shiny new Ford, open the passenger door and place the cardboard box in the well beneath the seat. Then he walked to the front and cranked the engine.

'Glad to be rid of him?' Anton was standing at the door.

'Yes.'

She turned back to the window as the car began to pull away. Her hands were trembling, and she clenched them in fists.

'He's gone.'

'Yes.'

'It's Mr and Mrs Mitchell again tonight, isn't it?'

She turned abruptly to face him. 'What did he want, Anton?'

He frowned, crossly this time. 'I told you. Business. It was business.'

'Why does it have to be secret?'

'Because it does,' he exclaimed angrily. 'It does.'

It was too much for her. She crumpled, shoulders shaking, reaching for her handkerchief, and turned away. Anton was beside her in a second; 'Shh shh,' his arm about her. 'Emmeline, please don't. It's nothing.' But she couldn't stop.

'Don't let him upset you.' He took her hand and gave it a squeeze. 'Dear Em.'

She wanted to tell him, 'No, Anton, it's you, not that oaf. I'm frightened for you,' but she couldn't. He would be angry, say she was silly.

'It's nothing,' he assured her. 'Just samples for a doctor I know in Baltimore. That's all. Hinsch said he'd deliver them for me.'

She lifted her face to him and he wiped a tear tenderly from her cheek.

'Are you bored, An?' she asked nervously.

He looked puzzled. Then the right side of his face twitched with irritation, but the smile was back in only a moment. 'Of course not, Em. I'm happy here with you. Very happy.'

'*Are* you?'

'Yes. Come on,' and he led her to the parlour door. 'It's five o'clock already. What can I do to help?'

But she stopped, pulling at his hand and turning towards him with a determined stare. 'You can be careful,' she said firmly. 'Please, Anton, please be careful.'

19

Saboteur

T HE NOTE WAS on the hall floor in the morning. Wolff
padded through to the bathroom and propped it against
the mirror while he went to the lavatory. He was surprised it
had taken so long, almost a week. Washed and shaved but still
in his dressing gown, he sat and read it at the kitchen table.

> Catch the ferry to Hoboken. Motor car waiting on the street
> outside the terminal at five o'clock. Driver in blue peaked
> cap, red card on the windscreen. Code word, Leuthen.

He'd arranged to meet Laura McDonnell at Burns' on 6th Avenue.
Volunteers were needed to distribute flyers at a strike rally, so
she had volunteered him. 'But if you have a rendezvous with Mr
Gaché I forgive you,' she said when they met at the restaurant.

Stop British Tyranny in Ireland. He handed back the leaflet.
'Telephone me tomorrow if you've any left,' he suggested casually.

'I'll have found someone more reliable by then.' She looked
down at her hands then up at him with a smile, her large eyes
twinkling with good humour.

'You said you were going to forgive me, remember?'

She laughed, and tossed her auburn hair. It had a wicked
lustre.

'I'll take some advice from Mr Devoy,' she teased.

*

The motor car was where it was supposed to be, its driver bolt upright behind the *Staats-Zeitung*. He refused to say where they were going but sat awkwardly at the wheel, his large hands squeezing it too tightly, as if he were wrestling the life from a large snake. He drove south-west towards Elizabeth, but clear of Jersey City he made a left off the highway, bouncing down to a fringe of woodland above the bay. Twilight was dropping to a darker blue, Bayonne winking on the opposite shore. Four large steamers were riding at anchor in a line, waiting for a berth at Port Newark. Somewhere, the thump, thump of heavy machinery echoing across the still water. Stamping hard on the gear pedal, then the brake, the driver brought the Ford to a sudden stop. A few yards ahead, in the long shadow of the trees, two men were climbing from a motor car. Wolff recognised Rintelen's slight frame. He greeted Wolff with a jaunty wave and walked briskly forward to offer his hand.

'Your visit to Dr Albert, it was satisfactory?' He was dressed like a theatre impresario in a homburg hat and ankle-length coat.

'Quite satisfactory, thank you,' Wolff said.

'Good. Well, we don't have any time to lose. First let me present Dr Ziethen.' He turned to his elderly companion. 'Step forward, Doctor. The doctor is a distinguished chemist and the designer of our bomb.'

'At your service.' Ziethen nodded stiffly. He had the air of an old soldier, sporting a thick grey moustache of a sort fashionable in Bismarck's day, but was dressed in a light grey sack suit like a prosperous New Yorker.

'Dr Ziethen is going to demonstrate his ingenious device,' Rintelen declared, rubbing his small hands with relish. 'Doctor, would you?'

They walked to Ziethen's motor car and their driver lifted a trunk down from the back seat. Inside it were at least twenty of the cigar-shaped detonator casings Wolff had seen in the ship's workshop.

'You drove these here?'

Ziethen blinked at him indulgently. 'Perfectly safe, Mr de Witt. Here . . .' and he tossed one to Wolff. It was surprisingly light; smooth and round at one end, flat at the other. Hollow inside but for a copper disc pressed and soldered halfway along its length, Ziethen explained; at one end of the device, picric acid, at the other sulphuric. It was simple but ingenious.

'You understand?' he asked.

Wolff nodded slowly. 'I think so. The acid eats through the copper disc and the device detonates?'

'Yes.'

'And you set the time by altering the thickness of the copper disc?'

'Correct,' interjected Rintelen. 'The beauty of it is, the acid melts the lead leaving almost no trace, so no one knows what caused the fire. But we will show you. How long, Doctor?'

'How long?' Ziethen lifted a watch from his waistcoat. 'Just a few minutes, I think. Yes.'

'No longer, I hope. We have a busy evening,' Rintelen observed, glancing impatiently at his own watch.

Ziethen had set one of his devices in the long grass a few yards away, its position marked by a white peg. They stood side by side peering into the gloom like naughty boys waiting for a firecracker. Wolff lit a cigarette and had almost finished smoking it when a blinding flame burst from the device at last: white-hot, stiff, twelve inches high and completely silent.

'You see?' Rintelen demanded.

It burned for less than a minute. Fifty-three seconds precisely, according to the doctor's pocket watch. Nothing remained of the casing but a few hot lumps of lead.

'Just a question of putting our firework in its proper place.'

Rintelen bent to pull the white marker from the ground. 'Your job, Mr de Witt,' he said, tossing it into the trees. 'But there are some arrangements I must make, if you will excuse me,' and he turned to stride back to the motor car.

'I've packed them in paper,' Ziethen observed, at his side. 'Try and keep them upright. Four will be enough, don't you think?' He coughed and looked down, shifting the scorched earth with the toe of his boot. It was made of fine Italian leather.

'Place them near some combustible material. They may not burn long enough to ignite a shell, but if you manage to, get a good fire going. Perhaps you know this.' He spoke ponderously and with a phrasing that suggested the flat farmland and long winters of East Prussia.

'And how long will the fuse – the discs – last for?' Wolff asked in English.

Ziethen hesitated, his hand drifting to his moustache. Was it supposed to be a secret or was he just surprised to be addressed in English?

'Three, four days. Until the ship is out of American territorial waters,' he replied in English.

'Gentlemen, please.' Rintelen summoned them to the motor car. He was standing in the circle of light cast by its lamps, a small briefcase in his right hand. It was seven o'clock but seemed later, darker. Wolff's driver was sitting behind the wheel of the other motor car with the engine running.

'Is our comrade ready, Dr Ziethen?' Rintelen asked.

The doctor was examining his boots, recalling the white flame perhaps, or his bank draft from Albert, or the little redhead at Martha's who crossed her legs just so. Or was it because he didn't answer to the name 'Ziethen' as a rule?

'Doctor!' Rintelen dragged him from his stupor. 'Please, Doctor. Does our comrade know all he needs to know?'

Ziethen glanced at Wolff, then nodded.

'Good.' Rintelen held out the case. 'So, Mr de Witt, the opportunity you have been waiting for.'

The case was made of light-brown leather and would have looked well in the hands of a Wall Street banker.

'You want me to . . .'

'Yes.' Rintelen thrust it towards him again. 'Hinsch is waiting for you.'

Wolff lifted it carefully by the corners, then by the handle. 'New York?'

'Hans, your driver, will take you there,' he said with a smile. 'Good luck.'

Wolff held the case steady between his knees as they crawled back to the highway. If Hans was anxious, he gave nothing away. Just obeying orders: weren't they all? There was nothing Wolff could do but sit tight until he was alone, a tenth of an inch of copper from incineration. If it didn't end badly on the road there might be an opportunity to dump the detonators in the Hudson. He felt calmer on the highway. For a time the rhythm of the engine acted like an anaesthetic, his thoughts drifting and dissipating, just as they used to when he pounded the hard-baked fenland lanes of home.

They drove down to the Jersey waterfront, rumbling cautiously along cobbled streets, between brick warehouse blocks and busy dockside bars, sailors staggering along sidewalks, stevedores emptying from a shipyard gate. Then on past a freight train wheezing in a siding, across the tracks, turning left at a mission chapel, pulling up at last beside a patch of wasteground.

'This is it?' asked Wolff.

Hans didn't answer but reached forward to extinguish the car's kerosene side lamp. On the opposite side of the street, a dockyard wall and the sharp silhouette of cranes, Manhattan bright across the water. Wolff reached into his jacket for his cigarettes. It was colder and his hand trembled a little. Perhaps it was fear. His chest felt tight, his head ached too. 'Look, do you have a light?'

'There,' replied the driver, nodding to the street. Someone close to the end of it was signalling with a small light, swinging it like a wrecker luring a ship to a reef. 'All right, we are coming,' he muttered, and he swung the Ford away from the kerb.

Hinsch greeted Wolff with his customary scowl. 'You're late.' He was standing by the wall with two burly longshoremen he introduced in heavily accented English as Walsh and McKee. Wolff recognised McKee as one of the men he'd seen at the strike meeting with the leaders of the Clan.

'The bombs?' Hinsch asked, pointing to the case.

'Yes.'

'Then put these on.' McKee handed Wolff a stevedore's cap and a threadbare woollen coat that was too small and made his chest feel tighter still.

'It is good,' Hinsch observed. 'You can go,' and he nodded to McKee.

'Hell's teeth, what am I . . . ?'

'The job you were paid for, de Witt,' he snapped in German.

At the end of the street they turned right and followed the wall for a hundred yards to the gates. Christ, they're not going to be fooled by a flat cap, Wolff thought, the briefcase brushing against his suit trousers. But McKee must have arranged everything because the guards let them pass without a word. 'Don't open your mouth,' he warned, as they walked across the yard. 'I'll see everything straight.' They stopped by the door of a warehouse and he disappeared inside, returning after only a few seconds with a sack. 'Put the case in this.'

Three piers ran at right angles to the quay, with three ships alongside. Munitions had been loaded aboard the nearest and an engine with empty wagons was waiting to leave the dock. Stevedores were shifting through its steam like wraiths, caught in silhouette against the arc lamps for a second, then away.

'The *Blackness* of Liverpool. Three holds: two fore, one aft,' McKee whispered as they walked towards her companionway. 'Artillery shells for the Russians. You know what to do?'

Yes, Wolff knew what to do. Christ, he hoped he wouldn't have to do it.

Groups of longshoremen were drifting towards the quay, their work over for the night. Two men stopped to speak to McKee, glancing at Wolff, at his shirt cuffs, at his suit trousers, at the sack.

'They're still in the forward hold,' McKee reported, shifting uncomfortably from foot to foot, his hand at his lip. The engine screeched a warning that made them flinch, and with an impatient whoosh of steam, began to trundle along the pier. McKee touched Wolff's arm. 'Will one hold be enough for yer?'

'I can't tell.'

He cleared his throat nervously. 'All right, let's get it over with now.'

The guards at the foot of the gangway were armed with rifles but dressed like storekeepers in cheap cloth coats and caps, gold badges pinned to their chests. Private security, Wolff guessed, perhaps something to do with Koenig or his contact in the café, the man with the old Empire moustache.

McKee sidled up to the one without a rifle. 'Brendan? McKee. The fella from Clan na Gael.'

'You're late,' the guard called Brendan grumbled. He was another Irishman. His eyes met Wolff's for a moment, his face florid, with the small broken veins of a drinker, a nasty scar splitting his top lip. 'For God's sake, couldn't you find this fella a coat that fits,' he complained. 'Look, put these on,' and he dipped into his pocket for three of the shiny badges. 'Anyone ask, you work for Green's. Green's Detective Agency. All right? And whatever you're doing, make it quick.'

One of Brendan's men escorted them up the gangway and they were met at the top by another. A junior officer was on watch beside him at the rail. He glanced complacently at their badges and away, flicking his cigarette end over the side in a shower of hot ash. Under the upper-deck arc lamps, sailors were stowing the ship's loading booms. Hatch number one over the for'ard cargo hold was sealed, hatch two still gaping.

'Hey, what yer doing?' They'd caught the eye of a mate.

'Green's,' McKee shouted back, pointing to his badge. 'Inspection.'

'Says who, Paddy?' the mate asked, stalking towards them, his shoulders rocking belligerently.

'Says me,' replied Wolff, in a military voice that startled them all. 'Says His Majesty's Government. This is a security inspection, a random inspection.'

The mate looked nonplussed. 'No one said . . .'

'It wouldn't be a random inspection if they had, would it, man?'

'You are, sir . . . ?' enquired the mate tentatively.

'Didn't I just say? I work for His Majesty's Government.' Wolff spoke with the cut-glass confidence of one who presumes to be recognised as an English gentleman even in a stevedore's cap. 'The hold next, I think. Number two.' His authority was vested in his broad *A* and his precise *aitch*: the sort of commanding performance possible only with subjects of the Empire.

The mate stared at him sullenly for a few seconds, then nodded obediently because he was from somewhere like

Birkenhead and lived in a two-up two-down with a family to feed on eight pounds, three and six.

Just what the hell am I doing? Wolff wondered as they escorted him to the lower deck. He hadn't the time to think it through; it was the smell of the thing now. He'd come too far for excuses.

'Stay here,' he demanded, releasing the dogs on the hold door, but he wasn't surprised that McKee ignored him: Hinsch must have instructed him to stay close. Inside it was damp and smelt of rotting vegetables, perhaps the ship's last cargo. The shells were stacked in two blocks, a gap the width of a man's shoulders between them, five hundred identical crates, a thousand, maybe more. If he didn't plant the detonators carefully, he would have the devil's own job retrieving them. Six crates from the left of the door and six crates up from the deck. 'Help me with this one, will you?'

They lifted it down and McKee produced a jemmy, forcing it with a splintering crack. 'Jesus.'

'Hey, what's going on?' It was the voice of the mate. Walsh was blocking the door. 'Just a little accident,' they heard him say.

The dim light kicked off the burnished steel of six high-explosive shells.

'This will do,' muttered Wolff. 'Here,' and he tossed one to McKee. 'A souvenir.'

'What the devil . . .'

Wolff looked at him scornfully. 'Pull yourself together, man, it isn't that sensitive.' In the space left, he placed two cigar detonators side by side.

'All right. Help me put it together.'

'What do I do with this?' McKee lifted the shell.

'Put it in the sack, of course.'

They slid the crate back into place and were looking for another when they heard raised voices in the passageway. The mate was plainly in no mood to accept the brush-off a second time. McKee looked rattled.

'I'll deal with it,' Wolff assured him.

Jaw set, feet apart, seamen at his back, the mate meant business.

'The captain, where is he?' Wolff commanded before he could speak.

His mouth opened then snapped shut like a fish expiring in a net.

'Well, man? Where is he?' Wolff removed his cap and slapped it against his leg, stroking his hair back in exasperation. 'You know you failed, don't you? You,' he said, directing a finger at the mate's chest, 'you failed.'

Why? Because the mate had allowed three strangers into a hold full of TNT. The badge? Anyone might wear a badge. Saboteurs might wear a badge.

The Dark Invader approved. Wasn't de Witt's performance proof of his own fine judgement? He heard the story from Hinsch, who'd listened to McKee's breathless account with something like grudging admiration.

'You enjoyed your adventure, Mr de Witt?' Rintelen enquired with boyish enthusiasm.

'Not especially,' replied Wolff tersely; he'd hated every bloody minute.

'So, you earned your money.'

They were sitting side by side on Martha Held's couch, his arm draped round Wolff's shoulder – like a couple of *Schwule*.

'We will wait for the dust to settle,' he said, leaning forward to pour the wine. 'Next week, perhaps.'

Wolff's glass chinked against the neck of the bottle. 'Next week?'

'Another ship, Mr de Witt.'

'I thought you wanted me to instruct your men?'

'Correct. You will. But it would be a shame to waste your talent.'

Wolff sipped his wine.

'More? Naturally, I will pay you for this too.' He shifted to the edge of the couch so his little brown eyes could dance about Wolff's face. 'Are you unhappy with this arrangement?'

'Not if the price is . . .' Wolff smiled wryly '. . . *correct*.'

'Then that is agreed. Good. Now you must excuse me.' He got to his feet, smoothing the same imaginary creases from his perfectly pressed trousers. 'I have something I must attend to. No, stay,' his small hand hovering above Wolff. 'Please, there is one thing more . . .'

'It's after midnight,' Wolff complained. He'd been wound so tightly all evening. 'Can't it wait? I'm tired.'

'I am afraid, no, it cannot.' Rintelen smiled shiftily. 'I will be back. Soon.'

But he didn't come back. Half buried in the couch, eyes closed between sips of wine, the time ticked into the early hours. Clara, the girl he'd paid for nothing, found him again. Why wouldn't she? It was the easiest money she'd earned in a long time. She sat with her head on his shoulder, sharing his glass of wine, and he was too tired and bored to care; too tired to get up and leave; too tired to resist when with a fragile smile she led him by the hand to her room. And although his mind was befuddled, he recognised he'd been played like a fool. The ship, the instruction to sink more ships, Martha Held's at midnight – why hadn't he rung Gaunt? – he'd been played the whole damn evening. And now the girl. I should be more afraid of Rintelen, he thought.

*

She folded his clothes and placed them neatly on a chair. Then she took off her silk dress and put it carefully on a hanger on the back of the door. Naked on the threadbare rug before him, a little spindly, a little knock-kneed, with gooseflesh on her arms and thighs, and an uncertain, almost innocent smile. Perhaps that was his imagination.

'I'm to look after you,' she said, avoiding his gaze. 'There's more wine – if you want it . . .'

'No. No. Thank you.' Someone should protect her, comfort her, offer her some tenderness.

'Lie back.'

Her burgundy bedspread smelt of cheap cologne, but not enough to mask the stale sweat.

'No. Lie beside me,' he said softly. 'Here. Just here.'

But she didn't lie beside him because it wasn't part of her routine. Instead she fucked him, bumping him like a German horse.

'Good?' she asked, collapsing beside him at last.

He brushed a strand of hair from her small face. 'Fine. Thank you.'

He didn't need to pay, she said – unless he wanted to offer more. His friend Gaché had settled everything.

20

Dissonance

T HE FOLLOWING MORNING he woke with a wooden mouth and an agonising sense of self-disgust. He was still nursing it and a strong coffee in his spartan sitting room when the telephone rang.

It was Laura. 'Mr Devoy has taken you at your word.' Her warmth made him feel worse. Of course he betrayed her every day, that was his job, but going with one of Martha's tarts, well, he felt terrible.

'The leaflets, silly,' she prompted. 'I can meet you at the Hoboken ferry terminal at ten.' The line crackled expectantly. 'It's to be our largest meeting so far.' She was willing him to say, 'See you there,' but he was glad he wasn't obliged to. Something out of the blue, a business meeting, he explained, not Gaché, no, ordinary work of the sort he might mention to the neighbours. It wasn't his best performance because he found it harder lying to women he admired, although he had had plenty of practice. Laura didn't disguise her disappointment and he admired her even more for it and felt another intense pang of regret.

Tired brown eyes in the mirror, struggling with a tie, it was a morning for reflection, a morning when the heart didn't seem quite tough enough. Men learn to live with suffering and adversity until it breaks them, often suddenly. Sometimes it is the same with lies. Judgement is swift, his mother used to say with her scrawny forefinger raised, and he'd almost come to believe her in the impenetrable darkness of a Turkish cell. Every new lie a stone in a sack – like the one he'd carried on to the ship the night before. Sometimes he wasn't conscious of its weight, sometimes he staggered beneath it – one day it would crush him. This morning his burden was a heavy one, and he was sure that was how it should be.

'For God's sake, man, you're doing your duty. If you can't love yourself more, learn at least to forgive yourself,' C had chided him once. *Pro Patria.* Behind his desk, C was able to draw a thick straight line between the man and the lie. In the field it was easy to lose the line. The soldier stares down the barrel of his gun at a nameless face but the spy laughs, calls his enemy 'friend', makes love to, then betrays, his enemy. Wolff was glad there was enough left of who he used to be to feel sick about it, or was that simply the drink and the image he couldn't shake off – of Clara counting her gratuity?

At a little before ten o'clock he caught a taxicab as far as Madison and, thankful for the clear air, walked the last few blocks to the Prince George. Satisfied he didn't have company, he crossed the lobby to the elevators and took one to the fifth. The doors opened on a bellhop balancing half a dozen pieces of luggage. Wolff nodded to him, stepped from the elevator, stopped, patted his jacket for a key, sighed heavily, then turned on to the stairs as if intent on returning to the first floor. On the third, he set off along the corridor to Mr Ponting's suite.

'You're late,' growled Gaunt. The room was full of tobacco smoke and for no obvious reason the curtains were drawn conspiratorially. Rising from the couch, a dapper young man he didn't recognise, and from the seat opposite, an old Secret Service Bureau lag he did.

Wolff looked Gaunt up and down pointedly. 'Mr Ponting is

a businessman.' The damn fool had come to their meeting dressed in his naval attaché's uniform, medal ribbons, all the trimmings.

Gaunt flushed angrily. 'Clearing the mess you left us last night . . . Impertinent,' he blustered. 'There wasn't time to change.'

'There would be if it was your life at stake,' replied Wolff coldly.

'Lieutenant Wolff, isn't it?' interjected the young man, stepping forward sprightly to offer his hand. 'William Wiseman. Expecting me, I hope.' He smiled engagingly, his thick brown moustache bristling like a squirrel's tail. 'Cambridge, wasn't it? Before my time; I was up at Jesus in '03.' Excepting his moustache, he didn't look old enough to have been at university in '03. Very English country house but with the quiet authority of one familiar with the world beyond its gates. He must have paid a good deal for his clothes. 'You weren't a boxer, were you?' he enquired, with just the suggestion in his inflection of time spent in America.

'A runner.'

'I'm a boxer.' Small and plump, he was no more than a hopeful bantam weight, but with a certain swagger. 'Well, I used to be,' he added with a regretful smile, the moustache twitching again. 'Just a scrapper now.'

'Yes, well . . .' Gaunt wriggled his shoulders as if he could hear the echo of the same ringside bell, ready to square up to all-comers. 'Sir William's setting up shop here, Wolff. Reporting . . .' he paused for particular emphasis '. . . to me.'

Wiseman raised his right eyebrow a little but said nothing.

'Officially, Sir William will be our man from the Ministry of Munitions,' Gaunt continued.

'Unofficially, we're Section V of MI 1(c). That's what the War Office chaps are calling our bit of the Bureau. Everything has to be a number or letter, don't it?' observed Wiseman smoothly.

'You, me, old Thwaites here,' he turned to his companion; 'we've become a traditional two-finger salute to the Hun.'

'Glad you're still alive, Wolff.' Thwaites limped a few steps to greet him with a handshake and a slap on the back. 'My leg?' he asked, following Wolff's gaze. 'Gallipoli. Lucky they left me with it.' He looked ten years older, thinner, his skin yellow like a smoke stain.

'A couple of crocks,' Wiseman joked, hand to his chest. 'Touch of gas at Ypres. But the brain still works, eh, Thwaites?'

'Can we get down to business?' Gaunt grumbled.

First Wolff wanted to open the curtains, and yes, it was possible, perhaps because he asked so humbly. It was a dreary November day and cold on the street, the hotel doorman blowing vapour into his balled hands, a baker unloading warm rolls in front of the restaurant opposite, the faces of passers-by bent into their scarves; no parked motor cars, no one loitering, no one where they shouldn't be.

'Your ship, the *Blackness* – she sailed this morning,' Gaunt called to him from a chair.

'Christ!' Wolff spun away from the window to face him. 'Rintelen said she was leaving tomorrow.' His heart fluttered like a tiny bird.

'Then he lied,' replied Gaunt, with something very like relish. 'I got your message but it was too late. Late again . . .'; even this opportunity to score points he took without shame. 'I couldn't get my people aboard her.'

'That's why he made me visit him at the club, and . . .' Wolff hesitated, his conscience pricking him hard, '. . . kept me there.' Lie back, he thought; goodness, he'd fallen over.

'I thought he trusted you.' Wiseman was gazing at him intently over his fingertips.

'No one trusts anyone in this sort of enterprise. He was making sure.'

'Three to four days before they detonate, you say?' enquired Gaunt. 'There's still time to get them off.'

'He may have lied about that too,' Wiseman noted, smoothing his moustache thoughtfully with the tip of his right index finger.

'Yes.' Wolff felt obliged to acknowledge the possibility. He loosened his tie a little, his collar slipping between damp fingers. Suddenly the room felt close.

'Look, there's time. My people are onto it,' said Gaunt empathetically.

'And they know . . .'

'Yes, yes. Hold number two. Six along, six up.' Gaunt sounded very Australian suddenly, a sure sign that he was losing his temper again. 'Sit down, Wolff, for God's sake.'

'You did the right thing, old boy;' this from Thwaites. 'No choice but to plant the things. As they say here in America, you're the ace in our hole. Can't risk your cover.'

Wolff nodded gratefully. He walked round the couch to join the circle. Gaunt was holding court at its centre in the only comfortable armchair.

'The real question is, how on earth is he doing it? Can you tell me . . .' Wiseman glanced sideways at Gaunt, '. . . *us* how he's smuggling these bombs aboard the ships?'

Of course Wolff could explain. Hadn't he just planted two of the damn things on the *Blackness*? The same unholy alliance: Irish and German. A spark from Roger Casement in Berlin, fanned to a flame by the presence of a prodigiously energetic man, the self-styled Dark Invader.

'Dark Invader . . .' Thwaites guffawed. 'That's a bit rich, isn't it?'

'He's an actor certainly,' replied Wolff, running his fingers through his hair reflectively. 'There's a little of that in all of us who do this work, isn't there? He knows what he's doing.

Firstly, forcing up the price of ammunition to the Allies – that's through a cover company . . .'

'Gibbons. Cedar Street,' interjected Gaunt. 'My Czechs are watching the place . . .'

'Dr Albert made me sign one of the company's contracts,' continued Wolff. 'Albert's the paymaster. Then there's Clan na Gael – Rintelen is encouraging the Irish to organise strikes in all the East Coast ports we use. Thirdly, the sabotage network – taking the war to us here in America;' and he told them about the envelope Koenig had passed over his greasy plate to the man from Green's. 'Koenig used to organise the security for Hamburg America, knows all the agencies I shouldn't wonder. I turn up like Santa Claus with my sack and a Green's detective gives me a badge. Result, two packages in the hold.' He frowned pensively. 'I expect Dr Albert is paying detective agencies at the other ports too.'

'*Quis custodiet*, what?' observed Wiseman. 'Who guards the guards?'

'The thing is,' Wolff leant forward to offer him his cigarette case, 'someone with a badge and a lot of balls can do whatever he damn well pleases.'

'And the cigar bombs, tell me about those, man,' demanded Gaunt, the springs of his chair groaning as he crossed then uncrossed his long legs. He was unsettled, he wanted to ask the questions.

'They're ingenious.' Wolff bent to light his own cigarette. 'Simple, inexpensive, easy to hide. They leave no trace – ingenious. The inventor is elderly, Bismarck whiskers, Prussian I would say. Got him to say a few words in English – he speaks it well and with an American accent – New York, New Jersey – so he's been here a while.'

'Do you have a name?' Gaunt was fumbling for a notebook.

'Only a false one, Ziethen.'

'You're sure it's false?'

'Not one hundred per cent . . .'

'Von Ziethen was one of Frederick the Great's commanders,' Thwaites explained.

'"Correct",' as friend Rintelen would say. 'And the code word for the operation was one of Frederick's battles: *Leuthen*.' Wolff drew heavily on his cigarette. He was apprehensive about the ship and impatient for Gaunt to leave. 'Is there any tea?'

Wiseman was watching him from behind his fingertips, as inscrutable as a plaster saint. 'It's not very warm;' but rising from the couch, he stepped over to the table and poured Wolff some anyway. 'Sugar?'

'Two, thank you.'

'Heard any word of this fellow, *Delmar*?' he drawled, handing Wolff the cup.

'No.'

'They're worried in London. The Admiralty has a source . . .'

'I know.'

'You do?' Wiseman raised his bushy eyebrows. 'London thinks the fellow's important, wants to know what he's doing here.' He sat down and took a pipe from his jacket. 'Inspiration, anyone?'

'Wolff needs to take a look in Rintelen's office,' replied Gaunt with quarterdeck confidence. 'It's all in there.'

Wolff would have liked to disagree; the 'Wolff needs to', he didn't appreciate. Irritatingly, it wasn't an unreasonable assumption. Contracts, accounts, receipts, the business of war in America expressed as a balance sheet; that Dr Albert was a meticulous record keeper he'd witnessed with his own eyes. Was there a securer repository available to him in New York than the *Friedrich der Grosse*? 'Our piece of Germany,' Rintelen called her.

'Do you think you'll be able to take a look?' Wiseman enquired, pulling at strands of tobacco.

A number of thoughts flashed through Wolff's mind as he considered his answer: that Rintelen would never trust him to be alone on the ship; that no one but the crew would hear the crack of a revolver in the cabin, and if they dropped him from the stern the tide might take him to Coney Island – he'd always meant to visit. He wondered how sorry Laura would be and resolved to ask her to dinner, and he remembered that the cabin door was secured with a basic mortise, the filing cabinets with something simpler, but there wouldn't be time to do more than glance through the files and some would be in code. And if he was caught he would shoot, and he would make a particular effort to finish Hinsch because that would be a genuine pleasure. He thought also that for a Bureau new boy almost ten years his junior, Wiseman was asking rather a lot, but that he managed it so graciously he was probably accustomed to getting his way.

'It's a question of opportunity,' he said flatly.

'Believe me, I'm sensible of the risk,' Wiseman observed with what at least sounded like humility; 'and we can't leave it all to Lieutenant Wolff.'

'It's his duty,' replied Gaunt.

'You know, I have some ideas . . .' Wiseman held a match to his pipe. The tongue of flame rising from its bowl reminded Wolff of the detonator, and with a frisson of anxiety the smell of rotting vegetables, a crate six up and six along the stack, and fifty Empire sailors.

'I have . . . some . . . some thoughts . . . I might share, Captain,' Wiseman puffed. 'Shall we leave these fellows and sort a few things out by ourselves?'

There wasn't anything more to discuss – it was a Navy show, Gaunt grumbled. But Wiseman persisted, oiling his ruffled colonial feathers with a charm that demonstrated perfectly why C had put his faith in a Secret Service rookie.

*

'Americans are dewy eyed about English aristocrats,' Thwaites observed when they'd gone. 'Sir William will be a great success here.'

Wolff got to his feet and wandered back to the window. 'I think that's what Gaunt is worried about,' he muttered distractedly. A motor car had broken down in the middle of the street and a plump lady in a preposterously large hat was standing in front of it with a crank in her hand, waiting for a gentleman to do the decent thing. 'He's careless,' Wolff remarked. 'You saw the naval uniform'.

Storm clouds were rolling in from the Atlantic, towering grey and shifting in an awkward image of the city. Different faces in the windows of the restaurant, a police officer strolling along the sidewalk, more cars, more people moving with purpose. There would be rain. Hard rain.

'Prickly customer,' Thwaites declared. 'Thinks we're taking over his patch.'

'Aren't we?'

'I suppose we are. But it's time to get on the front foot here.'

Thwaites had friends in America. He'd spent ten years in New York, most of them as a foreign affairs adviser for a newspaper. Charming, self-deprecating, the sort of upper-middle-class Englishman who went down well with everyone from millionaire steel magnates to State Department secretaries; a cocktail-party regular, a particular favourite on the Long Island summer circuit, a guest and special companion of the celebrated beauty, Edna May Lewisohn. How special was a matter of speculation because Thwaites' American friends knew him to be the soul of discretion – and in affairs of the heart at least he could be. Wolff had met him in Washington before the war and was so impressed by the ease with which he worked the room that he'd mentioned his name to the Bureau. If that meant he was responsible for drawing him into C's web, he was heartily sorry.

'I think we should work with the people here,' Thwaites continued. 'Get them onside. Sir William feels the same. Your Captain Gaunt seems to wants to do it alone . . .'

'He isn't my captain, Norman.'

'No, of course not, sorry old boy.' He waved his cigarette at Wolff apologetically. 'Damn fool nonsense. Look, there's a chap called Tunney in charge of the Police Department Bomb Squad; might have a word with him. Keep your name out of it, of course. Any objections?'

'Koenig . . .' Wolff had forgotten. 'I think the police are watching him already.'

'I'll ask old Tunney, he'll know.' Rising with the help of his stick, Thwaites limped across the room to a drinks tray. 'I'm having one, you? Know it's a little early but, well . . . whisky all right?' He was perspiring with the effort.

Wolff said that whisky was fine. For a while neither of them spoke. Thwaites was taking his time with the drinks. Across the street a storekeeper was rolling his awning, the wind had taken a little girl's hat and it tumbled along the sidewalk with her mother bent almost double in pursuit. Sharp splashes on the window.

'They let you down rather,' Thwaites said at last, his back still turned. 'Turkey, I mean. We all thought so.'

He glanced over his shoulder at Wolff, then hobbled back to his chair with both glasses, his stick hanging from his arm.

'Leaving you in the hands of those savages all that time. Here . . .' he placed Wolff's whisky on an occasional table, almost obliging him to take the seat opposite.

Wolff didn't want his sympathy, he wanted to forget – at least, he wanted to try.

Thwaites persisted. 'Made all of us angry,' he observed with a shake of the head. 'There but for the grace – what? Didn't think they'd leave you high and dry – not the old man, not Cumming.'

'Drop it, would you.'

'It's just – but if you say—'

'Yes,' he interrupted emphatically. 'Yes, I do. Yes, please.'

Thwaites nodded slightly. 'All right.'

Wolff stared at him for a few seconds longer, then walked to the chair and sat down. 'What was Gallipoli like?' he asked to fill the silence.

'Well, you know Johnny Turk.' Thwaites frowned and studied his glass for a few seconds before taking a long pull of whisky. 'Don't care for your Mussulman. Never have.' Thwaites didn't 'care for' anyone with a skin darker than his own and assumed other gentlemen felt the same way. 'A shambles, a bloody shambles,' he muttered disconsolately; 'the Dardanelles. Damn fool idea. I was lucky to escape with this in May,' he said, slapping the stick against his boot. 'The boys in my battalion say it was worse in the summer – hot as hell . . .' He took a little more whisky and swallowed hard. 'It isn't any better in France, is it?

The front had settled on the city and gusts of rain were rattling the window like bursts of gunfire. They sat in silence, Thwaites twisting his glass distractedly on the arm of his chair. The memory of that fly-blown foreign field where bits of Englishmen were left jigging on the wire had drawn the light from him.

'What a pair we are,' he said at last, lifting his glass and his chin. 'Another?'

'No, thank you, Norman.'

'I think I will,' he said, struggling to his feet again. 'Sure? No, well . . .' He poured himself another stiff one, his hand a little unsteady, then hobbled back to his chair. 'We'll win the war – with the Empire, with our friends here in America. Salute,' he said, raising his glass to Wolff. 'Trouble is, a lot of chaps are going to die before we do. We're too good at it, aren't we?' He slumped heavily into his chair and settled his leg in front of him. 'Killing, I mean.'

Wolff took another cigarette, tapping it lightly on his case. 'I don't know if we'll win,' he said, bending over the flame from his lighter, 'and I can't remember why it's important, can you?'

Thwaites may have said something about little countries like Belgium and international law. He may have said something of democracy and an end to autocracy. Then he said nothing for a while, sipping the question in the gathering gloom of the room.

'Why?' he muttered at last. 'Why?' Bent forward, elbows on his knees, holding his head and his gaze to the carpet somewhere between his boots. 'Why? For a boy called Roberts out there in no-man's-land who will always be crying for his mother; and for Lowe, the little Durham miner whom I brush from my jacket every morning; and the baker's son, Rees, who gives me a startled smile if I jostle a stranger on a train. Yes, Private Brown – he was so very sorry for the trouble he put me to, dying in the piss and the mud far from home. Yes . . .' he raised his eyes to Wolff. 'That's why it's important to me.'

Wolff gave a little nod and drew deeply on his cigarette.

'A thinking chap should wonder, yes,' Thwaites continued, settling back in his chair. 'Bound to have a few doubts, and you've been ploughing a lonely furrow here,' he smiled weakly. 'Still, have to avoid self-pity.'

Wolff leant forward to grind the end of his cigarette in an ashtray. 'I probably deserve that rebuke.'

They spoke for a time of the new arrangements: Thwaites was to take over the contact, run things the Bureau's way, with dead drops, a postbox, a safe apartment, and new names. 'I thought Mr Rogers would suit you. I'll be something German – Schmidt.'

245

From time to time, his man would make deliveries. 'Not a good valet but a stout fellow and very discreet. With me at Gallipoli,' he explained. Gaunt and the Service politics they would leave to Wiseman.

'And I almost forgot this,' he said, as they were standing at the door. Bending awkwardly, he removed a large envelope from the bag at his feet and offered it to Wolff. 'Letters from home, courtesy of our chief,' he smiled sardonically. 'You see, he has your best interests at heart.'

Wolff paid off the cab a few blocks short, conscious that someone watching his apartment might find and question the driver. The rain bounced on the sidewalk and seeped insidiously through his mackintosh, running round the brim of his hat into his face, the rumble and flash of the storm loosed like that black tide on a distant shore. Kinder. Splashing softly on his neck and hands. Thank God I'm alive and in New York, he thought. He felt an urge to run, sploshing with abandon through puddles, but he didn't because he was a spy and even small steps he took with care. The East Street gutters were washing across the sidewalk and the stallholders had abandoned their barrows for the shelter of doorways and the tables at Mr Romeo's Diner. From time to time a motor car crawled by with its driver hunched over the wheel, and a sad-looking shire horse was shivering between the shafts of a cart at the grocer's. As Wolff approached his apartment building he took in the opposite side of the street with the ease of one who has learnt to see everything but look at nothing. Five workmen were standing beneath the eaves of the library, their backs pressed to the wall as the rain cascaded from the roof in a curtain. Twenty yards further on, a short man in a derby hat and smart overcoat was conspicuously failing to make himself inconspicuous. Back half turned, peering furtively at the name above a tenement bell, blind or inept or both, he was breaking the first dark commandment: *The good spy will hide among the ordinary brethren.*

Nothing was out of place in his apartment; there'd been no uninvited guests. The maid lit a fire while he changed into dry clothes, then he settled in a chair beside it to read his letters. There was a note from C, thanking him and commending Sir William Wiseman; a long letter from his mother, and a small damp one from the Honourable Mrs Lewis in Violet's wispy hand. *A whirlwind romance, the sweetest man,* she wrote, *an old school chum of Reggie's.* Her breathless sentences made him smile. The Honourable James had swept her off her feet – a position, Wolff reflected wryly, she was quite accustomed to – and he'd married her within the month. The Honourable James wanted so desperately to volunteer but unspecified health problems kept him at home, serving King and Country in the City. *I know dear Reggie would want me to be happy. You do too, don't you, darling? Only, I haven't told James we used to be friends, he would be awfully jealous. We did have fun, didn't we, darling.*

Wolff closed his eyes and tried to recollect their lovemaking, but could conjure only opaque images of a sort that hardly did her justice. Was it ever possible to recall more or was that particular pleasure like a tiny bird with brilliant feathers that hovers for a moment in the sun before it flutters away for ever? Turkey was the sort of shit-brown memory he would never lose. 'Fool,' he muttered to himself as he bent to stoke the fire. He didn't love her, he wasn't jealous, but there would be no finer way to spend a wet afternoon than to share a bed with the new Mrs Lewis. 'Goodbye, Violet.' He kissed the damp paper, then cast it on the fire and watched it shrivel to ash. Later, he read his mother's letter, the one she always wrote; dutiful, patient, pious. Bent low over the escritoire in her Sunday room, her face framed by stray grey hair, her brow creased in concentration, the pen tight between her thin dry fingers; this, Wolff could imagine with the ease of a gallery Vermeer. And after, into the fire too, because Jan de Witt had neither lover nor living mother.

When her ghost had left the room he rang Laura. For something to do, he told himself disingenuously. *Don't get involved on an operation* was the third dark commandment. He'd slept with many women but broken it only once. After eight years the recollection still made him wince. Another brown memory.

Miss McDonnell wasn't at home, he was informed by her aunt's housekeeper. He left his name but no message. Absurdly, he was relieved. This is the dissonance of my life, he thought, a piece played on a badly tuned instrument, staring uselessly from another window into another street. Christ, it was going to be a long evening with only his tired memories and the little spy in the derby hat for company. Poor devil.

21

Opera Lover

U PTOWN ON THE same evening, Dr Anton Dilger was sipping champagne with his new friend while casting warm glances at an older and very dear one. The queen of the New York night was holding court beneath a crystal chandelier in the ballroom of the German Club with the press and rich box regulars at the Met in attendance. Those who didn't know Frieda Hempel thought her plain and a little matronly; those who did were caught in a glittering spell.

'She's worth more to us than a dozen old aristocrats in Washington,' Paul Hilken whispered at his elbow. 'Just look at Bodzansky. He worships her.'

Yes, the conductor was moonstruck; and I am too, Dilger reflected.

And yet she had greeted him in her crowded dressing room at the opera house like a stranger, large brown eyes only for Kahn, the railroad banking baron, and his friends. *Dr Dilger, isn't it? A pleasant surprise. I hope you enjoyed tonight's performance.* Performance. After so many months he'd forgotten that her performance didn't end with the orchestra or in a shower of carnations at the curtain, but only when she stepped from her dress in her chamber – and sometimes she was the self-conscious artiste in silken sheets too. She'd cut him because he'd spoken proprietorially, too eager to impress his new friend Hilken, yes, cut him, humiliated him, left him seething with embarrassment, just to remind him she was a prima diva who belonged to everybody and to nobody. Confounded, he was inventing lame excuses when a dresser found him, with an invitation: *Frau Hempel would like to invite the doctor and Mr Hilken to a reception to be given in her honour.*

Hilken was a member of the German Club. He was a member of a good many clubs, Dilger had discovered in the course of the three days they'd spent together. It was Hilken who'd persuaded him to enjoy some society, visit the homes of other Germans, share a box at the opera.

'There's nothing to be gained from hiding in the country with your sister. Live a little, Doctor. That's what people will expect,' Hilken had assured him. 'Then you can return to your laboratory with a lighter heart.'

Dinner one night at Delmonico's, the next at the Waldorf. By the time they reached the bottom of their first Latour, they understood each other perfectly. They were more or less the same vintage, good Germans both – Hilken from Baltimore – they shared the same dry sense of humour, the same shameless hauteur, the same taste in women. He was slight of build with the sort of boyish good looks that, in Dilger's experience, appealed to ladies who were ready to lie about their age. Of the laboratory and their work, they had barely spoken. 'We've used the first batch here and in Boston,' was all Hilken ventured of their operation, 'but that's Hinsch's business.' For the first time since arriving in America, Dilger had managed to forget why he was there for a few hours, to pass a night without waking.

Frieda was hanging from Bodzansky's arm now, smiling indulgently, head bent a little but with her eyes lifted beneath long lashes to his face. The conductor said something amusing and she laughed a perfect little portamento, lifting her hand gracefully, forefinger crooked as if grasping the neck of a violin.

'Applause, please,' Dilger muttered irritably.

'The Austrian Jew?' enquired Hilken. 'They say he worked for Mahler.'

Dilger didn't give a fig who the fellow had crept to; for goodness' sake, why did everyone make such a fuss of musicians? Then she caught his eye, amusement playing on her lips, and he loved and he hated her for provoking him, and he wanted her, and hoped she felt the same.

'Ah. That's a pity.' Hilken shifted at his side. 'I think we should leave.' He stepped closer, turning his back on the room. 'There's a club we might try.' The waiter was hovering with a bottle of champagne but Hilken waved him away.

'No, just a minute,' Dilger protested, presenting his glass. 'What's the hurry?' He'd only just managed to catch Frieda's eye.

'We should be careful.'

'I'm always careful.'

Hilken shifted his position again, sipping his champagne to disguise the turn of his head. 'The man in the dark suit – to the left of Mencken . . . see him?'

Short and dapper, hair swept back from a high forehead, military bearing, late thirties, a nonchalant air and easy to discover amongst the guests floating about the ballroom because he was almost the only man who wasn't in white tie and tails.

'Von Rintelen. He's using the name "Gaché" but a lot of folk here know who he is. It would be better . . .'

'I know,' interrupted Dilger. It had been the Count's last instruction: keep the operations separate, the circle tight, no chances, and he'd mentioned von Rintelen by name.

'But disappearing in a puff of smoke would be worse,' he declared with a tart confidence that he knew owed more to his determination not to let Frieda slip away than to an honest appraisal of the risk. She was drifting in to dinner on someone else's arm, a preening banker perhaps, a shipping magnate or manufacturer, the sort of club patriot who toasted the Kaiser one day and his enemies the next.

'You haven't mentioned my name to von Rintelen, have you?'

'Of course not,' Hilken retorted hotly. 'But you know, Hinsch sees a good deal of him.' He pressed two fingers to his lips anxiously. 'And he drinks too much. But I'm sure . . .' Precisely what he was sure of, and why, he wasn't at liberty to say because the subject of their whispered conversation began walking purposefully across the knotted pile towards them, his arms folded like a German genie.

'Hilken, what a pleasant surprise,' he said smoothly. 'You were at the opera? Mencken says Frau Hempel was sublime, but isn't she always?'

'Always,' Hilken replied, shifting his weight uneasily from one leg to the other. 'May I present my friend, Dr Dilger.'

Rintelen turned to gaze at him amiably.

'A German from the state of Virginia,' Hilken continued. 'And you studied at Heidelberg University too, Doctor?'

Yes, Heidelberg, Dilger said, and he'd spent a good deal of his childhood with his sister's family in Berlin. 'I was working in a hospital. Can't fight, I'm an American citizen.' Rintelen's smile was set like concrete but his gaze flitted restlessly about Dilger's face. 'I lost my cousin in the first few months,' Dilger continued, although he knew he was offering too much information, too quickly, 'and, well, I wanted to do something for . . .'

'Mr Gaché is a Swiss, Doctor,' interrupted Hilken impatiently.

Rintelen's eyes danced across to him for a moment, then back to Dilger. 'But he's told you,' he observed coolly.

'Yes.'

'What has he told you?'

'That you're a German officer.'

Rintelen nodded crisply. Another waiter was hovering at his

elbow with a bottle but he refused and Dilger felt obliged to follow his example. Perhaps it had been a mistake to accept the last time. The reception was over, the prima diva had left the stage. Patrons with the deepest pockets were to dine privately with her; the rest must step from the light and the warmth, edging out of the ballroom with flushed faces, champagne voices on the stairs, cloaks and hats in the lobby, carriages at the gate.

'You are a friend of Germany's, Doctor . . .'

'I *am* German, Mr Gaché.'

'Of course, yes.' Rintelen bowed his head apologetically. 'Then I can rely on your discretion?'

'You can.'

Those sharp little eyes were still trying to discover the truth in the lines of his face, chin raised slightly, sniffing the wind, scenting or sensing another story. Hilken had said Rintelen was cocksure but good at getting things done. It seemed absurd to Dilger; two men fighting the same fight in a fog of suspicion.

They talked stiffly for a few minutes more, of the latest from the Front, of Washington and Wilson's promise to keep America out of the war, then Rintelen made his excuses.

'He'll want to question me,' Hilken remarked gloomily as they watched him leave the ballroom. '"Can your friend be trusted?" – that sort of thing. There'll be a note at the hotel asking me to meet him at Martha Held's.' He paused, smoothing his trim little moustache. 'I don't know why he's so fond of the place; it's not as if he touches the girls.'

'You've nothing to worry about – if Hinsch has kept his mouth shut.' Dilger shook his head; honestly, he didn't care. He was tired of that sort of intrigue. Like the foul soup he mixed for the cultures in his cellar, the smell seemed to cling to him, assaulting his senses. An evening that had begun with promise beneath the sunburst chandelier at the Met was slipping into shadow. What did it matter that there were other men in her life, that she'd snubbed him and kept him waiting? She held his imagination in thrall. It was her world, she made its laws, and he was her servant to command because she could make him forget everything and everyone else. Forget and laugh quietly at the stupidity of it all. 'You see, Anton,' she'd said once, 'I'll play many parts in my lifetime.' Tonight he wanted it to be the lover.

Hilken was still speaking in a confidential tone as they walked down to the lobby, but he left at the foot of the stairs to summon a carriage. Two minutes later he was back with his cloak over his arm and a sly smile. 'The porter was instructed to deliver this on pain of death,' he declared, presenting a pink envelope on the palm of his hand like a tray. Dilger lifted it to his nose at once – as she must have known he would – and smiled as a kaleidoscope of memories danced through his mind to a head note of jasmine. Tastes, colours, the sweet ambered fragrance of Frieda's warm skin, and it wasn't necessary to read her letter to be sure it was a promise to be with him tonight.

'If I arrange a meeting with Hinsch for ten o'clock tomorrow, will that be satisfactory?' Hilken enquired artfully.

'Perfectly,' he replied.

In the end it wasn't satisfactory. Stumbling into clothes, room curtains drawn, Frieda in her tumbled sheets, back turned, awake but silent, and by the time he had reached his hotel, washed and changed, he was almost an hour late. He listened with only half an ear as Hilken gave an account of his evening with 'the Dark Invader'. 'Yes, he calls himself that,' he said disdainfully. 'He says they've planted bombs on a dozen ships, a train, a factory, and in other places, I forget where. There's no limit to his ambition, it seems.' He frowned, biting his

254

bottom lip thoughtfully. 'He's going to go down in a blaze of glory. Do you think Berlin expects him to? Your Count Nadolny?'

'I can't imagine he does,' Dilger replied distantly.

'Sure?' he asked, raising his eyebrows quizzically. 'Perhaps Rintelen's meant to fall. A "*fall guy*",' he enunciated it carefully in English. 'That's what they say in prison, I believe. Just cover for our operation.'

Dilger sat straighter, disturbed by the suggestion. 'That's too devious.'

'You think so?' He plainly didn't agree.

Hinsch chose to meet them in a smoky little café on the Lower East Side, the windows opaque with grease.

'No one will see us here,' he said without irony. 'Want something?' He clicked his fingers for the waiter and with a flick of the hand gestured crudely to the ripped leather bench opposite. 'Sit down.'

While they ordered coffee Hinsch played with his cup, a spoon, the cuffs of his blue suit, then his cigarettes, his head bent heavily over the table; so close Dilger could see a vein pulsing in his right temple.

'You don't look well, Captain,' Hilken observed. 'Too much beer?'

'Ha,' he grunted bad-temperedly. 'Too much beer, you think? I was doing my job. Haven't been to bed;' and to prove it, he ran a rasping palm over his chin. 'Where were you? Champagne in the Chelsea?'

'No, champagne at the opera. Not your sort of thing, but a very pleasant evening,' Hilken replied, breezily. 'Thank you for enquiring.'

Hinsch scowled but said nothing and for a minute or two they sipped their coffee in silence, avoiding eye contact, the purpose of their meeting crackling uneasily between them like electrostatic.

'You were on the Jersey side?' prompted Hilken at last.

Hinsch was examining his hands, picking distractedly at a piece of dry skin. After a few seconds he took a cigarette from his case, tapped it lightly on the top and lit it, inhaling very deeply.

'Captain?'

'Yes, all right, I heard you,' he replied crossly. 'Look, we have a problem.' He paused to draw long on his cigarette again.

'A problem? Come on, man, explain yourself.'

He ignored Hilken, his gaze settling on Dilger. 'How long will it take a man with one of your diseases to die?'

'What on earth . . .'

'No. Let the doctor speak,' Hinsch insisted. 'How long?'

'Which one?'

'Anthrax.'

'Do you know how he caught it?'

'No.' He ground the rest of his cigarette into an ashtray. 'Look, I haven't seen him; he's in hospital.'

'He's in hospital!'

'I said so.'

'Oh God.' Dilger leant forward with his elbows on the table, his forehead in his hands as if in prayer. 'I don't know, perhaps a week – less if he inhaled spores.'

'Calm yourself, Doctor,' Hilken whispered. He turned his head deliberately to check the café.

'There's no one. I've seen to that.'

'It seems as if you've seen to rather a lot, Captain,' Hilken remarked sharply.

'It wasn't my fault,' he replied indignantly. 'I told the fool, "No mistakes or you're done for."' The sick man's wife had contacted one of Hinsch's lieutenants at about half past eight, just as the Queen of the Night was making her first curtain call. 'He's in a ward at the Bellevue.'

Hilken stroked the end of his trim little moustache thoughtfully. 'Has he spoken to the police?'

'I don't know. The wife says he's a mess.'

'Has *she* spoken to the police?'

'She doesn't know anything.'

'Are you sure? By God, you better be sure,' Hilken declared fiercely.

'This is the end.' Dilger dragged his elbows back across the table as if the conversation was over and he was ready to rise. If it *was* the end, most of him didn't care.

'You give up too easily, Doctor,' Hinsch observed sourly. 'He knows nothing of you.'

'He knows you.'

'Not for much longer, Doctor,' Hilken interjected; 'not if your diagnosis is correct. But . . .' he paused, anxiously smoothing the end of his moustache again, his cuff retreating to reveal an expensive-looking wristwatch, '. . . we can't take a chance. Someone must visit him.' He sighed heavily and sat back from the table. 'As soon as possible.'

'That's madness,' Dilger exclaimed hotly.

'No,' he said quietly. 'It's the only way.'

'Why? What possible . . .' But the answer was written plainly in the determined lines of Hilken's face. Not money or flowers or a word of comfort; 'You're going to kill him.'

'You've done that already, Doctor.'

'He'll be in an isolation ward, but that might make it easier,' Hinsch remarked, scratching his beetle brow with a crooked forefinger. 'We need to finish him without a mark. How? What do you say, Doctor?'

He tossed the question with a gallows sneer – *doctor and*

opera lover, what do you say? – and the doctor flinched but said nothing because there was nothing he could say.

'I'm sure your people can manage it without any help from us, Captain,' Hilken replied coolly.

They sat in strained silence in the taxicab to their hotel but in the lobby Hilken took his arm and drew him into a corner. 'Difficult times. We serve the best way we can,' he said, thrusting his face close to Dilger in an effort to communicate his sincerity. 'You mustn't let it upset you.'

Dilger wanted to laugh but he felt a little sick. 'You know what upsets me most? That it doesn't upset me anywhere near enough.'

'Oh? Well, it's war,' Hilken offered tentatively. 'Look, I know it's early but let's have a drink.'

'You know we swear never to harm others.' Dilger closed his eyes for a moment, gathering the image of a brightly lit lecture room, a small dark painting of his great-grandfather Tiedemann high on the wall behind the professor. 'Before today, I still thought of myself as a doctor.'

'You are a doctor. Come on,' Hilken shook his arm. 'He's just another casualty, one more casualty.'

Over the next few hours Dilger's doubt and guilt reached fever pitch. But in the afternoon a bellboy delivered a second pink envelope from the opera. Dinner at the *Hofbräuhaus* on Broadway with Mencken, the newspaper man, and some German bankers whose names she couldn't remember, *and darling, collect me at a little before eight.*

Of the dying stevedore there was no mention in the cable to Berlin. It was sent in Agent Delmar's name, although he knew nothing of its content. An enciphered message slipped across the counter on Broadway and Dr Albert and his people saw to the rest. Dilger was fastening his shirt studs and the hotel valet was brushing his top hat by the time the signal began its journey up the stone stairs of the General Staff Building and along one of the many broad corridors the midday sun never managed to penetrate. The chief clerk in Section P presented it to Nadolny in a thin red leather file the size and shape of a fine restaurant menu, and the Count stood at the window behind his desk to consider its contents, turning his red intaglio ring and gazing out distractedly at the Reichstag.

'Send this by courier to headquarters, for the eyes of the Chief of the General Staff only,' he said, turning to his clerk. 'Actually, no. That is not necessary.' And placing the file on his desk he bent to write a line that stated simply the first phase of Delmar's operation had begun. 'Encipher and telegraph this to General von Falkenhayn – and you can show in Sir Roger.'

The two months since their last meeting had not been kind to Casement. He was thinner, his eyes more deeply set and the Count was struck by how slowly he walked down the room.

'You have not been well,' he said, shaking Casement's hand and directing him to a chair.

Casement dropped into it with a sigh of frustration. 'I'm kept idle and useless, Count. The men of my brigade are still treated as prisoners – I'm not much more than a prisoner myself. Is it any wonder it has brought me low?'

'But I understand you have barely enough of your countrymen for a company, Sir Roger,' Nadolny observed.

'There were assurances of arms and men for a rising in Ireland but I've been here more than a year and—'

The Count cut him off. 'I'm sorry, Sir Roger, I asked you to visit me to discuss a more pressing matter.'

Casement seemed startled. 'Is there something . . .'

'Your courier, Christensen – he has just returned from America?'

'Yes.'

'Did your Irish friends write to you?'

Casement said they had.

'Then perhaps you know your servant was caught spending the money they intended for you on a common showgirl he pretended was his wife.'

Casement's forehead creased with concern. He knew and it was plainly a source of pain. 'A misunderstanding,' he said. 'Christensen has spoken to me about it and I believe—'

Nadolny interrupted again. 'You can explain it to your comrades in New York, Sir Roger – it is of no interest to me.' He paused, leaning forward, his hands clasped in a fist on the desk. 'There is a much more serious matter, one that touches on the security of Germany. Your valet passed through Christiania on his way back to Berlin?'

'He did.'

'Our people in the city say he tried to make contact with the Head of the British Legation there – a man called Findlay.'

Casement's face was white with shock, his hands gripping the wooden arms of his chair tightly. 'I'm sure there's an explanation. I trust Adler completely – with my life. There will – there *is* an explanation, Count. Your spies may be—'

'Wrong? No,' Nadolny replied shortly. 'I have told you this as a courtesy, Sir Roger. We will question him.' Then, with a wry smile, 'but for now it would be wise to make other domestic arrangements.'

'Arrangements?' Casement seemed close to tears.

'Another valet.'

'You're not keeping him?' He began to rise.

'That depends on whether he is a spy.' Nadolny rose, too.

The meeting was over. 'Captain Maguerre and his men will escort you to your hotel. Your valet is there?'

'Yes.' Casement stared catatonically at the floor to the right of the desk.

'Sir Roger,' Nadolny prompted, stepping forward to touch his elbow. A few seconds more and he jogged it again. 'Sir Roger.'

Casement's gaze lifted to his face. 'Adler is a weak man, but he has a good heart and he's very fond of me. You won't hurt him will you, Count?'

'But a weak man could put our operation in America in danger,' Nadolny said, guiding him firmly to the door. 'You can be sure Captain Maguerre's men will have the truth from him.'

22

Black Tom

THE RENDEZVOUS WAS the Hoboken ferry terminal, as before, the black Ford parked in the same place, Hans the sour-faced driver reading his German newspaper. Written on the red card in the windscreen, the code word *Rossbach*. They drove through downtown Jersey City, round the canal basin and marshalling yards, then to the waterfront, Liberty in shadow a mile from the shore. A ribbon of light ran into the bay towards her and with a jolt Wolff realised it was the isthmus to the Black Tom yard along which the matériel of war travelled night and day on its journey to the battlefields in the east. 'The busiest munitions wharf in the country,' Laura had remarked as they'd gazed from Liberty across the narrow water.

'We're to meet him there?' Wolff nodded towards the strip. Surely it was madness to attempt such a thing. Hans wouldn't say but pushed on a little faster and after a few minutes it was plain that the road led to Black Tom and nowhere else. At the perimeter fence it bent away from the shore through marshland and along a stretch of abandoned railroad track, petering out at last at an iron gate. Beyond it the gable end of a warehouse and in the sooty yellow of the wharf lamps a loading gantry and the triangular points of dockside cranes like broken teeth in an old man's mouth. Opposite the gate, a siding choked with weeds and a dozen old boxcars, the black flag of the Lehigh Valley Railroad peeling from their sides. As Hans cut the engine, the door of the nearest slid open and the silhouette of a slight figure was caught for a second in the light of a shrouded lamp. Wolff stepped down from the Ford and pushed the door shut gently. Rintelen was picking his way across rough ground towards him, with Hinsch and two associates in tow. The smaller man tripped and cursed and Wolff recognised the voice of McKee, the Clan's fixer on the docks and his guide on the night he planted the bombs on the *Blackness*. Rolling like a ship in a storm beside him, the Bavarian butcher, Koenig, summoned no doubt to effect an entry. But this wasn't an ordinary yard, this was Black Tom.

'You know where you are?' Rintelen asked, offering his hand.

'This place must be a fortress.' Wolff sounded quite as concerned as he felt. What the hell were they proposing to do if they did get inside?

'I thought you liked an adventure, Mr de Witt,' Rintelen replied.

'Eleven. It's time.' Hinsch brandished his pocket watch. Koenig was already lumbering to the gate. Pushing a flashlight through the railings to the left of it, he directed the beam at the ground, flicking it on and off three times. His signal was answered immediately from the corner of the warehouse and after a few seconds the light began to approach the gate.

'That will be our man.' McKee's hands were thrust in his coat pockets, pulling it tight for comfort. 'The guards on the trains carry rifles – and on the dock for loading – but there's only a couple of fellas on the sheds at night.'

Their contact stepped up to the gate, his stevedore cap pulled low over a thin face and grizzled moustache. Koenig slipped him a packet, then turned to beckon them over.

'That's it, he's paid.' McKee's voice shook a little. 'We've an hour until the shift changes and a new watchman. No more.'

'For what?' No one was carrying a case like the one they'd given Wolff the evening he'd placed the detonators on the *Blackness*.

'Calm yourself,' Rintelen replied disapprovingly.

'I am calm,' he lied. 'I don't like surprises and this . . .'

'We are paying enough for your patience, I think,' Rintelen interjected.

'Have it your own way.' You bastard, he thought.

From the gate, the watchman led them round the warehouse and between sheds to the flat yard at the neck of the dock. A small works engine was shunting empty wagons into a siding, a railroad man at the switches, his face bent into his coat. To their right, a boiler house and chimneys and a windowless wharf building, a single dim lamp above its door, three men in its light, rifles slung on their shoulders. The watchman waved his flashlight and one of them raised his hand in acknowledgement.

'The main explosives store?' Rintelen enquired.

'One of them,' the watchman replied, a hint of Irish in his voice. 'There are more on the island. Most of the stuff is held in barges at the piers, so they can turn it round quick.'

'And that is the only door?' Rintelen took a small pocketbook and pen from his coat. 'How much explosive is kept in there?'

'It changes, Jim, don't it?' said McKee. 'Fifty, maybe a hundred thousand pounds. Crates mostly.'

Rintelen made a note in his book. 'In the yard at one time – the island too?'

McKee lifted his cap and scratched his head. 'A million,' he ventured. 'Maybe more.'

That went into the book too, and Wolff began to feel more easy. Rintelen wasn't there to plant detonators, merely to explore and plan. There would be time to raise the alarm.

They left Koenig and Hinsch and walked along the track towards the island, stopping from time to time so Rintelen could make notes of the distance between a pierhead and a storage shed, the 'correct' position of the pontoons and the places that were too well lit by the wharf lamps. Ahead of them always, and closer, the shadow of Liberty, glimpsed here through a cloud of steam, there between buildings or below the steel hook of a crane. Nobody challenged Rintelen, nobody asked why a man in a well-tailored wool coat and a homburg from Hermès was striding yards out on the dock; no one enquired because no one gave a damn. It was quiet because they were waiting for British ships, the watchman explained; there were barges of the 'stuff' at pier 4 and crates the length of a small city block on the wharf.

'Show me,' Rintelen commanded.

Most of the matériel was stacked at the railhead on the north side of the island. Hundreds of howitzer shells were standing on their base plates in the open as if in readiness for a push on Wall Street. Rintelen muttered something uncharacteristically profane: someone at the works with a little education had chalked 'Gott strafe Deutschland' on one of the crates. A couple of guards were stamping and blowing into their hands. McKee shuffled over to say his piece and very obligingly they turned and walked away. 'From Green's,' he muttered on his return. 'They say they're expecting three ships at dawn.'

'How much would you need for something like this, and those . . .' Rintelen nodded to the water between piers 3 and 4, '. . . those barges, Mr de Witt?'

'That depends on what's inside them,' he said cautiously.

'Shine your flashlight here.' McKee reached up to one of the crates. 'Can you read that?'

'Don't need to, Billy,' the watchman replied. 'They're Canadian Car from Kingsland. Three-inch shells. This lot's on its way to

Russia. The big stuff's from Bethlehem Steel, that's on its way to France.'

'Well?' Rintelen prompted.

'Not very much,' Wolff declared bullishly. 'A fire would be enough.'

'And those?'

'Ha.' He rapped his knuckles against a crate. 'Don't concern yourself with the rest of this stuff. They'll be picking up the pieces in Bronx County.'

Rintelen pursed his lips thoughtfully for a moment, then nodded, 'Enough.'

They walked back along the causeway swiftly and in silence. At the gate, a hearty pat on the back and more money for the watchman. 'For the love of old Ireland,' he remarked without irony as he slipped it into his breast pocket. They pressed Wolff to join them at Martha's. 'What better place to be at this hour?' Rintelen enquired with a disingenuous little smile. 'My own bed,' he replied curtly, and for once the German wasn't inclined to argue. 'But you must come to the ship tomorrow at eight.'

'Oh, must I?'

'If you want to work, yes,' he retorted in a clipped no-nonsense voice that implied he was happy to dispense with Wolff's services. Wolff promised to be there.

It was after midnight when he paid off the cab close to his apartment. The diminutive spy in the derby hat was loitering in a doorway down the street. To be sure I'm as good as my word, Wolff reflected, as he closed the sitting-room curtains. A mistake to appear flustered in front of Rintelen; a poor performance. An old ham with stage fright. He poured a whisky and sat with his eyes closed, breathing deeply. Just a few minutes, then he would leave a coded message for Thwaites. Tonight. No more blunders like the *Blackness*. The glass was at his lips when the sudden trilling of the telephone in the hall made him start. At that hour, it could only be the man he was preparing to call.

'Sorry to telephone so late, sir.' The flat unflappable voice of Thwaites' man, White. 'I'm ringing on behalf of *Royal*, sir. Mr Schmidt's compliments, he's anxious to speak to you. An offer of employment.'

'Very well, I'll visit Mr Schmidt . . .'

'At the office, sir.'

'The office, yes, of course.' To insist on the Consulate, well, it had to be urgent. 'I'm obliged to Mr Schmidt. I'll visit the first opportunity I have.'

He put the receiver down gently. First opportunity was their code for right away. Was his cover compromised? But Rintelen's cronies would have finished him and dumped his body in a boxcar. He didn't know, couldn't, and that was unnerving, so he put it from his mind and bent his thoughts to avoiding the spy in the derby hat. Off all lights except the lamp in the bedroom, change of hat and coat, revolver in pocket, stocking feet from the apartment, fire escape into the foul-smelling back court, the spare key to the building opposite hanging in the coalhole where he'd watched the drunken janitor leave it one evening.

It was a while before he found a taxicab and he was obliged to walk most of the way. The British Consulate was at 44 Whitehall Street in a brutal sandstone-and-brick building close to the elevated railway and an army recruitment office. Wolff walked along the street, then back, before slipping through the door. White was in the lobby and greeted him with a broad grin that suggested he was enjoying this new adventure as valet and spy. Why not? The last one had taken him on Mr Churchill's bloody goose chase to Gallipoli. The Bureau's new rooms were on the first floor, *Sir William Wiseman, Munitions* handwritten on a card at the door of his outer office. Perhaps Gaunt was resisting anything more permanent.

'Whisky, isn't it?' Wiseman asked. He must have come from dinner, breezing into the Consulate in his white tie.

Thwaites had a face like an undertaker's mute.

'You better tell me,' Wolff said impatiently. Englishmen always made a mess of bad news. 'Come on – spill it.'

'Sit down.' Wiseman waved the whisky tumbler at a large leather armchair in front of his desk.

'Is it my mother?'

'Your mother, old boy?' Wiseman handed Wolff the whisky and eased himself carefully into the chair opposite, Thwaites sitting beside him. 'No, not your mother. But I'm afraid it *is* bad news. The *Blackness* was lost – sunk. An explosion.' He jerked his hands out theatrically. 'Terrible luck.'

'Bloody incompetence,' chipped in Thwaites. 'The Navy should have dealt with it and I told Gaunt so.'

'Gone? Christ. Christ.'

'*Captain* Gaunt . . .' said Wiseman reprovingly, 'informed us this afternoon. Lost three days ago.'

'Were there survivors?'

'None, I'm afraid.'

'How many men?'

'Forty-five.'

'Christ.' Wolff closed his eyes, pressing his fingers firmly to his temple. When he opened them he would wake and know it for a nightmare. Just as he used to in the boxroom at the farm: always the graveyard hours. But Thwaites was speaking again: '. . . Gaunt says they tricked you. The fuse was set for two days, not four.'

'Christ. I told him I couldn't be sure.' He shivered and opened his eyes, his head still in his hands. 'I've sunk one of our ships.'

'No. They sank one of our ships, one more of our ships,' Wiseman insisted quietly. 'I know how you must feel but . . .'

268

'What sort of madness . . .' he interjected. My God, what had he done? To lose a ship and crew . . . no, they didn't know how he felt. How could they? 'I used to be a seaman.'

'Nothing else you could do,' Thwaites declared firmly.

'. . . forty-five men.' Wolff remembered the flat, pugnacious face of the ship's mate he'd browbeaten into letting him place the explosives. 'I could have stopped . . .'

'Rintelen's operation has sunk at least three this month,' Thwaites continued. 'There are Clan men in all the large ports – you said so yourself.'

'But the *Blackness* was me.' Rising quickly, Wolff stepped over to the fire, his mind clouded. 'I should leave, seek another path,' but he knew he didn't have the courage. He had delivered them to the enemy just as he'd done in Turkey, and he would pay for both in time because, in some way he perceived only dimly, that was how it always was, and should be.

'Our job is to stop him,' he heard Wiseman say from what sounded like a great distance.

'Yes,' he said flatly.

'Here.' The baronet was suddenly beside him, pressing the whisky into his hand. 'Come on, old fellow.'

'Yes.'

They sat in awkward silence, gazing into their glasses, at the patterns of the Persian rug, the embers in the grate; Thwaites turning his stick impatiently between thumb and forefinger, Wiseman with chin on bow tie, careful not to catch his eye. Fortitude, Wolff, their silence seemed to say; only a battle lost, the war to fight; you've blundered, but *'Was there a man dismay'd?'* Somewhere a clock with a Westminster chime struck two.

'Rintelen's going to attack the Black Tom,' he said at last.

'Oh?' Wiseman leant forward, his elbows on his knees.

'I was on the point of arranging a meeting to warn you.'

'Has he told you when?' Wiseman asked, staring earnestly at him over his fingertips, arrogant in a good-natured sort of way.

'No.'

'Is the fellow boasting?' Thwaites threw in. 'You said yourself he's conceited, Dark Invader and all that – Black Tom is a bit of a fortress.'

'It's nothing of the sort,' Wolff replied, and he told them of his visit; that the price of the ticket was a few dollars to a doorkeeper from the Clan, and that enough TNT was sitting on the dock to rock Liberty from her foundations with just toe rags from Green's to keep her safe.

'The Consulate would probably lose its windows,' he remarked matter-of-factly.

'Ouch.' Wiseman pulled a face. 'That would be unfortunate. Yes.' He patted his pockets, then rose and drifted over to his desk. 'Well, we have some ideas, don't we?' he said, addressing Thwaites. 'Ah, here it is.' He picked up a leather pouch from the desk and began tearing at tobacco, pressing the shreds into his pipe with a key. 'You see, Norman has made contact with his friend in the Police Department Bomb Squad – you were right, he's on to this fellow Koenig. Takes a dim view.' Striking a match, he lowered it carefully to the bowl. 'Have to find the right balance,' he gasped between puffs. 'He wants to have his cake and eat it. Doesn't want us to interfere, but will take what he can from us – isn't that so, Norman?'

'He's one hundred per cent,' interjected Thwaites. 'Thinks Rintelen's men are behind a fire at a munitions factory in Pennsylvania too. Haven't told him about you, of course. Police Department's full of Irishmen.'

'We'll expose Rintelen in the newspapers, use Norman's friends on *The Times* and the *New York World*,' Wiseman said.

'Only we need to offer some proof.' He took the pipe from his mouth and began inspecting it carefully. 'Yes, this cabin of Rintelen's,' he offered casually, 'the one where he keeps his records – any chance?'

The springs of Thwaites' chair groaned as he shifted awkwardly. Wolff glanced over at him but his head was turned away.

'I'll try,' replied Wolff deliberately.

'Yeees,' drawled Wiseman. 'After today, the sooner the better.'

'Of course,' he retorted indignantly. 'Of course.' Was Wiseman trying to make him feel guiltier? 'Look, can't you just make Rintelen disappear?' It wasn't a solution C encouraged, but after the *Blackness* . . .

'Thought of that,' said Wiseman, sitting back in his chair. 'One of Gaunt's Czech footpads – trouble is, the network would still be in place. And you – it might compromise you.'

'I see.' But I don't care, Wolff thought, running his fingers through his hair wearily. Or am I being naïve? He wanted to stay in America, the sun shone a little brighter even in winter, and if he left he would never make love to Laura.

'Cigarette?' Thwaites leant forward with his case. 'The thing is, our friends at the *World* need names, payments, meetings; they want someone at the top – in the embassy perhaps – to stir it up on the eve of a presidential election.'

'And Delmar,' Wiseman chipped in. 'London keeps pestering. They're convinced there's something.'

Wolff bent to Thwaites' match then leant back, inhaling deeply. 'I'll do my best.' What else could he say?

'Well, this might help,' said Wiseman, reaching into his waistcoat and removing a pocket watch.

Wolff raised his brow quizzically. 'With what, precisely?'

'It's a Ticka, a hidden camera. Look,' Wiseman held it upright between thumb and forefinger; 'dummy face. Lens here in the winder, the shutter release this tiny catch at the bottom. Here,' he presented it on his palm to Wolff. 'The film is loaded on a reel. Twenty-five exposures. Save you taking too many notes.'

'Needs a good deal of light, doesn't it?' He'd heard tell of the Ticka but had never needed to use one. 'Look, I'll do what I can.'

They sat for a while in uncomfortable silence, the shadows of the fire dying on the walls, a winter chill creeping into the room.

'You must be shattered,' Wiseman observed at last, his voice soapy with concern. 'White will whistle up a taxicab.'

Wolff said it was better if he made his own arrangements. They wished him good luck, shook his hand and Thwaites urged him to put the *Blackness* from his mind.

'But what an explosion,' Wiseman exclaimed, stopping suddenly at the door. 'Like a German push. Worse.' He was plainly stirred by the thought, shamelessly so. 'Not the ship,' he added hastily, 'the Black Tom yard – can you imagine, in a presidential election year?'

Walking on the cold street, Wolff turned this remark through his tired mind for a time. There had been the glint of an idea in Wiseman's eye. Rattle the windows of the White House. Something to tip the balance and bring America into the war, he thought, blowing warm vapour into his hands. Crossing Bowery, he slipped on the frozen sidewalk and shortened his stride. He was cold and empty. *How should I feel?* In the twisted logic of the Bureau, the ship and her crew were just small pieces. Perhaps Black Tom, too, in time. Like those decoy attacks favoured by generals in France, frightfully clever chaps who could see 'the big picture'. Had Gaunt made any effort to remove the bombs from the *Blackness*? Did they decide on the alternative in the interests of what they perceived as a greater good? To question everything was to know nothing and to make everyone your enemy.

On Chambers Street, he managed to hail a cab. It dropped him short of his apartment and he used the janitor's key to creep back through the yard into the building. He needn't have bothered; the man in the derby had left his post. Four o'clock and in another hour the city would begin to stir. The Russian in the flat above would slam his door, then clatter down the stairs on his way to work at the Fulton Street fish market; while in the kitchen the landlord's eldest daughter would feed the range and boil hot water for the family; and if the old lady on the ground floor was awake she would open her window and place a saucer of milk on the ledge for the cats.

Wolff took off his coat and hat, he took off his shoes and jacket, then rolled himself in the bedcover. 'I don't laugh enough,' he muttered, closing his eyes. Violet used to make him laugh.

23

The Moment

Timing waits for opportunity, C liked to say, and a good spy is the one who recognises and seizes the perfect moment without hesitation.

'What were you expecting to happen?' Wolff exclaimed when von Rintelen greeted him with the *Shipping News* the following evening. In black and white on page two – the *Blackness*: hull, crew and cargo lost in an explosion at sea to a cause unknown. 'But not to us,' Rintelen observed with a yelp of laughter that set Wolff's teeth on edge. 'Good judgement – you see, Hinsch?'

'Yes,' Hinsch conceded, turning to acknowledge Wolff with a nod and a grudging smile, 'you've done well.' They were true comrades – who could doubt it? A toast! Rintelen insisted; and because he was a gentleman with a generous paymaster, his wine was good.

They were sitting in his office cabin, the newspaper open on the delicate lacquer table, anchored by their glasses and cigarette cases. 'Wine is the only thing the Franzmann does better than us,' he remarked, inspecting the bottle. 'I will send some cases home. Quicker than waiting for our army to conquer France.'

'Let's talk about tomorrow,' said Hinsch, opening his rough hands on the table. 'The *Linton*, a small freighter, about four thousand tons. Grain and some artillery shells. There should be no difficulty.'

'Our associates are responsible for the security,' Rintelen explained.

'Irish associates?' Wolff enquired.

'Friends of Sir Roger's, yes.'

'Those chaps from Green's,' Wolff persisted. 'I met them, remember?'

'McKee is there to get you aboard,' said Hinsch sourly. 'All right?'

Wolff reached for his glass. 'All right.' He didn't want to lose his new advantage. 'Once the grain catches, well . . .' he paused to sip his wine, '. . . you can imagine.'

Rintelen *could* imagine: satisfaction was expressed plainly in every middle-aged line of his face. Wolff was reminded of his promise: *I'll buy what I can and blow up what I can't.* His preference was distinctly for the latter. They discussed the number of detonators and the rendezvous, and Rintelen boasted of his 'other operations'. 'The Dark Invader's empire grows,' he joked. 'And what do you say to this, gentlemen?' Rising quickly, he stepped over to his cabinets, took a key from his jacket and opened the middle one. A wafer tumbler lock, Wolff noted, and one of the simplest. The two other cabinets appeared to be sealed the same way. 'Here.' Rintelen lifted a file. 'Clear the glasses, would you?' Then he opened it on the table. 'Recognise this?'

'Black Tom.'

'Yes, I drew it myself,' he said with a smug smile. 'I have given it some thought and the correct thing to do is land by sea, here . . .' he prodded his map with a well-manicured forefinger; '. . . a boat to pier four to place them on barges . . . here and here. It is the best way to make it look like an accident. So,' he said, straightening his back, 'what do you think?'

Wolff was sure his opinion was of no importance and Hinsch may have thought the same because he shook his head but said nothing.

'The time isn't right, I know,' Rintelen continued; 'we must wait, but it's important to have a plan.'

He closed the file and picked up the bottle to fill their glasses once more. This time Wolff refused. 'I must go.'

'You have a dinner engagement?' Rintelen enquired, leaning forward as if inviting a confidence.

'Something like that,' he said casually. 'Don't trouble, I can make my own way.'

'That won't be necessary. I will have a guide take you to the gangway.'

'Still a question of trust?'

'Of manners,' Rintelen lied; it was something he did smoothly too.

But for once there wasn't a sailor on station in the passageway. Rintelen seemed to hesitate, his hand lingering on the rail: 'If you don't mind.'

Wolff had already taken a few steps down the companionway. 'Of course not.'

'Then I'll leave you.'

Wolff turned to offer the flicker of a smile – 'Until tomorrow, Captain' – then continued down the companionway. A few seconds later he thought he heard a door swing to behind him but he didn't risk a glance. Was this the moment? There might be no better. He wasn't going to sink another ship. He'd tried to think it through a hundred times; he'd hidden in corners, picked locks, made excuses, fought his way off the ship and felt his heart freeze as he plunged from her side into the bay, but hours of imaginary effort had left him with no more than a great leap of faith. Should he stay and hide or leave and then try to bluff his way back aboard? He pushed through heavy stateroom doors to the top of the main companionway, acknowledging a passing steward with a smile. By the time I reach the bottom I'll know, he thought. If Rintelen was watching the gangway to be sure he left the ship it would be over in minutes, but if he did leave and then tried to return with a story, the watch officer might insist on an escort. By now he was a companionway and a passage of fifteen paces from the shelter deck, another forty from the seamen at the top of the gangway. Wolff, you can never know, he told himself. You're here now, you're alone. He pressed his pocket and felt the heft of the revolver. Do it now. You must.

'Can I help you, sir?'

A steward had stepped from a cabin in third, apron about his middle, duster in his hand. What the hell was he polishing at that hour on a ship without passengers? Like a lonely middle-aged hausfrau taking out her frustration on the silver.

'I know my way,' Wolff replied haughtily.

The steward shuffled back to let him pass. At the end of the corridor he turned right and kept walking towards the last companionway. Fear was his driver; the cold controlled fear that sharpens perception and urges one to action. He had to lose himself and quickly, but higher. If the main companionway was amidships, there would be another towards the stern. From there he could climb back to 'A' deck and find a corner somewhere close to Rintelen's office. Turning on his heels, he walked back through the cabins on the port side of the ship. At the foot of the main companionway a petty officer was issuing orders to two seamen. They turned to acknowledge him but he passed with only a supercilious glance, the first-class gentleman and friend of the captain. He touched his forehead; it was wet with perspiration, and he was conscious of his shirt clinging to his back. Come on, you fool.

At the polished mahogany doors of the dining saloon, he was forced to turn on to the open deck where second class was accustomed to promenade at sea. Leaning on the rail, a young member of the watch was smoking a cigarette. As soon as he saw Wolff he tossed it guiltily over the side and straightened his back, a crooked forefinger to his cap. Twenty sharp paces then back inside, pantry on the right, head steward's cabin on the left, ahead of him the foot of the stern companionway. He climbed it quickly but like a gentleman, battling the urge to take the steps two at a time. As he approached the top he heard the murmur of voices through the door of what was either a lounge or smoke room. A junior officer, to judge by the hoops on his sleeve, was holding the handle, his back turned to the passageway. Don't hesitate, Wolff told himself, not now, not for a second; sharp suit and coat, saboteur or spy, he will know me for one of the Dark Invader's men. And if the officer did glance over his shoulder he said nothing.

I'm shaking, Wolff thought, how strange, and he tried to concentrate on breathing deeply. If Rintelen sees me, I'll say I came back to speak to him.

But nobody noticed him as he made his way for'ard again and a minute later he was in the starboard passageway, only the width of a first-class cabin from Rintelen on the port side, torsion wrench in one hand, pick in the other. Come on, come on, he muttered under his breath as he felt for the lock. Voices suddenly somewhere, a door swinging to, but he was in, panting quietly, his back to the cabin wall. He couldn't risk the electric light but enough was spilling through the porthole for him to move freely. It was half past ten: settle, disturb nothing and pray. Two hours, perhaps three. If only I could smoke . . . He sat and listened for steps in the passageway, a steward, a search party, but minutes slipped by in plush silence. He took off his coat and checked his gun and the watch camera; he considered his route from the ship and concluded again that there was only one. Then he leant forward and placed his head on the table, wristwatch ticking in his ear, tick, tick, tick, carrying him to the future and to the past, twisting an uncertain contour through hopes and memories, but alive always to the present: a motor car on the quay, the rattle of cable on the boat deck, the striking of the bell.

He left the cabin an hour into the First Watch. Softly along the carpeted passageway, clutching the barrel of his gun like a club, a few yards only to the first turn, a few more to the port side then back; on his right, suite six, five, the door of number four. He bent close: nothing, not a sound, and no telltale splinters in the lock. It took only seconds to open. Pitch black, and he remembered von Rintelen dropping the deadlight and drawing the curtain. No one spoke, no one was waiting, the cabin was still. He switched on the wall sconces just long enough to be sure of no surprises. Everything was in its correct place, neat pencils and paper on the tabletop, floor lamp close by, the oak cabinets just in the loop of its light. He stared at them for a few seconds, breathing deeply. All right, from the left to the right, see what there was first and keep the files in order. It took no time to pick the lock.

'How on earth . . . ?' In the top drawer, there were dozens of copies of telegrams to the National City Bank of New York authorising munitions purchases and the harbour dues for Allied ships. Names, cargoes, sailing times, all the intelligence a saboteur or submarine needed to sink a ship, and most of them sent from the Consulate in Whitehall Street. Yellow slips in date order. He thumbed through to 6 November and found the SS *Blackness*. 'Clever bastard.' Rintelen had someone inside the bank that the Allies used for their business.

In the next two drawers, intelligence on other targets: gun foundries, factories, railroad routes and bridges to blow before a munitions train, grain stores, ports east and west, and the Dark Invader's plan of the Black Tom. But the gold was in the middle cabinet. 'I knew you would have to,' Wolff muttered under his breath. Every one of the Kaiser's pfennigs, every mark, because meticulousness is a state of mind and accountants like Dr Albert are born to their figures. In one ledger, the million-dollar munitions purchases of Gaché's cover company; in another, the handfuls of grubby greenbacks paid to men with Irish names. The paper trail of the network's activities: so much stuff it frightened him. Follow the money and the payroll regulars, he told himself, settling at the table with the ledgers. Glancing through the accounts of the cover company he could see that Albert had authorised millions of dollars to force the price of war matériel up and prevent it falling into the hands of the Allies. All he'd done was feed the machine. He must have recognised it because the defrayments stopped in September. Of more use, three large account books of payments to the members of Clan na Gael, to Jim Larkin and the other strike leaders, and half a dozen detective agencies in as many ports.

Thumbing through the files in the cabinet, he was able to cross-reference the lines in the ledgers with receipts signed by Paul Koenig and others. Some he photographed as evidence, the rest he carefully noted in his pocketbook. Then, at three o'clock, he began hunting for the identity of Rintelen's contact at the National City Bank. No reference in the accounts, no contracts, no receipts. Turning to the last cabinet, he was fiddling with the lock when a sharp noise in the passageway made him start. What was he thinking? He'd almost forgotten he was in danger. Crossing to the table, he picked up his revolver and switched off the lamp. The shuffling of feet, a light knock at a door further down the passageway.

'Franz,' hissed someone with a young voice. 'Are you there?'

Wolff breathed a little more easily. Some other business? Personal. Casement's sort of business.

'Franz! It's me.' But no answer came.

Wolff listened impatiently to his retreating steps. At twenty-five minutes past three he turned on the lamp again. Half an hour only, he couldn't risk more. In the middle drawer of the third cabinet, a brass strongbox, the lock a simple pin tumbler. He reached inside with both hands: 'What the hell!' Lifting the box had triggered an alarm like a London bobby's whistle.

Damn you. His hands were trembling so much the pick rattled in the lock. Damn, damn, damn . . . Half a turn left, then right, then left, and the alarm cut out. Silence, but for the ringing in his ears and the thumping pulse in his temple. He snatched the revolver from the table and stood shaking in the dark. What now? The alarm had sounded for what felt like an eternity but was only seconds, so if no one was sleeping in the neighbouring cabins, perhaps . . . He switched the lamp back on and pulled the strongbox closer. I'm a fool, he thought; remember Turkey.

Two feet by one, large enough for a ledger and a stack of papers, and a simple electrical alarm concealed in a false bottom. On the spine of the ledger: *Secret Section.* The pages were laid out like an ordinary account book but the recipients were denoted by a number and the disbursements coded in five-letter groups. But they'd been careless with the loose paper. On top of the bundle there was a contract with the New Jersey Agricultural Chemical Company for certain scientific services. It was signed by a Dr Walter Scheele of Hoboken. Wolff's thoughts jumped to the doctor with the grey walrus moustache and Jersey drawl who'd demonstrated his cigar bomb in the field: he'd wager good money they were one and the same man.

In the same papers he found the receipts he'd signed for Albert with a false name and one authorising a cash payment to Laura McDonnell. Of the rest, the most intriguing were large transfers to two accounts bearing the baroque signature of a Mr Paul Hilken of the Norddeutscher Lloyd Shipping Line. Wolff photographed them both and twenty pages of the coded ledger. By the time he'd locked the strongbox away it was after four o'clock. Cursing himself for a fool, he checked the cabin carefully to be sure everything was as he'd found it, then slipped into the passageway. But no one troubled to ask his business as he retraced his route. The ship's watch had changed a few minutes before and was still wiping the sleep from its eyes. So much for Rintelen's 'good German crew'. Bloody hell, he thought, I might pull this off. At the head of the gangway a young Third greeted him with a cheery 'Good morning'.

Wolff took refuge in ill temper. 'If you say so.'

The lieutenant was a little taken aback. 'Working late, sir?' he ventured.

'Don't ask a friend of the captain's what he's doing,' Wolff replied, brushing past and on to the gangway. Relief and something close to euphoria washed through him as he rattled down to the dock. Damn you, Rintelen, damn you, Gaunt, you too, Cumming, he thought. I've done it! He was in range of a shot from the ship but they weren't going to kill him because they were stupid and complacent. That's it, let me waltz away with your secrets.

The quay glistened like a sheet of black ice. For the first time he noticed fine rain on his face and it was good. He walked at a steady pace, his hands deep in his pockets, the warm gun-steel a comfort still, careful to concentrate on the end of the pier, careful to avoid the splashes of light cast by the dockside lamps. As he approached the terminal his pulse quickened and he tightened his grip on the revolver. To reach the street he would have to pass under the arch in the embarkation gallery; twenty-five dark yards through a forest of steel girders. He was suddenly very conscious of the sound of his steps crunching the loose cinders. A second later his heart jumped at a shadow ahead and to the left – it was a straggle of rope dancing on the breeze. Then he was under the arch and his stride lengthened, one, two, three, casting about for movement, five, six, seven, almost halfway – but Christ, there was someone. Scuffing feet and at the corner of his eye a shadow. A second later another glimpse: the man from the street, his Bill Sikes, the little spy in the derby hat. Close, so close, a few yards; he must keep walking – but Rintelen will know by the morning. That can't happen. No.

A giant leap and swinging blindly: Wolff caught him on the left cheekbone with the grip of the revolver. A throaty groan and he staggered sideways, head dropping, defenceless as Wolff's fist cut under, driving his chin up again. He toppled back, his shoulders thumping heavily to the ground, prostrate, gasping for breath. Too dark to see his eyes, his features contorted in pain, trying to raise himself on one elbow, clawing at the concrete. Wolff stamped on his hand, then dropped a knee to his chest, clubbing him with the grip again. His head fell, blood in his eyes, blinking, unable to speak, a look of abject terror, trying to curl his body but locked by Wolff's arm and knee. A small man, middle years, with a poisonous little moustache. A nothing man. But from somewhere he'd produced a knife and with his free right hand caught Wolff at the top of the thigh. Still prone, but with the strength of fear, he lunged a second time. They wrestled for control of the blade, Wolff's weight forcing it down, down, down to the shoulder and in hard, into bone. The man screamed in pain: 'Please.' But without hesitation Wolff drew it and thrust it back, to the hilt, to the heart. With a jerk and a sad little gasp he died, Wolff straddling him like an exhausted lover, the derby rocking on its crown a few feet away. And what was there to read in the dead man's face? Astonishment, outrage, fear, disappointment.

Later Wolff could recall only images of his journey home – and the face. Wiping blood and prints from the handle of the knife, he remembered, and hiding the body in the tangle of steel. He dumped his own coat somewhere. There was a taxicab and this time he took it to the door of the building on East 5th. Inside his apartment he poured a whisky with a trembling hand, then another. His trousers were clinging to his legs: it was his own blood, from the gash in his thigh. What a fucking mess. He'd killed before but only once and in self-defence. For months after, he'd hated himself. Was this the same? Did it matter when thousands were dying every day? He was the enemy and he tried to stick you, he thought. But weren't you going to finish him anyway – the little man in a derby hat?

By the time he'd dressed his wound, the world was spinning. At its soft edge, he heard the bang of the Russian's door upstairs and the hum of dawn on the city's streets, and feeling sick he limped through to the bathroom and threw up in the lavatory. 'What a state,' he muttered, collapsing on the bed. I won't sleep, he thought, but he did.

24

A Fever

THERE WAS A deposit box at a bank on Broadway. Two keys: Thwaites' man had the other. Make the drop before they find the body. But it was a struggle the following morning, moving in a fog of pain and memory, careless of his dress and customary toilet. He limped out at eleven and felt better for the winter air. Tomorrow it would be December. Flurries of snow were chasing down the street and the low sky promised more. On a balcony opposite, a woman was taking in some stiff-looking laundry, while the stallholders below hunched disconsolately in their coats, their horses stamping and steaming between the shafts. An old Chinaman hobbled into the library to search for a Dickens or just a warm corner, and the dead spy lingered in his doorway. I'll move, Wolff thought; I was going to have to anyway.

The taxicab dropped him at the bank because he was bone-weary and too sorry to be careful. He signed out the black deposit box as *Mr Rogers*, placed his notebook and the watch camera inside, then watched the clerk carry it away – just to be sure. Walking down Broadway he stopped at a public pay station to telephone Thwaites: *Rogers from Western, sir. Yes, a parcel for Mr White. For collection, yes.*

Replacing the handpiece, he closed his eyes and leant his head against the booth. Perhaps it would save lives too, seamen like the crew of the *Blackness* and the next ship they were expecting him to sink. Would he be able to risk making the rendezvous? He should have told Thwaites about the *Linton*. What if they've found the body? His head was spinning; a little faint, he needed to sit somewhere warm, a coffee, a cigarette, something to eat.

He chose an Italian place just off Broadway. He knew it was expensive because the waiter looked at him disrespectfully. No tie, a day's growth, scuffed boots, he was dishevelled, a little dissolute. He ordered coffee, some eggs, and lit his cigarette, ready to play the usual game of joining pieces, words, something like Consequences. If the Germans found the body, they'd kill him. Who else could have finished the spy off? He had lived with Wolff for days, part of the bloody street furniture. The tobacco was making him giddy. Am I prepared to take the chance? He thought perhaps he owed it to the *Blackness*. Peculiar, even after Turkey, after Germany and a blade inching to his throat, it was difficult to draw the line. The feeling for life captured closest to death was a compulsion, prowling the edge of an impenetrable forest, like a twilight figure tested in a medieval romance.

The waiter served the omelette and he picked at it for a while. His thigh ached and he resolved to see a doctor in case the wound was infected or needed stitches. Perhaps he was poisoning himself.

In the event, he spent the afternoon in his apartment, his eyes closed but very much awake. Rising at seven, he limped into the hall and for a time stood gazing at the telephone. He hadn't seen or spoken to her for a fortnight; he'd written to her once and thought of her often, but it was foolish to call her when, if things went badly, he would fail to make the appointment. Tomorrow, he'd telephone her then.

*

286

The first rendezvous was with Rintelen's driver, Hans, at the ferry terminal. Will he drop me at the entrance to a dock or throw me in it? Wolff wondered as he stepped inside the Ford. He felt ridiculously calm, too tired, too low, and that was dangerous because it was in just such a frame of mind that mistakes were made. 'It's important to be a little afraid,' C liked to say. Wolff had brought the revolver, but its weight was an unpleasant reminder of the night before. In the event, Hans dropped him at the dark end of a dockyard street close to the Jersey Canal basin with the instruction: 'Walk the rest of the way.'

'Why?' Wolff wanted to know.

'Safer,' he said with a shrug.

Would it be here then, slipping and stumbling on frozen cobbles? Dock wall one side, four-storey warehouse on the other; can't run, can't hide. He tried not to limp because that might arouse suspicion. A hundred yards ahead, two men stood in the shadow of the wall. He watched as one of them lumbered over to the gate and into a circle of lamplight. Too fat to carry out an execution, he thought, and if that was Koenig, his companion would be McKee.

'You're late,' they grumbled, but McKee shook his hand warmly. They were a little on edge but that was only to be expected at the dock gates. There was nothing else remarkable in their demeanour, no awkwardness, no hidden glances, no reluctance to look him in the eye.

Koenig's contact opened the wicket at exactly midnight. The men from Green's were as obliging as ever; McKee carried the explosives on to the ship and Wolff was permitted to place them in holds fore and aft. 'Simplest so far,' McKee observed, handing his gold badge back to their guide; 'experts, so we are.'

Hans was waiting in the Ford. 'I'm to take you to Frau Held's,' he said in an efficient monotone. Wolff didn't argue. It seemed safe to assume that an invitation to sprawl on the great lady's leather couch and sip champagne meant they were not intending to finish him off tonight. The little spy was still in his hiding place, hat wedged between stiff thighs, eyes wide open and resentful at the indignity of the death meted out to him. Wolff shook his head vigorously to clear the image from his thoughts and leant forward to stare out blankly at the passing streets.

At the club, Martha greeted him in person, squeezing his hands like an affectionate aunt. Their Swiss friend was waiting in her private drawing room, she informed him with the disingenuous smile of the demi-monde. 'And there is someone else who is hoping to see you – a certain young lady. You haven't visited Clara for a while, Mr de Witt.' She contrived to sound hurt.

Rintelen was standing in front of the fire, gazing at a silver photograph frame. 'Herr de Witt.' He placed it carefully back on the mantelpiece between a pair of china swains. The room was chintzy, the paper a gaudy pink like a doll's-house bedroom. 'The evening was a success?' Rintelen enquired. He might have been speaking of a musical soirée.

'An effortless performance, yes.'

'But you have hurt yourself . . .' Rintelen gestured with a peculiar chopping motion of his open palm to a chair. 'You must sit down – please.'

'I caught my leg against something on the ship. It's nothing,' Wolff replied. It was damn careless of him; what was he thinking? 'Look, why do you want to see me?'

'Champagne?' Rintelen lifted the bottle from an ice bucket and poured two glasses. 'We must celebrate our victories, even the small ones.' He wiped his hands carefully on a damp cloth, fastidious in everything always, dapper in his fashionable suit, his white waistcoat and Ascot tie. Damn the fellow. 'I'd like you to visit Boston for me,' he said, gazing down at Wolff from the hearthrug. 'McKee has collected some more Irishmen, but they'll need to be . . .' he paused to slip into precise English, '. . . shown the ropes.'

Wolff nodded slowly. 'All right.'

'Good. On Friday then.' Rintelen lifted his champagne, examined its colour, dancing in the firelight, then raised it to his thin lips.

'Is that all?' Wolff enquired impatiently.

'More champagne?'

No. No thank you. Look, it's late. Two o'clock.'

'But you will stay here, of course.'

'No.'

'As you wish.' He had settled in the chair next to Wolff. 'Sir Roger's servant, Christensen – when did you last see him?'

Wolff said he couldn't be sure, but not for many weeks, perhaps September.

'Do you trust him?'

'No, but he's Sir Roger's,' Wolff hesitated, 'friend.'

Rintelen nodded deliberately. 'Berlin says he has spoken to the British.'

'Oh?' The band round Wolff's chest tightened a notch or two. Slowly, casually, he sipped his champagne, hiding for a few seconds behind the glass before lowering it slowly. 'What has that got to do with me?'

Rintelen raised his eyebrows. 'You are angry?'

'Tired, that's all.'

'I see. Well, Christensen admits he has been in contact with a British diplomat called Findlay. In Christiania, I believe. Berlin has had its suspicions for a while and wants to know if you think he is . . .'

'Clever enough to be a spy?' Wolff interrupted. 'I hardly know him – just the journey here; I didn't care for him much. He does have . . .' he sighed and reached into his jacket for his cigarette case; '. . . it isn't important.'

'It might be.' Rintelen leant forward earnestly, his rodent eyes chasing about Wolff's face again. 'Please finish.'

'Just, he has a great hold on Sir Roger's affections.'

'Yes,' Rintelen said, examining his well-manicured hands. 'He told his interrogators the English offered him money to spy on Sir Roger but he refused. What else can he say? Count Nadolny is concerned for our operations. He wants to know who Christensen has been in contact with – both here and in Berlin before he came.'

Wolff shook his head sharply. 'No idea. As I say, I barely knew him.'

Rintelen was gazing at Wolff intently. Something sharp in his manner suggested he knew more than he was prepared to say. 'I'll ask Hinsch to make some enquiries,' he said at last.

'Good, yes.' Wolff perched at the edge of the chair. 'If there's nothing else?'

'I wonder if . . .' Rintelen hesitated. 'No, not now, Herr de Witt. Not tonight.' He smiled weakly. 'You must rest your leg.'

Hans drove him most of the way home. The last two blocks he limped, half expecting to find a shadowy figure stamping snow outside the library. But the street was empty, no one had broken into his apartment, no one had slipped a secret message beneath his door: thank the Lord.

The following morning, he was woken from troubled sleep by the telephone and a cautious voice inviting him to Mr Schmidt's residence to discuss another offer of work. *Would it be possible at two?*

Thwaites' safe apartment was on the west side of Central Park at the top of a new block that was respectable but busy enough to be anonymous; home for the most part to aspiring young couples with money for only one domestic and old ladies put out to grass by their families.

'My dear fellow,' Wiseman came forward to greet him, 'well done. Let me shake your hand. A marvellous haul. Come and sit down. You're limping, are you hurt? White, a chair if you please.'

They were gathered at a table in its small sitting room – Gaunt, too – before them papers, pocketbook, the photographs he'd taken on the ship. To judge by the cigarette smoke, they must have been poring over the stuff for a couple of hours at least. It had been no great matter to decipher the ledger, Wiseman informed him, sliding a photograph and a hand-written transcript across the table. 'Norman, why don't you take us through it?'

'Some you know already,' Thwaites observed, grinding his cigarette into an ashtray. 'Thousands of dollars to the Clan for its help with the strikes and with the sabotage campaign, payments to Larkin and some of the other agitators; to three detective agencies – Green's here in New York, and this . . .' he said, running a bony forefinger down the flimsy, 'May the third this year to a chap called McCarthy for what friend Albert calls *a service to His Majesty at the Anderson Chemical Company in Wallington* – that's in New Jersey.'

'There was an explosion at Anderson's on that day – three men killed,' Gaunt interjected. As usual, he looked out of sorts. 'You see – I told you it was important we lay our hands on these files.'

'And how right you were, Captain.' Wiseman smiled at him patiently.

'Five days later another payment,' Thwaites continued;

'this time *to Dr Scheele for scientific services* . . . your Dr Ziethen?'

'There's a contract?' Wolff nodded to the photographs. 'You have an address and a company name.'

'We're checking. The thing is, a few days later the SS *Langdale* was damaged by fire. The doctor's special scientific service perhaps? Almost all these entries in the ledger . . .' he lifted the sheets, '. . . can be matched to some misfortune aboard one of our ships or in a munitions factory. May the tenth: *explosion at Dupont in Carneys Point*; May the thirteenth: *SS Samland catches fire at sea*; May the twenty-fifth: *another explosion at Dupont*, and so on and so on . . .'

'Yes,' Wiseman frowned. 'Rintelen's been busier than we thought, and for longer.'

Gaunt dumped his hands on the table, leant forward to speak but changed his mind, content instead to glare at them defensively.

'And the source at the bank?' Wolff enquired.

Wiseman said, 'Working on that, aren't we, Norman? Friend of a friend on the board of the National City, you know – he's making discreet enquiries. One of the clerks churning out munitions purchases – Irish or German, I shouldn't wonder.'

'Agent B-1 in Albert's ledger,' Thwaites chipped in. 'He should be easy to spot because he'll be wearing the best suit in the bank.'

The audit trail was pretty straightforward. It wandered up and down the East Coast, to Canada and even to someone with an Irish name in San Francisco. 'No limit to the fellow's ambition, really,' Wiseman remarked with admiration. 'And this chap Hilken in Baltimore – know anything about him?'

Wolff said he didn't.

'Norddeutscher representative in America,' Wiseman declared. 'Father before him too. Rich it seems, and Norman's newspaper pals say he's thick with the German smart set. So why is he picking our friend Albert's pockets, eh? Tea, anyone?' Half turning to the door, he shouted: 'Do the honours, would you, White?'

'He'll be paying for German sailors caught by the blockade,' rumbled Gaunt. 'Look, what are we going to do—'

'That's what I thought at first,' interrupted Wiseman, lifting his hand apologetically, 'but it seems not. My banking friend tells me those payments come from an account in the company name. Is it possible . . .' he paused, his moustache playing above a clever smile, '. . . well, that he's our Delmar – if not – the contact to Delmar? We've talked about another show, two networks with the same old woman holding the purse strings. Albert counts everyone else's coppers, why not Delmar's too?'

'Delmar, Delmar, Delmar.' Gaunt pushed his chair back impatiently. 'Could be nobody! Just a code word – let's talk about Rintelen. I think it's time we told the Ambassador. He can take it to the President.'

The kitchen door opened and White reversed through it with the tray.

'Over here, yes, on the table,' said Wiseman with a sigh of what may have been exasperation. 'Clear those photographs, old boy. Sugar?' he asked, chin raised enquiringly to Gaunt.

'Two.'

Gaunt sat forward again and the table instantly felt smaller.

'I'm sure you're right, Captain,' Wiseman cooed, 'only, our masters do have a bee in their bonnet about old Delmar. Won't let me rest. I think we should take a little look at Mr Hilken. Keep 'em happy, what? No lemon, I'm afraid. Here we are,' he presented Gaunt with a china cup; 'damn it, no cake either – what were you thinking, man?'

White said he was very sorry.

'As for Rintelen,' Wiseman continued, 'I'm sure the President has more pressing concerns. No. We thought, drip, drip the story to Thwaites' newspaper pals and the city police.'

'Once they've got it you'll lose the bugger.' Gaunt had turned a high colour. 'You must . . .'

'Politics,' said Wiseman, pushing a cup in front of Wolff. 'Bound to go down badly – Huns blowing up factories and ships, interfering with commerce. Public won't like them turning the country into a battleground – politicians won't like it with an election round the corner. Small steps, Captain, let's help America make up her mind which side she's on – nudge her in the right direction.'

If the police arrested the Dark Invader, things would become messy, he said, glancing at Wolff. He wasn't the sort to blab under pressure but the city's finest could be very persuasive. Putting him out of business mattered the most.

'Enough here to see off old Gaché and his business, Scheele, Koenig and those rogues in the detective agencies,' he remarked, stirring his tea slowly. 'As for the Irish – well, it ain't a crime to take German money – look at all the fellows on Wall Street – the best we can hope to do is embarrass them, there's nothing we can magic up here,' he waved his teaspoon over the table, 'nothing that will put more than the foot soldiers away. And we mustn't drag you into all this,' he said, turning to gaze at Wolff; 'you might look like a provocateur. We've got to keep our hands clean. Don't want the President thinking we've been flaunting the laws of his country too. Besides,' he paused, stroking the end of his moustache thoughtfully, 'we need to keep you in play.'

Wolff didn't reply. His first thought was the body of the little spy; Rintelen would surely know by now. Strangely, his second was of Laura.

'Sebastian,' prompted Thwaites.

'You look tired,' said Wiseman, oozing sympathy. 'Your leg? Must let a doctor have a look at you. Accident?'

Wolff lifted his eyes to the ceiling for a second. 'I had to kill one of their men,' he said, dropping them to Wiseman's face.

'Oh?' the baronet returned his gaze impassively.

'Messy business. He stabbed me. I stabbed him. Anyway, if they've found his body the game's up for de Witt.'

For a few seconds no one spoke, Thwaites shuffling his papers, Gaunt swilling the dregs of his tea. They must have killed, thought Wolff, just not a man in a bowler hat, not close enough to smell his breath or feel it hot on your cheek.

'Can we move him?' Gaunt asked at last.

Wolff said he didn't think so; it was probably too late.

'And von Rintelen, have you seen him since?'

'To drink champagne;' and he told them of the risk he'd taken in making the rendezvous with McKee, of the dockyard and boarding the ship, and the meeting at Martha's. While he was speaking, Gaunt rose from the table to prowl the sitting room like a caged bear. 'What were you thinking, man?' he blurted at last, unable to contain his anger. 'Isn't one enough!'

'You mean the ship?'

'Of course I mean the bloody ship,' he shouted.

Thwaites intervened: 'Steady on . . .' but he was swept aside as Gaunt's pent-up resentment broke in a torrent. 'You gave Wolff too much rope,' he declared, addressing himself to Wiseman. 'Now this – another ship, another bloody . . .'

'It hasn't exploded yet,' the baronet observed calmly.

'But he shouldn't have put us—'

Wolff slammed the palm of his left hand on the table: 'It won't explode.' He rested his head in his right hand. 'Look, that's why I did it. I couldn't trust you . . .' the words tumbled wearily from him, '. . . not after the *Blackness*. Did you mean to? I wonder. I couldn't take the risk, and they'd have asked someone else – and it was easy, you see, they knew it would be . . .'

Thwaites touched his elbow gently. 'Sorry, old boy, don't have a clue what you're talking about.'

'I pierced the end of the detonator.'

'The cigar bomb?'

'Drained the acid, so if you want some evidence for the police, you can arrange for the detonators to be found on the ship – she's the *Linton*, West Quay . . . sails tomorrow – there's just time.'

No one spoke for a few seconds, Wiseman easing back from the table, his languid gaze settling on Gaunt.

'Jolly clever of you, Sebastian,' said Thwaites, slapping him heartily on the back; 'clever and – well, bloody brave.'

'Hear, hear,' Wiseman chorused.

Gaunt hesitated, then offered his hand. 'I say, sorry, Wolff.'

Wolff didn't care much for his apology. He didn't care very much for anything. The pain in his leg was worse, throbbing bone-deep; it was almost impossible to think of anything else. Their conversation he heard in snatches as if at a distance, barely marking his consciousness, the page blank, his eyes wandering from hands to faces – Gaunt fidgeting with a pen, Wiseman's enigmatic smile – as if through the frosted bottom of a bottle.

Thwaites bent to his ear: 'You're coming with me. We need to get you to a doctor.'

'I'm fine. I'll stay in bed,' he muttered thickly. 'Honestly – fine. Can White arrange a taxicab?'

'Norman's right,' said Wiseman firmly. 'Must keep you safe. We need you, the work's not over yet;' this with a teasing smile.

'You can afford to disappear for a few days. Goodness, by tomorrow all Captain von Rintelen's friends will be doing the same.'

25

The News in the *World*

'C AREFUL WHAT YOU say, Doctor,' Hilken cautioned. Albert's fear seemed to crackle down the telephone line. A mistake to trust so many secrets to an inflexible and guileless man. Breathing like a blacksmith's bellows. When he found his voice, it was thin and querulous.

'Have you seen it? They have it all – almost all . . .'

'Pull yourself together, please,' Hilken bristled angrily. 'Tell me – carefully, mind – who has what?'

'In this morning's *New York World*, my name, and payments linking me . . .'

'I'll read the newspaper.' What was he thinking? 'A time for cool heads, Doctor.'

But the second Hilken hung up the receiver his own thoughts clouded with the worst possibilities, and by the time his driver fetched the motor car to the front of the house he was on the point of ordering his wife to pack their cases. He felt trapped behind the glass in the back and insisted on sitting beside his chauffeur. Gazing out on streets he'd known since he was a child, he trembled with resentment at the thought that he might have to leave. Life was good in Baltimore, business was good, a fine house in a streetcar suburb, the country club, a pillar of the German community: the name Hilken meant something in the city. I shouldn't have become involved, he told himself.

But what choice did I have? He was an American and a German but not, like Dilger, he was 'an American first'.

The Hansa Haus was a brick-and-timber folly in the high renaissance style, with gable windows set in a red-tiled roof, the shields of the Hanseatic cities painted on its walls. It had opened just before the war, the new home to German interests in the city, just a few streets from the port. Norddeutscher Lloyd was on the first floor, across the corridor from the Consulate. It was half past seven in the morning and the New York papers were delivered at a quarter to eight. Hilken counted the minutes in yards, pacing the length of his office until his assistant knocked lightly and entered with a copy of the *World*. '*Sabotage*' and '*German*' jumped out from the front page and a picture of the spy '*Mr Gaché*'.

'That's it then,' he muttered, spreading it open on his desk. But glancing through the story he found no mention of his name, and when he took the trouble to read it properly he felt a fool. It was the end for von Rintelen's network, all right. There were details of attacks and of the bomb maker – a Dr Scheele of Hoboken – some Irish names, a reference to the military attaché, von Papen – it wasn't clear why – and beneath an unflattering picture of Albert, the caption: '*German commercial attaché bankrolls destruction*'. The investigation into the sabotage ring was being led by a Captain Tunney of the New York Police Department Bomb Squad, '*an officer of great experience and tenacity*'.

An editorial called for robust action to stop Germany waging war in America. '*The time may come when this country will be forced to take sides*,' warned its writer. '*This illegal campaign has only succeeded in bringing the point of decision closer. It has cost British and American lives but no one has lost more than Germany.*'

'So says the *World*,' Hilken muttered in disgust; the newspaper was in the British camp – most of them were. He'd been expecting something like this to happen – too many people seemed to know the Dark Invader's business. It might have been a great deal worse. If that was all they had, he was safe. There were no references to the only man who tied the networks: Hinsch. Berlin would expect them to batten the hatches for a few weeks, then resume their operation in the New Year. But a salutary lesson, he reflected, wiping newsprint from his damp hands; someone had signed one of those damn contracts of Albert's, taken his money, then squealed to the press and the police.

Sitting at the desk, Hilken wrote two short letters, the first to Albert advising him to go to ground for a while, to avoid the Broadway office, the embassy and anyone named in the story, and under no circumstances speak of their arrangements by telephone; the second to Hinsch, suggesting the same. Then he instructed his assistant to send a man to New York with both letters: 'but take this telegram yourself.' He scribbled Dr Dilger's name and address in Chevy Chase on an envelope. 'The message is simply: *Laurel 1700*. Do you have that?'

For a while, he tried to settle to the business of the shipping line. He took lunch at a downtown restaurant with his father and they spoke of the war in Europe and the rise in shipping stocks. In the afternoon he telephoned his wife to say he would be late home and lost his temper with a junior clerk who had paid too much for repairs to one of the line's ships. But churning always in his thoughts, the glass phials locked in the safe on the floor above, the newspaper picture of Gaché startled in a hotel lobby, and for the first time a nagging fear of exposure. At three o'clock he locked his desk and door and, dispensing for once with the services of his driver, set out in the motor car for the Washington highway.

*

New York police headquarters was an extravagant beaux arts cathedral of a building in the heart of Little Italy, the city fathers hoping to impress the divine majesty of the law on the criminal class. Come unto me, Norman Thwaites reflected, gazing up at its new copper dome from the corner of Center and Broome; come, and I will throw you into jail. It reminded him of the basilica they were building in Paris to atone for old socialist sins. He didn't care for the French. He didn't care for Bolsheviks, Jews, gypsies, or Negroes, and there were a lot more of them in New York than there used to be. Some were joining the Police Department, Tunney had told him, but not as many as the Irish. He'd met the captain of the Bomb Squad before the war at the old headquarters on Mulberry Street where Teddy Roosevelt had made his name as a commissioner. In those days the *World* had paid all his bills and on its behalf he had wasted hours in cheap cop saloons trying to wring stories from Tunney. It was not – as the editor-in-chief had remarked caustically – 'a productive relationship'. Things were different now, new times, new headquarters, and he limped into its white marble lobby not as a supplicant but at the invitation of the captain and the deputy commissioner.

'Sit yourself down here, Norman. Coffee?' Tunney pulled a chair away from his desk. 'No, let's have something stronger?'

'Coffee.'

'Coffee, yes.' Tunney stepped over to the door and spoke to a clerk in the outer office. Thickset, early forties, but already struggling to contain his neck in his high-buttoned uniform, he had a square no-nonsense face and shopkeeper moustache. He moved and spoke like a man who was proud to have begun on the street and wanted you to know it.

'Was the paper grateful?' he asked, pulling his chair closer.

'Most grateful. Did you like the reference to "*an officer of great experience and tenacity*"?'

'I'm afraid that officer has lost your "Mr Gaché". He sailed yesterday – I was mad about it, ready to knock heads . . .' Tunney leant forward a little, gazing intently at Thwaites, '. . . but you don't seem very surprised – or upset.'

'No.'

'Well, Norman, I was,' Tunney said hotly, 'until I read this.' He nudged a black loose-leaf memorandum book across the desk. 'This is Koenig's. Found it in his apartment. Lots of code names and initials – know most of 'em now we've worked him in the interrogation room.' He paused, his eyes narrowing aggressively at the recollection of the scene. 'One of ours was being paid by him, you see. It's there . . .' He gestured towards the book on Thwaites' lap. 'Agent 6 or B.P. turns out to be Otto Mottola of the NYPD. Tipped off von Rintelen. The bomb maker Scheele's gone too.'

'The ship?'

'Holland America Line, the *Noordam*.'

Thwaites took out his own pocketbook and made a note.

The clerk brought in coffee and shuffled round the desk with cups as Tunney described the course of his investigation. They had caught the spy at the bank with a copy of a British cable in his pocket. 'Scheindel, from Bavaria and the Bronx. He was making good money – twenty-five dollars a week on top of his salary, but it wasn't enough – he wanted an Iron Cross as well.' Tunney grunted with amusement. 'Probably deserved one.'

'Dr Albert?'

'Washington says "stay away",' he said with a resigned shrug.

'And the Irish?'

Tunney frowned, his chin dropping to his chest. His collar looked even tighter. 'We've dealt with the detective agencies . . .'

'Our own people are going to handle security on the quays,' Thwaites interjected.

'If you mean Clan na Gael – it isn't a crime to take money from the Germans. You British have your friends on the payroll in this city, I reckon. Must have got your information on von Rintelen from somewhere.' Tunney pushed his chair back suddenly, rose and turned to the window. Winter dusk was settling on the city, the lights hard and bright in the office buildings on the opposite side of Grand Street. He's Irish too, Thwaites reflected; or what passes for it in this city.

'We're friends, aren't we, Norman?' Tunney asked. It didn't sound as if he cared one way or the other. 'Because I know you're holding out on me.' He turned back from the window. 'All right, you're doing your job, protecting your man, but—'

'What do you want?'

'I want your informer to tell me what happened to my man, Kelly.'

Thwaites inspected his nails for a moment. 'You had someone inside?'

'Not inside. A hustler, a con man, ran a few errands for us – a familiar face on the street. He was working a tip-off.' Tunney had sat at the desk again and now leant forward over his crossed arms, his uniform rustling tight at the shoulders. 'They fished him out of the bay with a boathook four days ago . . . I don't like that. Kelly was working for me. Koenig swears he knows nothing, no one knows – but your man might.'

'There was someone who helped us,' Thwaites admitted cautiously. 'This man of yours, he drowned?'

'Murdered. Stabbed in the heart.'

'I see.' Thwaites cleared his throat. 'I'm sorry.' His eyes were fixed on the policeman's shield. 'Of course, I'll ask him, Captain. If I can reach him. After all this . . . ' he lifted Koenig's file, '. . . he will be keeping his head down. They might be chasing him.'

*

Laurel was a dormitory town on the Royal Blue with nothing to distinguish it from half a dozen others along the line but a sanatorium for the treatment of nervous diseases and a thoroughbred racetrack. At weekends in summer, punters from the capital caught a train to its little brick station, then a bus to the course; on every other morning the town's menfolk made the journey in the opposite direction, returning at seven in the evening. During the day the station was haunted by an old man in dirty blue denims who blew his whistle, spat and offered advice whether it was asked for or no. The temperature close to freezing, old Joe hovered at the stove in the ticket hall, puffing on a corncob pipe as if he'd stepped from the pages of a Mark Twain story. Anxious to avoid him, Hilken parked behind the station and sat at the wheel gazing into the darkness for a plume of steam. He expected Dilger to be on the 4.45 from Washington. He was bound to be jumpy, reflected Hilken wryly, remembering the state he had worked himself into.

But the doctor confounded his expectation. Tipping his hat to a lady, summoning Joe and the cart for her trunk, he sauntered through the steam and smoke with his hands in his overcoat pocket, the Good Samaritan at ease with his neighbours. Hilken stepped from the motor car to greet him.

'Pleasant journey, Doctor?' he enquired, for something to say.

'I wasn't followed, if that's what you mean,' Dilger replied laconically.

They sat side by side in the front of the car, a copy of the *World* open on Dilger's knees.

'I think we do nothing for now, do you agree?' Hilken said.

'And if Hinsch is in tomorrow's paper?'

'He will keep his mouth shut. It's in his interests . . .' Hilken sighed heavily. 'You know, we always said this might – would – happen in time. Berlin said so too.'

'Yes.'

They sat in silence for a while, their breath slipping down the windscreen, then Hilken said: 'You should come to Baltimore for Christmas.'

'The problem we spoke of before . . . Hinsch's man with the disease . . .'

'The man in the hospital? That was dealt with satisfactorily.' Hilken shook off his driving gloves and blew into his hands. 'I'll tell Hinsch, no more. Keep away from the Irish. Until the dust settles. Perhaps after Christmas. The Secret Service and the police will take a close look at all the German sailors here – it's the end for the *Friedrich der Grosse*. But there's no reason to assume it will go further – to Baltimore.'

'Is it worth it, Hilken? What have we achieved?' Dilger shook his head slowly. 'I would have done better service for Germany in a hospital.'

'Doctor, three ships in the last month. A thousand remounts lost to the Allies – and Rintelen's network did some good work – look.' He snatched the newspaper from Dilger's knees, peering in the gloom at a list on the front page. 'Ships, the Dupont factories, Canadian Car and Foundry – small things but it isn't finished yet.' It was foolish but he was angry with Dilger for sharing his doubts. 'Your Count Nadolny chose you – and the letter you told me about, from the Chief of the General Staff – Falkenhayn?' Clumsily, he was trying to stiffen not just the doctor's resolve but his own. 'It's *our* duty to Germany,' he said resentfully. 'And, Doctor, in a few months you'll be able to leave the United States.'

The thought hung in the cold air between them. A train – the twenty past the hour – was pulling into the station. The next one from Baltimore would be carrying the first commuters home.

'You're risking a great deal, Paul, I know,' Dilger acknowledged apologetically. 'You know I'll do my duty. It was never the Count's intention that I should stay for long. I'm going to train someone to do the work when I'm gone.'

'Can you?'

'It isn't difficult.'

Hilken nodded. 'As you wish, but do nothing for now. Visit Frau Hempel in New York. Come to me, your sister can come too. There's always a good party at the Baltimore Germania Club.'

They talked for a little longer and made half-hearted plans for a second visit to the opera, perhaps a weekend at the Hilken beach house on Long Island or the Dilger farm in Greenfield. At a quarter past the hour, old Joe stepped out of the ticket office again and a few minutes later the track began to sing.

'I'll catch this one,' said Dilger flatly.

'And the glasses at the Hansa Haus?' He'd just remembered the phials in the safe.

'Throw them in the sea or leave them in the safe – as you wish.'

'Simple to replace, you say?'

'If you know what you're doing.' Dilger had opened the car door and was perched at the edge of the seat. 'I'm going to instruct my brother.'

'Your brother?' Hilken didn't disguise his astonishment. 'Is he a doctor?'

'He's a brewer.'

'A brewer?'

'Yes. A good one.' Dilger stepped down stiffly, smoothing his coat then rising on his toes to encourage feeling back into his feet. 'Don't worry, Hilken, he's perfectly capable.'

'And he can be trusted?'

'He's a good German.'

And once you have taught him to culture your diseases you will leave your simple brother the brewer and your simple sister and return to Germany with your opera singer. Doctor, Hilken reflected as he watched Dilger walk to the station, you're more cold-blooded than I thought.

'The Secret Service wants to kick it into the long grass,' Wiseman said to Thwaites in the grill room at the Astor that evening. 'It's made 'em look foolish. And the President's people don't want anything to raise the temperature with Germany this close to election year. They're happy to leave it to the police.' He put down his knife and fork and dabbed his moustache with his napkin. 'How about your Captain Tunney?'

'He wants help.' Thwaites paused. 'It may be awkward.'

'Oh?' Wiseman enquired, turning to catch the eye of the waiter. 'Ask the sommelier to bring another, would you?' he commanded, flicking his hand at the bottle.

'Tunney's lost one of his runners,' Thwaites explained. 'Chap called Kelly. Thinks he was murdered by Rintelen's crew. Sore affronted.'

'Perhaps Wolff can help—'

Thwaites interrupted. 'Sorry, I should have been clearer. This fellow, Kelly, well, he was stabbed – through the heart apparently.'

Wiseman checked the glass he was raising to his lips. 'Ah.' It hovered there for a few seconds as he considered the implications, then he took a sip. 'And he hasn't any idea who—'

'No. But he would appreciate our assistance. He's a determined sort, I'm afraid. I think he's going to worry away at it.'

'Kelly, you say.' Wiseman was gazing reflectively into the body of the restaurant, crystal twinkling in the candlelight, gentlemen in white tie, their ladies in satin, a murmur of contentment and money, punctuated by the ring of silver. 'Wonder what it is like to kill a fella with a name,' he remarked at last. 'Have you? Don't think we should mention it to Wolff. His conscience is a little fragile.'

26

Christmas Ceasefire

Rest, the doctor ordered, so they moved Wolff to a boarding house on Lexington, Thwaites' valet to play nurse. For a time he drifted in submarine darkness, babbling of home and a man in a derby hat. But by the third day he was well enough to hold his tongue and order his thoughts, turning his back on blue hills to stroll along Broadway, a free man, engineer, a speculator – he needed some risk – with his particular friend, Miss Laura McDonnell of Philadelphia. Head on pillow, turned to the bright window, he wanted her as a man desires a pretty woman, but for her faith too: in the pursuit of liberty and the ruin of great empires, a just and equal society; for her conviction that no other cause was worthy of great sacrifice. The nature of her brave new order didn't impress Wolff as much as her belief that it would be built in time. 'Bolshie,' Thwaites and the wise men of the half-world they shared would say, but Wolff didn't care for their opinion.

On the sixth day he discharged himself from their care to resume life as Jan de Witt, and he was pleased to.

'You're still here then,' Laura said, when he telephoned.

'I would have called but – well, you must have seen the papers.'

There was a long silence.

'We could meet for lunch,' he ventured.

'I'm glad you're safe. But my friends say I—'

Wolff interrupted. 'You don't sound glad.'

'Oh, it's so difficult on the telephone,' she blurted in exasperation. 'Our friends are anxious. Trust no one, they say, until we can be sure – and it's been weeks since . . .'

'I know. I'm sorry,' he said, with complete sincerity.

Another silence, but when she broke it he heard the old mischief in her voice: 'And I'm busy. Tomorrow I have a meeting in the morning, and I'm visiting Mrs Newman in the afternoon . . .' she paused deliberately, '. . . at three o'clock.'

'I see.' He smiled. 'Thank you.'

The windows of his East Street apartment were opaque with frost, the stove cold and his bed unmade. He scraped away a square with a penknife and examined the stiff faces of passersby, the empty doorways and windows opposite. 'Trust no one,' the Clan had warned Laura. So they were still looking for their traitor. Wolff had toyed with the idea of moving to somewhere safer uptown for Christmas but standing in the bare sitting room in his overcoat he resolved to leave at once. Just two small cases and he clattered down the stair to his landlord for the last time, handed in the key, a few dollars, and as cover, a post office address for mail he wasn't expecting to receive. Then he took a cab to Grand Central and another to the Plaza Hotel, where he paid for a comfortable six-dollar-a-night room with a bath.

The following morning he telephoned Casement's sister. She was pleased to hear from him, but resentful that he'd neglected her. 'So much to discuss . . . Roddy was asking after you . . . if you can come to tea . . .'

Punctual, at three, he lifted the broken gate in the picket fence and crunched down the path. Nina Newman was watching for him and opened the door as he was shaking the snow from his hat.

'Laura is visiting, did I say?' she asked, taking his overcoat. 'She's just arrived.'

Wolff had prepared with care: a sober grey suit and Tyrian purple tie – just a hint of something radical. Combing oil into his hair, he'd discovered a suggestion of silver at his temples that left him out of sorts, then ashamed of his vanity. She was so much younger, perhaps fifteen years.

In the middle of the little sitting room, the same dusty armchair throne, but this time Laura was to hold court. Still pink from the chill, she rose to greet him with an arch smile. 'Quite a coincidence.'

'A happy one,' he replied.

'So much has happened, Mr de Witt. So much,' Nina Newman gushed, directing him to the chair at Laura's side and taking the one opposite. 'Roddy's in despair. It's the Germans.' She leant across to the mantelpiece for an envelope she'd left in anticipation. 'He writes that *". . . no man was ever in such a false position . . . I'm sick at heart and in my soul . . . swines and cads of the first order."* The Germans are killing him, Mr de Witt – not the people, of course – the government . . . and that man, his valet – Christensen – says the British asked him to spy on Roddy – to murder him, I shouldn't wonder.' She paused to contemplate this perfidy with furrowed brow, eyes deep set and brooding like her brother's.

'I'm sure he's safe.' Laura touched her hand. 'Don't you think so, Mr de Witt?'

'In Germany, yes,' Wolff replied distantly, his thoughts still with a slippery bastard called Christensen. 'If he doesn't do something—'

'And who can believe that, that . . . Norwegian – Christensen?' Nina interjected, twisting the end of her handkerchief. 'What does Roddy see in him? He's a thief, duplicitous – that business with his wife . . . he's in Berlin and Roddy's too sweet-natured . . .' She rattled on unhappily for a few minutes more before excusing herself to make some tea.

'No one in the Clan trusts him,' Laura observed, touching her hair, drawing his gaze.

'Roger?'

'No!' she exclaimed indignantly. 'Adler Christensen. Only— ' she bit the corner of her lip, uncertain whether she should say more.

'Berlin doesn't trust Christensen,' he prompted.

'Oh?'

'Von Rintelen said so. Asked my opinion.'

A sharp little shake of her head, auburn hair catching the light from the window: 'First the brigade in Germany, then Christensen; some people are questioning his judgement. It was Roger who asked the Clan to help your German friends. Did you know?'

'No,' he lied.

'Yes,' she said quietly, guiltily. 'Perhaps I've said too much.' Her sea-green eyes were earnest and beautiful. 'But you knew Christensen – is he a traitor? Did he know about . . . well, all those things in the newspaper?'

'You don't approve of sabotage?' He raised his brow quizzically. 'At Liberty Island you pointed to the Black Tom yard and said—'

'I remember. But has Mr Gaché's adventure helped us – Ireland, I mean? I don't think so.'

Wolff gave a small shrug. 'If you get your guns, and if—'

He was interrupted by the chink of china, and the conversation belonged to Nina again. She had read the stories of German sabotage too – fussing with their cups – and she was sure her Roddy wouldn't approve. Wolff caught Laura's eye but she frowned and looked away, her hands clasped in her lap, pulling her skirt tighter over her thighs than she might have wished if she'd known.

'The Germans are going to give us a bad name,' Nina exclaimed.

'She doesn't know Roger as well as she thinks,' Wolff remarked later, as he walked with Laura to the station. With the last of the light the snow was turning to ice, the sidewalk treacherous, and she accepted the offer of his arm.

'Perhaps in this one thing,' she said defensively.

In more than this, Laura, he thought with a wry smile.

'Gaché, I mean von Rintelen, has gone, but I expect you know,' she continued.

'I guessed.'

'But you're still here . . .'

'Yes, I am.'

'Have the police spoken to you?'

He'd been expecting her to ask: 'Tell the Clan "no".'

'That's unfair.' She shook her arm free.

'But your friends in Clan na Gael think there's a spy?' He turned to face her.

'Mr Devoy and the rest of the committee say so.'

'And they think it's me,' he prompted.

'No,' she said too quickly, avoiding his gaze. 'Everyone is under suspicion.'

'I proved my worth.'

'I'm sorry. It's horrible,' and she began to walk on alone.

'Hey,' he followed her, offering his arm again. 'For what it's worth, I don't think there is a spy. Rintelen was careless, that's all.'

'Can we talk about something else,' she pleaded; 'please.'

So Wolff asked her to join him for dinner – 'the day after tomorrow,' she said. Then he told her he'd moved to the Plaza

313

– 'Please say nothing to your friends'– and he could see she was uncomfortable with their first secret, this small conspiracy of silence, but not enough to refuse. Even in this I'm a spy, he reflected, sipping whisky in the solitude of his hotel room. What can she see in this fellow, de Witt? Perhaps some principle – he was anointed by Casement – perhaps danger and the pull a woman feels for a certain sort of man, an Antonio with his ice-cream cart.

Dinner at the Café Francis; Laura in a white evening gown from Paris, a gift from her father, she said, because he was ready to pay a king's ransom for her to look like a 'proper' lady. They were easy together and de Witt spoke as much truth about the past as he dared, but for the most part he listened as she talked with passion of her hopes. 'I admire you,' he declared, 'you're so full of life;' and she blushed with embarrassment and pleasure at the warmth in his voice.

The following day, they went shopping on Broadway, and the day after, Wolff heard her speak at a women's suffrage meeting and lost his temper when a couple of Christmas drunks had the temerity to heckle.

'We're having dinner with Laura's father – the Catholic Club of all places,' he confided to Thwaites when they met at the safe apartment. 'New territory for me.'

'Oh? Business or pleasure?' Thwaites enquired slyly.

'I'm fond of her,' he said, rising to pour another drink; 'so, yes – pleasure and a little business. I'm enjoying New York. Don't you think I deserve that?' He brandished the bottle. 'For you?'

Thwaites shook his head. 'She may be spying on you.'

Head bent, forefinger to his lip, he grappled with this thought for a moment: 'She's not duplicitous. But indirectly – yes, it's possible. Who knows what her Clan comrades ask about me?

I expect they're like us.' He smiled and raised his drink in an ironic salute.

'Won't give you C's lecture, because you gave it to me,' Thwaites replied, contemplating Wolff over the rim of his glass. 'Just hope you know what you're doing.'

'Oh, I do,' he lied. Then, as a sop, 'She's my only way into Irish circles here, and if the Germans kick off another campaign . . .'

But as soon as he floated the thought he was angry with himself – it wasn't how he wanted their friendship to be.

'I say, are you listening?' Thwaites pushed his leg playfully with the end of his stick. 'I'm telling you about your old friend, Hinsch.' He ignored Wolff's sigh. 'He's back in Baltimore. Hilken too. Missing Martha's tarts, I dare say. Oh, Christ!' he exclaimed. 'Fucking Turks.' He was struggling to rise from his chair – 'Sorry about the language, old boy' – perspiring with the effort and pain.

'And you want me to make the contact.'

'I think my leg's worse today,' he muttered, leaning heavily on his stick. 'We're pulling out of Gallipoli, you know. Such a mess. Awful bloody mess.'

'What do you want, Norman?' Wolff stood up and walked over to the drinks tray.

'Another gin.' He slumped back in his armchair. 'I'm so damn stiff. Must be the cold.'

'I mean, Hinsch,' said Wolff, thrusting a glass at him.

'Sir William wants to know what you think.'

'What I think?' Gazing down at Thwaites, his hands in his trouser pockets, easy because for once no one else's opinion mattered: 'I think – wait. It's too soon to do anything – they're still looking for a spy. The Irish know I'm here so the Germans will know too.' Reflecting for a moment: 'Dr Albert's still in New York?'

'Pretending to be the perfect guest.'

'He would be my first contact again.'

'When will you try? The thing is, Sir William has to tell London.'

'I'm sure C's first thought will be for my safety,' Wolff observed with mordant sarcasm. 'Tell him what you like.'

Thwaites shook his head disapprovingly, pulled at his ear, shifted restlessly, sipped his drink, then smiled brightly, like a burst of winter sunshine: 'After Christmas then.'

Wolff was guilty of a small injustice. As C pushed his Rolls from village to village his thoughts often turned to Wolff and his business in America, in particular the troubling text of a signal intercept in the briefcase beside him.

The officer prisoners at Donington called their camp 'the zoo', but to Cumming's eye it was something closer to a palace. He didn't hold with the mollycoddling of the enemy's young gentlemen. The commandant was a fusspot called Picot, no longer fit for active duty. But after bitter coffee and the usual conversation about the war, he had the decency to surrender his office and a roaring fire. Cumming waited with his back to it, pondering whether he should attempt the interview in his indifferent German. From the lawn in front of the hall, excited English and German voices and the thump of a football reminded him of the ceasefire in no-man's-land the previous Christmas. By order there would be no fraternisation with the enemy this year and, after so many thousands more casualties, who would wish to attempt it?

There was a sharp knock at the door and it was opened unbidden by the prisoner. Captain von Rintelen cut a less imposing figure than Cumming had imagined from the descriptions he'd been given, but his smug smile suggested he was quite as self-regarding.

'My name is Smith – Captain Smith,' Cumming declared in English.

'Like the captain of the *Titanic*?' Rintelen remarked. His handshake was limp and careless, and Cumming was startled by the strangled pitch of his voice. Taken with the spirit of the house perhaps he was dressed in a brown wool suit like a country squire. 'You have come from Admiral Hall?' he asked, settling in a chair at the desk. 'How is the Admiral? I enjoyed our conversations. There is a bond between naval officers, the sea, don't you think? It is always the same. After the war we will be friends.'

'Yes, I'm sure. As you say, the camaraderie of the sea.' Cumming smiled benignly. 'And I want to take a little of your time – a few small points I'm hoping to clear up.'

'But you understand my position?' Rintelen opened his arms and his hands in a helpless gesture. 'I'm an officer of His Majesty's navy, there is nothing . . .'

'Yes, yes,' Cumming interrupted. 'Delmar, Captain, who is he?' and dipping into the pocket of his uniform jacket he produced the square of signal paper. 'This was sent from your embassy in Washington two days ago. It says,' he paused, lifting it a little so he could observe Rintelen above its edge; 'it says, "For Count Nadolny, General Staff, Section P. The Irish advise that the New York police are satisfied they have broken network. Delmar now ready to resume operations New York, New Jersey, Boston, Baltimore, Newport News. Require start date for Phase 2. Hilken estimates a cost of 25,000 dollars. Answer immediate. Hinsch."'

Rintelen was still smiling but the corners of his mouth looked a little tighter.

'What do you think of that, Captain?' prompted Cumming. 'Nadolny's running another operation – you knew of course?' He waited for Rintelen to speak, resuming after a few seconds when he showed no inclination to do so. 'You're surprised, I can see that,' he guessed, 'Hinsch didn't tell you. I thought Hinsch was your man.' He paused again. 'Twenty-five thousand dollars. A lot of money. What do you think Delmar is going to do with it?'

Rintelen shrugged. 'I cannot say.'

'Guess.'

'Go shopping on Fifth Avenue?' Rintelen gave a yelp of laughter, but it sounded brittle.

'I think Delmar's network in America was more important to Berlin than yours,' Cumming observed. Perhaps Rintelen agreed because he was uncharacteristically silent. Impossible to shut the fellow up, Admiral Hall had said, but too clever to let something of consequence slip.

'Come on, come on.' Cumming banged his stick down sharply on the brightly polished parquet floor. 'Do you know Delmar or don't you?'

'Surely you would not expect me to say so if I did,' he replied stiffly.

Cumming glared at him for a moment, then shuffling awkwardly through the narrow gap between the wall and the desk, lowered himself into the commandant's chair. The football match was over and the prisoners were being summoned to lunch by handbell like the pupils at a preparatory school. Rintelen pointedly took out his pocket watch: 'If there's nothing more?'

'You don't understand your situation, Rintelen,' Cumming snapped at him. 'You came ashore as Emile Gaché, as a spy.'

'You are threatening me, Captain Smith?' Rintelen laughed, grimly. 'I was taken from the ship by your boarding party.'

'That's as may be. You were travelling on false papers. Your army shot Miss Cavell for less.' Cumming lifted his chin pugnaciously. 'You must have read about her case in the New York papers.'

Rintelen didn't reply but returned his gaze without flinching.

'You know you were sacrificed by your Count Nadolny – yes, you smile, but this –' Cumming tapped the signal in his jacket pocket – 'this is proof enough. You were making too many waves in New York, things were becoming difficult for the other network – Delmar was more important than you. It was simple enough to shut you down: a word to the newspapers and the police and . . .'

'Real-ly, Captain Cumming.' The patient smile slipped, the faultless English too and he leant forward to smack the palm of his right hand on the desk. 'Yes, I know who you are, and your Secret Service – I know who is responsible for putting me here. Was he working for you or for Admiral Hall? It does not matter. But now we are finished,' and he began to rise.

But Cumming wasn't finished. Threatening, scowling like a playground bully, then coaxing with more bitter coffee and some sympathy. He pressed hard because Rintelen expected him to. He learned nothing more of importance but he had learned enough, and when the prisoner was taken away he placed a call to the director of Naval Intelligence to tell him so. 'As we feared, Admiral.' He knew he was betrayed and he knew it was by a British spy, and although Cumming hadn't probed deeper for fear of giving something more away, he thought it likely Rintelen would have named his chief suspect 'de Witt'.

'Do you think he's informed anyone?' Hall enquired, pensively. 'We may have picked him up before he was able to.' But it was impossible to say and because they couldn't, they would have to take a chance.

'It was always going to happen like this,' Hall observed, 'Rintelen doesn't know Delmar . . .'

'. . . We're pushing Wolff's luck.'

'No alternative,' Hall said, and reluctantly Cumming agreed – no alternative. And yet, waiting beneath the great Gothic entrance arch for his motor car to be delivered to the steps, he was troubled by the recollection of almost the same risk taken two years before. Wolff had spent nine punishing months in a Turkish jail and it had almost broken him. Hadn't they said 'no alternative' then?

1916

27

Inconvenient Truths

THE CHILDREN RETURNED with their nanny at dusk, then Frau Albert in the motor car, the chauffeur following her up the steps with an armful of parcels. A few minutes later Wolff glimpsed the silhouette of her full figure at a second-floor window before a maid drew the curtains. White stone house in the neo-classical style, six storeys, quiet tree-lined street in a fashionable part of the Upper East Side: the man the papers had dubbed an *architect of terror* lived well. Have the neighbours forgiven you? Wolff mused, as he waited at the wheel of the motor car. Well-to-do people have short memories. The worst crime a gentleman might commit in what the real-estate sharks were calling the Gold Coast streets was to lose one's money. The sabotage story was already last year's news; the headlines of that morning's *World* were of a rise in the country's gold reserves, and shipyards too busy to handle new orders, the President ready to embark on his 'America First' tour of the Midwest. Besides, the German gentleman in the bowler hat who walked briskly home with cane and case every evening did not cut a dangerous figure – or even a memorable one.

Gaunt's runners had logged his routine, his contacts, and the traffic in and out of his Broadway office. 'Just as you'd expect,' the naval attaché reported. 'Leaves home at seven thirty, spends all day at his desk, home again at eighteen thirty sharp. No mistresses, no trips to the theatre, no restaurants. No fun. He might be keeping his head down, but you know, I think he's just a dull man.' Distant father and husband, grumpy with the servants, a Polish maid had confided to one of the runners. 'A real bringer of joy,' Gaunt had observed drily.

Wolff glanced at his watch, extinguished his cigarette, then stepped down from the motor car. I'll shake my chains at him, he thought with a smile; an unpleasant smell too close to home. The street was wreathed in threads of a freezing mist that put him in mind of the afternoon he had wandered in Hyde Park with his first confused thoughts of Casement and the operation. It was almost twelve months to the day. Had the smog cleared? He hardly knew.

Once in a while a taxicab ground down to a hotel on the corner, and there was a trickle of commuters from the omnibus stops on Madison and Park, collars up, hats down, gazes fixed on the sidewalk: ordinary men with tan leather cases, well-pressed suits and regular office hours. Wolff watched them without envy. Bowler and cane, straight back and steady gait, Albert was easy to spot even in the mist, almost gliding from one puddle of yellow lamplight to the next.

All right, give him a few more yards. Moving with the precision of a Patek timepiece, two, three, four, and Wolff was away, stalking across the street, into his path.

'Dr Albert.'

'I am sorry, I don't know you . . .' But then his expression changed from puzzlement to alarm, like a cat's paw ruffling the surface of a calm sea. 'De Witt!'

'*Mr* de Witt, if you please,' Wolff replied in German. 'I would like a brief word . . .' and he took Albert's arm. 'There's a car across the street, Doctor.'

'What are you doing here?' He shook himself free. 'Our business is over. I've nothing to say.'

'Let's not draw attention to ourselves. I suppose you know your office is watched?'

'I've nothing to say,' he repeated icily and he tried to push past, lifting his stick in a half-hearted threat.

'I wouldn't, Doctor. Please stay calm. Goodness, a contract is a contract – you of all people should understand that!' Wolff grasped his arm tightly this time. 'Just here, Doctor.'

'I've nothing to say to you,' he protested again, but he permitted Wolff to guide him to the car. They sat side by side in the front, Albert's thin face in shadow, his eyes sickly in the light of a streetlamp.

'Your contract was terminated when our associate was obliged to return to Germany,' he declared flatly.

'Oh? Has Germany surrendered?' Wolff asked sarcastically.

'What do you want, Herr de Witt?'

'I wish to continue serving His Imperial Majesty on the same terms.'

'I told you, your contract is terminated. Captain von Rintelen has gone. Detained at sea by the British . . .' he paused to consider his words carefully; '. . . his former associates are of the view he was betrayed.'

'Not by me. My record speaks for itself.'

'That's as may be. I have no part to play in those kinds of—'

Wolff interrupted: 'Save it for the police, Albert. We both know the war here in America isn't going to end with this small setback – only to be expected, in my view. Your Rintelen was a man of vision, no doubt, but careless. Who's in charge of things now – Hinsch?'

Albert's features were stiff and cold, like a bureaucratic corpse.

'Make the contact for me.' Wolff reached into his coat for a slip of folded paper. 'Hinsch can leave a message at this address.'

After a moment's thought, Albert dipped his index and fore-finger as if plucking the paper from a muddy pool. 'Don't come to my home again.'

'That depends on you. Do your duty, Dr Albert.'

'I always do my duty, Mr de Witt,' he said in English, releasing the door. 'It is not necessary for a Dutchman to remind me of my duty.'

He climbed carefully from the car, then crossed the street without a backward glance. Wolff observed him in the light above the portico, standing below an entablature carved with a laurel garland, in his bowler hat, a hero for the new age.

Days, a week went by, a fortnight, and every morning a note from Thwaites, a telephone call or a summons to a meeting: *London's impatient, old boy, terribly concerned. Does Albert suspect you? Visit him again. Go to Baltimore and see Hinsch, why don't you?* Wolff said that London could go to hell.

With Laura's assistance he was going up in the world – by elevator to the fifth floor of a new brownstone block on the Upper West Side, a well-appointed bachelor apartment with a fine view east over the Hudson. They'd seen a good deal of each other at Christmas, dining first with her father – florid and opinionated and a voice to whip the froth from a pint of stout at fifty paces – then at her sparrow aunt's home. Wolff was a student of friendship. Priests, politicians and publicans, soldiers and scientists, matrons and maids, he'd inveigled his way into the confidences of them all. Mr McDonnell had presented no great challenge. 'I like yer,' he had declared while his daughter was away from their table. 'You're a practical man like me. That's what Laura needs.' And as a favour to her he had used his friends in the archdiocese to find Wolff somewhere 'respectable' to live.

Thwaites dismissed his new arrangements as *'foolhardy'*. Good cover, Wolff argued, and it sounded quite plausible.

'And who, pray, is paying the rent on this new apartment?' Thwaites asked.

'Me, Norman, as you ask – from the fruit of my labours on behalf of the Kaiser.'

'Damn cheek!' Thwaites complained.

But some sober nights Wolff paid in dreams, too, as he had done in the past – confused images of ten years' service, waking in the dark, sheets damp, his conscience rocking like an upturned derby hat.

One evening Laura dragged him to the opera to hear the soprano, Frieda Hempel; he took her to the Clef Club where the pianist Jelly Roll was playing ragtime. There were meetings in draughty halls, more talk of votes for women, of Ireland and Empire, lively debates in which she played a full and passionate part, always impatient for change, determined, but also funny. For all her strong convictions, she took no offence at his teasing and was quick and merciless in her turn. She wasn't an elegant woman, and she didn't have a figure like Violet's to turn heads; she was shorter, with generous curves, her gestures and speech often hurried as she wrestled with an idea or an opinion; pretty but not in a conventional way, sharp intelligence always apparent in her face. Wolff had decided on reflection that her eyes were robin's-egg blue, the finest he'd been privileged to gaze into.

Thwaites liked to remind him that the growing warmth of their friendship was supposed to serve a purpose. But Laura was careful not speak of Clan na Gael's activities and Wolff made no effort to coax them from her – until one Sunday afternoon, the last in January.

A briny wind was chasing blue-grey clouds westerly across the river, rattling the flag ropes at the Blessed Sacrament School and shaking dead twigs from the trees in front of the church. They had arranged to meet at four o'clock, but it was only a few blocks from his new apartment, so with time to waste he arrived early and was waiting on the sidewalk when members of the Clan began leaving the parochial house. Shrugging on their overcoats, hands planted on hats, bent double into the wind as they hurried along the street to the omnibus stop. Only John Devoy spoke to him.

'Waiting for Laura?' He shook his grey head disapprovingly. 'She knows what I think of ye.'

'I'm sure everyone knows what *you* think, Mr Devoy.'

Right hand gripping the iron railing, left in a fist at his side, Devoy glared at him like an old bar-room brawler living on his reputation. Wolff returned his stare defiantly.

'Tough one, aren't ye?' Devoy muttered. 'More of a man than that fella Christensen, I'll give you that.'

Wolff acknowledged this small olive branch with a smile.

'I hear you did good work for the Germans.' Devoy frowned, his eyes lost beneath his shaggy Old Testament brow. 'Just mind you're careful with our Laura, now.' He wagged a biblical forefinger; 'I know she'll be careful with you.' He scrutinised Wolff's face for a few more seconds, then nodded and walked away, turning the collar of his well-worn coat up against the wind.

'It's just Mr Devoy's way,' Laura said, when he related the substance of their conversation. She was cross and upbraided him for arriving early.

'Ashamed of me?' he asked provocatively, the wind sweeping them along the sidewalk in the direction of Central Park.

'How can you suggest such a thing?' she chided.

'You spoke to Devoy about—'

'Mr Devoy asked me,' she interjected defensively.

'You told him you'd be careful not to tell me anything.'

'Oh! For goodness' sake!' she exclaimed, and she pulled her arm free and turned to face him, exasperated and at the same time beguiling. 'What did you expect me to say to him? It doesn't mean I don't trust you. How can you say so?' Her eyes were blazing with indignation, and Wolff loved her for showing no respect for the difference in their ages. But was she protesting too vehemently? 'We have to be so careful, especially at this time,' she declared. 'Things are happening at last,' she added, filling the pregnant silence. 'It's difficult – Mr Devoy knows you're a friend of Sir Roger's.'

'I know. I'm sorry.' He reached into the dark space between them to take her hand for the first time. Perhaps she blushed, he felt her tense, but she made no effort to withdraw it. 'But I don't understand,' he said. 'Why is my friendship with Roger an issue? Is it Christensen?'

'Things are happening,' she repeated. 'Sir Roger and Mr Devoy don't agree about, well . . .' her voice fell away.

'Guns?' He took a half-step closer to her. 'It's about guns to Ireland then.'

'No. Not really. I can't say.'

'Of course not,' he replied quickly, but his tone was a little rueful. 'Come on, it's too dark and chilly to argue in the street.'

'Are we arguing?' She sounded anxious.

They chose a quiet trattoria a few blocks from the park, and once they'd settled her hand crawled across the gingham tablecloth to rest lightly upon his: 'You do understand?' Her face was pink with cold and confusion. 'Please, Jan,' she pleaded, 'don't sulk.' That made him smile, and he gave her hand an affectionate squeeze.

'Of course I trust you,' she whispered, a little crossly this time; 'I couldn't be friends with someone I didn't trust.' She was lost in thought for a moment, biting the corner of her bottom lip. 'Everyone's in a flutter, you see – even more than usual.' She glanced round the restaurant, then leant closer. 'The rising in Ireland – it's going to happen – soon – there are plans. And there are German guns. Only, not everyone agrees – Sir Roger thinks we're making a mistake.'

'A mistake? Why? I thought – but you mustn't tell me more,' he said earnestly.

'But I trust you – you see? And I want you to rejoice with us.'

He closed his eyes momentarily and gave a regretful shake of the head. 'It's too early for rejoicing . . .' then after a pause, 'I shouldn't have asked you.'

'Why?' She smiled and reached for his other hand, clattering a knife against a plate and drawing the gaze of the waiter. 'Don't worry. Put it from your mind – and you didn't ask, I offered.'

But she was wrong. He'd drawn it from her, tempting her into an act of faith. As they ate and spoke of other things, he considered the intelligence she had given him with something close to dismay. *I shouldn't have asked*, he'd said to her with sudden clarity. Perhaps he'd hoped she would have the strength to hold her secret close. It was too late to put it from his mind, but he didn't wish to hear more.

'You seem distracted,' she observed. 'I'm sorry, I shouldn't have brought you here. It's a simple place.'

No, he assured her, it was perfect in its simplicity; and for a time he tried to bend his mind to easy conversation. But later a Polish pianist played in the restaurant, his bony fingers stroking the keys, and the aching poignancy of his music was almost too much to bear. *Why did I press her?* And during one short piece Wolff felt, then shaped, the

330

conviction that Laura could never know. *Never*. He wouldn't hurt her.

A Prelude in E minor by Chopin, she told him, as the manager helped her into her coat. 'But it's rather sad.'

Wolff met Wiseman the following morning. Gaunt and Thwaites were at the safe house too. They had summoned him to talk about the Germans and he sensed at once that they were bristling for a fight. 'You must go to Baltimore,' Wiseman insisted, as soon as the terse pleasantries were over. They were taken aback when Wolff agreed at once, even a little disappointed. Wiseman offered his reasons, although it was hardly necessary: 'Can't hold off any longer. Our masters have intercepted a wire authorising Agent Delmar to resume his activities. Been on holiday, what?'

For an hour they sat in the stuffy smoked-filled sitting room discussing Wolff's best course, although there was really only one. 'Our chaps down there will let you know when Hinsch is aboard his ship,' Wiseman said. 'It's asking a great deal, I know.' He was always charming enough to sound grateful. 'Rough customer, Hinsch,' he continued. 'He may not be pleased to see you.'

Wolff was sure he wouldn't be.

'Didn't expect you to roll over and offer your tummy like that,' Thwaites observed when they were alone. 'Quite took the wind out of Sir William's sails.'

'Is that possible?' Wolff enquired.

He made light of his sudden acquiescence, falling back for an explanation on the first word in the Bureau's lexicon, the word to trump all other words: duty. The truth? In so far as he was able to perceive the truth, his decision owed more to guilt than a sense of duty. Guilt, because even when Thwaites enquired, astutely perhaps, how things were 'with your Fenian girl', he chose to say nothing of plans for the Rising. He wasn't entirely sure why. He'd meant to – and he knew it was topsy-turvy to chase a new secret in Baltimore in order to feel a little better about concealing the one Laura had shared with him: trading lies and loyalties.

I will tell them about Ireland – soon, he decided. I will. I have to because they are with the enemy. Casement, his garrulous sister, Laura . . .

Did he have a choice? There were boys from the fenland villages he knew well, stumbling with fear in their hearts into no-man's-land, trench whistles ringing in their ears. In this together, C would say. But wasn't that merely the shell of duty, like Norman Thwaites fighting for lads he'd left on the Turkish wire? Was there sense in such thinking? Where would it end? Was it thinking at all?

As he slipped out of the safe apartment, he remembered that his mother used to upbraid him in verse, the old cliché about the tangled web we weave when first we practise to deceive. Christ, he'd been practising a long time. And now he was struggling with confused feelings, searching for a way to unravel some of the threads he'd spun, because . . . he admired Laura more than he should. He wanted her. Did he love her? He wasn't sure, but if he didn't quite yet, he knew he would soon. He'd stepped from a high building and the sidewalk was rushing towards him.

So, a month after his encounter with Dr Albert, Wolff caught a train to Baltimore, and from its new railway station took a cab round the harbour basin to the hard-working dockland district of Locust Point. At its eastern edge, in the shadow of the city's historic fort, stood the Bremen pier where thousands of German immigrants had stepped ashore in the country they wished to make their home. In the years before the war, Captain Hinsch's ship, the *Neckar*, was often to be seen there. Her last voyage had brought her to the pier with passengers and cargo a fortnight after the pistol fired in Sarajevo led to the outbreak of general hostilities. Since then, she had travelled no further than a cable distance to her new berth among the tramps and colliers plying their smoky trade from the wharfs at the tip of the point.

It was a cold day but blue, the sun bright on the water. The harbour ferry was steaming out of the old clipper yard on the opposite shore, the breeze whisking its plume away to the west in a horizontal line. Beyond the roof of a low shed, Wolff could see the frayed and faded house flag of Norddeutscher fluttering from the *Neckar*'s foremast, and walking round it to the wharf, her sharp black bow. She was larger than he'd imagined, five hundred feet in length, riding high and rusting in the slack water of the dock. At the foot of her gangway, a junior officer was supervising the unloading of supplies from a wagon. Wolff introduced himself and, with the determined authority of one used to addressing Germans in uniform, asked to be taken to the captain.

The skipper of the *Neckar* filled his little chart room. It was the first time Wolff had seen Hinsch in uniform, immaculately groomed, clean shaven, blond hair combed with a little oil: his sour expression was the same.

'What are you doing? You shouldn't have come here,' Hinsch declared belligerently.

'Albert gave you my message?'

He gave a curt nod.

'Well?' Wolff prompted.

'The British have von Rintelen,' he snapped. 'Stopped his ship, took him off.'

'Are you accusing me? They stop most ships,' Wolff observed coolly; 'they stopped mine.'

'They arrested him – not you.'

'I'm more careful. You saw yourself how—'

'And the stories in the newspaper?' Hinsch interrupted. 'You know nothing about those? Koenig was arrested . . .'

'You're blaming me?'

Hinsch glowered at him for a few seconds then looked away, his right hand trailing across a chart to a pair of dividers. 'It might be you – or an Irishman – I don't know. It's over, anyway. Finished.'

'Over?' Wolff looked pained. 'Don't take me for a fool. Mind if I sit down?' He perched at the edge of a swivel chair bolted to the deck before the table. 'Are you in charge of the new operation? Look, Hinsch, you know what I can do – I'm not German, and yes, I want to be paid – paid well – but this work suits me, and I have my reasons, you know them well enough. You don't like me – I don't care much for you – but we want the same thing.' He paused in hope of acknowledgement but the lines on Hinsch's face seemed to indurate like clay. 'I'm not here as a suppliant but as an enemy of the British Empire,' Wolff added testily. 'Berlin gives the orders and I was sent here to be of service.'

'There is no operation,' he retorted. 'I've said – no work.' He spoke without respect, as if he were upbraiding the least member of his crew. 'And if I change my mind, I know how to find you.'

Wolff shrugged. 'Have it your own way. I'll contact the embassy – or Berlin.' It sounded lame but it was all he could think of to say. He stared at Hinsch for a few seconds more, refusing to be intimidated by his enmity, then picked up his hat from the table and dusted a speck from its band. 'I can find my own—'

'There was a body.'

Wolff started, his right hand frozen over the hat. 'What?' he barked impatiently to disguise his confusion.

'You know about this, I think?' Hinsch asked, searching his face.

'No – and perhaps I shouldn't.'

'The police are asking questions. It was one of their men.'

Another frisson of anxiety. 'A dead policeman?' Wolff heard himself say.

'A nobody. An informer, but working for them,' Hinsch squinted at him suspiciously. 'They found his body in the bay, but he was killed at the terminal in Hoboken – stabbed, then thrown in the water,' he paused, his eyes flitting away, 'by someone else, I shouldn't wonder. They'll catch the killer, they say – won't let it lie. They spoke to the crew of the *Friedrich der Grosse*,' he paused again, lifting the dividers to stare down the line of them at Wolff. 'Perhaps they'll want to talk to you. Best be prepared.'

'Yes,' said Wolff, 'yes, I will be,' and he tried to smile.

Slowly down the ship's gangway, slowly along the quay, concentrate on walking slowly, head up right, eyes to the front, determined not to falter in view of the bridge. Hinsch suspected but didn't know. The Germans must have disposed of the body. Did the police have a description of de Witt? He'd tried to bury the memory, but bastard Hinsch had spat on it and burnished it until it was bright again. He must warn Wiseman and Thwaites. He would have to tell them he'd failed to find a way back inside the operation too. Hinsch wasn't going to contact him – not in a month of Sundays. Or was he looking for an excuse to give up?

Confused, disconsolate, he walked a little way from the dock-yard gates to stand at the kerb for a taxicab. From a sailors' bar close by, drunken voices, a snatch of Southern song, although it was only one o'clock in the afternoon. After only a few minutes he changed his mind and set off for the station, relieved to be on the move. It was simple enough to follow the curve of the street round the harbour, the downtown skyline always ahead of him. Half an hour at a brisk pace and he would take a horse-drawn cab from one of the piers on the waterfront for the final mile. The wind was freshening still, obliging him to keep a hand to his hat but lifting his spirits a little. In another place, in different shoes, he would have run, chasing away frustration and his sense of foreboding. He was a little breathless – he knew he was out of condition – the rhythmic click of smooth leather soles, fast enough for sideways glances from strangers, but not fast enough to free him from his own cutting thoughts. At the corner of Light Street and Lee, he broke his stride, shuffling round a carter who was scooping oats back into a sack he'd emptied on the sidewalk. 'Watch your feet,' he grumbled, but Wolff ignored him, brushing his bent shoulder as he stepped from the kerb, checking his stride again for an oncoming cab. In a moment it was upon him, clopping, squeaking, jangling, barely worthy of a second look except that it was *him*.

Christ. You again.

Behind the driver, the broad frame and large head of his passenger: Captain Friedrich Hinsch, like a stout German nemesis. His eyes found Wolff and lifted away before the cab flashed by.

Wolff watched the cab trotting along Lee Street and slow down to cross Charles. Then he began to follow, skipping, breaking into a run – he wasn't sure why – instinct and experience and anger and something furtive in the man's expression, something . . . Perhaps it was a waste of time, but what had he got to lose? Weaving along the sidewalk in the shadow of shopfronts lest Hinsch look over his shoulder, tripping and fighting for his feet, one block, the next, and pausing to search busy Sharp Street before racing on to turn right at a junction when he could go no further. By then he'd lost sight of the cab but on he pressed; to his left a high wall, ahead the Italianate tower of what might be a church. A tram rattled past, drawing to a halt twenty yards in front of him. Shouldering his way carelessly through the queue at the stop, he realised suddenly that he was chasing along a railroad wall and the tower was above the entrance to another of the city's stations.

Parked beneath a canopy ahead of him, were three motorised cabs and the burgundy hack he'd been chasing. Hinsch had gone.

'Your fare?' he demanded, a greenback between his fingers. The driver nodded to the station entrance.

Inside its oak-panelled hall, Wolff pushed to the front of a line. 'An emergency,' he explained to an old lady with sharp elbows. 'A friend, broad, blond hair, thick accent, heavy grey overcoat, critical I find him.' No one asked why. The ticket seller complained but spoke to his associates at the other counters all the same. 'To Washington, mister, the Royal Blue,' he informed Wolff when he returned, then, casting heavy-lidded eyes to the hall clock, 'She's due about now.'

Wolff took the ticket but not his change and ran helter-skelter through the barrier and down two flights of stairs to the lower level, pausing only to confirm the platform number. The passengers were aboard the train, the railroad workers uncoupling the electric locomotive that had guided it through the city's tunnel. Was Hinsch at a window? He had seven yards to cross from the shadows at the bottom of the stair to a carriage. The guard's whistle reminded him they were at war – would it always? – and the heavy clunk of doors: *Damn it, just get on, why don't you?*

There were only four carriages. Wolff walked quickly to the second. Was Hinsch even on this train? he wondered, as the engine took up the slack, and then: it's the final nail if he sees me. But it didn't matter really. Hadn't he decided already there was nothing to lose? Then he remembered Laura.

28

Delmar

THERE WAS NOTHING to do but wait – wasn't that most of a spy's life? Thankfully this was on a broad leather bench in the parlour carriage, comfortable in the best tradition of the Royal Blue Line. Wolff glanced at his wristwatch – a gift at Christmas from Wiseman. It was an hour and a half to Washington so he would be arriving after dusk. Until then he couldn't even be sure he was travelling on the same train as Hinsch. Better to sit tight than risk giving himself away. He'd noticed on the station board there were stops – Relay, Annapolis Junction, Laurel – but he didn't expect a saboteur to have any business in a small town. All the same, he kept a close eye on the platform at Relay. Beyond it the train rumbled pleasingly through flat grassland dotted with neat brick and white weatherboard farms, the low sun blinding in the glass. A conductor punched his ticket. Two suited men and a sailor left the train at the next junction. Then onwards, gathering speed, but only for a few minutes before slowing again. 'Laurel. This is me,' the middle-aged lady opposite said, encouraging him with a pointed look at her portmanteau. 'I should have put the thing in the van but it's such a short distance.' Wolff was still hauling her bag to the carriage door when they chuffed into Laurel.

'You're so kind,' she drawled in a Dixie voice. 'My brother will be here to take it, I'm sure.'

*

Stooping to the window, he could see a file of people emerging from the little brick station, some with luggage, others to meet passengers, their faces lost in shadow. An old railroad worker was pulling a trolley along the boardwalk platform. Parked in the yard at the side of the station were a buggy, a wagon and two automobiles. With a hiss and hollow groan, the train came to a stop. Seconds later a barrage of opening and closing doors, and the Southern lady was urging Wolff to step down to the platform. He was turning to make an excuse when Hinsch swept past the window. Fortunately his gaze was fixed on those who'd already left the train.

'Are you going to help me, sir?' the lady prompted him, her voice rising in agitation. 'If not, perhaps you'd do me the courtesy of calling Joe the stationmaster for me.'

That wouldn't be necessary, he assured her. He was leaving the train too, and pulling the brim of his hat lower, he lifted the bag on to the platform, then offered his hand to her: 'Madam.'

She gave him a coy smile. She was of an age when, in Wolff's experience, a woman was most likely to be grateful for the attention of a younger man, and it suited him well enough to offer it. Bending over her bag, he shuffled sideways in time to see Hinsch shake hands with a smartly dressed man at the station door. Hat, mackintosh, about five-ten, slim build, but at thirty yards and in shadow, it wasn't possible to distinguish his features. His cramped shoulders suggested he was ill at ease, and he may have said something of the sort because Hinsch turned to look back along the platform. If he noticed Wolff and his new lady friend, he thought nothing of them because his gaze did not settle, and a second later he was distracted by a blast of the train's klaxon, like the trumpeting of a dying elephant.

'Is everything all right?' she enquired. 'Look, he's here at last.'

Stalking towards them was a well-built young farmer, to judge from his clothes. She scolded him, then introduced him as 'Tom Brown, like the schooldays' – fishing for Wolff's name in return. 'Curtis,' he said. Over the farmer's shoulder he saw Hinsch conduct his associate into the ticket office.

The train began to trundle out of the station and those who had left it were making their way down badly lit steps at the back of the building on to the street, or to the vehicles on its west side.

'Will you be staying in Laurel long?' Miss Brown enquired, patting her hair artfully with a gloved palm. 'Not long,' he said, just a little business. He pretended to watch brother and sister walk away, taking in the stationmaster unloading packages from his trolley, the empty platform, and in the vehicle park the one remaining motor car, a Winton; at its wheel a man with jowls and a bushy moustache, eyes closed, chin nodding on to his chest. The station door was behind Wolff, facing the platform; there were windows at the front and back of the building, and a large one to the side, its blind half drawn. Crouching to do up a shoelace, he could see beneath the blind into the ticket office and beyond this the glass door of the waiting room. Hinsch was at the stove and his associate went to sit beside him but he had barely settled before he was up again. He was plainly anxious and Wolff guessed the meeting wouldn't last long. Rising, he slipped out of his overcoat – it was the last thing Hinsch had seen him wearing – and began to stroll along the platform.

'Washin'ton this side,' the wizened stationmaster volunteered. He hadn't replaced the bulb in the lamp above the door and the only light was spilling yellow through the windows.

'You comin' in, sit by the stove?' he asked. 'Fifteen minutes till the next 'un.'

Later, perhaps, Wolff replied.

*

The waiting room extended a few feet from the station façade so passengers could gaze along the platform. Wedging his shoulders in the angle of the wall, Wolff was able to peer through a slit window in the side across to the reflection of the room in its main one. Hinsch was still by the stove, his companion standing beside him. They were a thickness of brick from Wolff but it was impossible to distinguish their features in the glass or hear more than the murmur of their voices.

Then the image was moving, the stranger drifting to the window, and Wolff heard him say in German, 'No. Look, tell Hilken two weeks and not a day longer.' Hinsch must have replied because the stranger turned to gaze at him, his back still to Wolff. If he moves his head the other way, he might see me here, he thought. He was trusting to luck and the deep shadow beneath the hipped roof.

'I'll need a ticket and more money,' the stranger said. 'Money for Carl too.'

Was he a stranger? Wolff wasn't sure. Dark hair, slight wave, strong jaw, slim but tall, heavy overcoat with a fur collar, and something in the way he held himself that was familiar. Perhaps one of the gentlemen at Martha's, but not a sailor. He would know a sailor.

'Carl knows what he's doing, I've told you,' the man said irritably.

Was he Delmar?

The image softened as the man walked towards the stove and out of earshot. But a couple of minutes later he was back, peering up and down the platform this time, his nose to the glass, too close for more than a murky reflection.

'When did you say your train was due?' The stranger didn't wait for an answer. 'The case is with Carl in the motor car. When we go out there, please don't mention my plans to . . .'

But the rest was lost as the station door to Wolff's right swung open, forcing him to step smartly from the corner.

'Baltimore and Noo York in five,' the stationmaster hollered as he stepped out to the platform.

He must have drawn the gaze of the stranger at the waiting-room window. Wolff could sense him there. Is he watching me? I should be carrying a suitcase, he thought.

'Noo York,' the old man called once more.

Slowly, stiffly, Wolff ambled along the platform, glancing through the window of the ticket hall. The waiting-room door was ajar: they'd gone. He walked on past the old man and his trolley and a military man in a blue dress coat; stepping round the luggage of a young couple who had just arrived and were arguing about timekeeping. A few yards more to the corner of the building and he paused, pretending to consult his watch. He gave an impatient shake of the head and half turned to search the vehicle park at the side of the station. A large motor car was jigging across the rough ground and as it swung right its lamps caught two men dropping down the steps. A few seconds later it came to a halt and Hinsch and his companion crossed its beam again. Wolff watched them walk a little further, to where 'Carl' was waiting at the wheel of the Winton. They were only a stone's throw from the platform but it was too dark to see the stranger's face. That he was German and involved in something nefarious, Wolff could be sure of. Why else would Hinsch drag his carcase to a place like Laurel? Was this Agent Delmar? If Wolff moved closer he was certain to arouse suspicion. And if he didn't, he had nothing.

He was still weighing the risks when Carl turned on the lamps of the Winton. Stepping into the beam, Hinsch reached into his coat for his money, which he began laboriously counting from his left hand to his right.

That's right, thought Wolff, play it by the book again. Are

you insisting on a signature for Dr Albert? Wolff could imagine the stranger's frustration. Help him, my friend, why don't you? And as if pulled by invisible strings the stranger stepped forward, snatching at the money. There were angry words, the stranger shaking his head with incredulity. Then he turned abruptly to speak to Carl, his face full in the light and white like an apparition: strong jawline and chin, high brow, thin lips. And Wolff knew he'd seen the fellow before.

The howling of the klaxon made him jump and drew Hinsch's gaze up to the platform. He was plainly intending to catch the train because the rest of their business was conducted with some urgency. The stranger opened the passenger door and removed a case from the well in front of the seat. From thirty yards, Wolff could see it was brownish, an unusual shape, perhaps a doctor's bag, and not heavy because he lifted it from the car with ease. Hinsch took it from him almost gingerly. A final word and a cool handshake, and nodding curtly to Carl he turned towards the steps. The train was pulling in at Wolff's back, its carriages casting a sickly light on the platform.

The engine came to a stop with a gasp of steam and the stationmaster's cracked voice was straining to be heard over the clatter of doors and chatter of Washington commuters: 'Laurel, this is Laurel.' From the window of the ticket hall Wolff watched as a conductor directed Hinsch to a carriage at the head of the train.

It's all about the case, Wolff realised. That's why we're here.

It was peculiar, about the size of a doctor's bag, yes, but more rigid. The care with which Hinsch was nursing it was striking. He gripped the handle so tightly his knuckles were white and his arm tense, and he was holding it awkwardly, away from his left leg. As Hinsch climbed to his carriage Wolff turned to race down the station hall and out to the steps above Main Street. The Winton had reached the entrance to the vehicle park. Was Carl going to turn right or left? Careless, Wolff launched himself at the steps, two at a time, brushing someone aside, deaf to protests, eyes fixed on the street below.

What did the occupants of the motor car see? Shadows. Perhaps the silhouette of a man sprawled on the steps and another offering his hand and some frank advice. Was it a patch of ice or just too much ambition in a pair of expensive shoes? His left foot slipping, spinning like a dervish, but falling, cracking his elbow, his hip, then his knee; and the Winton's number plate was gone before Wolff was able to think of more than the pain in his side.

'Just piss off,' he hissed at the man who stopped to a wag his finger. It sounded very English.

By the time he'd limped up the steps the train had left the station. He sat on Hinsch's chair by the stove and stared into the coke fire, his thoughts drifting through Martha's rooms, to the union rally in Hoboken and back further to the sea crossing and Berlin. He still had the face; he needed a spark to place it, just a word, an image, an object.

It was the case. No matter how hard Wolff tried to concentrate on other possibilities, his thoughts returned to an image of Hinsch's associate lifting it from his motor car. He was still considering it when the next train to New York was called. Rocking gently in the parlour carriage, left leg out before him – his suit torn, his knee bloody – he closed his eyes to consider its colour and shape again. The task absorbed him completely. What do I know? he asked himself. That I associate the case in some way with my memory of this man; that they handle it carefully; that he called it a 'case' but it looks like a medical bag – is he a doctor? It's the sort of bag people notice, so why does Hinsch want the thing?

He was asking questions he couldn't hope to answer. He knew he should concentrate on the one he could.

Wisps of memory like the tails of light from streetlamps as the train raced on: Baltimore, to Aberdeen, Wilmington, Philadelphia – a whirligig – dizzying, round and round in a blur until he heard a cultivated American voice shout 'Steady', and suddenly the medical bag was flying through the air on a safety line. There was a seaman's face at the rail, a grey Channel sky, arms raised in the stern of the pinnace to catch it, and a well-dressed passenger in a coat with a fur collar, turning to glance for'ard for just a second, tired eyes, thin straight lips, square jaw.

Wolff had to stand and walk the length of the carriage. It was you – in the ship's boat! And the bloody bag. They must have questioned you at Ramsgate. Why? Because you're a German and an American. But you'd visited Germany. What did they ask you to do, Delmar?

So many questions: 'When will we visit Herr Hilken?' – 'Will you introduce me to Frau Hempel?' – and money, always. But what they were doing didn't trouble him in the slightest. Carl was as happy as a clam, fat fingers squeezing the top of the wheel, peering into the darkness. For Anton, for the money, for Germany, in that order.

'How far now, Carl?'

Carl glanced at Dilger, a happy smile lifting the corners of his thick moustache. 'Not far, Anton. Thank God! Should have put on another pair of socks.'

Carl was six years older but he'd always looked up to his younger brother. 'You got my share of the brains, Anton,' he often joked. He was a fine brewer, but a poor businessman. 'It's good of you to find him something,' their sister had said when he explained that Carl was going to help in the laboratory. He didn't say why it was necessary and Emmeline didn't ask. Carl would be a capable technician, once he learnt how to be careful. 'Easier than a good beer,' he'd observed, 'but nothing to enjoy.' A few days into his new work he'd suggested using the basement to brew some – 'There's room, Anton' – and sulked when Dilger had told him not to be ridiculous.

'Look out!' The Winton swerved to avoid a buggy at the roadside.

'Sorry, Anton. The pig had no lamps.'

They were approaching the creek, only twenty minutes from home.

'Did Captain Hinsch say when he wanted the next batch?' Carl enquired tentatively.

'We didn't agree a date.'

It had been a bad-tempered meeting, although it wasn't necessary to say so.

'I think you're ready to handle the cultures on your own,' Dilger observed. And you'll have to, he wanted to confide, but it wasn't the right time. He would tell his sister first. He felt guilty leaving them and worried about what would happen to the laboratory when he'd gone. Was it right to have embroiled Carl? Sooner or later someone would make a mistake and the police would roll up at the door of the little house in Chevy Chase; but he would have gone. It would be Emmeline and Carl on the front page of the papers. Before I leave I'll tell him he can walk away, he thought, but he knew his brother wouldn't. For the first time in a long while Carl felt important. 'I'm a spy,' he'd boasted, over a tub of their evil-smelling soup. 'Will Berlin give us medals?' 'I expect so,' Dilger had lied.

Now he closed his eyes and pinched the bridge of his nose. This was dishonourable.

347

'All right, Anton?' Carl touched his shoulder. 'Headache?'

'Tired, that's all.'

'Well, nearly home,' Carl said, swinging the Winton right into 33rd Street.

And there was the Dutchman, de Witt. 'Sniffing about,' Hinsch had dropped into their conversation sheepishly. 'Berlin's not sure about him.'

Not sure? What the hell did he mean by that? Hinsch had shrugged. 'New information.' Dilger had said nothing to his brother. He wondered if he ought to. Hinsch had urged him not to worry: 'Keep your shirt on, Doctor, I'll fix de Witt.'

'Our sister's waiting,' Carl observed, as the Winton pulled up in front of the house. 'Wonder if she could fix me something.' It was midnight but the lights were on in the parlour and before he could cut the engine Emmeline was at the door.

29

13 February

'Y OU CAN'T BE sure.'

Wolff said he was as certain as he could be of most things. If they didn't believe him they might return to their beds.

And Gaunt held up his large hands: 'Just an observation, Lieutenant, that's all.' He wasn't the bastard he used to be. As the Germans say: *Not the cock who crows on the dungheap any more.*

'Testing. Quite right,' said Wiseman, ready with his emollient smile, palms flat on the top of his desk, perfectly groomed even though the clock in his office had just struck six. Another hour before the sun would begin to creep down the many floors of Manhattan's skyscrapers – and another before it reached the street – if it was able to.

'Delmar was sent by Berlin – so was the fellow Wolff saw last night at the station. If he isn't Delmar, he's probably working with him. I'm inclined to believe he is,' Wiseman said, easing back in his chair. 'Lots of questions. First of all this doctor's bag – why? What's the fella got in the thing? Fuss he made on the ship – must be something breakable – nastier than Ma's best china, I warrant.' He smiled weakly at Wolff.

'A bomb?' Gaunt suggested.

'In a medical bag? Too conspicuous.' Wiseman's moustache twitched with amusement. 'Imagine – Hinsch on the train – an old lady in need of assistance – if you can't save her, my friend, why are you dressed for the part?' He leant forward, planting his elbows on the desk, his fingertips together. 'Is he a doctor?' he asked, pressing them to his lips. 'And why Laurel? German American, you say, Wolff. Might have been travelling on false papers. But we need the names of everyone the Navy brought ashore at Ramsgate . . .' He raised his chin enquiringly.

'Last week of May,' Wolff replied. 'Travelling first class.'

'Check them all. London to organise,' Wiseman was directing his gaze to Thwaites. 'Coffee, anybody? Think your chap can organise some, Norman?'

'Managed it in a Turkish trench,' Thwaites remarked laconically.

Wolff stood up and walked to the window, shielding his body with the curtain. He'd summoned them to the Consulate because it was more discreet than the safe apartment in the early hours.

'They clock on at eight,' Thwaites called from the door.

'Same funny little chap,' Wiseman added. 'Only does a day shift.'

There was a taxicab at the recruiting office; further up the street, a delivery at the Custom House, and a few early business birds were striding out from the South Ferry subway, tightly buttoned-up in their grey overcoats from Brooks Brothers.

'There's something you should know,' Wolff declared, his voice rising to command their attention. 'The German spy I killed . . .' he paused, reluctant to admit his mistake: too late. 'The thing is . . . he was a police spy, not a German one, I'm afraid.'

Wiseman picked up a pen and began turning it in his right hand, his gaze fixed on his desk blotter, and Thwaites was contemplating his shoes. 'Christ,' Gaunt exclaimed under his breath. 'Christ,' he intoned again, plangently this time, craning forward as if he was scrutinising a dangerous creature. 'You can't distinguish friend from foe, can you?'

'Can anyone in this business?' Wolff remarked provocatively. For once, Gaunt's anger would be welcome – but he was struggling to articulate it: 'After the ship, it's the damnedest thing . . .'

'Ah, coffee,' interjected Wiseman in a 'not in front of the servants' voice. 'Well done, White. Over there, please, expect you know how everyone likes it.' The silence was filled by the polite tinkle of china cups as Thwaites' man placed the tray on a table between the windows. 'Plenty of sugar for the lieutenant,' Wiseman suggested, with an impish glint in his eye. Does he know about the police spy? Wolff wondered, or is it simply that he doesn't care?

'There may be repercussions with the police but we haven't time to worry about them,' Wiseman observed the instant the valet closed the door. 'Delmar. We have his scent – let's get after him. We've got the Czechs in Baltimore, haven't we? Well, tell them to wake up. Better still, go there, Norman – see to things. What's Hinsch got in his medical bag? What's he planning? Captain Gaunt and I will inform London.'

'You asked, "Why Laurel?"' Wolff placed his cup on the desk. 'That's undrinkable.'

'You know?'

'A guess. The station's halfway between Baltimore and Washington. I think they've used it before – they seemed to know the geography of the place.'

'So you think he's in the Washington area. Let's see if London comes back with a name for us.' Wiseman contemplated Wolff over his fingertips for a few seconds, then said: 'And Hinsch – do you think he'll see de Witt again? – only if it's necessary, of course?'

Wolff shrugged: 'It's possible. He doesn't trust anyone who was part of the von Rintelen operation – but I have a reputation.'

*

When they'd said what they wanted to, Wolff went to his apartment, poured a breakfast whisky, then another, and fell asleep on the couch. He woke in the middle of the afternoon but lay under a blanket, gazing at the shadows on his ceiling. 'Don't worry about the police,' Thwaites had said to him after the meeting at the Consulate. 'We'll manage it.' It was plain enough from his voice that he had known for some time. 'Sir William doesn't want to deflect you,' he explained. 'These things happen. You were protecting yourself.'

These things happen was the kitchen philosophy of his mother when a treasured object splintered into a thousand pieces on her flagged floor. It wasn't an adequate explanation for six inches of steel in a man's chest or the astonishment he'd left frozen on his face.

It was dusk and the shadows had gone when Wolff was roused from his couch by the telephone. His hand hovered over the earpiece, in two minds whether to answer.

'So you are home.' She sounded piqued and pleased.

'It's been a couple of days – that's all,' he teased her.

'But there are things I wish to discuss with you – I have no engagements this evening,' she said sheepishly; 'I know it isn't ladylike to say so.'

He laughed. 'But you're free of that sort of idle convention, aren't you?'

He felt guilty in the taxicab to Laura's apartment but not enough to dampen his anticipation of pleasure in her company. She looked very much a lady in a finely pleated ivory gown. Her aunt fussed over her like an old priestess at a sacrifice. 'Isn't she beautiful?'

'She means well,' Laura said as he escorted her to the waiting motor car. 'It's just that sometimes she treats me as if I were a village girl in Ireland,' she paused, colouring a little, 'in need of a match.'

'I see,' he smiled affectionately at her. 'But she's right, you look very beautiful.'

She blushed deeper, like the pink of a wild hedge rose, turning her face from him but not before he caught the suggestion of a smile.

They chatted and laughed as she described her last suffrage meeting in a rough neighbourhood on the Lower East Side. An Italian mama had taken exception to the barrage of insults her son was directing at the platform and chased him from the hall.

They were to dine at Sherry's, one of the best and dearest restaurants in town. Why? she asked. For the hell of it, and in honour of St Valentine, to celebrate his birthday in a fortnight's time, but mostly for the enjoyment of her company, he said. He didn't need to pay Sherry's prices for that, she assured him.

A perfectly supercilious French waiter showed them to their table.

'Parisian,' Wolff observed.

'Have you been to Paris?' she asked. 'I want to travel, I feel so uneducated – I haven't left these shores. My father says not while the war's on – not after the *Lusitania*.'

'And you always obey your father?' he teased.

'No. But I don't like to trouble him unnecessarily,' she said defensively. 'He's very patient with me, but protective.'

'And he's right to be careful,' Wolff remarked, conscious of the irony.

He ordered oysters – Blue Points – then English pheasant, and she requested the consommé and chicken fricassee, accompanied by wine that wouldn't embarrass the waiter. For a time they spoke of Europe, the cities Laura hoped to visit when the world was at peace, and his memories of them before the war.

'We always speak of the future and how things should be, never – or hardly ever – of the past,' she observed. 'I know so little about your life – your childhood in Holland and England, and South Africa, that's all, and yet it's as if we've been friends for ever.' Embarrassed perhaps that her voice betrayed too much warmth, she began to concentrate on her plate.

'We are good friends,' was all he could think to say. She lifted her gaze to his face again and offered him a hesitant smile, a promise and a rebuke. 'We are good friends, aren't we?' she said softly, inviting him to say more, her eyes sparkling like the sun on the sea. He wanted to please her, to reach for her hand and shape the words: *Laura, I love you.* He wanted to tell her, *It's true, I love you, and that is the truth.*

'What is it?' she asked. 'You look unhappy.'

'No, how can I be?' he lied, the knot in his chest twisting tighter. 'I think I must be the luckiest man in the city.'

'Just the city?' she asked.

'All right, the world,' he heard himself say, and he tried to smile. He probably made a good fist of it after so many years' practice.

'Do you really think so, Jan?'

'Yes. Don't you believe me?'

She seemed younger and, for once, vulnerable as if she wished to speak of her feelings but was uncertain of the grammar.

'Now, there's something you said you wanted to discuss with me,' he declared, trying to jolly them both. 'New curtains? A dress? Shoes? Your best friend is considering a proposal of marriage from someone called Rockefeller? No – a part in Mr DeMille's new picture – abducted by a bandit.'

'You know me so well, Mr de Witt,' she countered with a happier smile.

She was going to help a new campaigning group called the National Women's Party, she said. Tired of being ignored by the President, they were going to picket the White House, and, if necessary, break the law. 'Look at our sisters in England – they were prepared to go on hunger strike,' she observed, the battle in her eyes again.

Wolff said he was glad she'd been able to dine at Sherry's first. She laughed and said she wouldn't speak to him if he was going to make fun of her. But he wasn't, he assured her; he was full of admiration – always.

After dinner he suggested they visit a club but she wanted him to take her home. They sat very close in the taxicab although it wasn't necessary, almost shoulder to shoulder, her thigh brushing against his at every corner, her hands resting lightly in her lap. She had used some more scent in the ladies' room at the restaurant. They didn't talk and he sensed she was excited and tense too. A few blocks from the apartment, she turned to look at him, her face so close he could feel her breath on his cheek.

'Would you like to dance with me? I have a phonograph and some records,' she said.

He laughed. 'You are a most surprising woman.'

'Isn't that good?' she asked, but not in a simpering voice.

'It's wonderful.' He reached for her hand and squeezed it affectionately. 'Wonderful.'

Their eyes met but her gaze fell almost at once, and to cover her confusion he asked: 'Does your aunt dance well?'

It was her turn to laugh. 'I don't think so. I haven't seen her dance.' Her eyes flitted up to his again. 'But she's with friends – she's visiting the Sisters at the Sacred Heart Covent.' She began to giggle like a schoolgirl and soon he was shaking with laughter too, her head resting against his shoulder.

It was a handsome apartment, paid for by her father but furnished to her aunt's taste with dark Victorian pieces, potted plants and bad portraits of Laura's immediate family. They had been executed to burnish the McDonnell name, she said, oil on canvas to cover the stain of poverty and famine. The maid took their coats and brought Wolff a whisky. They sat opposite each other by the drawing-room fire, the spell broken for a time as Laura spoke of her aunt's concerns and their routine at home. Her aunt was a prisoner of her upbringing, poorly educated, with no appetite for books and very religious. 'The perfect chaperone for Father's daughter,' she quipped. 'But she's wise enough to recognise that at twenty-three I know my own mind. She won't support votes for women but is happy to help raise money for Clan na Gael, and we've held meetings here in the apartment.'

He nodded and sipped his whisky.

'Were you in Baltimore to see the Germans?' she enquired suddenly. Her voice shook and he wondered if she was afraid of her thoughts and anxious not to let the conversation flag.

'So you know there are Germans in Baltimore?'

She laughed – 'A quarter of the city, I believe.' She laughed a good deal; it was one of the things he loved about her, but this time it sounded brittle. 'And Captain Hinsch is one of them,' she said.

'You know Hinsch?'

'Sometimes he's mentioned by members of the committee.'

'Yes, I saw Hinsch. It wasn't a very useful meeting.'

'I'm glad. I think it's too dangerous – after the Rintelen affair. No good will come of it.'

'But you're ready to break the law by chaining yourself to the railings of the White House.'

'Yes,' she replied distantly, her hands turning restlessly in her lap. For a few seconds neither of them spoke and she avoided his gaze, nipping the corner of her mouth uncertainly. 'Would you like to dance?' she asked at last.

'Yes,' he said.

'Are you sure?'

'Yes, Laura, of course. Shall I?'

'No, the phonograph's here.' Rising quickly, she stepped over to a tall cabinet in the corner of the room.

'Allow me.'

'No, no, I can manage. Father says it's a good one,' she said, lifting the top. 'A diamond disc – although I don't know what that means.' Her hands were shaking so much that it took quite a time to slip the record on the turntable: 'Silly me.' Then she turned the handle at the side of the cabinet and dropped the needle on the disc, wincing at the thump and crackle of protest. 'Sorry.'

He had risen, and now he walked towards her. 'A waltz, then.'

'Yes.'

'I'm not very good.'

'Nor am I.'

He offered her his hand and she took it, her eyes fixed on his white tie. He stepped closer, placing his other hand at her waist: 'one, two, three' – and they were off, waltzing stiffly; one turn and two turns, and – three – and – four, and he could feel her relaxing and relief in the music – and growing elation in the warmth and their movement. They danced the length of the disc without speaking and when it was over he dropped his hands as he knew he should. She looked at him and smiled with more confidence. 'You *are* good.'

'So are you,' he said.

'Do you think you could manage . . . ?'

'Yes.'

So they danced again, closer, wearing away the hideous purple rug, dizzy with excitement, certain enough now to look each other in the eye; sweeping round in a cloud of perfume and to the rustle of her satin dress, the chandelier too bright but her hair lustrous in its light: drunk, cavalier, forgetful. This time when the music stopped he didn't release her hand but bent to brush it with his lips.

'Thank you,' he said.

She raised heavy-lidded eyes to his, a small frown at her brow: 'You can kiss me, if you like' – and he did.

When he finished, his forehead resting against hers, she smiled happily and whispered, 'Don't stop.' And he bent to her again, holding her close, arm about her shoulders, her hair brushing his cheek, soft lips quivering with desire – with love.

In the corner of the room, the *tissh*, *tissh* spitting of the phonograph disc, like a limping timepiece.

'I love you,' he said when they broke apart.

'Do you?' she asked, her eyes glittering with a film of moisture. 'Yes.'

'I'm glad because I love you.'

They stood there, silent, content, her head against his cheek and his mind empty of anything more than his feelings for her. Then she said, 'I'm so happy, Jan. So many good things have happened today;' and he was suddenly afraid of something in her voice, the promise of a confidence. He kissed and stroked her hair but said nothing.

'Don't you want to know why?' She was a little hurt, lifting her head from his shoulder to gaze up at his face. 'I want to tell someone, you see—'

'If it's Clan business, you shouldn't,' he interrupted, bending to silence her with a rough kiss – and for a time she let him.

'But it's important. I want you to . . . I only heard today – and you're Sir Roger's friend,' she persisted. 'It's to be Easter, you see. It's decided – and Roger will be there – with guns.' She smiled, craning up to kiss him lightly on the lips. 'Do you remember what you said the day we met? You spoke to the Clan, and you said it was time to prove we had the guts to do more than sing about dying for Ireland. Aren't you pleased we're going to at last?'

'Of course,' he said.

'You don't look pleased. Please be happy – this is what we've been hoping for – freedom at last.'

'I'm sorry,' he kissed her forehead, 'it is wonderful news. I'm just anxious for Roger, that's all. It won't be easy, even if the people rise together against the British.'

'I know, but it *is* something to celebrate, isn't it?'

Something fine, he said, but a sad cold wave was washing through him. In an effort to suppress it he kissed her hair and her cheek and her neck, holding her very close, until with trembling breath and parted lips she turned her face, and he kissed her passionately, deeply, with all the love he felt for her. *Why? Why did you speak of it?* She was still trembling when they broke apart and he said in a broken whisper, 'I must go.' She squeezed him tighter, clinging to him as one who has known little, perhaps nothing, of men. Eyes firmly shut, stroking her hair, for a while he couldn't speak as sad, cutting thoughts waltzed round his head to the *tissh, tissh, tissh* of the diamond disc phonograph. *Why did you tell me?* But to even ask was another lie. The blame was his alone. She trusted de Witt – she loved him.

'I must go,' he said with more determination. She spoke but it was barely a whisper, and her words were lost at his shoulder.

'I'm sorry, I didn't . . .' he said, pulling away to examine her face.

Her large eyes lifted shyly then dropped. 'You don't have to go. You can stay,' she said.

'Your aunt will be home, and . . .' he understood and was afraid for her. 'I . . . I think I should leave,' he stammered.

'Would you like to make love to me?' She turned her face up with *I can, I will* eyes, and he felt a frisson of desire and at the same moment guilt that she was offering her love for the first time to a man like him. *Tissh, tissh, tissh,* the revolving phonograph, as if possessed by the spirit of her maiden aunt, and Laura looked down, disconcerted that he hadn't spoken or kissed her. 'You can, it's all right – I love you,' she whispered.

'I love you, Laura,' he said with quiet sincerity. 'Please believe me – that's why I'm going to leave.' He bent to kiss her but she'd turned her face away, pulling from him, hurt and perhaps a little ashamed.

'You're very beautiful and I want you,' he said. 'It's just . . .' but he couldn't think how to explain. 'I love you,' he said again, but this time it sounded like an excuse.

'I'm glad. I love you too,' she declared brusquely, her back turned as she lifted the needle from the disc.

And now she wanted him to leave at once. 'I'm sorry. I do love you,' he said again in the hall, his coat over his arm.

'Why are you sorry? There's no reason to be,' she said, but wouldn't look him in the eye.

'Yes, there are many reasons why I should be sorry,' he said bitterly; 'but it doesn't matter now . . . it's gone, done . . .'

'No. How can you say so?' and she stepped forward, laying her hand upon his arm. 'It's just pride' – and she lifted her eyes to his face and blushed. 'What a hussy you must think me.'

'You're surprising, beautiful, clever and I want you very much – I love you,' he repeated, drawing her close. 'Please kiss me.'

Standing across the road from her apartment, gazing at her lighted windows, he could still taste that last kiss, smell and feel her pressed to him; and when for a moment he shut his eyes she was beckoning him back to be her lover. He stood in the empty street, the railings and the sidewalk were white with frost, his coat open, head bare, the cold pricking his face and hands. He was lonely, he hurt and he hated himself even more, though he knew he'd done the right thing for once; just too late.

There was a taxicab at the end of the street but he wanted to walk, striding out in his best shoes, slipping, almost falling, too angry to care. By the time he reached the Albemarle Hotel it was midnight.

Wiseman answered his door in slippers and a silk dressing gown, its pocket sagging with the weight of a revolver. Raising an eyebrow, he enquired with his customary composure, 'Are you all right, my dear fellow? You did take care, didn't you? They keep a pretty close eye on me here.'

Wolff hadn't taken the trouble he should have.

'Another drink?' Wiseman asked, gazing pointedly at his tie and tails. 'Whisky, isn't it?'

'No.'

Wiseman brandished the decanter. 'You don't mind if I . . .' and poured himself a glass. 'Sit down.'

'No.' Wolff took a deep breath. 'There's something you should know.'

'You're a bit out of sorts, I can see that. Are you in some sort of difficulty?'

'I haven't murdered anyone else, if that's what you mean,' he gave a bitter little laugh, 'yet.'

'That wasn't what I meant,' Wiseman replied quietly. 'Sit down, why don't you?' and he indicated the couch opposite with his glass.

Wolff shook his head impatiently. He was standing with his back to the door, tapping his hat against his leg. 'There's going to be a rebellion in Ireland – at Easter.' He spoke hurriedly and mechanically like someone repeating instructions. 'Not sure of the precise date – perhaps Easter Sunday – don't know – there will be German guns – don't know when they'll be landed – Casement will be part of it – not sure how much of a part – there are difficulties between him and the Clan and the leaders in Dublin. How good is my source? Good.' He took another deep breath. 'That's it. That's all I know.'

Wiseman had listened with the faintly superior air of a university don coaxing a temperamental undergraduate with nods and smiles. 'You're quite sure about this?'

'Yes.'

'They aren't trying to smoke you out?'

'They – whom do you mean?' he snapped.

'The Irish, the Clan, or the Germans – perhaps they fed her this information to test her, or you, or both of you.'

'You know then?'

Wiseman acknowledged it with a slight nod.

'No, it's true,' he said, wearily. He'd said what he had to say and he didn't honestly care whether anyone believed him.

'I see,' Wiseman drawled, leaning forward, elbow on his knee and chin on his knuckles like Rodin's *Thinker*. 'Do you think you can learn more?'

'No, and please don't ask me to try.'

'It must have been a difficult evening for you,' Wiseman observed politely.

'It was fine,' he lied.

'Sure you don't want a drink?'

'I'm sure. Look, there's no reason for me to stay in New York, is there?'

'Do you want to go to Baltimore?'

'I don't know – yes – somewhere.'

Wiseman considered this for a moment, sipping his whisky. 'Perhaps Baltimore is best.' Then, in his soapiest voice, 'You've done well, old boy. I don't have to tell you how important this might be. I know you're tired – go home. Rest.'

Wolff left him to encipher his signal to London. Task complete, Wiseman may have gone back to his bed and was perhaps still sleeping the sleep of the righteous when, at daybreak, Wolff caught his train to Baltimore.

30

A Baltimore Valentine

F ROM THE SINGLE grimy window of Thwaites' hotel room it was just possible to see the tips of the cranes on the south side of the harbour.

'Better not to be too close, I hope you agree,' he said, sweeping newspapers and an edition of Tacitus' *Histories* from his bed. He had signed in as *Schmidt* and was dressed in a sack suit like a travelling salesman. His runners were staying at a flophouse on the south side, in spitting distance of Hinsch's ship, the *Neckar*.

'That Masek's a taskmaster.' The bed springs groaned as Thwaites perched at its edge. 'His people hate the Germans, you know, which is all the better for us. Why don't you settle in, then we can go over there.'

Wolff was on the same corridor. The room was damp and smelt of stale smoke and the window wouldn't close. He inspected himself in the spotted mirror above the basin. His eyes were red rimmed so he bathed them in cold water. Then he changed into an old pea coat and boots. They left the hotel separately and took separate cabs to Locust Point. Masek met them in a dark little basement bar a few streets from the Norddeutscher Lloyd dock. The owner was also a Czech, he informed them, and for the right price could be trusted to hate Prussians too. Their host brought strong black tea and they sipped it and listened to Masek's report of comings and goings to the ship.

'No Hinsch, then?' Thwaites enquired, blowing the steam from the top of his glass. Briefly, at the foot of the ship's gangway, came the reply. He was seen with a large black man, a stevedore. They'd spoken for a minute, then Hinsch had given him a package.

'The Negro isn't Irish, is he?' Thwaites remarked with an unpleasant little laugh. 'So of no interest to us.'

Wolff wasn't sure. 'Hinsch may have found some of his own people.'

One of Masek's runners was inside the yard, another at the gate, two more at the flophouse or in the bar, and there was nothing for Wolff to do but wait. Rather than contemplate the stains on the hotel wallpaper, he left Thwaites to his Tacitus and walked down to the waterfront. His route took him through a salty neighbourhood of brick terraces and cobblestone streets, taphouses, whorehouses, markets and missions, empty warehouses and decaying timber wharfs that brought to mind London's docks and Portsmouth and a score of other ports over almost as many years. At a place called Fell's Point he stopped to gaze at the last of the sun on the water. A stiff breeze was rocking the oyster boats and beating loose halyards against the masts. From the other side of the harbour the long, empty echo of a ship's horn. Keep moving, keep busy, concentrate on the operation, he said to himself, but the ache in his chest was there – as if he'd been kicked by a horse. Closing his eyes, he could see Laura looking up at him expectantly, a small surrender that only served to sharpen his pain: and what was his pain? Love, loss, regret, guilt, anger, hopelessness – all those words and ones he didn't remember or had never known.

Thwaites was waiting in the hotel lobby. 'Where have you

been?' he hissed, pulling Wolff roughly aside. 'You came here to do a job – Hinsch is at the Hansa Haus – the Negro too.'

They parked in front of a row of shops on the opposite side of the street, about fifty yards from the main entrance. Masek recognised their motor car and wandered over, stepping up to the back seat. 'My man there,' he said with Slavic disdain for prepositions. 'Front automobile showroom. Hinsch inside with Hilken two hours, but that nothing strange – here always.'

Wolff looked at Thwaites sceptically. 'So no need to get excited.'

'We need to be with him all the time,' he replied coolly. 'If you haven't the stomach for it . . .'

'All right,' Wolff held up his hand, 'I know.'

Masek patted him on the shoulder. 'Pretty girl – Brooklyn. I remember you. Followed you for Captain Gaunt.' Sliding down the seat, he pulled his peaked cap over his eyes – 'Masek have nap' – and like a dog he was asleep and snoring gently in minutes. Wolff lit a cigarette and watched the lights go out in the large office building opposite. Clerks from the downtown business district were striding home along the Charles Street corridor or queuing for streetcars to the suburbs. The tinkling of a bell signalled the approach of another and the scramble for a seat. 'You know it's Valentine's Day?' Thwaites remarked. 'Did you send your Irish lady a card?'

'Chuck it, will you?'

'Just killing time, old boy. But I say, you're not . . .'

'Shut up, for God's sake.' He nudged Thwaites with his elbow. 'There's our man,' and turning to wake Masek, 'Hey, you, any idea who the other two are?'

They were standing at the main door, the Norddeutscher house flag flapping above their head. 'Hinsch – and that is Hilken in wool cap – the Negro do not know and . . .' Masek pointed over Wolff's shoulder, 'Hilken's driver.' A large burgundy-and-orange Packard was drawing to the kerb a few yards from the group.

'The Negro's carrying something – looks like a present for his mother,' Thwaites observed sardonically. It was wrapped in brown paper and tied with string.

With a curt nod to his companions, Hilken walked over to the motor car and stepped into the back. The driver was plainly expecting another passenger because he stood waiting at the open door.

'We should follow the black man,' Wolff declared.

'Because of his parcel?' Thwaites sounded sceptical.

'Because Hilken and Hinsch won't be doing their own dirty work. Hilken isn't comfortable with – look, here we go . . .' Hinsch had shaken hands with his companion and was lumbering towards the motor car.

'Hurry up, you ox,' Wolff said between gritted teeth. The black man had set off at a good pace, faltering only to wave at one of the city's gaudy yellow cabs. 'We can't wait – you go after him, Masek – don't lose him.'

Thwaites stepped out to start the motor car and was bending over the handle when the Packard pulled away. He limped back slowly, was caught at the first set of lights, then the second. 'Come on, man, come on,' Wolff grumbled. Masek flagged them down outside the bank at the corner of Baltimore and Charles Streets. 'Where you been?' he railed. 'Go west – go straight.' They caught up the stevedore's cab at the City Hall and followed it without difficulty through cobblestone streets to the harbour. Beyond the old wharfs at Fell's Point it turned south-west into new docklands, through a dark tunnel of warehouse walls broken only by glimpses of the navigation lights on the shore, emerging after a mile in a neighbourhood of workers' rowhouses.

*

Morahan's Bar was the last building in a parade of rundown shops, at the edge of a salt marsh; opposite, a dockyard gate and chain-link fence. Single storey, windows part boarded, it was a hard-drinking place for run-ashore sailors and stevedores with piecework wages to blow in an evening.

'What do you think?'

Masek rubbed his little beard: 'Think dangerous.'

'Yes.' Wolff took a deep breath. 'I think so too. Have you got a gun?'

Thwaites patted his pocket.

'Then give it to me.'

'I'm coming,' he protested.

'Not with your leg – not in that suit,' Wolff insisted. 'Masek – you come.'

The Czech touched his cap facetiously. 'Du bist der Chef.'

'We're Germans,' Wolff muttered, stepping out of the car. 'I'll do all the talking.'

But as they were crossing the street the stevedore appeared on the threshold of the bar again. He must have thought nothing of the approaching sailors because he pushed the door ajar and called to someone inside. His companion was young, white, well built and dressed in a longshoreman's cap and short coat. Cradled in the crook of his right arm was the parcel.

'Got a light?' Wolff asked in German, stopping a few yards short of them to fumble for a cigarette.

Masek nodded. 'Sure.'

The stevedore seemed to barely notice. He whispered something to his associate, then watched him walk beyond the circle of light cast by the parade lamps.

Wolff bent over the guttering lighter flame. 'Hold it steady, man,' he protested loudly. The stevedore gazed at them for a moment then stepped back into the bar.

'Stay with him, Masek,' Wolff said. 'Take this,' and he handed him the revolver.

The meadow at the end of the parade was soft underfoot and thick cord grass grew at its edge. Stumbling forward a few feet, Wolff found a path and, presuming the young man with the package had taken it, he pushed on quietly, weaving first away from the road then back, the faint glow of light from the wharf buildings behind the fence his guide. It didn't take long to catch him. Sinking to his knees, Wolff watched the longshoreman make his way from the meadow up to the road and across to the fence. He bent over his toes to tug at the bottom of the wire: it lifted like a curtain. Then, slipping under, he ran for the cover of a warehouse. Bloody idiot – I should have kept the revolver, Wolff thought, as he scrambled after him. On the other side of the wire, he crouched to gather his bearings – twenty or so yards, three warehouse buildings, no lights, no sign of a guard. He struck out fast and low to the nearest. Back pressed to it, the first thing he noticed was the smell of shit, then a restless murmur like the breaking of waves on a distant shore, and in the seconds it took to reach the front of the building he realised that the dockyard was full of horses. Covered stables occupied two sides, an open corral the third, the administrative block along the fourth – the Union flag flying from a pole above the door. Beyond this, the dock and the dim lights of two large ships.

What the hell was he doing here? Were the ships the target, or the horses? It was a British remount depot. He'd seen a place like it in a New York park, and there were half a dozen more on the East Coast. Horses and mules to haul British guns, bring up the rations, and carry the luckless into no-man's-land; from Midwest pastures by train, then sea; no passport, no neutrality – big business. A precious investment guarded by careless nightwatchmen: or was Hinsch paying them to turn a blind eye? If so, to what end?

A whinnying, the scraping of hooves and Wolff was suddenly conscious of the horses shifting in the old warehouse at his back, their shoulders shaking the planking. It was lit by only a few dim lamps so he could see no further than the first pen, but its darkness seemed to have a pulse, to breathe, move with a will, inexorably, like the tide. There was something else too – fear. Close by, an animal snorted and whinnied, startling its neighbours. Christ, he wished he had the gun. Treading lightly on tiptoe, he advanced towards the central feeding aisle. At the corner of the first pen he paused to place the movement on the opposite side. Creeping forward a few more steps, he could see the horses stirring in the second pen, pressing together, heads high in distress. Another step, and brown packaging in the straw at the gate, a wooden box with its lid open, phials, a glass syringe with a cork on the needle, and he knew it was the contents of Delmar's case. Crash, a horse kicked at the gate and, shying away, exposed in the murky light of a wall lamp, the poisoner and his poison, motionless, his face covered by a mask, the syringe upright in his right hand like a priest holding the host. Then he was hidden again and on the move, the horses buffeting the slats as he tried to force a way through to the first pen. If he's running, he isn't armed, Wolff reasoned, and he isn't thinking clearly.

Releasing the bolts on the gate, Wolff eased his way in among the horses. The longshoreman was in a blue funk. Had he dropped the syringe? Terror was infectious too, borne in the air from pen to pen, screaming, sweating, restless enough surely to worry even a corrupt nightwatchman. Ahead in the darkness the fence creaked and he heard a sound like the slapping of a horse's haunches; yes, closer, closer, and he tensed to spring – but the poisoner was ready too. His needle missed Wolff's face by inches. Instinct must have made him flinch. Grabbing the man's right arm, holding the needle away, in desperation Wolff tried to gouge his eye with a thumb; the beasts shouldering them, locked in their dance. Then, thrusting at the man's chin, pushing the facemask up, the needle dropping, Wolff knew his enemy was stronger, and for a second he remembered: *Christ, it was like this with the man in the derby hat.* A shower of glass and liquid as the syringe splintered in the poisoner's hand and, grunting with fear, he loosened his grip. Wolff struck hard at his throat and he staggered back, grasping for some support. But a horse kicked out, catching him below the knee and he fell, then Wolff kicked him again – in the head – again, and again – in the back, his sides, again, again.

'All right,' Wolff gasped at last, 'the syringe, what was in it?' But the young longshoreman was curled tightly in a ball, his face hidden by his rubber gloves. 'Come on,' Wolff bent over him, shaking him by the collar. 'What was in the syringe?' He slapped the man's head with the palm of his hand and shook him some more. 'Tell me or I swear to God I'll make you eat the stuff.'

'Anthrax.'

'Anthrax?' Wolff grabbed his coat and was dragging him to his feet when someone at the entrance of the warehouse called, 'McKevitt, that you?' A Southerner, an old voice trembling with fear. 'McKevitt?'

Wolff shook the longshoreman again: 'You McKevitt?'

He dropped his hands at last. 'Yeah.'

'Who's that?'

'That's Flynn and he's got a gun.'

'Has he?'

'Yeah,' McKevitt drawled. 'Here – over . . .' he tried to shout. Wolff caught him hard in the mouth. He tried to cover his face but Wolff punched him again and grabbed his hair, slamming his head once, twice, against the stone floor until he lay there unconscious. Then Wolff pushed through the horses to the gate, let himself out and turned to pick up the box of phials.

'McKevitt?' The old nightwatch was advancing slowly with a cavalry revolver.

'Flynn? I'm working with McKevitt.'

'Just wait there, mister.' He waved the revolver at Wolff. 'McKevitt said nuthin about anyone else.'

Wolff kept walking: 'I brought the stuff for him.'

'Don't want to know about that – don't wanna know nuthin'. Where's McKevitt?'

'He didn't say where he was going.'

'Now hold it there. You ain't from here, are you?' This time he levelled the gun at Wolff. 'Where you from?'

'Sure you want to know? I mean, best not to – best let me get on. You got the money, didn't you?' Wolff was close enough to register the uncertainty in Flynn's weatherbeaten face. 'You see, what you don't know can't get you in trouble, can it?'

'No, no, reckon you're right,' he said, his voice quaking. Wolff stopped beside him and gazed down into his rheumy drinker's eyes. 'Forget you saw me – that would be best for you, Flynn.'

Then he left the way he had come, discarding his coat by the fence. It was stained with the contents of the syringe.

'Is that the parcel?' Thwaites enquired, as Wolff climbed into the motor car beside him.

'This? This is Delmar's box,' he remarked grimly. 'Fetch Masek – we need to leave – at once.'

On the journey to the hotel he told them what he'd seen and done.

The little he knew of anthrax he'd learnt as a boy growing up on a farm; a contagion in horses, cattle, sheep – a killer.

'Evil,' Thwaites declared, and he repeated it many times, and that only the Germans would behave so dishonourably. 'Are

372

you afraid you might be infected?' he bellowed over the roar of the road.

Wolff said he was too tired and hungry to be afraid.

'And the poisoner,' he shouted, 'did you kill him?'

'Knocked him out.'

'Pity.' He glanced across at Wolff. 'You should have, you know – killed him, I mean. He saw you.'

'For God's sake, man,' Wolff exclaimed, thumping the door of the car. 'What do you take me for?'

At the hotel they wrapped the box in brown paper as before and wrote on it: *Handle with Care*. Their courier caught the last train to New York. 'I'll telephone Wiseman – warn him it's on the way,' said Thwaites. 'Have a bath, old boy, you smell of horse shit and you should,' he hesitated, 'well, you know – you have to be careful.'

Later, they sat in his room and drank too much whisky – *antiseptic*, Thwaites called it. After a time he observed with the tearful sentiment of the tipsy that no one could doubt they were fighting a war for civilisation. 'You – you – you've had your doubts, I know,' he slurred, 'but you can see now, can't you – you can see what we're up against.' Wolff sipped his drink and wondered why poisoning animals made it a war for civilisation when so much that was an abomination had been done already. He was confused and a little drunk, exhausted too – he ached all over. Was the poison working through his system?

Thwaites prodded his knee. 'I know what you're thinking – you – you're thinking "animals – just animals" – but what if they're using it on us, eh?'

'Then why poison horses?'

'Who knows how far this Delmar will go. I don't understand why, why . . . a doctor would do such a thing.'

373

Wolff gazed at him for a few seconds. 'Men like us have to, well, prove we belong somewhere.'

Thwaites looked at him quizzically. 'Don't . . . don't . . . follow . . .'

'A bad joke, that's all.'

'You know there have to be laws, Wolff,' he muttered, then louder, 'There . . . there have to be limits – without them there's no civilisation.'

31

Breaking the Seal

THERE WERE TELEPHONE calls, telegrams, and on the second day Thwaites caught the train to Washington, but he was back in the hotel at dusk. 'We're to sit tight while they put the pieces together.' Time had meant little to Wolff in a Turkish cell with only dreams and memories to measure the dark hours between interrogations. A wristwatch and a square of leaden sky made for harder time, the hours trickling like grains of sand through a glass. Too bored and restless to read, he sat on his bed wrapped in a blanket, fighting the future, his past, civilised society and his feelings for Laura. After a few drinks he recalled her large blue-green eyes gazing up at him with a smile; a few more and he wanted to kick down the door.

'Are you sick?' Thwaites enquired warily.

'Aren't you? Delmar may be halfway across the Atlantic.'

'Ah. I see.' Thwaites couldn't disguise his relief. 'Don't worry – Masek's people say there's nothing unusual. Hinsch is still aboard his ship, Hilken in his Hansa Haus. The man at the remount depot may have kept his mouth shut.'

Wolff didn't think so.

'This anthrax – it's very nasty,' said Thwaites uncomfortably. 'You know, Sir William thinks you should see someone.'

'Oh?' He muttered impatiently. 'It isn't necessary, I feel fine.' It was a lie; he felt terrible – hungover and out of sorts.

'Don't be an ass,' Thwaites chided. 'It's for your own good – and mine.'

The Johns Hopkins Hospital was a five-minute cab ride, its tissue culture laboratory on the third floor of a red-brick neo-Gothic block that resembled the station hotels of the last century.

'I've told Sir William I want to keep you a while,' Dr Reid said, breezing into his office in a spotless white coat; 'a few tests, a skin and a blood culture.' He bent over his desk, distracted for a moment by some paperwork. He was a tall man with boyish features and a shock of ginger hair he must have spent most of fifty years trying to tame. 'Blood,' he muttered in his Scots American brogue; 'blood,' and lifting his gaze to Wolff at last, 'How are you feeling? Any shortness of breath, sneezing, light-headedness? Fever? Any itching or blisters?'

No aches and pains that couldn't be placed at the door of a longshoreman with fists the size of dinner plates, Wolff assured him.

'We'll see. Put this on, would you,' and he handed Wolff a surgical mask. 'Just a precaution, and please – don't touch anything.'

As old as man, he explained as he guided Wolff along the corridor to the tissue laboratory. *Bacillus anthracis*: one of the biblical plagues. Grazing animals ingested or inhaled its spores from the soil and once they were infected they could spread the contagion to man. 'Through the skin or sometimes by breathing in the spores – tanners and wool workers have picked it up from animal hides. Here we are . . . no, no, let me get the door,' he said, placing a firm hand on Wolff's arm. 'Don't touch anything, remember.'

His laboratory was larger and better equipped than most, perhaps; brighter than some, with arched windows facing south, and emptier than many at midday, with just a single research student bubbling a flask at a bench.

'This won't take long,' Reid declared, summoning his assistant with a wave. 'Cutaneous infection from a diseased animal is the most common cause – the tiniest unseen abrasion on your skin is enough, or by touching eyes, nose or mouth.' He was busying himself with a microscope and some slides. 'Here, this is a gram stain – it's the rod-shaped bacilli between the cells.' Wolff bent over the eyepiece. The bacilli looked unnervingly like tiny jointed worms and he said so. 'If you've spoken to Sir William, you'll know . . .'

Reid had closed his eyes and was shaking his head irritably. 'I live here now and whatever dirty little war is being fought behind the backs of the authorities . . .' He sighed heavily. 'Yes, it can be used as a weapon. It spreads quickly – horses brushing against each other. If you're asking me about people . . .' he paused, his gaze fixed on the microscope slide. 'It's a zoonosis. Human-to-human transmission is rare. The reservoir for the infection is the animal.'

For a few strained seconds they stood in silence while the laboratory assistant laid syringes and dishes on a surgical trolley. Reid reached for some rubber gloves. 'You can thank the Germans for this test,' he said with a sardonic smile.

He took some mucus from Wolff's nose, some blood from his arm; he examined his mouth for ulcers and his skin for blistering, tapped his chest and prodded for signs of soreness. 'I'm fine,' Wolff repeated, hoping to God it was true.

'Yes, you're probably free from infection,' Reid conceded a little reluctantly. 'Too early to be sure. Did you bring some things?'

But Wolff refused to stay. 'I'll let you know if I find any blisters.'

'Too late by then,' the doctor observed savagely. 'Want to know how you die?'

'No. You can spare me the details.'

They parted without a handshake even though Reid was wearing his gloves. But as Wolff was approaching the end of the corridor he came bounding like a camel in pursuit, his white coat flapping about him. 'Do you read German?' He thrust some medical papers and a book into Wolff's arms. 'Put them in the mail when you've finished, if you please.'

Wolff was turning away again when Reid grabbed his arm. 'Just a minute.' He waited for three nurses to rustle by, then said, 'Since Wiseman came to see me I've given this . . .' he hesitated, searching for a suitable corridor euphemism, '. . . problem. I've given this problem some thought, and it occurs to me the clever thing about *Bacillus anthracis* is that it would be easier to target than most diseases.'

'I'm sorry, Doctor, I don't . . .'

'Look, it's in those papers,' he reached a finger across to them. 'Just a possibility – I hope I'm wrong. I'm sure I'm wrong,' and with a curt nod he walked away.

The summons to the British Embassy in Washington was delivered by telegram the following morning. Thwaites wanted to drive. They arrived in the middle of a downpour and were escorted without ceremony up the ornate oak stairs to a salon on the first landing.

'You must be frustrated,' said Wiseman, advancing across the silk carpet to greet them. 'It's taken an age.' They shook hands and he drew them into the circle of chairs about the fireplace. The room was furnished with pretentious gilt pieces of a sort favoured by diplomats of all nations. The King-Emperor hung above the black marble chimneypiece and on the longest wall a large canvas of British soldiers engaged in another battle.

'Congratulations the order of the day again,' said Gaunt from his place at the hearth.

'Plaudits from everyone,' agreed Wiseman, squeezing his hips into a fragile-looking fauteuil. 'Agent W – the toast of Whitehall.'

'How gratifying,' Wolff replied.

'Must be.' Wiseman smiled weakly. 'So, let's begin. We've tested the poison, spoken to C, the Admiralty, the War Office, the British Army chaps here, and we've enough information to be sure the Germans are trying to infect everything on four legs we buy – horses, mules, cattle.'

'Evil bastards,' Gaunt murmured.

'There have been fatalities.' Wiseman leant forward, elbows on his knees; 'London says five British sailors on horse transports – and a newspaper here reported another – a stevedore in a hospital just before Christmas.' His gaze rested pointedly upon Wolff: 'You've seen Dr Reid?'

'I'm fine,' he said, with more confidence than he felt.

'He's sure?'

'Yes.'

Wiseman relaxed back in the chair. 'This whole thing has been an almighty cock-up. The damn fools in the War Office who organise the supply of horses kept it to themselves. C says they admit to more than a dozen outbreaks of anthrax in the last three months – that's thousands of animals destroyed at depots or tipped into the sea – no one is entirely sure of the precise number. Infections have been reported at five ports on the East Coast and on goodness knows how many ships – the last the *Brownlee*, two weeks ago. The Admiralty dismissed it as poor animal husbandry. Well, biological warfare – who would have thought it?'

'I don't understand,' said Gaunt, stooping to stir the fire. 'Why are they killing animals?'

'Only a sailor would need to ask.' Wiseman observed with an

indulgent smile. 'An army can't feed or fight without horses and mules, Captain; it can't move. The Americans have sold us hundreds of thousands already. We're getting through horses pretty quickly, aren't we, Norman? Thank God we don't publish those casualty figures.'

Thwaites coughed. 'Depressing thought.'

For a few silent seconds it hovered in the room.

'And Agent Delmar?' Wolff prompted. 'Did London come up with a name?'

'You were right. He's an American doctor,' said Wiseman, rising to his feet. 'Doctor Dilger – Anton Casimir Dilger;' and leaning on the back of his chair he trotted through the facts he'd gathered as if intent on making up the lost time. A bacteriologist he had consulted knew of a Dr Dilger and was able to find papers on tissue cultures he'd written before the war. The family were Germans from Virginia, his father a hero of the Civil War. 'The rum thing is that old man Dilger stayed in America to breed horses. Ironic, don't you think? Berlin must have run our Dr Dilger as a separate sabotage operation, with Hilken to handle financial affairs and Hinsch to recruit and run the necessary . . .'

'Scum,' Gaunt chipped in with venom.

'. . . network. German and Irish, no doubt,' Wiseman continued with a twinkle in his voice. 'They've kept things tight. If you hadn't followed Hinsch, who knows how long it would have been before we picked up the scent.'

Wolff raised his eyebrows: 'Are you confident we still have it?'

'Sent a fella to the Dilger farm yesterday – he spoke to some people. Dilger's living with a sister just a few miles from here. The cheek of the man – he's listed in the directory as a "physician".'

Thwaites sighed heavily. 'Isn't it time to give this to the Americans?'

'Your leader has thought of that.' Wiseman paused, putting his palms together as if in prayer. 'London says, "Ask our Ambassador." The Ambassador says, "Proof." He can't – won't – take it to the White House without proof. President Wilson wants to keep the temperature with the Germans low. He's campaigning for re-election on the slogan "I – kept –"' and Wiseman drew it in the air, '"us – out – of – the – war".'

'The phials, the syringe – aren't they satisfactory?'

'British propaganda.' Wiseman had taken his seat again and was contemplating Wolff over his fingertips. 'What do we have that can't be dismissed as bad husbandry or propaganda? Goodness, it isn't easy to believe.'

'Poisoning animals, food, water supplies – I suppose we've been doing something of the sort for centuries,' Thwaites remarked gloomily, 'and now it's the turn of the scientists. Is that progress?'

'I dipped into the Bible last night,' Wiseman said, 'half remembered something from Revelation;' and screwing his eyes tightly shut in concentration he intoned in a fire-and-brimstone voice: *'When he had opened the fourth seal, I heard the voice of the fourth beast say, Come and see. And I looked, and behold a pale horse: and his name that sat on him was Death, and Hell followed with him.* There,' he exclaimed, opening his eyes again, 'the seal's broken and behold death on a pale horse.'

For a few seconds there was silence.

'"The Black Bane",' muttered Wolff at last.

Wiseman lifted his chin quizzically.

'Anthrax. The last pandemic in Europe killed thousands.' Wolff paused, turning the thought. 'There haven't been cases at the Front?'

Wiseman shook his head in disgust. 'Honestly, I don't think the War Office has a clue how its animals die. Has enough of a job accounting for . . .'

Wolff cut him short. 'No – soldiers. How can we be sure the Germans aren't poisoning our soldiers?' He leant forward distractedly, his gaze fixed on the carpet, as if the answer was waiting to be teased from its fibres and motifs. 'Reid gave me some medical papers – the enemy has chosen wisely. For one thing, anthrax is deniable. A disease found in horses and cattle – it's a silent killer. Look, we're struggling to convince our own Ambassador it's a weapon, aren't we? Secondly,' he said, counting it coldly on his fingers, 'delivery. The enemy has targeted American horses and mules as a reservoir of infection. It's easier to operate here. The British pay through the nose for diseased animals, then obligingly ship them to the boys at the Front. A gunner harnesses his battery team, the Army Service Corps bring the supplies up to a field kitchen on the backs of mules, a soldier in a reserve trench pats the neck of a cavalryman's horse as it passes – spreading the contagion is that simple.'

They were staring at him uncomfortably. Gaunt opened his mouth as if to speak, then shut it again with a frown. The light in the room was fading, the rain rattling against the windows.

'Influenza, the plague, even cholera would jump no-man's-land in time, like gas shifting with the wind,' Wolff observed quietly. 'The enemy is taking less of a risk of infecting his own men with anthrax.' He paused to breathe deeply. 'And it seems to me fear of the disease would be the most potent weapon. Dead horses, dead cattle – diseased carcases on the battlefield – anthrax spores grow quickly and survive for decades. Are they infecting our cattle too? What about the supplies we're importing from America? If soldiers believe they can catch the disease from their animals or food, well, they'll panic.'

'Steady on,' Wiseman interjected. 'We have no proof, Wolff. There's nothing . . .'

'We haven't, Sir William,' Wolff snapped back, 'but if we don't look, we won't find.'

Thwaites shifted uncomfortably beside him. 'You really think they would go that far?'

Wolff shrugged. 'I don't know . . .' he hesitated, then said forcefully, 'Yes. Yes. They've used gas – we've used it too. They've bombed civilians – the Allies have too. So why not this? There are no limits, Norman.'

There was another oppressive silence. The rain still lashing the building, the heavy Empire clock still ticking, and distant English voices drifting up the stairs.

'I don't believe they've gone that far, or intend to,' Wiseman declared at last. 'For one thing, animals infected here would die before they reached the Front. We don't have any evidence they're—'

'We're guessing,' Gaunt interrupted gruffly. He was still clutching the poker, flexing his fingers as if he was itching to beat someone over the head with it. 'Catch this bugger Dilger and we can be sure.'

'Quite right. We must pay him a visit.' Wiseman's gaze floated between Wolff and Thwaites. 'After the time we've wasted, the sooner the better.'

But they should eat first, he said, and he ordered beer and sandwiches, fussing around them like a baronet's butler. Perhaps he was feeling guilty about his magisterial use of the collective pronoun, or just that he was sending them into the pouring rain on what he suspected to be a wild goose chase. No violence on the President's doorstep – the Ambassador was insistent, he informed them with an ironic smile. 'But if he's there . . .' he paused, stroking the end of his moustache thoughtfully with his forefinger, '. . . well, we can't let him go.'

32

Manhattan 03656

THE DILGER HOUSE was just fifteen minutes' drive from the embassy. They parked beneath a dripping cedar on the opposite side of street.

'Folksy,' Thwaites observed. 'Can you imagine him living in this place?'

'Respectable American doctor living in a respectable part of town,' Wolff declared, wiping condensation from the windscreen. Thwaites offered his cigarette case and they smoked and listened to the rain drumming on the motor car and trickling through a rip on to the rear seat. The patch of sky Wolff could see through the canopy of the cedar was many shades of grey. The lights were on in most homes already, glowing with contentment, even self-satisfaction. Behind new lace curtains and plush draperies, bankers' wives padded through rooms without memories, furnished from the same stores in just the same way. The Dilger house was dark.

'He's gone, hasn't he?' Thwaites remarked, winding down his window a little to flick his cigarette end into the street.

Wolff rebuked him: 'Wrong sort of neighbourhood,' although he hardly cared. 'Let's take a look at the house.'

'We'll be soaked.'

'This is a good time. If the sun comes out, so will the neighbours.'

'All right,' Thwaites muttered between gritted teeth.

Wolff's jacket and trousers were wet through before they reached the porch and the rain had worked its way round the brim of his hat and inside his collar. They pulled the bell and waited a few minutes to be sure the place was empty. 'Let's look round the back. Friends of friends, if the neighbours have the temerity to ask.'

Kitchen, dining room, rented furniture and the walls were bare but for a large photograph in the sitting room. Five narrow steps down to a cellar door and two small windows. He squatted on his haunches and wiped the rain from the glass – empty but for a workbench, a sink and some rough shelving. How much more would the doctor need?

'Anything?' Thwaites asked. 'If I bend to look I won't get up again'.

'I don't know – perhaps.'

'Has he gone?'

Wolff shrugged. 'Probably.' The Dilgers seemed to have made an effort with the garden, planting spring bulbs in the borders, and the earth at the back fence had been broken recently too.

'I've looked at the door – we can force our way inside,' said Thwaites, turning back to the house, 'if you keep an eye . . .' His mouth snapped shut in surprise. A woman was standing beneath the eaves in a winter coat and sou'wester.

'Who are you?' She was softly spoken, unmistakably of the South.

'Frau Dilger?' Wolff enquired.

'Yes.'

'My name is von Eck – my friend here is Mr Schmidt. If you'll excuse the discourtesy, I'll keep my hat on.'

She pretended to smile. 'What are you doing here?'

'I hope I haven't startled you. We're friends of a friend – may we speak inside?'

'Whatever your business, I'm sure it can't be with me.' She moved closer to the door, her face hidden by the sheet of water cascading from the roof. 'Is it Dr Dilger you wish to see? My brother isn't here, I'm afraid.'

Wolff took a couple of steps closer. 'We've come from Baltimore – associates of Mr Hilken.'

She was considering him carefully. Perhaps she had a kind heart and would take pity on them. His jacket was clinging to his back. 'Mr Hilken asked me to put your mind at rest on a few matters.'

'Oh, I see,' she said, taking a key from her pocket. 'Then you better come inside.'

She invited them into her kitchen but no further, and she rejected Wolff's offer of assistance with her coat. A handsome woman, early forties, a thin straight mouth like her brother's, the same determined jawline and dimple in the chin.

'We're making a puddle on your floor.' He smiled reassuringly.

'I'm sorry if I appeared rude. I have to be careful now I'm on my own.' Her voice shook a little and she wouldn't look him in the eye.

'Have we missed Dr Dilger?'

'Yes.'

'When do you expect . . .'

'I don't. You said you had a message. Please give it to me.'

'For you *and* your brother, Miss Dilger,' Wolff replied. 'Is he at the farm, or in New York perhaps?'

Her eyes flitted up to his face, then away. They were a warm brown-green colour. 'He's visiting Germany – Mr Hilken knows that.' She shuffled to her left, perhaps consciously putting the broad oak table between them.

'But not yet,' Wolff remarked. 'We were told he was here.'

'Well, he's gone.' She was staring at Wolff defiantly now,

unflinching, her small dry hands clasped beneath her chest. 'I'd like you to go too.'

'I'm sorry, Miss Dilger.' Wolff slapped his wet hat down on the table. 'I don't want to inconvenience you, but we have a few questions.'

'Leave.' She glanced at the door.

'Please don't,' he said in an aggrieved voice.

'I'll shout – my neighbours . . .'

'No one will hear you,' Wolff gestured to the rain beating at the window, 'and it isn't necessary.'

'Who are you?'

'Please sit down.'

She didn't move.

'Sit down,' he repeated firmly, and this time she did.

'Where is Dr Dilger?'

'I've told you.'

'I saw him myself only a few days ago,' he lied.

'He sailed from New York yesterday.'

'The ship?'

'The *Rotterdam*.'

Wolff nodded. 'Did you know?' Their eyes met, the colour rising in her cheeks. Then she looked down at her hands. 'Know?'

'Know what your brother was doing?' He leant closer, forcing her to look up.

'My brother's a doctor. I don't know who you are – but a doctor visiting his family – he's on – was on – vacation, that's all.'

'Your brother was a cheap poisoner,' Thwaites interjected harshly. 'Instead of treating the sick he's been culturing disease. Where? – here?'

She shook her head. 'My brother's a doctor.'

*

387

She denied it, refused to even countenance the possibility, but he read shame in her face, heard it in her voice. Not the details perhaps, but she'd guessed and turned a blind eye. It wasn't so unusual, even among the God-fearing. Wolff touched Thwaites' sleeve. 'I'm going to look around.'

The main rooms of the house were empty of the past, just as he'd expected them to be. He found a photograph of the doctor on his sister's bedside table and took it from its silver frame, and in the sitting room a family group with young Anton at the feet of the soldier-patriarch. Finally, he clomped down the stairs to the basement and was reaching for the door when he suddenly froze, his fingers just touching the handle. In the kitchen above, Thwaites' abrasive German, then a sullen silence punctuated by the scraping of a chair leg and the rain at the window. But it wasn't a voice, a noise, that had startled him; it was a smell – the faint but sharp odour of the slaughterhouse – or so he imagined it to be. This is the place, he thought, here beneath Miss Dilger's kitchen. He pushed open the door and turned on the lights. White walls, sink, trelliswork bench, home-made shelves; just as he'd seen it through the window. Everything had been scrubbed with bleach and yet the sickly-sweet smell of decaying blood lingered like a bad spirit. Inspecting the room carefully, he found only shards of glass which he wanted to call a Petri dish, but it was impossible to be sure.

'What did he use, Miss Dilger?' he asked her at the kitchen table. 'An animal of some sort – blood?'

She didn't reply. She couldn't look him in the eye but kept twisting, twisting her lace handkerchief tighter.

'Whatever it was – it smelt awful,' he explained to Thwaites. 'Here in this basement.'

'Culturing disease in the house?' Thwaites exclaimed, incredulous. 'You must have known,' Wolff said to her. 'What about your neighbours – did you think of their safety?'

She began to rise – 'Leave my house.' Her lower lip was quivering, the first tear on her cheek – 'Leave, leave, leave' – then she bolted for the door.

Wolff held Thwaites' arm – 'No, let her'– and flinging it open she ran out into the rain.

'Don't you feel sorry for her?' he asked.

Thwaites scoffed. 'No, I damn well don't.'

'Don't you see? She's been betrayed by someone she loves.'

'Left her things,' Thwaites joked, lifting her coat from the back of a chair. Her clasp bag was on the table, just large enough for powder, a handkerchief, some money.

'Rummage through the coat, would you?' Wolff reached for the bag and emptied it on to the table. Just a respectable middle-aged lady's essentials, although he was surprised to find a Levy lipstick. He opened her pocketbook and thumbed through the pages.

'Nothing,' Thwaites declared, dropping her coat back. 'Bills from a grocery store and her key.'

Wolff looked up at him blankly, her pocketbook still open in his hands.

'Come on – what is it?' Thwaites prompted him.

'Notes, some telephone numbers – just . . .' he hesitated, swallowing hard, '. . . numbers – probably family,' then closed it deliberately and slipped it into his breast pocket. 'Let's go.'

They pulled the back door to behind them and scuttled across the street. The motor car had sprung some more leaks. Thwaites uttered a profanity and ran his sleeve over the driver's seat. 'We're sinking.'

'There's something I have to do,' Wolff said, sliding on to the passenger seat. 'I'll need your revolver. Can you drop me at Union Station?'

Thwaites stared at him intently. 'This thing you have to

do . . .?' He paused, waiting for Wolff to accept his invitation to explain. But Wolff just looked away. 'Look, whatever it is, you should tell me, it might be—'

'It isn't – not to you or Wiseman.'

Silence but for the rain beating on the canopy. A motor car sploshed by with its lamps blazing. Wolff was gazing impassively at the windscreen, misted with their breath. 'Is it her?' Thwaites whistled softly. 'It is.' He slapped his palm on the steering column in frustration. 'Remember C's rules, I said.'

'Yes, you did.' Wolff dipped into his jacket for the pocketbook. 'Last entry.'

Thwaites flicked through to the page. 'This number?'

'Zero, three, six, five, six. It's Miss McDonnell's.'

'And you think . . .'

'I don't know. I'm going to find out.'

33

To the Edge

WOLFF TOOK UP his post before dawn, loitering in doorways as New York began to rise. A clear cold city day in March, a day for thick socks, gloves and a muffler, walking at a brisk pace, and coffee and eggs in a smoky café. But Laura's apartment wasn't on that sort of street. He tried to keep on the move, shifting his position, drifting between blocks, brushing shoulders and smiling at businessmen fixing their hats on the doorstep or striding the sidewalk to the subway. He was exchanging short words with a man who had charged him with malicious intent when a motor car came to a stop close by and flashed its lamps once. A moment later Masek's pinched face appeared at the driver's window.

'Have breakfast,' he said, as Wolff climbed in beside him. 'I watch apartment. Café three blocks,' and he pointed over his shoulder with his thumb.

Wiseman had sent Masek in a Consulate car. 'She not know Masek,' he explained. 'I follow – no trouble.' There was no denying it would be simpler. Slight of frame, penetrating gaze, Masek had the air of a poor scholar at a provincial university, threadbare but respectable, fingers stained yellow by tobacco, the sort of man you might pass on a New York street without a second glance. They didn't say much because it was business, but shared cigarettes and took it in turns to doze. Then, at nine o'clock, Laura appeared at the door, sifting through the morning mail, placing it in a portfolio she was carrying, adjusting her hat and tidying strands of hair. As Wolff watched her pass he felt a desperate urge to leap out of the motor car and ask her outright: 'Have you seen Dilger? Do you know what he does?'

Masek glanced across. 'Don't worry. I look after her.' He reached for the door handle.

Wolff nodded. 'Leave me the car keys.'

He didn't see them again for six hours. Only once did he risk leaving the motor car to stretch his legs. At one o'clock he moved the Ford to a small lot further from her apartment but with a view of its third-floor windows. There was a lamp on in the drawing room where they'd danced and he thought he saw a figure fleetingly at the curtains, although he couldn't be sure. He wondered if it was Laura's aunt until a taxicab dropped her at the door a short time later. Then Laura appeared, head bent, a frown on her brow as if she were pondering the shape of her next suffrage speech or the rising in Ireland or just the sound of her footfall on the sidewalk. 'She caught train to Chambers Street, number 51,' Masek said, settling in the seat beside Wolff. 'A bank – something to do with church – took lift to tenth floor. She was there a long time. Masek very bored, tired, hungry, think British should pay him more.'

'Mention it to Captain Gaunt, why don't you?' Wolff remarked.

Masek smiled wryly. 'She come down at last – speaking to an old man, grey beard, bushy like this,' he held his hands beneath his chin, 'brown jacket – patches here and here,' and he touched his elbows.

'Devoy,' said Wolff; 'one of the Irish leaders. Clan na Gael meets in a judge's office above the bank.' It was where he'd met Laura for the first time.

'She talk to the old man few minutes then go. Think she heard bad news. Looked sad. She cry a little on train.'

Wolff felt a pang. 'Something the old man said to her?'

Masek shrugged.

They took turns to stretch their legs and grab something to eat. Masek returned with a bottle of liquor and five packets of cigarettes. 'We find men to help us?' he suggested.

'Tomorrow – if we need to.'

But the little Czech didn't have time to remove the top from his bottle before a taxicab drew up to the kerb. Laura appeared at the window, glancing up and down the street. Without a word, Masek pushed the starter and slipped the Cadillac into gear.

After a couple of minutes the door of the apartment block opened and Laura stepped out to speak to the cab driver. She looked anxious, her right hand to her temple. Turning most of a circle, she checked the street again, then walked back to the door.

'Not a good spy,' Masek observed laconically.

'I think she'd take that as a . . . hello.' Dilger was scuttling across the sidewalk, his hat pulled down over his face. Swinging at his side was the brown leather doctor's bag he'd given to Hinsch in the parking lot at Laurel.

'Is it him?' Masek enquired.

'Yes, it's him.' His bloody bag had been sitting in Laura's apartment. Now it was in the back of the cab between them.

Masek swung the Cadillac out of the lot.

'Not too close.'

Masek gave Wolff a reproving look.

The last of the sun was blinking in the windscreen as they drove west towards the Hudson. The taxicab turned left on 12th Avenue to run along the river, stopping briefly for lights at the Recreation Pier. They tried to keep their distance but Masek was afraid they would lose the cab in the evening traffic.

'You think it's a trap?' he asked, braking for another set of lights. 'Why this woman? I think it's because of you.'

'I think so too,' Wolff said. 'I'm not sure why. Perhaps they suspect me, perhaps they're testing her.'

The traffic was flowing left on to 14th Street and Wolff was expecting the cab to do same, but at the junction it pressed on along the waterfront towards the abandoned piers running into the river opposite Castle Point. They bumped over granite setts in pursuit, passed empty and boarded warehouses, navigation buoys rusting on their sides, the carcase of an old tug on stocks, cranes, cables and carts, the dockyard detritus of decades that might have been heaved from the river by a great harbour wave.

'Drop back,' Wolff commanded. It was dusk now and if the cab driver had a mirror he would notice their lamps.

A few hundred yards more and the cab turned to the right and was lost behind a warehouse.

'Pull up, they're stopping.'

Masek guided the Cadillac into the shadow of the same building.

Reaching under his seat, Wolff lifted out a waxed canvas package.

'Honey and plenty of money.' It was Thwaites' service revolver.

Masek frowned. 'Don't understand.'

'Nor do I,' said Wolff. 'Wait here.'

It was just a few yards to the corner of the warehouse. The taxicab had come to a halt at the entrance. Parked beyond it were three more motor cars, the largest Hilken's burgundy-and-orange convertible. Dilger had climbed down from the cab with his bag and was offering to help Laura but she was in no hurry to rise. Two men came out of the warehouse, the elder of the two, Devoy, his Old Testament beard sickly yellow in the light spilling through the open door. He shook Dilger's hand, then leant inside the cab to say a few words to Laura. She had sheltered and delivered the doctor and her task was complete. Wolff was relieved when, a moment later, the taxi pulled away. He waited with his back pressed to the wall as the cab turned in a large circle to return the way it had come. Devoy had escorted Dilger into the warehouse and shut in the light. But by the dim glow of the city Wolff could see the silhouette of a driver lounging against the hood of a motor car. He was going to have to take a chance. Cocking the revolver, he put it back in his pocket, took a deep breath, then stepped forward like a man with an urgent appointment to make.

The chauffeur heard his footfall. Stamping guiltily on his cigarette, he turned and was plainly relieved to find a stranger. Heart pounding, Wolff opened the door of the warehouse and glanced inside. 'They're in here?'

'Yes, sir.'

He felt a moment's relief: the corridor was empty, gloomy, double doors at the end, to the left an iron staircase. Stepping lightly, quickly, damp fingers round the grip of the gun, he paused at the door to listen to voices and judged them only feet away. Christ, I should burst in and shoot the bastard, he thought. Instead he settled for the stair, moving carefully in the darkness, a steadying hand to the wall as he felt his way up the last few steps. The door at the top was stiff and he needed to ease it open with his shoulder. He misjudged the pressure; it grated and he froze, holding his breath, expecting a shouted challenge or the ring of boots on the stair. A cold night but he was perspiring, his shirt clinging to the small of his back. Through the open door a confused echo, movement, voices, someone speaking English, issuing instructions perhaps. After three or four minutes he was calm enough to try again.

This time he was able to prise it free without a sound and in the blue light from a gallery of broken windows he could see a broad iron gantry, thick with dust and glass and pigeon shit. In a pool of light on the empty warehouse floor beneath it, a dozen men stood about a table, most of them dressed in pea coats and woolly bonnets, and in their midst the distinctive shaggy grey head of John Devoy.

Dropping to his knees, Wolff emptied his pockets, placing the revolver carefully by the door, then crawled forward until he was almost directly above the lamp and in the middle of the circle. He could see Dilger in the shadow at its edge, whispering to a heavily built man with a moustache who looked like Carl, the driver of the Winton in the station lot at Laurel. The medical bag was sitting on the table.

Bang. Wolff almost jumped out of his skin as the door beneath the gantry swung heavily to, starting pigeons from the rafters and making the men on the floor flinch. A few seconds later Hinsch rolled into the light with Hilken in tow at his heels.

'Doctor, you can speak to them now,' he announced in his thick English.

Dilger muttered something Wolff couldn't catch in reply and stepped up to the table.

'I'll be going, then. Until tomorrow.' Devoy was shuffling from the circle. 'Good luck to youse all,' he declared, addressing his remarks in particular to the men – his men. 'Beidh an lá linn. Remember – our day is coming.'

Dilger had removed from his bag, gloves, a mask and a box of phials like the one Wolff had taken from McKevitt.

'My brother's shown you what you must do?' he asked, turning to his companion with the horseshoe moustache. Someone replied very sullenly in the affirmative.

'Be sure to wear these when you handle both the phials and

the sugar cubes.' Dilger held up the mask and gloves. 'If you don't, you'll . . . well . . .' He paused to let them ponder the consequences. 'If you're careful you should have no difficulty; it's a simple procedure.'

'Do not let the enemy catch you,' Hinsch barked. 'Throw the empty phials over the side.'

Over the side. Christ. Shifting his shoulders, Wolff craned further out from the edge of the gantry to examine the men more closely. Their clothes, their gestures, one man lifting his cap to scratch a bristly scalp, another slouching against an old packing case, the bored silence, the careless ease with which their minutes slipped by, as if whiling away the early hours of a watch at the rail of a ship: Wolff knew these men. He'd seen them beaten by the sea, wrestling with warps on a heaving foredeck; he'd seen them paralytic and gazing at the stars, heard them grouse, terrified then elated; he'd seen them in all moods, all weathers.

'. . . and if you can't use the syringe,' Dilger was telling them, 'use the sugar cubes.' He'd taken a small package from the box. 'Wait as long as you can – a day or two days from port would be best – no sooner. That is most important – vital. Any questions?'

'And these gloves will be enough to keep us safe?' one of the men asked, with just the suggestion of Irish in his voice.

'And a mask, yes,' Dilger replied. 'Anything else?'

No one else spoke. They'd clearly been well schooled by Dilger's brother.

'Good,' said Hinsch, nodding to Carl.

Wolff watched Carl disappear from the ring of light, returning a minute later with two packages wrapped in brown paper and string. He lumbered into the darkness like a fat German

Santa, repeating his delivery until there were eight parcels on the table. The dust-dry spirit of Dr Albert floated about the warehouse as the sailors stepped forward to sign for a parcel and pay. They left at once, cradling their packages in the crook of an arm or against their chests, relieved to be away, their pockets jingling with money earned for Ireland's cause. Did they know they were poisoning not just the animals but soldiers too? A lot of thoughts flitted through Wolff's mind as he lay on his side in the filth. That Casement couldn't know. That it was a bargain without principle, shaped by someone subtler – a man like Nadolny. No, Roger couldn't know, not Roger, not Laura. They were being used by ruthless men, servants of their own empire, Devoy too perhaps, and Ireland. And what the hell to do about it?

With the sailors gone and no one to address, Dilger and his companions were speaking in no more than a conspiratorial whisper. It made the warehouse feel a colder, a more dangerous place. From the little Wolff could gather they were house-keeping, with mention of Devoy, travel arrangements, security checks: it was impossible to be sure. The doctor picked up his medical case and they began to drift from the light, pausing only at its edge for a few more words and long handshakes. Hilken said something funny and there was a little nervous laughter. They were on edge and wanted to be away. A moment later the door beneath the gantry banged again, the circle of light disappeared and Wolff was alone. His shoulder and hip were numb and he'd strained his neck peering out over the iron lip, but he lay still a few seconds longer, breathing deeply. Somewhere above him the beat of pigeons' wings. I've spoilt my coat, he thought, with a wry smile. He was too relieved to care.

From his vantage point in a derelict shed, Masek had watched

Dilger and the others leave the warehouse. Minutes later he saw Wolff do the same.

'The doctor travelled with Hinsch,' he observed as they walked to the motor car. 'Maybe go back to your friend Miss McDonnell.'

But Wolff didn't think so. 'Drive me to a telephone, would you?'

The duty clerk at the embassy in Washington was wet behind the ears. Sir William was dining with the Ambassador and shouldn't be disturbed, he declared, and certainly not for a man who refused to give his name and wasn't prepared to share his business. It took ten minutes and the sort of language more commonly heard in a sailors' whorehouse before Wolff bullied him into delivering a note.

'Find Dilger?' Wiseman asked as soon as he picked up the mouthpiece.

Wolff told him what he'd seen. Eight seamen, eight ships perhaps, he couldn't say for sure. 'They were instructed to wait until the end of the voyage before they infected the animals – horses and mules, I suppose – I don't know.'

For a time the line crackled emptily.

'Our soldiers.' Wiseman sounded shocked even on a bad line. 'They're attacking our people, too.' More crackle. 'My God. I can't quite . . . their own countrymen. It's come to this?'

'Yes.'

Another long pause.

'The best men in my battalion were Irish.' Wiseman's sigh was long and audible from two hundred miles. 'Sugar cubes, you say. Harder to find.'

'Yes. If we want to catch Dilger we'll have to . . .'

'An American citizen, what can we do?' Wiseman interrupted. 'No, we have to stop those sailors, and stop the enemy sending more.'

Another silence filled only by the fizzing of the phone, as if a thought was taking shape on the wire.

Wolff spoke first: 'I won't recognise all of them but if the War Office and the Admiralty can hold British merchant ships here in port – the least we can do is check for Irish names.'

'Actually, there's another way,' said Wiseman, a little too casually. 'A better way.' This time the line seemed to spit portentously. 'That's if you're willing, Wolff?'

34

Inside the Hansa Haus

F OR ONCE MR Paul Hilken informed his wife by telephone that he would be working late at his office in downtown Baltimore. It wasn't necessary or customary, but in the last few days he'd surprised her, and himself, by being attentive – even affectionate. It's the uncertainty, he reflected, as he sat waiting for the call. He was frightened he would lose the things that made being married to a man like him tolerable. Hinsch had organised everything, taking it in his ungainly stride. No evidence, he said, no laboratory and no one who would dare speak to the authorities. To be sure, he'd sent the longshoreman caught with the poison to the West Coast: at least, that was what he said.

'And the doctor?' Hilken protested. 'If they find him . . .'

'They won't. Now, in God's name behave like a man,' Hinsch had upbraided him.

Hinsch was a brute, but a clever one, Hilken mused. Their relationship had changed: he'd always tried to bully, now he expected to be obeyed, and when he'd asked Hilken to wait at the Hansa Haus for a telephone call, it was issued as an order.

In the hall below his office, seamen from ships washed up by the war were gathering round the piano, as they did most evenings. A few cheap beers, a distribution of letters from home, and by nine o'clock they were ready to sing. Floating up the stairs a Plattdütsch shanty he'd heard countless times since the beginning of the war. At one time he used to hum the tune. There was a sudden swell as the door opened and his clerk brought in more papers: victualling orders, ships' repairs, the day-to-day business of the Line. He tried to settle to them but found it impossible to anchor his thoughts.

'Is it true?' Miss Dilger had demanded on the telephone. 'Was my brother doing what they said – those diseases?' She'd been quite hysterical. All lies, he'd assured her; spies trying to discredit Germany. It wasn't the first time the enemy had tried this sort of propaganda. 'Believe me, Miss Dilger, they made up the story because they hate us and hope America will as well,' he'd said, and she was desperate to believe him. She had scrubbed their basement and repeated her brother's lies to neighbours and spies without question or complaint. When Hilken had spoken of patriotic duty she had cut him – 'I love my brothers,' she'd said, and that was enough. When the time was ripe, Carl Dilger would resume the work and she would cook, clean and look the other way as before.

'Is that Mr Hilken?' he heard someone say. After so long, the tinkling of the telephone bell had startled him and he'd dropped the receiver. 'Mr Hilken?' The line crackled and hissed like an old phonograph. 'Mr Paul Hilken?'

'I'm Hilken,' he replied.

'John Devoy.'

'Yes, Mr Devoy, I've been waiting for your call.'

'Your friend's gone.'

'You're certain?'

'Of course I am – I saw him go aboard myself.'

Hilken closed his eyes and took a deep breath. *Thank God.*

'Are you there, Hilken?'

'Yes, I'm here,' he said, 'thank you, Mr Devoy. Thank you. A weight off my mind, I can tell you.'

Perhaps he'd said more than was wise because the Irishman growled something inaudible and hung up the telephone.

Hilken was too relieved to care. He'd said harsh things about the Irish after the von Rintelen affair, but honestly, thank God for them! He took another deep breath: they'd almost tied up all the loose ends. What a state he'd worked himself into. Rising from the desk, he stepped into the corridor to instruct the clerk to arrange for his motor car. Then he poured a drink. He was carrying it to one of the armchairs at the hearth when there was a sharp rap at the door.

'Yes.'

There was no response. 'Come in,' he shouted impatiently in German. This time the visitor knocked more forcefully. Exasperated after a tense evening, he walked back to the door, ready to give him the sharp edge of his tongue. The stranger was dressed as a petty officer in a pea jacket and bosun's cap, his face thin, his eyes dark and hostile.

'Hello, Hilken,' he said, barging into the room.

They'd talked about breaking in and rummaging the safe but the Hansa Haus was never at rest. From a doorway across the street, Wolff had listened to the pianist thumping out the old tunes and the singing of a rowdy chorus. Some of the songs he'd learnt in a Wilhelmshaven beer cellar when spying felt like an adventure and a respectable profession for a gentleman. 'Every night sing – wait until they sing,' Masek had counselled. 'Then they will be too drunk and sad to notice a stranger.' Somewhere in the shadows of the street he was waiting to be sure Wolff was safe. He must have noticed Hilken at the first-floor window, and watched Wolff turn up the collar of his coat and cross the street to follow a group of seamen inside.

*

'Who are you?' Hilken stammered at last.

Wolff placed a hand in the middle of his chest and gave him a shove. 'This won't take long. I see you have a drink – why don't you sit and finish it?'

'How dare you touch me,' he protested, angrily brushing Wolff's arm aside. 'Who the hell do you think . . .'

'I'm de Witt.'

That Hilken knew the name, and was unhappy to hear it, was written plainly enough in his face. 'If it's business – make an appointment with my clerk.'

They were standing toe to toe like cowboys squaring up in a saloon, Wolff a few intimidating inches taller, broader and set with the confidence of a man who knows he can take a punch and return it with more than equal measure. 'Sit down,' he commanded. Hilken glared at him but his shoulders dropped, and a second later he turned to walk over to his desk, anxious to place four feet of mahogany between them.

'It's a business proposition,' Wolff said, pushing further into the room; 'if that helps a chap like you make sense of it. You see, my clients know all about your activities – you're trying to poison our soldiers – and our horses. Killed at least one American, I hear, you and Hinsch, and Dilger.'

'I don't know what you're talking about.'

Wolff's features settled into a bored expression, his forefinger trailing lazily along the edge of the desk until it came to an ugly silver paperweight, a ship's dog in a sou'wester. He picked it up, testing its heft in his hand. 'Well, of course you know. You don't do the dirty work – you pay people like McKevitt. You settle the bills. You helped Dilger set up his laboratory – goodness, what would your president say if he knew a German spy was culturing anthrax a few miles from the White House?'

Hilken lifted up his glass, inspected his drink, then placed it gently back on the desk. 'He'd recognise it for British propaganda,' he said, affecting indifference.

'Well, of course I was expecting you to suggest something of the sort. I wouldn't be here if my clients . . .'

'Can we stop this pretence?' Hilken sneered.

Wolff shrugged; '. . . my friends didn't have proof. Your associate, Dr Albert – an excellent bookkeeper – he made a very careful record – you have accounts at two banks in New York, don't you? I'm sure the *Baltimore Sun* – oh, and the Secret Service – would be interested to know why a German diplomat implicated in a sabotage campaign is paying you thousands of dollars. No, just a minute, let me finish,' he said, holding up his hand. 'You see, he was foolish enough to entrust his accounts to von Rintelen, who kept them in an oak filing cabinet, the middle one of three, if I recall.'

Hilken had turned a sickly white. 'And Miss Dilger,' Wolff continued, 'we visited her – I'm sure you know by now. Do you think she'll be strong enough to lie when the police and newspaper reporters are on the doorstep?'

Carefully replacing the paperweight, he stepped over to the hearth, holding his hands to the glowing embers. 'Think of the disgrace, Hilken, a saboteur helping a foreign power. If they don't execute you as a spy they'll put you in prison. What will the other members of the Baltimore Germania Club say, and your business associates, your father, your wife – does she love you enough to wait for twenty years? You know, you won't be able to afford to keep the girlfriend – Miss Johnston, isn't it? Perhaps the newspapers will speak to her too.' He stared disapprovingly at Hilken. 'But it doesn't have to be like that. We're not interested in you – it's Hinsch and his people we want – his contacts in the ports – the network – most of all the sailors at the warehouse last night – yes, I know all about that. I want their names and their ships. I know you kept a record. Was it for Albert?'

Hilken's gaze was flitting blindly about the room as he tried to manage his fear. 'Albert,' he repeated with dismay.

'I was sure it must be,' Wolff continued. 'It doesn't matter. All that matters is that you give me the ships and the men. Eight men.'

'How the hell . . .' Hilken was so astonished he forgot he was afraid, but only for the briefest of moments. 'You want me to be your creature?'

'A small enterprise. An exchange. I want those names.'

'Even if I were inclined – I don't have that sort of information here.' He paused, then added with less conviction, 'And I wouldn't give it to you if I did.'

'I know, you're a German patriot.' Wolff smiled patiently. 'But for a few names – is it worth the sacrifice? – your life, liberty, the pursuit of happiness—'

He was interrupted by polite knocking at the door. For an unguarded second, hope flickered on Hilken's face before his expression settled in a sullen frown.

'Who is it?' Wolff demanded.

'My clerk. I expect he's come to collect the papers I was working on.'

Another knock at the door. 'Mr Hilken? Müller, sir.'

'Let me see,' said Wolff, waving Thwaites' revolver at the documents on the desk.

They were invoices and orders, nothing of importance. Wolff handed them back, then gestured with the gun to the door.

'Your driver's waiting, sir.' The clerk sounded bemused. Hilken handed him the papers and they spoke briefly about the next day's business. He was clearly surprised to be going through the diary in the corridor. 'Is everything all right?'

Perfectly, Hilken assured him, and was on the point of closing the door when he checked, his forefinger across his lip. 'The victualling of the *Breslau* – I almost forgot – it needs a signature.' He turned back to his desk for a pen. 'Tell my driver I'll be down in ten minutes.' He bent over the document the clerk presented to him and wrote his name. Wolff realised it had been a mistake to let him even as the door was closing.

'Your offer,' Hilken said quickly. 'I might be able to collect this information – it will take a little time, just a few hours. Of course, I'd want Dr Albert's accounts in return.'

'Has Dilger gone?'

'Yes.'

'And the anthrax – you still have some?'

Hilken examined his nails. 'A little.'

'Where?'

'That's Hinsch's concern,' he replied evasively.

'And you're going to culture more?' Wolff asked, walking to one of the windows overlooking the street.

Another long pause. 'We haven't talked about it.'

Wolff knew he was lying. 'And Dilger – are you expecting him back or is his brother going to culture it?'

A streetcar, perhaps the last of the night, pulled up to the stop outside the building and a drunken sailor stumbled up its steps, tripping and almost falling at the top.

'No, Dr Dilger's gone and won't come back,' Hilken said in a neutral monotone.

Hilken's Packard was parked at the kerb, the driver's back against the bonnet, a cigarette burning between his fingers. A noise seemed to startle him; he turned sharply to look down the street but at what, Wolff couldn't tell.

'You know, Hilken, I could knock you down.' He stepped away from the window and closer to the desk. 'I could shoot you. Or you could give me the names I want – the sailors and their ships. They're here, aren't they?'

'No. I don't . . .' he hesitated, taking a step sideways behind the desk. 'I'll shout for help. My clerk, and there are thirty . . .'

407

'You can try,' Wolff levelled the gun at him. 'It might be the last thing you do. You're wondering if I'm bluffing . . .' He *was* bluffing, but it was invested with fifteen years of quiet menace.

'I haven't got the names.' Hilken's voice shook. 'I haven't. Not here.' He was lying.

Wolff was upon him before he had time to raise a word, striking him hard on the left cheekbone with the grip of the gun, then a punch to his right side. As he fell, Hilken struck his head on the edge of the desk. Dazed, whimpering, he sprawled on the floor beneath it, Wolff on one knee beside him, breathing hard, the revolver raised to strike again. 'Tell me,' Wolff gasped; 'tell me.' The words came to him like an echo from his Turkish prison cell, and in that instant he was gazing up at a sunburnt face with a full moustache, dark smiling eyes. Hilken tried to curl into a ball. 'Please. I don't . . . just, just . . . please don't . . .' he mumbled between fingers. And this time the echo was Wolff's own voice. *Christ.*

'The drawer,' Hilken said. 'The drawer.'

'Which one?'

'Right – top right.'

'Stay there,' Wolff commanded.

A black file, papers in date order, and glancing through, a sheet with a list of eight ships.

'The *Richmond*, the *Lagan*, *Oberon* . . . ?' He pushed Hilken with his shoe.

'Yes.'

'And the sailors' names?'

'Devoy has those. Only Devoy – that's the deal.'

It made sense and it sounded true. He had the ships at least, that was a start. 'All right. I'll contact you tomorrow. Time for you to collect the names of the people you are using in the port, and an opportunity to think about how much you enjoy being a pillar of society. What a hard thing it would be to give up.'

'But what if I . . .' Hilken was struggling too obviously for something to say, his thoughts at the end of the corridor or in the hall or in the shadows of the street.

'Just give me the key to your room.'

The clerk had gone, his desktop empty but for a rectangle of writing paper and four sharp pencils in perfect parallel lines. Wolff locked Hilken in his office with a fleeting prayer: *Please God, the oily bastard's in there a long time.* It was galling to acknowledge but he knew his clumsy attempt at blackmail was going to fail. I've shot Wiseman's bolt and hit very little, he thought, as he walked quickly along the corridor to the stairs. Large payments from a foreign diplomat to a business-man's private accounts were proof of nothing but profiteering, and wasn't that just the sort of enterprise to make America richer still? Perhaps he should have tried harder. It was the recollection of Turkey, his own torturer – well, he couldn't – just the thought made him sick. The ships, he had the names of the ships.

The singing had stopped and someone was trying to stroke the old piano through the Moonlight Sonata. The party in the club below was over and a commanding voice and the clatter of furniture suggested the stewards were clearing the tables. If Hilken's clerk was organising a reception committee, it wouldn't be here, he thought. At the bottom of the stairs the doors of the club swung open and a sober-looking merchant officer stalked out with his hat under his arm. Wolff followed him from the building but waited in its shadow and watched him climb into a horse cab. Parked a few feet from the entrance was Hilken's Packard – the driver had retreated behind the wheel – and striding along the sidewalk opposite, two smartly dressed men, heads bent in conversation. Midnight on a chilly downtown street in March, well lit, almost empty, nothing out of the ordinary or so it seemed, but his heart was pounding. Where the hell was Masek? He could feel the danger creeping over his skin.

Sidewalk to sidewalk on the brightest streets, bending his mind to movement, faces, footsteps, a reflection shifting in a shop window; a route through downtown Baltimore; *and if I'm lucky I'll find a cab.* Cursing Masek as he walked, because at such times it was important to blame someone. On Baltimore Street he was startled by a drunk who lurched out of an office doorway to ask for money.

'Get lost,' he muttered angrily. Half a block further on he was sorry he hadn't found a nickel or dime. Baltimore was so empty, so still, the sound of his own footsteps was unnerving. It reminded him for just a moment of Conan Doyle's *The Poison Belt*; the gas cloud that wipes people from the world, leaving its streets to machines.

Beyond the Custom House he began to breathe more easily. A few blocks to the harbour basin, on into President Street and he would be there. *What happened to you, Masek?* Ahead of him now, the chimney of the new pumping station; on his right the lights of the city dock. Damn stupid to check in to the hotel under the same cover name; what was he thinking? Careless, as if it was over, when it was never over. He tightened his grip on the revolver.

Two sailors staggered from an alleyway with their arms draped around each other and began to weave along the sidewalk away from him. He slowed a little, seeking some assurance that they were the harmless drunks they appeared to be. They were disconcertingly well-built men, the sort he used to baulk at tackling on the naval college rugby field. Drawing closer, his pulse began to quicken again. There was something wrong. What? He was close enough now to hear their shuffling foot-steps. Footsteps, footsteps. They were rolling home in silence.

I'm a fool. It was a performance. He'd known a lot of drunken sailors, he'd often been drunk himself and he could remember quiet moments, but not at turning-out time, not in a street, not with an arm round a buddy.

Christ. Here we go again; and he set off across the street, checking for just a second to avoid a passing carriage. Only three blocks more to the hotel; and if the bastards came for him, he'd fire one over their heads. They were sober now all right, keeping step through one junction, and the next, and past the pumping station, men on the graveyard shift smoking at its gates: *They won't take me here.* But a few more yards and they made their move, breaking across the street towards him. Turning smartly, steadying himself, he took aim: 'Halt.' For a second they did, but only for a second, edging forward step by step like children in a playground game. To be sure they knew these were his rules, he yelled: 'Another and you're dead.' But the larger of the two seamen kept coming. *Have it your own way then*; he was close enough to be sure he'd hit something. He squeezed, the revolver kicked, the seaman crumpled, the shot echoed for ever – or so it seemed because at that moment he felt a searing pain in his shoulder. A scream locked behind his teeth, and he spun round to confront a man with a bullet head and blue eyes, his mouth slightly open and his knife raised to strike again. Wolff tried to level the gun but he felt weak and someone was holding his arm. There were more men – three – a tangle of arms and fists and boots. Then an agonising jarring in his chest, and through a blinding kaleidoscope of shapes and lights he fell. *I'm going to die.* He was lying on the cobblestones and he'd never felt colder. *I love you, and I'm sorry.* He tried to shape the words but couldn't move his lips. *That's it then – over, over. Hadn't it all been a bloody waste.*

35

Attrition

M ASEK WAS FOUND floating in the harbour. They left Wolff
where he fell. The doctors at the Johns Hopkins Hospital
did all in their power, without hope. The blade passed within
half an inch of his heart and he'd haemorrhaged too much
blood to recover, or so they said.

Beyond the bright white confines of the hospital, the thick
cotton sheets, the perfect bed corners, the laboratory coats and
starched aprons, a dirty little battle was fought over his body
in the press and on Capitol Hill. The Baltimore *Evening Sun*
broke the first story. *The stabbing in our streets of a Dutch
engineer united the sympathies of the citizens of this city*, its
columnist, Mr Mencken, observed; *but this newspaper understands that the unfortunate Mr de Witt is neither Dutch nor an
engineer. He is a British spy.* The newspaper's well-informed source
was also able to reveal that a Norwegian sailor called Christensen
had told the authorities in Berlin that the same spy had
tried to induce him to betray the Irish patriot, Sir Roger Casement.

The answering shot came in the *New York Times* under the
headline: 'Germans attack America again'. The newspaper had
seen *incontrovertible evidence* implicating German diplomats
and *respectable American businessmen* in another sabotage
campaign. *Using the ships and premises of the Norddeutscher
Lloyd Line as cover, ruthless men have sought to undermine
this country's interests and security*, its editor wrote in an

opinion piece. *German Americans must now show where their true loyalty lies.* A few days later the *New York World* was able to reveal that police were investigating *shocking* claims that German agents in America were using *a terrible new biological weapon. With help from sympathisers in this country, German agents are infecting animals with anthrax in the hope of striking at Allied soldiers and their supply lines on the battlefields in France.* In the course of this attack, at least one American dockworker was infected and had died, the paper claimed, and it printed a picture of a prominent Baltimore businessman with the caption: *Mr Paul Hilken has denied any role in the campaign.*

By April, Congressmen were debating it on the floor of the House and a senator called on the presidential candidates to pledge that they would do all in their power to end 'the secret war' being waged by Britain and Germany on American soil. Finally the German diplomat, Dr Albert, was asked to leave the country and efforts were made to arrest his associates. For a time the police search for the guilty men pushed the glad tidings of record-breaking export sales to the Allies down the page, and the slaughter on the battlefield at Verdun inside.

Wolff knew nothing of his celebrity. Later, when he thought of the weeks he had spent at Johns Hopkins, he could remember only disparate images: a nurse with eyes a little like Laura's lifts a cup to his lips; a fly struggles in a single thread at the angle of the ceiling; hushed voices, the yellow shaft of the morning sun through a chink in the curtains they never seemed able to close; and in the afternoons the shadow of a maple tree dancing tirelessly on the wall.

Then, as conscious minutes became hours, Thwaites' valet reading in a bored monotone at his bedside: *'There pass the careless people / That call their souls their own . . .'*

'Oh Christ, have some pity,' he mumbled, and White jumped

up, excited: 'Them's your first words,' and he made Wolff smile: 'You shouldn't blaspheme, sir, not after what you've been through.' And after that they all came. Gaunt paced his room, barely making eye contact, a quip about nurses' ankles, a promise to 'see to Hinsch', and a present of *The Life of Horatio, Lord Nelson* by Southey. Thwaites refused to tell him anything but left a small bottle of brandy, and Wiseman brought some letters from home, and the news of the Easter Rising in Dublin. 'Army wasn't ready – in spite of our warning,' he said with a resigned shrug, 'but the rebels didn't have enough support anyway.'

'Were there German soldiers?'

'None, and the Navy intercepted the guns they'd sent – oh, and that damn fool Casement was captured by a local bobby almost as soon as he stepped ashore.'

A nurse brought Wiseman coffee and he joked and flirted with her as she rustled about the bed in her well-starched uniform, refolding corners, plumping pillows. When she had gone he reached into his briefcase and lifted a stained sheet of paper. 'Remember this? You should – you spilt your blood for it.' It was the list of ships Wolff had taken from Hilken's office. 'We found it in your jacket,' Wiseman explained. 'Bloody fools didn't look, or didn't have time to. Anyway, we identified the sailors. Their captains detained them as soon as they left American waters, and we had a reception committee waiting for them in France. They didn't have much idea what they were doing – thought it was just an attack on our animals.' He paused, patting the mattress in a show of applause, then said with feeling, 'Well done, really, old chap. Well done. Only sorry it ended for you in hospital.'

Wolff smiled weakly. The whole damn business made him feel low.

'You're tired,' he said, rising, brushing the creases from his trousers; 'thoughtless of me.'

'No, no, I'm sorry.'

Wiseman gazed intently at him and for a second their eyes met. 'Is something troubling you?'

'Yes. Roger Casement – you said they'd taken him?'

Wiseman couldn't quite conceal his surprise. 'Yes, *we* have,' he said with careful emphasis. 'He's being held in the Tower of London of all places – makes more of him than he deserves, if you ask me.'

'And after that?'

'He'll go on trial for treason. Does that concern you?'

'Yes, it does.'

He nodded thoughtfully. 'Well, you should know, the other Irish leaders were shot.'

A few days later Wiseman arranged for a guard in the corridor outside Wolff's room. 'You're not that popular,' Thwaites explained. 'The Germans will probably leave you alone but Sir William's concerned about the Irish.'

The doctors tried to refuse Wolff newspapers but he insisted that boredom would set back his recovery. They all carried Casement's appearance in a London court and the prosecution's case that he was a traitor. 'Not to the Irish people,' his sister, Mrs Agnes Newman, told the *New York Times.* 'He is an Irishman captured in a fair attempt to achieve his country's freedom.'

Only at the end of May was Wolff permitted to leave the hospital. Wiseman rented a handsome weatherboard beach house on Long Island. An attentive young lieutenant from the embassy called Keane travelled with him in the motor car.

'Can't we go to New York?' Wolff asked, a little pathetically.

But he loved the house. Perched alone at the top of a dune, with picture windows and a veranda looking out to the Atlantic, he was content sitting for hours watching the tide roll in up the beach and out again. Sometimes he could see only the dark shadows on the sea's surface, but they passed, and at night its shushing helped him sleep. Most days were bright with a stiff onshore breeze whipping fine salt spray in his face. It was on just such a day in June that Wiseman and Thwaites came bumping up the track.

'We're celebrating,' Thwaites shouted, lifting a hamper from the motor car. 'The Royal Navy has engaged the enemy at Jutland – a complete victory – at least that's what our people are saying. Apparently the Germans are saying the same.'

'Another stalemate then,' Wolff remarked.

'Make up your own mind, old boy.' Wiseman thrust a bundle of newspapers at him. 'On such a lovely day even a draw is worth celebrating.'

They spread a blanket on the beach in front of the house. The food was from the Waldorf, 'because even if we're pretending, we should do it properly,' Wiseman said. Cold fried chicken, salmon and mayonnaise, veal, tongue, cheeses, pickles, jellies, cakes: a great deal more than they could manage. 'Emergency rations in case we stay the night.'

As they ate and drank, Thwaites entertained them with the story of the visit he'd made to the home of a millionaire socialite. 'Showed me an album of photographs – honestly, I almost fell off my chair. There was old Bernstorff, the German Ambassador, cavorting with a couple of young things, neither of them his wife – who isn't that young. I said to myself, "Norman, that picture is priceless" – so I stole it. That's the sort of education you get working for newspapers. And, well, stop the presses – there will be red faces in the German Embassy tomorrow.'

After lunch Wiseman lay snoozing in the afternoon sunshine, his moustache twitching beneath his boater like a fat mouse.

'Don't you want to know what's happening to Hinsch and the others?' Thwaites asked as they ambled along the shore. 'Don't you care? They almost killed you.'

'I honestly don't. Glad to be given another chance, that's all.'

'Hinsch is in hiding somewhere. Hilken's still at his desk. We've thrown a lot of mud but not enough of it has stuck.'

'So there's nothing to stop them trying again?'

Thwaites stopped to gaze at the sea. 'It's beautiful here.'

'Very.'

'There's something you should know.' His gaze was fixed on the horizon. 'The New York police, actually Captain Tunney of the Bomb Squad, is taking an interest in de Witt.'

'Because of the man in the derby hat?'

Thwaites looked blank. 'I don't . . .'

'The police informer I . . .'

'Yes,' he said quickly, 'the police informer.' He glanced at Wolff, then down, drawing the point of his stick over the wet sand. 'I've tried to convince Tunney it's nothing to do with you.'

'But he doesn't believe you.'

'No.' The pattern he was drawing with his stick resembled the criss-cross grille over the window of a prison cell. 'But you don't need to worry,' he said. 'Sir William is sorting it out.'

'Oh?'

'I think I'll let him say.'

Wolff smiled weakly. 'As you wish.'

A short time later, Thwaites announced that he was driving back to New York. A meeting with a newspaper reporter, he said. It was the sort of smooth polite lie they told each other all the time. Wolff said he was sorry, and Wiseman pretended to be surprised but joked that there wasn't enough food left for him anyway.

And when he'd gone they retreated from the advancing tide

to the veranda to gaze at the rippling gold and grey of the evening.

'You heard about the New York police?' Wiseman enquired eventually. He leant close to fill Wolff's glass. 'The President's people are going to hold them off. Don't want a scandal.' He lifted his champagne to the dying light. 'This isn't bad. Actually, it's bloody good – 1911. What do you think?'

'Yes, it's good. Thank you.'

'Yes, it is.' He lifted the glass to his lips then lowered it again without drinking. 'Unfortunately there is a price for fending off our friends in the police. Thing is, President Wilson has promised the people he won't allow foreign spies to flout the law, and it's an election year, so it's a promise he wants to keep.' He offered an ironic smile. 'What's more, we're supposed to be the good boys. The President's on our side, well, his advisers are . . .'

Wolff interrupted: 'So you want me out of the way?'

'They do, old boy, they do. Persona non grata, I'm afraid.'

For a while they didn't speak, their silence filled with the sea's sad cadence.

'Perhaps it's for the best – it isn't safe for you here,' Wiseman said at last. 'When America comes into the war this nonsense will be . . .'

'You think she will enter the war?'

'I do. One last heave, I say.'

'But it isn't nonsense, is it? The death of the informer.' Wolff swept his hand across his eyes. 'I did kill him.'

'Yes, you had to.' Wiseman shifted his chair a little to look Wolff in the eye. 'And you were extraordinarily brave. HMG owes you a great debt of gratitude. It owes me the price of the best champagne I could buy to thank you properly on its behalf,' and he raised his glass in salute.

'I thought we were toasting the victory at Jutland?'

'Course not. Another costly stalemate. It would be a waste of good champagne.'

Wolff smiled weakly. 'You know, I've done nothing of real worth.'

'Now you're fishing for compliments, old boy.'

'They'll culture more poison. Probably send another von Rintelen.'

'Of course they will,' he huffed, 'it's a war – goodness, a bloody brutal one. A war of attrition. We've enjoyed a few victories, that's all, we haven't won it. But when they come back it will be harder. The President has told his advisers America must start protecting its interests more vigorously – happily, those interests correspond with our own.'

He paused to sip his champagne, his lips smacking a little. 'It's one of those little ironies thrown up by war that the more trouble the enemy causes us here in America, the better we like it, because our hosts are losing patience.'

The tide had crept up the beach and would soon be at the full, the sea quite calm, a feathery trail of mist lifting from its face but a shining firmament above.

'When do I leave?' Wolff asked, offering his cigarette case.

'No, thank you. My pipe,' Wiseman said, tapping his blazer pocket. 'Soon, I think – a fortnight? Is that all right? White will accompany you.'

'That isn't necessary.'

'We think it is. Don't want you dumped over the side like a sick horse.'

Wolff bent to the flame he was cupping in his hands and inhaled deeply. 'I've a favour to ask.'

'Ask away.'

'Something I must do. Actually someone I must see. I'd like a driver for a day, perhaps two.'

Wiseman frowned thoughtfully. 'Do you think that's wise?'

'No.' Wolff drew deeply on his cigarette. 'No, it isn't wise. It *is* something I must do.'

'I see.' Wiseman took out his pipe and spent a few minutes preparing and lighting it. Teeth clamped on the bit, he muttered, 'Just this pipe, then bed.' The tide was high now and breaking gently thirty yards from the house. Soon it would turn and draw away from the fringes of the earth.

'This business with the poison – the anthrax,' he said, inspecting the bowl of his pipe. 'I don't mind telling you, Wolff, it's shaken my faith in the march of man, or for want of a better . . . civilisation. Is that an inevitable consequence of war, I wonder – any war?'

Wolff examined the back of his hands. 'I have a friend who says only a great moral cause is worthy of such sacrifice. Is ours a great moral cause?'

Wiseman sighed. 'I don't know. Perhaps it is too late to ask.'

The Consulate Cadillac collected Wolff from the beach house two days later. It was midday when they parked outside Laura's apartment on the Upper West Side. He didn't expect her to be in at that hour. Campaigning for a new world, he thought, instantly ashamed of his cynicism. He sent the driver to eat and sat gazing at her front door. An old lady hobbled out to a waiting carriage and a short time later a concierge helped a nurse and her young charges to another. There was a chance that he would be there for hours. He was torn between impatience to see her and relief that he couldn't. In the many idle hours of his recovery he'd often pondered what he might say. He couldn't explain, and why would she believe him if he said he loved her? He was sorry and he hated what he'd done; that much he should say, he had to say.

When the driver returned from lunch Wolff instructed him to leave his hat and jacket in the motor car and join New

York in the park. Was Laura there too? It was an overpoweringly hot afternoon; he guessed the thermometer was pushing ninety-five. An expensively dressed young couple came out of the adjoining block and floated arm-in-arm along the street. At three o'clock, Laura's aunt took a cab west towards the river. Oppressively stuffy in the Cadillac, by half past three he'd smoked his last cigarette. For God's sake, he thought, what's the point of hiding? He felt a little better in the sunshine, leaning against the scorching bonnet and meandering short distances, the heat shimmering over the sidewalk. I'm glad to be alive in spite of this, of everything, he reflected, and if he felt a little weak and tired of waiting he was sure it was the right thing to do. It was possible he would be there all evening.

But it didn't happen like that in the end. At a little after five o'clock he saw her walking briskly from the direction of the Columbus Circle subway. She was wearing a cream dress and floppy sunhat to protect her fair skin, wisps of hair escaping as always, lifting her left hand to tidy them away, and again after only a few steps; leather portfolio in her right hand; bending into her stride, unmistakably a woman of purpose. He felt sick with confusion but at the same time full of joy and sudden, crazy, crazy hope. He began to walk towards her – *when will she see me?* – but she was occupied with her thoughts. He could imagine the little frown of concentration hovering at her brow. Taking a shaky breath, he stepped lightly into the street, his gaze fixed on her advancing figure.

He was a few yards from her when she lifted her head and caught him there. She stopped abruptly, eyes screwed tight shut, an anguished expression, and biting her lip. Then, dropping her chin so her face was hidden by the brim of her hat, she set off again, her pace quickening with every step.

'Laura,' he called. His voice sounded distant, uncertain. 'Can we talk?' He tried to step closer, but she raised her hand as if to push him away.

'Laura, I want to say . . .' but he wasn't able to – not yet. 'Please stop. Please speak to me.'

'Leave me alone,' she said in barely more than a whisper. He was at her side, step for step.

'Did you know about Dilger? Doctor Dilger?'

She ignored him.

'Dilger – you were sheltering . . .' He was trying to engage her, but her stride didn't falter. 'Look, I know what you must think of me. I'm sorry – believe me – I didn't want to hurt you. I didn't think I would . . .' Words stuck in his throat again. Without thinking, he reached a hand out to her.

'If you were a gentleman, you'd leave me alone,' she said quietly, her voice shaking with anger.

She's right, he thought with sudden cold clarity, like a drunk in a fleeting moment of sobriety. 'Of course, if you wish . . .'

'How can you doubt it?' and she glanced up at him, her blue-green eyes sparkling with a fury that cut deeper than the German sailor's knife.

'Yes, I'll leave,' he said softly. 'I wanted to say how sorry I feel – and that I did – I *do* – love you.'

She ignored him, lifting the hem of her dress to lengthen her stride, almost scuttling, frantic to cover the last few yards to her door. That was almost the end of the affair, but in her hurry to escape she tripped and, pitching forward, dropped her portfolio. It burst, spilling papers on the sidewalk. 'Oh God, no,' she cried in frustration.

He bent down to help her, anchoring as many as he could, their hands close as she scrabbled for the papers with her nails, one hand still to her hat. He couldn't see her face but he saw her shoulders rise and fall heavily as she struggled to control her feelings, and a few seconds later he heard her strangle a sob.

'Oh Laura, I'm so sorry.'

And then she looked up, her lower lip trembling, her fine eyes wet with tears. 'How could you? How could you?' she asked, and the dam burst, her words flowing in an agonising torrent: 'Who are you, who – how could you when I loved you? – but I don't know you – you betrayed Roger – and Nina – everyone – you let me love you, and you lied – liar! You liar! Liar!'

He tried to touch her but she brushed his hand away. 'Liar! What do you care – liar – you care for nothing, no one – I don't even know your name – liar,' and with a heart-wrenching groan she rose from the sidewalk, papers clenched in her tiny fist, and turning to the door – somehow she managed to find the key – closed it quietly behind her. He could hear her sobbing in the entrance hall and a moment later saw her silhouette at the pane of blue glass to the left of the door. She was bent almost double in tears.

'Laura.' He rapped on the door once. 'Laura, let me in – please.'

There was only a thickness of glass between them but she didn't turn to look at him or reply.

'Laura, I love you. Please,' he pleaded, longing to cherish her. But she wasn't going to open the door. She couldn't forgive him and perhaps she wanted to punish them both, because she stood crying at the window for at least ten minutes. Wolff waited in silence beside her.

Then, standing straight and without a backward glance to the shadow in the glass, she walked away. He followed her footsteps across the mosaic floor and heard the elevator doors open and close and knew she'd gone. Her leather portfolio was still lying on the sidewalk, papers fluttering in the gusts from passing cars. Moving slowly and in a mist, he painstakingly collected them all and posted the portfolio through the letterbox.

A few days later, he took a passage to England.

36

The English Sickness

BERLIN WAS NOT the city it used to be. Everything was changing and for the worse, Anton Dilger reflected as he shuffled from the platform on to the station concourse. He could read it in the creased face of the factory worker beside him in the queue, and in the rheumy eyes of the old lady with her eggs to sell at market, and he could hear it in the frazzled voice of a mother scolding the children at her skirt. Greyer, grubbier, thinner, the city was shrinking from the fine-figured lady she used to be into a street urchin. Every day of the three months he'd been home had brought new sadness. He shut his eyes for a second, trying to force from his mind the scenes he'd witnessed in Karlsruhe just a few days before, but he could hear an endless echo of them in the huff and rumble of the station.

His sister, Elizabeth, had taken it sorely when he had announced, after only a few weeks, that he was leaving Berlin to become a surgeon at a hospital closer to the Front.

'You've only just come back to me,' she had protested.

'Karlsruhe, isn't so far,' he had assured her.

Count Nadolny had tried to persuade him to stay, too.

'Take some time, but we need you here,' the Count had insisted. 'Things are worse in Germany – open your eyes, you'll see.'

And here I am again, he thought.

*

It was five in the afternoon and the queue for cabs stretched across the front of the station and round the side. Too impatient to wait, he threw his bag on his back like a soldier's knapsack and set off at a brisk pace. It was a fine June day and he hoped some vigorous exercise and sunshine would lift his spirits a little. But it was impossible to walk away from the war. Cripples begging in front of a church; at a street corner a gang of women in flat caps and bloomers, wielding picks and shovels as their menfolk at the Front used to do; and crossing the Tiergarten in silence a column of fresh young recruits – passers-by turning away, frightened to look them in the eye.

Walking on, the sun blinking, blinding through the trees, Dilger's mind was confused with angry thoughts, his chest tight with the unconscious pain of memory. Only the death of his sister's son, Peter, had hurt him like this before. Perhaps he'd been naïve not to understand the enemy's hate sooner.

In his first week home, his sister Elizabeth had asked him to visit a family in the working district of Wedding in the north of the city. The widow of the footman, she'd explained; the poor man had been killed a few months after her Peter and they had no money for a doctor. Dilger had found the family at the top of a tenement block, mother, grandmother and nine pale children in two rooms and a kitchen. The flat was almost empty of furniture and their clothes were riddled with more holes than a Swiss cheese. The youngest was lying listless in her cot, a scrap of skin and bone.

'How old is she?' he'd asked.

'Almost two,' came the reply. Shocked, he had berated the mother for neglect and she'd burst into anguished tears. What could she do with so many mouths to feed and no money? Scraping by on 120 marks a month, she said; they couldn't even afford the local food kitchen, and the ration of milk had been cut to a pint a day. They were living on tea and potatoes. 'We're all suffering from the sickness,' she'd sobbed.

'From what?' he'd asked.

'The English sickness,' she said.

Before he left he gave her some money and perhaps they'd eaten a little better for a few days. When he had described the visit to Elizabeth, she had said it was the same with most of the families in the district. 'You don't understand, Anton, you've come back from the land of plenty. It's the same in every city – your English sickness.' The curse of the blockade, the enemy's grip on the Atlantic – hadn't he seen it with his own eyes? Fleets of British ships loading grain, cattle, horses, shells, and America growing fat on the trade while Germany wasted away. His old neighbours in Chevy Chase called it 'neutrality'. 'If we don't win soon, we'll all be sick,' his sister had observed.

She was watching for him now at a window and greeted him on the doorstep. 'Oh Anton,' her voice quivered a little, 'I'm sorry – it must have been awful;' and she kissed him and gave his hand a comforting squeeze. He tried to say something but could manage only a crooked smile. The maid took his coat and he carried his own bag to his room, falling on the bed, breathing slowly, deeply. When he was calmer he rang for some tea and a hot bath.

They didn't speak of what he'd seen in Karlsruhe at dinner. Elizabeth told him she had visited the Zoological Gardens as they used to do every Sunday, but the gaiety had left the place. No concert band, no beer, only empty tables.

'And the colonel?' he asked, picking at his food. 'Have you heard from him?'

She reached for her handkerchief, as she always did when he mentioned her husband. 'He's well,' her voice was tense, 'but his regiment has been engaged in the fighting at Verdun.'

'Oh,' he replied as casually as he could, then, because he had to, 'I'm sure he'll keep well, Elizabeth.'

'Yes,' she said mechanically, because that was also the polite thing to say.

Then she scolded him gently, just as she had when he was a boy: 'You've hardly eaten anything, Anton – when so many go without food.'

After dinner they sat in her gloomy drawing room for ersatz coffee, and he drank the last of the colonel's French brandy. The clock on the mantelpiece was still silent in his nephew's memory. The photograph of him playing with Peter at the Dilger farm was on a table to the right of the fireplace; there was another of them both in uniform beneath the mirror.

'I read about the attack in the newspaper, Anton,' she said at last, leaning forward to touch his hand lightly. 'What is our world coming to?'

Then it tumbled from him, in bursts like machine-gun fire.

'They celebrate Corpus Christi with a festival in Karlsruhe,' he said. 'After the church services, there's a circus for the children – Hagenbeck's. It's famous for its elephants and lions. I heard the planes, then the anti-aircraft guns, but I . . .' he paused for a moment, too choked to continue; '. . . you see, the children were making so much noise no one in the big tent heard the enemy – anyway, I don't know how many bombs were dropped . . .' He paused again to take a deep breath. 'The children were wearing white robes from the church procession and they were ripped and bloody – terrible, terrible injuries, little arms and legs – we did all we could but . . . and the mothers trying to identify the bodies – oh God.' He let out a long sigh. 'We were operating all night – children – children are different, aren't they? It wasn't war – a crime – it was a crime. The papers say two hundred people killed – seventy children, and more injured: a church festival, Elizabeth. A church festival.'

428

She tried to hold him as she used to do when he was a child, but he pulled away from her. 'I didn't realise – it *is* a fight for our survival – the survival of the German race. Corpus Christi. Ha!' He wiped his cheek with the back of his hand and reached for his glass. '*Do this in remembrance of me* – isn't that what they say?' Then, after a pause, 'Sorry – what a performance.' He took a sip, the glass shaking against his teeth. 'I'm tired.'

'You've left the hospital, Anton?' she asked quietly.

'Yes.'

Silence.

'Will you try for one here?' She sounded anxious.

'No. No, I don't think so.'

Another silence.

'You know Emmeline wrote to me,' she said at last. 'She says some men were chasing you – Englishmen. They talked about your work – your experiments.'

He grunted crossly.

'She says they were spies. Don't be cross with her, Anton, she sent them away – she's worried about you, that's all.' She hesitated. 'I'm worried about you.'

He stood up abruptly. 'Yes. Well, she shouldn't – you shouldn't worry.' He spoke more sharply than he meant to because he felt guilty.

'Well, we are,' she said firmly. 'Emmeline says you've changed – I've noticed it too.'

He shrugged carelessly. 'Hasn't everybody? Isn't that war?'

She paused, her gaze steady. 'Will you see your Count Nadolny?'

'I don't know. Perhaps,' he said evasively, then, reluctant to lie to her, 'Probably – yes.'

Elizabeth's face was set in the determined expression they all had from their father. Feeling awkward, he stepped away from her to rest his elbow beside the silent clock on the mantelpiece.

'What will he ask you to do?'

'I don't know if he'll ask me to do anything,' he replied coolly.

'Promise me you won't do anything dangerous. Promise me.'

He smiled at her concern but wasn't sure what he should say. 'I don't know what—'

'Promise.'

'I'm not a soldier, like your Peter or the colonel.'

'Promise'; the pitch of her voice rising.

'I promise.'

Her gaze dropped to her hands, cupped in her lap. 'Promise me you won't do anything dishonourable.'

'Elizabeth,' he exclaimed, hurt by the implication that he might. 'Only my duty.'

She took a deep breath. 'War – this war – people are not themselves. The bitterness. Perhaps because it touches us all so. I don't know who will win – if it is even possible—'

'We must win,' he interrupted.

'Yes, yes,' she said, shifting impatiently on the edge of the settee, 'we will, Anton, I'm sure. But when it's over we must live with ourselves – with what we've become.'

'Didn't you hear me say – we're fighting for survival?'

'I don't know, Anton,' she replied quietly, 'but we must hold true to what is good, in others and in ourselves. Our father was so proud of you – his clever son, the doctor. You have the gift to heal – to help those who suffer. I'm sure he'd want you to use it. But I've said enough, I know.' Lifting her dress a little, she rose and took half a step towards him. 'You know we love you, Emmeline, Carl, Josephine, Butzie – all of us. Peter loved you too,' and she reached out to touch his arm. 'Please be careful.'

They didn't speak of the Count in the following days but he considered what she'd said, drifting through parks and through galleries, sitting in cafés where he paid too much for very little. In the new Kaiser Wilhelm Church, too, the blues and reds and yellows of the memorial glass dancing at his feet, and although he wasn't a believer he tried to say a prayer for the children of Karlsruhe. He telephoned Frieda Hempel but her house-keeper said she'd left to sing to the old Emperor in Vienna. One evening he visited a seedy club near the Anhalter Station with doctors he knew from his time at a city hospital. To pretend he was merry he drank too much, and when at last the girls came high-kicking on to the stage he felt ashamed. 'Thinner than before the war,' one of his companions remarked, with the carelessness of someone who spent most of his waking hours triaging the wounded. To forget, I must work, Dilger told himself, and he remembered thinking the same after Peter's death: only in action will I find release.

A baking hot day at the end of June, dressed in a light-blue suit from Wanamaker's like an American gentleman. Stifling on the tram, seated next to an old man with a summer cold, wheezing, and wiping his nose on his sleeve. Walking the last few stops, and the Military Veterinary Academy was extrava-gantly decked in imperial bunting. 'The Crown Prince of Prussia visited this morning,' the professor's assistant informed him as they walked along the whitewashed corridor. Professor Carl Troester was at his desk, tall and pale in the sunshine pouring through the window behind him. The room was extraordinarily bright, clinical like an operating theatre. Count Nadolny was rising from the chair beside him with a pleasant smile: 'My dear Doctor.' As he stepped forward his reflection was mirrored in the glass-fronted cabinets lining the walls, and for a moment it was easy to imagine he had many faces: dark-brown eyes appraising Dilger carefully, the signet ring pressing his hand, a gentle reminder always of his authority. 'Appalling.' He shook his head. 'So many children – a religious festival. I was just saying to the professor, it is impossible to imagine the enemy could mistake a striped circus tent for a military target' – he shepherded Dilger to a chair – 'and you operated on the children? What a shock.'

'You're our second important visitor of the day,' Troester observed with a distant smile. 'You saw the flags? The Crown Prince came to see some of the research we're doing on new vaccines.'

'And our work?' asked Dilger. 'Did you show His Royal Highness our work?' Startled by his hostile tone, Troester was unable to think of something to say.

'I didn't think it was wise, Doctor,' Nadolny remarked, coming to his rescue; 'not after the fuss in the American newspapers. We must let the dust settle.' The sun was full on his face, smoothing lines and the duelling scar from his skin. It seemed to Dilger he enjoyed its heat, his eyes almost closed, like the skinks that used to bask on walls at the family farm.

'You achieved so much in America,' said Troester, finding his voice. 'An experimental operation that yielded notable successes. So unfortunate it ended the way it did.'

'I blame myself, of course,' Nadolny declared. 'De Witt surprised us all. I should have taken more care. And I'm afraid Sir Roger Casement was a poor judge of men – rather an innocent – but that is the past and the future is our concern, isn't it, Professor?'

'Always, Count,' Troester replied stiffly, recognising the question as a gentle rebuke. The door opened and an orderly brought in the coffee. 'Thankfully we're not reduced to drinking acorns yet,' he observed, lazily stirring sugar into his cup. 'We will be if things carry on as they are.'

'The doctor has seen how things stand at home with his own eyes,' the Count said, turning to address Dilger more directly.

'You know, America was merely a setback. Your – our work isn't over – it can't be.' He paused, gazing down at his hands long enough to indicate that he was preparing to say something of importance. 'The Chief of the General Staff has given me authority to expand our operations – to improve the delivery of these germs . . .'

'Germs, Count?' Troester snorted contemptuously.

'To harness the deadly force of nature, shall we say. New targets – new weapons—'

'What sort of new weapons?' Dilger interjected.

'Well, we will consider everything – we must.' He inclined his head quizzically. 'I hope you agree?

They were staring at Dilger, inviting him to reply. Troester removed his pince-nez and wiped his face with his handkerchief. 'One of our doctors is proposing we drop liquid cultures of plague bacilli from Zeppelins,' he declared, inspecting his glasses carefully. 'But there are other possibilities – cholera perhaps.'

'We need someone with experience to explore the possibilities,' Nadolny explained; 'direct an experimental laboratory.'

In the corridor outside the office, the sound of breaking glass and the clatter of a tray.

'Clumsy fool,' Troester muttered.

'And the Crown Prince?' Dilger enquired. 'Will he be invited to visit this new experimental laboratory?'

Nadolny smiled. 'I know why you ask – and you're right, there is a certain hypocrisy. No, it will remain secret . . .' he paused, examining his nails thoughtfully. 'But it's part of the science of war now, whether the rest of the world is ready to acknowledge it or not. The enemy will do the same in time; he'll have to – it's the future.'

Troester was shuffling papers on his desk impatiently. It was too hot in his office. *I'm perspiring so profusely they'll think I'm afraid*, Dilger reflected as he gazed beyond the

433

professor to the window and the stern face of the Charité opposite. His sister had told him that the hospital was founded by the Prussian King to treat victims of the plague. But that was then; this is now, he thought. They were at the beginning of a new century, a new age.

37

Of Innocence

C SENT THE new office boy to escort Wolff to London.
'What happened to Fitzgerald?' Wolff enquired.

'Didn't care for the work, sir,' came the reply. 'He enlisted –
probably in this latest show.'

The show was the British offensive on the Somme that had
begun on the first of July, just four days before. His young
chaperone, Lieutenant Snow, was full of the news and confident
that victory was at most weeks away. The *Times* correspondent
in France sounded a more cautious note, describing the battle
as 'ninety miles of continuous chaos, uproar and desolation'.
Just the fog of war, Snow declared, shaking the newspaper
excitedly. Wolff said he would wait for it to clear. His eye had
been caught by a small piece on an inside page, confirming
that the King was to 'degrade the traitor' Roger Casement of
his knighthood.

At Charing Cross Station they were held at the platform barrier
while the wounded from a hospital train were loaded into
ambulances. 'Haven't stopped,' Wolff heard a guard grumbling
to a passenger; 'so many we're diverting to Paddington.' A crowd
had gathered in the Strand to cheer the wounded as they swept
by. Snow spent ten minutes searching for a taxicab before
tentatively suggesting they leave the luggage and walk. 'If you're
feeling strong enough, sir?'

It was the sort of hot white-sky day that made London seem drabber and oppressively close. Christ, wasn't it good to be home, Wolff thought with a pang of regret, what with its dirty little buildings and khaki uniforms, Coleman's and Wright's, 'Enlist today' and 'Let your conscience be your guide, boys', while in Trafalgar Square well-heeled women shook their tins for the limbless. He longed for the shade of a canyon street and the view to the Hudson from his last apartment, and, well, lots of things it was foolish to contemplate.

They had drained the lake in St James's Park so the Army could build barrack huts; it wasn't the pleasant place to walk that it used to be. Soldiers showed no respect for things they couldn't polish. Lieutenant Snow was anxious because they were late, and C was unpleasant to people who were late. Wolff trailed faithfully in his wake, very short of breath. He'd spent the daylight hours of the Atlantic crossing wrapped in a blanket on the promenade deck and his evenings brooding and drinking in his cabin. A comfortable invalid, at least; he had Sir William to thank for easing his passage.

The doorman at The Rag recognised him although it was a year since his last visit. He would have made a good spy. Cumming was waiting in the same private room, with its guns and spears and portraits of Empire soldiers. Advancing with just one stick now and a broad smile of welcome – 'Good crossing? First class, wasn't it? Suppose you deserved it' – peering at him through his gold monocle, in his particular way – 'you're thinner.'

'Probably. Yes.'

They sat in the same leather armchairs by the hearth. 'Did the war seem a long way from America?' he asked.

'Not when the Germans are trying to kill you.'

'I meant the fighting in France. The newspapers say you could hear the guns firing for this new offensive in London. I didn't hear them.' He removed his monocle and inspected it for a few seconds, then slipped it back in his eye. 'Country's expecting a decisive victory.' There was just the suggestion in his voice that he didn't share the general optimism. 'I hear there are a lot of casualties.'

Wolff nodded slowly. There was nothing he could say that wouldn't sound either bitter or trite.

'Sir William thinks we can expect more trouble in America,' C continued. 'Our lawyers say anthrax is illegal –' he laughed grimly – 'illegal! Be sure and tell the police, I told them. But the politicians are a-flutter. They want to know what will happen if the Germans try the same thing here – with something nastier perhaps. "What about civilians?" they ask. "I don't know," I say; "ask your scientists." "You must have spies," they say; "find out what they're thinking" – as if it were as simple as marching another battalion over the top.' C leant forward, his large sailor's hands resting on top of his stick. 'I've tried to understand why I find the use of these diseases so shocking.' He sighed heavily. 'It's a long way from the Battle of Trafalgar, isn't it?'

For a while neither of them spoke, C restlessly tap-tapping his stick against his shoe. Lifting his Punch-like chin at last, he asked: 'Did Roger Casement know about the anthrax, I wonder? He put the Germans in touch with the Irish in America, didn't he?'

'He wouldn't have approved.'

'Well, Wolff, you must have a higher opinion of him than the rest of us,' C remarked tartly. 'Count Nadolny was handling both Casement and Dilger. So I think we can assume . . .'

'Another reason to hang him, I suppose?'

'I don't think we need another reason.' Cumming was fidgeting, trying to keep his temper. 'Ironic that you were betrayed by the same man, don't you think – that Norwegian sodomite Christensen.'

Wolff shook his head a little. 'Actually, I'm glad. It was a relief.'

'You're a strange fish. Did you know Casement was like that, by the way?'

'No,' he lied.

'I don't think I believe you.' C bent his head to one side, gazing at him thoughtfully. 'We will hang him, you know. How do you feel about that?'

'Does it matter how I feel?'

'No, not really, I suppose. There's a lot of bitterness, you see. They – we – put him on a pedestal, didn't we? No one's inclined to be forgiving, not the way the war's going – and not with Irishmen dying in khaki for their country.'

'I'm sure there will be plenty of his compatriots who think he's doing the same.'

'There may be some, yes,' he conceded. 'Not sure they'll feel the same when they hear about his proclivities.'

'Why would they?'

He looked awkward, even shifty. 'Not my business – Special Branch are handling those things. I think it . . .' He hesitated, ready to say more, then thought better of it. 'Anyway, thought you should know.'

'Know?'

'That they're going to hang him.'

'You're very sure.'

'Yes,' he said firmly, 'I am sure.'

Wolff tried to sound matter-of-fact. 'I'm sorry.'

'Don't hate yourself for it, Wolff, you're not responsible. The bloody fool should have stayed in Germany.'

There was another long silence, with C scrutinising him through his damned monocle like Reid at the hospital in Baltimore. 'You're battered and bruised but safe – I'm glad,' he said, levering himself from his chair. 'I must let you go.'

They drifted towards the door. 'Take a few weeks' leave. I can see you need a little more time to recover.' Then, more jauntily, 'And I almost forgot, you've been promoted – Commander Wolff. Thoroughly deserved – congratulations.'

Wolff said thank you, and he supposed he was grateful. In the taxicab to Devonshire Place, he wondered why, and reasoned that it was probably natural to take pleasure in promotion even if he despised most of what he'd done to earn it. His apartment was clean, tidy, empty and soulless. Returning to it after so long, he felt like Mole in *The Wind in the Willows*, catching on the breeze the telegraphic current of the past, not happy times but thrilling ones. The housekeeper had folded Violet's scarf and placed it on the arm of a couch. She must have left it the night he'd spent ashore from the ship, just a few months – or was it weeks? – before she'd become the Honourable Mrs Lewis. Lieutenant Snow had seen to his luggage and it arrived within the hour. He didn't unpack: he was sick of the closeness of the old city already.

First thing the following morning he sent a telegram to his mother, then took a taxicab to King's Cross. Rumbling north felt like a journey through his life, a familiar roll call of stations and memories, home on leave from the sea, undergraduate outings at Cambridge, and school visits to Ely, the ship of the Fens, its lantern tower brilliant in the July sunshine. At King's Lynn Station he paid a cab to drive him the last few miles across the Great Ouse into the open Lincolnshire farmland, drained and settled by the Dutch for centuries and more recently by his own family. Hamlets, isolated farms and the breeze from the Wash shaking the hip-high barley and wheat, still a few weeks from harvest. Above all, a vast tent of sky: wondrous as a boy, wondrous still. He thought perhaps that something of him had been shaped by its moods, its emptiness, its deep summer blues and angry winter greys, the shifting chiaroscuro of the Fens, clouds scattering and amassing in infinite variations, like a great unfinished symphony.

The farm was a mile from the village of Gedney, a large but undistinguished red-brick house and three low barns sheltered by trees. His grandfather had purchased the land with money he'd earned as a merchant captain with the Netherlands Steamship Company. It was the old man who'd taken him to school every day, rising before six to harness the horse and chaise.

The cab dropped him at the gate and he carried, half dragged his bags to the farmhouse. His mother discovered him bent double on the step.

'Trying to catch my breath,' he gasped.

She gave him a quiet smile of welcome and he rose to kiss her cheek.

'You look older, Sebastian,' she observed with characteristic bluntness. 'Are you unwell?'

'I'm getting better.'

She nodded. 'You look more like your father.'

She led him into the kitchen and he sat at the old oak table as she prepared their supper of boiled ham and potatoes. I'm older but she's just the same, he thought, as he watched her at the range, her grey hair – had it ever been anything else? – swept severely off her face in a bun, small like a chapel mouse but spirited, and sometimes fierce. A practical woman, strong, she liked to say, in the knowledge that Christ was her sword and shield. While she peeled and chopped and stirred he spoke of New York skyscrapers and the Statue of Liberty. As always, she listened with mild curiosity but asked no questions. 'I don't want you lie to me,' she'd explained once.

Later, she talked of the farm and how hard it was becoming to work with the young men away. The Baker boys had gone and John Vickers from Gedney Marsh, she said, and the Kidbys of Green Dyke had lost their eldest son already. It was a sin, and she'd told the minister so after chapel. '"Stop preaching nonsense," I said – my goodness, it was there on the wall above his head – "Thou Shalt Not Kill".'

She made Wolff say grace before supper and after it they wandered the farm together, the sun dipping into the barley. 'Will you stay for harvest?' she asked. He said he'd try to.

'It's a good life here, you know. A good Christian life.' She sounded sad, perhaps because she knew it didn't mean as much to him as she'd always hoped it would. 'We must hold on to that in these times.'

They stopped at the eastern edge, beyond it the old sea bank and the salt marsh stretching out to the Wash. Above them, an exaltation of larks chirruping gladly, a sound that always conjured this place for him.

'It's harder for clever people to be happy – sometimes it's a curse,' she said suddenly. 'I used to say that to your father. Do you have a lady friend?'

'There was someone for a time. She decided she didn't like me.'

'Was she a good woman?'

'Yes.'

'She might change her mind. Perhaps you'll persuade her.'

'Perhaps – one day.'

'Or there'll be someone else.' She threaded a grey hair behind her ear. 'Goodness, after this war there'll be plenty of women to choose from.' Then, pointedly, 'You'll be forty soon.'

He turned away from her to gaze out to the darkening sea. Is she lonely? he wondered. Perhaps she was worried about the future of the farm, the comfort of family, and grandchildren in old age. But if she wanted those things, she wouldn't say so.

There was no electricity at the farmhouse but she lit the oil lamp he'd always used and carried it up to his bedroom. Everything was how he'd left it when he went up to Cambridge. There was almost nothing to change. Black cross on white-washed wall, a few sticks of homely furniture, a single bed and a shelf of books. He picked up a favourite his grandfather had given him as a boy, its spine broken by over-eager young hands. It told of the voyages of famous Lincolnshire explorers, Flinders, Franklin and Bass, and Vancouver from King's Lynn. They had played their part in nurturing his restless spirit.

Over the next days, he rose early and rolled up his sleeves to repair fences and clear ditches, climbing up on the old barn to replace the broken tiles. In the afternoons he wandered through green lanes choked with kingcups and cow parsley, skirting fat wheatfields and striking across the old salt pans to the sea. Striding home late one evening, the sound of a tolling bell rolling across the fen from the tower at Gedney touched him deeply. Sempiternal, mysterious in childhood when death was so confusing – especially his father's – it was now an affecting reminder of the war and the poems White had read to him in hospital of ploughboys who would never grow old.

'Say a prayer for John Vickers,' his mother said, as she was readying his lamp a few hours later. 'He was only nineteen. He shouldn't have gone. He wasn't the sort to be a soldier.'

The following day Wolff rode the old cob into the village and ordered the newspapers. 'Do you want to know?' he asked his mother, spreading them on the kitchen table.

'Is it bad?'

'*The Times* is calling it the Battle of the Somme. It says: *fighting intense – another day of spectacular gains – relentless advance.* I don't know,' he paused, 'but I'm sure the correspondent doesn't either.'

There was a report that troubled him more, although he didn't speak of it to his mother. Somewhere on all the front pages was a column or so for Casement. His friends were seeking a reprieve but most of the newspapers were determined he should hang. To be sure they carried the public with them, they were blackening his name.

'Are you all right?' his mother enquired.

'Yes. Fine,' he said, 'fine. I think I'll chop that wood in the stable.'

'Don't exhaust yourself.'

Swinging the axe with all his strength, splintering the log in two, and again in four, and another, and another, full of rage and disgust at the cruelty. C had known, of course. 'They're going to hang him,' he'd said with certainty. He'd known that the police were ready to tighten the noose. Wolff could recall the distaste in his voice when he spoke of Casement's 'proclivities'. Whitehall was intent on a double death, trying him for treason, then again in the press for immorality, on the front page, forcing the stories of soldiers dying on the Somme inside.

Crack. The log splintered into four with one blow, leaving him gasping and the stable spinning. Christensen in the cemetery; his forefinger trailing down a marble bust. 'I copied it from his diary,' he'd boasted with a sly grin. 'You'd be surprised what there is in there.' And now Special Branch was leaking it to the jackals on Fleet Street. Wolff picked up a log and hurled it at the wall. How was the *News of the World* reporting it? *Nobody who sees the diary will ever mention Casement's name again without loathing and contempt.* Peddling poisonous stories of liaisons with Indian boys to blacken his character. Is this what we're fighting for? he wondered. Putting the axe down, he sat in the straw to smoke a cigarette. I didn't bring him to this, he reflected in its haze, but I did betray him. He'd lied to a lot of people, betrayed some and been betrayed, all in the name of duty. He'd betrayed Roger, then used him to betray others – Laura. Christ, the irony of it. Two people with a vision of how the world could be better, so the sacrifice wasn't a waste. For that, they were intent on casting Roger Casement down, from saint of the Empire to sinner and degenerate, falling to at least a rope's length. Sickening. And Commander Wolff wrings his hands and feels guilty.

He was still brooding when his mother called to him an hour later – and when he went to bed that evening and rose the following morning. 'Something's troubling you,' she observed at breakfast. 'No. Still a little tired,' he lied, because how could he explain?

In the days that followed, he read of appeals for clemency from Ireland and America but also more calculated poison, more calumnies. This is what Laura will believe I am, he thought. Why should it matter? But it preyed upon him continually. He walked his old routes still but not with the same unconscious pleasure. If I'm well enough, I might run, he reflected, fast and hard, outpacing his shadow like a middle-aged Peter Pan. Drop it like a hat and stick at the cloakroom of a London club or in an armchair in one of its smoke-filled rooms. But no, his part was always with him; he'd brought its sadness home to the fen, to his family's sky-filled fields, out to the salt marshes and into the secret lanes where he'd run easy as a boy.

'There's a telegram for you, Sebastian,' his mother said when he returned one afternoon. 'Behind the clock.'

It was a summons to the Admiralty signed by C.

'We should start harvesting next week,' she said, gazing at him over her spectacles. 'We'll be short if you go.'

'I'll come back.'

'I've got five women and Griggs who's too old to fight, Atkin the butcher's boy from Long Sutton, and our neighbours will help when they can.' She closed her eyes, the care lines obvious in the lamplight. 'I expect I'll manage.'

'I'll come back – I said so.'

*

His instructions were to report to Naval Intelligence at precisely four o'clock the following day. He arrived in his old country suit, patched at the elbow, flannel waistcoat, green tweed tie.

'You've caught the sun. You look healthier but like a bumpkin,' C observed as they walked slowly up the stairs to Admiral Hall's office. 'Disrespectful, Wolff.'

The Director of Naval Intelligence was on the first floor of the new building, with large south-facing windows overlooking Horse Guards Parade. The white stone heart of our Empire, he'd once observed to Wolff, with its view of 10 Downing Street, the Admiralty, Parliament and the Foreign Office and, craning east, the top floor and roof of the War Office.

Hall greeted him with a reproachful frown. 'Undercover, are we?'

'No, sir.'

'Well, sorry to drag you from your fields then. Thought you might help us win the war. Sit down.' He retreated behind his desk but remained standing, hands resting on the back of his chair. 'Last night there was an explosion at an ammunition depot in America – the largest.' He paused, blinking furiously. 'Are you smiling, man?'

'Was it the Black Tom yard?'

'You think it's sabotage?'

'Ask von Rintelen. You still have him, don't you?'

'Captain Gaunt thinks so too. Two million pounds of ammunition and explosive – broke windows twenty-five miles away and damaged the Statue of Liberty. Like the Somme, Gaunt says – how the hell he knows, I can't imagine,' Hall observed dryly. 'But that isn't why you're here.' He reached down to a file and slid a piece of paper from it across his desk. 'Take your time.'

It was an enciphered signal in number groups of five, bearing the legend at the top: BRITISH EMBASSY, PARIS. Rendered in English beneath:

French advise arrest of German agent. Sugar and glass phials
in possession contain *Bacillus anthracis*. His orders to infect
animals in holding pens close to Allied front line. Received
anthrax and instruction in use at laboratory in Berlin from
man he called DELMAR.

Wolff lowered the telegram to the edge of the desk.

'Seems your Dr Dilger is set on turning this into an industry,'
Hall remarked grimly. 'Who knows what else his laboratory is
cooking up. I suppose it was naïve to hope the fuss in America
would end it all.'

C leant forward to place his large hand on the telegram. 'One
of our people needs to question the German agent,' he said. 'I
don't expect we'll get any more but . . .' He was deliberately
avoiding Wolff's eye.

For a time no one spoke. Admiral Hall stepped out from his
desk, dragging his fingers across its bright surface. 'Can you
imagine the panic out there if the public thought it was under
attack from some disease?' A battalion of soldiers was stamping
rhythmically beneath his window. Turning, it began to advance
on Downing Street in close order. 'The War Office is setting
up a new experimental station so some of our scientists can
run tests on anthrax and a few other diseases . . .' he paused,
leaning closer to the window, '. . . just to see how we might
fight an attack – understand what we're up against.'

Wolff was conscious of C fidgeting uncomfortably beside him.

Hall turned to face them again, a short broad silhouette
against the window. 'The scientists aren't going to tell us what
Delmar is planning and where. The Army is circulating a confidential memorandum to intelligence officers urging them to
be vigilant – the Home Office is doing the same with the police.'
He paused again, then said, as if to himself, 'Just a damn shame
we didn't dispose of Dilger when we had the chance.'

'For God's sake, have you ever stabbed a man?' Wolff asked with a cold fury that surprised him too. 'So close you can smell him, feel his beard against the back of your hand, wriggling, biting – then that last little gasp. Christ.' He was shaking his head. 'The Germans – Nadolny – would have found someone to take his place – wouldn't you?'

The incredulous silence was broken only by the distant beat of marching feet. Then Hall exploded: 'Who the hell do you think you're talking to, Commander?'

'Was it you?' Again, Wolff was surprised to hear his voice trembling with passion. 'Did you instruct the police – instruct Special Branch to give the newspapers that poison?'

'Sir,' C prompted him quietly. 'Did you give the newspapers Casement's diary, sir?'

'I'm here to tell you how contemptible—'

'You're here, Wolff, because I ordered you to come,' C said, struggling to his feet to stand above him. 'I thought you might be of use but I see—'

'As you ask, yes,' Hall cut in belligerently. 'Yes, I asked Special Branch to circulate extracts – to politicians, bishops, the King – they have a right to know. I have a copy here, if you'd like to look – if you have the stomach for it. Perfectly genuine,' he sucked his teeth; 'the man is a disgrace. But you knew that, didn't you?'

'And libelling him in the newspapers is your idea of decency and duty?'

'Don't be a bloody fool. He was a traitor . . .'

'Not to Ireland.'

'There are Irishmen dying every day out there for their country and the Empire.' Hall gestured angrily to the window. 'Those few misguided souls calling for a reprieve – radicals, Americans – need to understand this man's nature. He knew what he was doing when he introduced the Germans to his friends in America – he probably knew about Dilger and his diseases – he's a traitor, he's a sodomite – he's a moral degenerate . . .'

'Tawdry – it wasn't enough . . .'

'No. Shut up before I – you fool. Shut up and listen,' Hall commanded icily. 'This isn't about Casement – it's you – your guilt. If it wasn't, I'd have you thrown in a brig – just pull yourself together. You did your duty – you did what was right. Now get the hell out of my office before I change my mind. Oh, and Wolff, for God's sake see a doctor. You're cracking up.'

And Wolff did leave – meek like a lamb. He left because there was nothing he could say with integrity. Blinker was right, and bleating, wringing his hands, just made him a hypocrite. In the Admiral's outer office, heads were bent over desks, sideways glances, silence. Wolff passed them in a daze, slowly, one foot in front of the other like a bandsman slow-marching to the Mall. He was fumbling with a bent cigarette and his lighter at the Admiralty entrance when C limped over to speak to him.

'Would you like me to do that?' he asked.

'I can manage.'

'Go home. You're not ready.'

'Ready?' Wolff gave a shaky little laugh. 'Ready?'

'I think you should see a doctor. There's someone . . .'

'Is he good with a bad attack of conscience? No, thank you. I don't need a doctor.'

'You do need more time. My God, you almost died. Go home, Wolff – that's an order.'

'Yes, I will.'

C's Rolls-Royce was parked at the kerb a few yards away. He took a step towards it, then checked. 'I don't know if I should say this, but I expect you'll work it out for yourself in time. This is the best thing that can happen to Roger Casement. I don't mean the attacks on his reputation – the diary.' He sounded disapproving. 'No, his execution – his death. If you'd been a

448

little less confused about your own part in it all, you'd have
. . . well . . . He wasn't much of a rebel, was he? He'll be a
bloody good martyr. Dying is the best thing he can do for his
country –' he corrected himself at once – 'his cause.' He pursed
his lips thoughtfully. 'Actually, I think we're making a mistake
– can I still say "we"?' He sighed heavily. 'It won't be the first
we've made in this war, will it?'

Wolff nodded slowly.

'I hear he's being received into the Roman Church – that
will help, of course.' He swung the end of his stick at a cigarette
packet, neatly driving it into the gutter. 'This place used to be
spotless – they've let the Army into St James's Park, you know.
Anyway, I have—'

'One more thing,' said Wolff abruptly. 'Turkey – did you . . .'
he was struggling for the words, with his feelings. 'I wanted to
ask, were you going to . . .'

C's small grey eyes were fixed intently on Wolff's face, the
monocle dangling on its string for once. 'If you're trying to ask
whether anyone betrayed or abandoned you – no, Wolff.' He
shook his head sadly. 'We think the worst of everyone, don't
we? No. No one betrayed you. Now go home.'

'Nine months – you could have . . .'

'Go home,' he repeated firmly.

Wolff heaved a lungful of smoke. 'All right. Yes. I will. Soon.'

At nine o'clock the hangman released the trapdoor in the
execution shed and the prison bell tolled once for the benefit of
the crowd. There was some cheering, mocking, then silence.
Roger Casement was pronounced dead at nine minutes after
nine o'clock on the morning of 3 August 1916. He would have
been hurt by the cheering, Wolff thought as he stood waiting
for the notice to be posted at the gate. He wouldn't have
understood why anyone would wish to cheer the death of another.

Women and a few men with the sickly yellow faces of munitions workers, chatting, joking, flirting; city clerks in bowlers and ready-to-wear suits; mothers and young children, some with breakfasts or mugs of tea from local shops that had opened early to offer 'a service'. The sort of gathering a prince several degrees from the throne might expect at the opening of a library. Just to say they were there, Wolff thought. And me?

At the back wall of the prison, thirty Irish men and women were bent discreetly in prayer. At the front, a prison warder was pasting whatever proclamation there was still to be made on the gate and the crowd was pressing round him for a part in this final scene. *Judgement of death was this day executed on Roger David Casement in His Majesty's Prison of Pentonville in our presence.*

There was no one for Wolff to say sorry to, no one to comfort; he didn't believe, so he couldn't say a prayer. But he was there to keep watch, as he knew she would be doing through the early hours in America. For Laura then, for Roger and his sister, for Reggie Curtis and the little man in the derby hat whose name he'd never known, and for others – the men who even at that hour were advancing across no-man's-land on the Somme.

At the station he bought an evening newspaper and read the report of Casement's last hours. He'd mounted the gallows' steps firmly and commended his spirit to God. Then they had buried him in an unmarked grave, like many who were dying at the Front.

'So this time you *have* come back.' She smiled and stepped aside to let him through the door. 'We started on the barley yesterday.'

'I'll take the wagon over at six tomorrow.'

'They won't be there before half past seven.'

'Half past seven then.'

450

And in September he would burn the stubble, for miles the fields aflame, flickering in the night sky as far as the eye could see, plumes of choking brown smoke – like the torment reserved for the unjust on the last day, his mother said – until it settled at dawn on the fen, so dense it was easy to stumble and fall, but only for the hours it took the sun to rise and a fresh breeze from the sea to blow.

1918

EPILOGUE

The Director, MI 1[c]
Whitehall Court
Westminster

24 October 1918

My Dear Admiral Hall,
I have this minute spoken to Commander Wolff about his mission to Madrid and taken possession of his report of the same. Regrettably, Wolff was unable to gather any intelligence of value. I know the scientists at the Porton Down Experimental Station were anxious to speak to Dilger in person, but in the few minutes Wolff was able to have with him he was adamant he would not co-operate, even if he were well enough to do so. Perhaps the consolation to be found from this sorry state of affairs is that the Germans are aware the game is finally up, they are beaten, and are determined to prevent us laying hands on those who know the full extent of their biological weapons research and campaign.

There is nothing I can add to Commander Wolff's rather colourful report, other than to say I thanked him for his assistance and assured him that, God willing, the end of the war was only weeks away and I did not anticipate there would be a need to call upon his services in future. When I enquired whether he would be returning to his crops and animals he did not reply, but asked if Wiseman was still in charge of our operations in America. I said he was still Head of Section but that I was sure he would be of the opinion it was too soon for Wolff to go back there. He acknowledged this advice with his usual insolence: he understood the risks perfectly well, he said, but de Witt was dead and he would be travelling as himself.

You and I both know a change of name will not save him from his Irish enemies there but it would have been a waste of my breath to say so.

Yours sincerely,

(signed) Cumming

MI 1[c] Report 376 Cdr S. F. Wolff
Date: 23 October 1918
Subject: The Fate of Enemy Agent Dr Anton Dilger

After a leave of absence of two years, the Director of MI 1[c] contacted me by telegram October 10, instructing me to report to the SS Bureau office the following day. Captain Cumming informed me the Service had received intelligence from the British naval attaché in Madrid that a man calling himself Alberto Donde had been seen in the city. Admiralty sources and the American Embassy in London suggested Donde was the German agent, Dr Anton Dilger (code name Delmar), responsible for culturing the anthrax used in attacks upon British soldiers and livestock in the autumn of 1915 and spring of 1916.

Testimony from the interrogation of German spies indicates Dr Dilger spent the intervening years at a laboratory in Berlin investigating the more effective delivery of anthrax and the culturing of other diseases that might be used against the Allies.

Captain Cumming informed me signals intercepts raised the possibility that Donde-Dilger had travelled to Madrid without the knowledge of his masters in German Military Intelligence. With an end to the war in sight, the doctor was deemed to be a source of some embarrassment to the German General Staff.

Captain Cumming asked me to undertake the operation because he knew I was one of the few people capable of confirming that Donde and Dilger were one and the same man. It was important for the long-term security of the Empire that the Service reach him before our American and French Allies, he said.

My orders were to:

1) Establish beyond doubt the identity of Donde-Dilger.
2) Discover the purpose of his visit to Spain.
3) Offer him British protection in return for information about German biological weapons research.

I took passage at once and arrived in Santander on October 13. Unfortunately the Spanish flu has taken such a toll on the country's railway service that it was another forty-eight hours before I was able to catch a train to the capital. Madrid was in the grip of the disease; its trams have stopped running, its buildings are draped in black, the church bells toll from dawn to dusk and the people walk its streets in fear. A hundred thousand Spaniards have died already, and one of the many thousands more infected was Senor Alberto Donde. Our naval attaché, de Saumarez, had learnt from his contact in the Guardia Civil that Donde had admitted himself to the city's German Sanatorium.

I arrived at the hospital with fruit and a book at approximately five o'clock in the afternoon and was told Senor Donde was very ill and unable to receive visitors. Fortunately the German nursing staff were too hard pressed to be vigilant and with the help of a Spanish orderly I was able to locate Donde. The sanatorium was full of very sick people but Donde had been allocated a private room.

Although much changed, I recognised the face of the man

in the bed at once. Dr Dilger was asleep, struggling to breathe, his fevered skin tinged with blue and there was blood on his pillow. It took no particular knowledge of the disease to see that he was dangerously ill. After a few minutes he opened his eyes and saw me there. I didn't expect him to recognise me because I was wearing a mask but he gave a short laugh and said: 'De Witt.' I said that I was sorry to see him in such a state, a remark he found amusing. Throughout our short conversation his eyes never left my face. They were larger than I remembered because his cheeks were thinner and drawn tightly from the cheekbones. He said very little because every word was an effort, his speech punctuated by a cough that racked his body and left him clutching at his abdominal muscles. It was impossible not to feel sorry for the man.

I wasted no time in explaining to him the purpose of my visit. The war was almost over and his country's Secret Service was searching for him with the intention of bringing him to trial for treason. He interrupted me to point out painfully but forcefully that he was not an American citizen, but a subject of His Imperial Majesty the Kaiser. That was as maybe, I said, but Germany would not be able to protect him, that in peacetime he would be an embarrassment, a much easier one to eradicate than the stench he had left in the cellar of his house in Chevy Chase. Something sad in his expression suggested he was quite aware of his situation.

As instructed, I offered him immunity from prosecution in exchange for information about his activities and the biological campaign. This offer provoked a fit of coughing and a nosebleed and it was a while before he was well enough to speak. Britain and America were 'dishonourably starving the German people into submission', he said, but its armies were undefeated and a time would come when they would fight again and 'secure the final victory'. Nothing would induce him to serve the enemies of the Fatherland, nothing, he declared with great feeling. I reminded him that his brother and sisters were in America and might be tried for treason, but if he agreed to my terms they would be offered protection too. Before he could answer, a German nurse entered and tried to drive me from the room. As far as Dilger was concerned, our conversation was over and he had rejected my proposition out of hand, but I asked him to consider his precarious position and that of his family and left him an address where he could send a message. I said that come what may I would visit him again in the morning and wished him a peaceful night.

Although I was with him for only fifteen minutes I was left with the impression that he enjoyed an abiding hatred of Great Britain and would ever be her implacable enemy; for the country of his birth he felt nothing but contempt. He cut rather a sad figure, consumed not only by the disease but by his anger. It was half past five in the afternoon when I left the sanatorium. Walking out to the street in search of a taxicab I noticed a German diplomatic motor car parked at its gates. Only later was I able to identify the man at its wheel as the naval attaché, Commander Krohn.

I spent the evening at our embassy in the company of de Saumarez, who arranged for a car to take me back to the sanatorium first thing the following morning. But at six o'clock I was woken by the lieutenant hammering on my bedroom door. His police contact had informed him by telephone that Senor Donde had died of the Spanish influenza a few hours before. His death was sudden but it did not strike me as strange. I made my way to the sanatorium without delay, in the rather forlorn hope of retrieving some intelligence from his personal effects. I explained to the duty doctor and a hospital matron that I was an old comrade and friend who knew the late Senor Donde's family well. The German naval attaché, Krohn, was with Senor Donde to the end, they said; he was making all the necessary arrangements, and they refused point-blank to let me see the body. I was in no doubt they had been schooled and were repeating their lines, and that they were very afraid. After a few minutes of fruitless wrangling they instructed a watchman to escort me from the sanatorium. A short time later, I climbed through a window at the side of the building and found my own way to Dilger's room. But it was not his any longer: his body had gone and his bed had been allocated to another victim of influenza. Stopping a nurse in the corridor, I said I was Commander Krohn's assistant at the embassy and would she please take me to Senor Donde's body.

It was lying beneath a stained sheet in a makeshift mortuary with twenty others, the case containing his few belongings on the floor beneath the table. Pulling back the sheet, I confirmed it was the body of Anton Dilger. There were red fingermarks and signs of bruising about his neck consistent with strangulation. I cannot be certain but am of the view that Dilger's last visitor was there to ease his passage, a simple task with one so weak. Commander Krohn was surely acting upon orders from Berlin, but the doctor may have hastened his end by mentioning my offer of protection for information. His case had been searched already, its contents thrown thoughtlessly back inside. I checked the seams of his clothes, his shaving kit, pulled the spines from his books; there was a photograph of the opera singer, Frieda Hempel; another of his father; and one of Dilger and a companion with horses – the inscription on the back: 'With your nephew Peter on the farm'. The only other item of note was a decoration: the Iron Cross Second Class. A label on the case suggested it was to be sent to a Frau Elizabeth Lamey at an address in Berlin.

Anxious not to be discovered beside the body, I slipped out of the hospital and returned to the embassy where I sent a coded signal with the news of Dilger's death to Director MI 1[c] at the SS Bureau and DNI at the Admiralty. The following day (October 18) Dilger was buried in a mass grave for victims of the influenza virus in one of the city's cemeteries.

(signed)

Commander Sebastian Wolff RN Retd

Historical Note and Sources

The plot of *The Poison Tide* is drawn from real events and the lives of those who took part in them, a story of what was and might have been. For those who like to pull the threads of the history from the fiction, here is a brief outline of the unvarnished facts and some of my sources.

As the armies of the European powers marched into battle in the summer of 1914, Irish leaders in America met the German Ambassador and his military attaché to discuss support for a rebellion. The former British diplomat and humanitarian campaigner Sir Roger Casement was present at some of their meetings. Since leaving government service he had become a prominent supporter of Home Rule for his native Ireland.

With the intention of pressing Ireland's cause in person, Casement left America in the autumn of 1914 and took passage to Germany. Adler Christensen travelled with him as his valet. Slipping through the British blockade of the Atlantic they reached Christiania, as Norway's capital Oslo was called at that time. During their short stay in the city Christensen approached the British Legation and offered to betray Casement. He spoke to the minister at the Legation, Mansfeldt Findlay, and presented him with confidential papers including a German cipher for which he was paid a small amount. From their conversation with Christensen the British inferred his relationship with Casement was probably of 'an improper character'. It was the first suggestion they received that Roger Casement was engaged in a homosexual relationship, an offence punishable with imprisonment at the time.

Christensen would later tell Casement and the German authorities that the British had taken him from a hotel lobby and interrogated him but he had refused to give them any information. For many details of Casement's life, love and politics I drew on Brian Inglis' biography, *Roger Casement*. Reinhard Doerries' books *Prelude to the Easter Rising* and *Imperial Challenge* were a source for the German-Irish connection, as were *My Three Years in America*, the memoirs of the German ambassador in Washington, Count von Bernstorff.

In Berlin, Casement's principal intelligence contact was Count Rudolf Nadolny of the General Staff. As the head of Section P, Nadolny was charged with masterminding covert operations against British and French interests in America and elsewhere around the world. Although the papers relating to Section P's activities were destroyed at the end of the war, we know from coded telegrams sent to the German Embassy in Washington that Casement furnished the count with the names of Irish republicans who would be prepared to assist with 'far-reaching sabotage in the United States'. In return Casement was allowed to visit prisoners of war in Germany and recruit his Irish Brigade, much as I relate in *The Poison Tide*.

Casement arrived in Berlin with great hopes, confident the Germans were 'fighting for European civilisation at its best'. But isolated from comrades and decision-making in Ireland and America, and cast down by his inability to persuade his countrymen in the camps to join his brigade, he suffered an emotional collapse. In December 1915 he wrote with characteristic humanity that, 'it is dreadful to think of all the world beginning the New Year with nothing but Death – killing and murdering wholesale, and destroying all that makes life happy

. . . I feel very sad, and it has been the most unhappy Christmas I have ever spent.' By then he had learnt from his friends in America that his 'treasure', Adler Christensen, had been spending money raised for their living expenses on a girlfriend.

Robert Monteith's *Casement's Last Adventure* offers a first-hand account of Casement's time in Germany and his attempts to recruit an Irish Brigade. His friend, the Princess Blücher, wrote of Casement's visits to her in *An English Wife in Berlin*. At the other end of the social scale Madeleine Doty's *Short Rations* is a vivid account of the effect of the British blockade on the lives of the ordinary Berliners that she knew.

The news that a date had finally been set for a rising in Ireland reached Berlin on 17 February 1916. A telegram from the German Ambassador in Washington announced 'revolution shall begin Easter Sunday'. The Irish requested up to 50,000 rifles, machine guns, field artillery and German officers. Count Nadolny offered only 20,000 rifles. Casement was landed from a U-boat on 20 April and arrested after only a few hours ashore. The trawler carrying his guns was intercepted by the Royal Navy. He was tried in London and condemned to death. To undermine the case of those seeking his reprieve, Captain Hall, the Director of Naval Intelligence, circulated salacious extracts from his diaries with details of payments made for sexual services and his descriptions of breathless encounters with young men he had met on diplomatic missions for His Majesty's Government. For accounts of Casement's execution at Pentonville Prison and the opinion of the public at home and abroad, I drew on newspaper reports, in particular the coverage of the *New York Times*.

The aristocrat at the heart of the German–Irish intrigue had lost patience with Casement long before the Easter Rising. By the spring of 1916 Count Nadolny's principal concern was the sabotage campaign he was orchestrating against Allied interests in neutral America and on three other continents.

In the Prologue to *The Poison Tide*, Count Nadolny echoes German Staff thinking that the war would be unprecedented in its reach, fought not just by soldiers but by the people. 'It will,' the War Book of the German General Staff predicted, 'destroy the total moral and material resources' of the enemy. The conflict was framed in terms of a Darwinian struggle. 'War gives a biologically just decision . . .' the influential German general Friedrich von Bernhard wrote, '. . . not only a biological law, but a moral obligation, and, as such, an indispensable factor in civilisation.' Or, as Count Nadolny predicts in my story, 'victory will be secured by those who prove the fittest'. If victory was a 'moral obligation' then the means used to secure it were of little consequence. The British First Sea Lord, Admiral John Fisher, put it like this: 'the essence of war is violence. Moderation in war is imbecility.' And in this Total War everyone would play a part – scientists and doctors too.

Preparations for a German biological weapons programme seem to have begun in early 1915. Count Nadolny directed its operations for the General Staff, while Professor Carl Troester was responsible for the culturing of anthrax and glanders bacilli at the Military Veterinary Academy in Berlin. How and when Anton Dilger was recruited and why he agreed to risk his life serving German interests in his native America are matters of speculation. His involvement in the campaign, the help he received from his family, the house in Chevy Chase and the network of Albert, Hinsch and Hilken was much as I relate in *The Poison Tide*. To help my story I have changed the chronology of his activities in the United States, some of his family relationships, but above all the target of the campaign. There is no evidence to suggest Anton Dilger and his associates were intending to attack Allied soldiers or civilians, only the horses, mules and cattle they needed for the waging of the war.

The German General Staff did consider using biological weapons against soldiers and civilians. On 7 June 1916 the naval attaché in Madrid, Commander Krohn, sent a telegram suggesting the contamination of rivers with cholera bacilli, but his proposal was rejected. A few months later the Staff was presented with another, this time for the spreading of plague. A military doctor, *Oberstabsarzt* Winter, argued the dropping of plague bacilli from Zeppelins on English ports would infect local populations and cause general panic. The idea seems to have interested the new Chief of the General Staff, General Ludendorff, but it was categorically ruled out by the Surgeon General. 'If we undertake this step,' he wrote, 'we will no longer be worthy to exist as a nation.'

There were many rumours of German biological attacks on both Allied soldiers and civilians. In 1917 the British Home Office instructed the police to take precautions against anthrax. A few months later civil servants reported information from a French source, 'that the enemy had inoculated a large number of rats with plague, and they intended to let them loose in the United Kingdom from submarines and aeroplanes.'

The General Staff considered the infection of horses and other livestock as an attack on military supplies and a legitimate act of war. Nadolny's biological warfare programme grew in scope and reach with Section P agents operating not just in the United States but against Allied interests in Rumania, Spain, Norway and South America, too. This campaign is covered in detail in Thomas Boghardt's book, *Spies of the Kaiser: German Covert Operations in Great Britain during the First World War*.

Culturing and then infecting the animals required more effort than many German agents were prepared to make. After the war scientists in Britain and elsewhere were able to mill anthrax spores to something like a dust that could be used more effectively in a high explosive device. In 1925 Winston Churchill wrote of 'pestilences methodically prepared and deliberately launched upon man and beast . . . Anthrax to slay horses and cattle, Plague to poison not armies only but whole districts – such are the lines along which military science is remorselessly advancing.' No doubt this thought was in the mind of Prime Minister Churchill when in 1942 he authorised the testing of an anthrax bomb that might be dropped on Nazi Germany. But it was the Japanese War Ministry that was to invest the most money and time in the development of a biological warfare programme during the Second World War. Within the walls of its Pingfan Institute, three thousand scientists, technicians and soldiers worked on a range of diseases to be used in an offensive, including typhus, typhoid, cholera, plague, smallpox, tuberculosis, glanders and anthrax. They concluded that anthrax bombs would be the most effective and more than two thousand were developed and tested experimentally.

Anthrax is still regarded as one of the most potent biological threats. The accidental release of anthrax spores from a weapons facility in Sverdlovsk in the former Soviet Union in 1979 resulted in seventy-nine cases of anthrax infection and sixty-eight deaths. Scientists are particularly concerned about the release of spores in an aerosol by a terrorist group or in a dirty explosion. Colourless and odourless, the spores might travel many miles before disseminating. In 1993 a report by the US Congressional Office of Technology Assessment estimated the release of 100 kilograms of anthrax spores upwind of Washington, DC, would result in anything from to 130,000 to three million deaths – a death rate that would match the impact of a hydrogen bomb on the district.

For the effects of anthrax and the history of its use I consulted a number of books and medical papers, and I am grateful to Professor Alastair Hay of Leeds University who spared time to go over some of these areas with me. More on the secret history of chemical and biological warfare can be found in *A Higher Form of Killing* by Robert Harris and Jeremy Paxman.

'A higher form of killing' was the epithet Fritz Haber used to describe his invention of poison gas. Although there is no evidence to suggest Haber met Anton Dilger, he did have some contact with Count Nadolny. In *The Poison Tide* Haber expresses his firmly held view that in war the scientist belongs to his country and must bend his efforts to victory. The Anton Dilger of my story stands shoulder to shoulder with him in contending talk of a humane death is nonsense and there is no ethical difference between blowing a man to pieces in no-man's-land and poisoning him in a gas attack. Clara Haber's opposition to her husband's work is well documented and is believed to have been the significant factor in her decision to commit suicide at their home in Berlin, just days after the first German gas release on the Western Front.

Dr Anton Dilger died in Madrid of complications associated with Spanish influenza a few weeks before the end of the war. By the autumn of 1918, the State Department in Washington was actively seeking his arrest with a view to indicting him for treason. Carl Dilger always believed his brother was murdered by German intelligence 'because he knew too much'. The most valuable source for the little that is known of Dilger's life and death is Robert Koenig's biography *The Fourth Horseman: One Man's Mission to Wage the Great War in America.*

Captain Franz von Rintelen enjoyed a longer and more peaceful life. After three years' imprisonment in America, he returned first to Germany then to England, where he died in 1949. The story of the espionage network he built using the personnel and contacts of the German shipping lines, his unholy alliance with Irish America, Black Tom and his campaign of sabotage can be found in his own colourful but self-serving memoir *The Dark Invader.* Many characters who appear in *The Poison Tide* are also there, including his contact to the Irish on the docks, Paul Koenig, and Dr Walter Scheele, the inventor of the cigar bomb the network used against British ships and American munitions factories. Another valuable source for the activities of the saboteurs was Captain Thomas Tunney's account of his time as the head of the New York Police Department Bomb Squad, *Throttled! The Detection of the German and Anarchist Bomb Plotters.* Chad Millman's *The Detonators* offers a good general account of the campaign and the post-war attempt to bring the German agents and their American collaborators to justice. From all of these books I took as much as was useful for my story.

The Poison Tide is set at a time of some confusion in both the British and German intelligence services with rival agencies competing for influence and resources. Today, the British Secret Intelligence Service – or MI6 – is the principal body responsible for the gathering of information from overseas, providing, in its own words, 'the global covert capability to promote and defend the national security and economic well-being of the United Kingdom'. But at the beginning of the First World War it was just one among a number of intelligence agencies.

Founded as the Foreign Section of the Secret Service Bureau in 1909, its first chief was the redoubtable Commander, later Captain, Mansfield Cumming of the Royal Navy. It was Cumming's habit of initialling classified documents in green ink as 'C' that gave rise to the tradition of the head of the Service being referred to as C. By 1914 the 'SS Bureau' or 'Secret Service' was operating from a large flat at 2 Whitehall Court in the centre of London, a short distance from the Admiralty and the War Office. Its cramped premises at the top of a mainly residential block reflected its lowly status. Cumming had to fight to prevent the SS Bureau being swallowed up by the War Office's Military Intelligence Directorate. During the war years it was referred to variously as the 'SS Bureau', the 'Secret Service', the 'Special Intelligence Service', even 'C's Organisation', and its official designation was MI 1(c). For simplicity I elected in *The Poison Tide* to refer to MI 1(c) as the 'Secret Service Bureau', the 'Bureau' or the 'Service', and to Cumming and 'Blinker' Hall of Naval Intelligence by their final ranks of captain and admiral respectively. More details of the foundation of the Service and its early operations can be found in the official history written by Keith Jeffery: *MI6: The History of the Secret Intelligence Service 1909–1949*; Christopher Andrew's *Secret Service*; and Alan Judd's *The Quest for C: Sir Mansfield Cumming and the Founding of the British Secret Service.*

Nowhere was the rivalry between competing intelligence agencies sharper than in America. Until the winter of 1915 British efforts to counter the German sabotage campaign were led by the aggressive and flamboyant naval attaché, Captain Guy Gaunt. He did not welcome the arrival of C's new station chief, Sir William Wiseman, or acknowledge his presence to be necessary. But Wiseman and the agents who worked with him brought a new professionalism to British espionage operations. It was a time when old secrets were a little less closely guarded, and in the years after the war some of C's best agents published their own accounts of the 'New York Front'. Norman Thwaites wrote the memoir *Velvet and Vinegar*, and the old spy and Germany hand, Hector Bywater wrote of 'trade craft' and his service in America in *Strange Intelligence.* Captain Guy Gaunt's autobiography *The Yield of the Years* was also a useful source. A more scholarly account of Section V's work in America can be found in the article by Richard B. Spence, 'Englishmen in New York: The SIS American Station 1915–21' (*Intelligence and National Security*, vol. 19, no. 3).

For my hero Sebastian Wolff, I drew from the background of another of C's spies, the Anglo-Dutchman, Henry Landau. Born and brought up in South Africa, Landau was fluent in

German, Dutch and French. In 1916 he was recruited by C to direct the Service's network in occupied Belgium. Landau's account of his war was published as *Secrets of the White Lady*.

For all the efforts of spies like Landau, the single most valuable source of intelligence on the German war effort was gathered in a room measuring twenty feet by seventeen in the Old Building at the Admiralty in London. Room 40 was the home of the Naval Intelligence Division's code-breakers. Within four months of the start of the war they were reading all the German navy's principal codes. German Foreign Office signals proved harder to crack, but in the spring of 1915 a copy of its diplomatic codebook was captured in Persia. Through 1915 and 1916, the Director of Naval Intelligence, Captain Hall, was able to read telegrams from the German Embassy in Washington. Room 40 intercepted at least thirty-two signals relating to German assistance for the Irish, including confirmation in February 1916 that there was going to be a rising against British rule at Easter. It was from the code-breakers in Room 40 that Hall learned of the activities of Agent Delmar and the German biological warfare programme. My source for the work of the code-breakers was Patrick Beesly's *Room 40: British Naval Intelligence 1914–18*.

More of the background to the story, features, profiles and photographs, can be found on the website www.andrewwilliams.tv

Finally, I would like to thank my editor at John Murray, Kate Parkin, for helping me shape the story; Caroline Westmore for easing the book's passage to publication in a tight time frame; Jane Birkett for copy-editing the manuscript; Lyndsey Ng for publicity; my agent, Julian Alexander; friends and family, in particular Kate, Lachlan and Finn for their enthusiasm and patience. I hope the reader finds enough of the spirit of the times in my story to forgive the liberties I have taken with the history.